Outback Desire

Savage splendour… Intense heat…
Men who really are towers of testosterone…

In January 2006, By Request
brings back two collections containing
three favourite romances by our
bestselling Mills & Boon authors:

OUTBACK DESIRE
Outback Heat by Emma Darcy
The Outback Nurse by Carol Marinelli
Outback Fire by Margaret Way

HIS VIRGIN LOVER
Mistress on Loan by Sara Craven
The Mistress Deal by Sandra Field
A Passionate Proposition
by Susan Napier

Outback Desire

OUTBACK HEAT
by
Emma Darcy

THE OUTBACK NURSE
by
Carol Marinelli

OUTBACK FIRE
by
Margaret Way

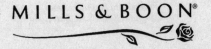

MILLS & BOON®

MILLS & BOON and MILLS & BOON with the Rose Device
are registered trademarks of the publisher.
Harlequin Mills & Boon Limited,
Eton House, 18-24 Paradise Road, Richmond, Surrey, TW9 1SR

OUTBACK DESIRE © by Harlequin Enterprises II B.V., 2006

Outback Heat, The Outback Nurse and Outback Fire were first
published in Great Britain by Harlequin Mills & Boon Limited in
separate, single volumes.

Outback Heat © Emma Darcy 1998
The Outback Nurse © Carol Marinelli 2001
Outback Fire © Margaret Way, Pty.,Ltd 2001

ISBN 0 263 84647 4

158-0106

Printed and bound in Spain
by Litografia Rosés S.A., Barcelona

OUTBACK HEAT

by

Emma Darcy

Initially a French/English teacher, **Emma Darcy** changed careers to computer programming before the happy demands of marriage and motherhood. Very much a people person, and always interested in relationships, she finds the world of romantic fiction a thrilling one and the challenge of creating her own cast of characters very addictive.

**Don't miss Emma Darcy's fabulous new novel:
TRADED TO THE SHEIKH
On sale in February 2006, from
Modern Romance™!**

CHAPTER ONE

HEAT enveloped her like an oppressive blanket as Angie left the air-conditioned taxi and headed up Queen Street Mall to the Hilton Hotel. It was sticky, humid, enervating heat and the city was sweltering in it, typical for Brisbane in January. It would be hotter in the outback, Angie reflected. Weatherwise it would be the equivalent of jumping out of the saucepan and into the fire...if she got the job.

But she could cope with that. Angie clung to the idea she could cope with anything as long as she got Brian Slater out of her life. Committing herself to a year of working as a governess on an isolated property in the outback seemed ideal for making a clean break and forcing it to stick. No easy come-backs in that situation. She would be right out of Brian's reach, in every sense. Besides, the heat there was dry, not like this sauna sizzle on the coast.

Entering the hotel was pure bliss. She scooped the hot weight of her hair away from the back of her neck to let the cool air erase the dampness that had gathered there. The curls tended to frizz on days like this so pinning it up would have resulted in tendrils wriggling free. Better to let the shoulder-length mass hang, rather than risk an untidy appearance. First impressions were important in a job interview.

She examined her image in a mirror. No damp patches on her dress. The soft lemon colour looked fresh and cheerful, not too bright against the golden tan of her skin. It suited her, complementing her brown hair and amber eyes. The button-through style of the dress was smart, without being overly professional, the right touch, she hoped, for a governess.

Satisfied her lipstick hadn't bled and she still looked respectably turned out, Angie checked the time. Five minutes left before she was to meet the man who could give her an effective escape from the emotional mess she was in. It might be cowardly to run from it but she didn't care. She was too vulnerable to Brian's persistent pursuit of her while ever she remained in Brisbane. She needed this job. Really needed it.

The directory by the elevators listed the Atrium Room on the sixth floor. The interview was to take place in the lounge area adjacent to the restaurant. As Angie rode up to her eleven o'clock appointment, she worked hard at keeping nervous tension at bay, taking slow, deep breaths and mentally rehearsing her answers to obvious questions.

It wasn't easy to project a composed and confident front when she felt so churned up over the situation that had developed with Brian. Somehow she had to put him out of her mind, as well as out of her life. The next half hour or so was critical to winning her best opportunity to do that. She fiercely told herself to concentrate all her energy on impressing the man she'd come to meet.

Skylights above the Atrium Room provided a large pool of natural light for ferns and other tropical plants to flourish. The softly cushioned cane furniture in the lounge area was inviting, more a pleasant social venue than a business one, Angie thought, but undoubtedly intended to put the applicants at ease. She was wondering how many were to be interviewed as she scanned the occupants of the lounge; couples, groups of ladies, one

lone man. The moment her gaze locked on him, Angie
felt a frisson of shock.

She hadn't formed any expectations...just a man of
the land, needing a governess to supervise his children's
lessons from the school of the air. He emanated strength.
He wore an aura of strength. He looked carved out of
some hard substance that didn't belong to ordinary flesh
and blood. Bred to endure, Angie thought, and she felt
intimidated by the impact of a power she'd never encountered before.

He saw her, nodded an acknowledgment and rose to
his feet, preparing to greet her with civilised courtesy.
He wore city clothes; grey trousers, blue shirt, nothing
to mark him as an outback man, but the clothes were
totally irrelevant. He was impressively tall and broad-
shouldered, yet with a wiry leanness that suggested he
could move fast and efficiently if action was called for.
There was an almost animal maleness about him that
seemed to deride any form of civilisation.

Darkly tanned skin was stretched taut over strong facial bones. Although he looked too toughened by life to
be called handsome, he had the kind of face that was
stamped with an innate authority, compelling attention
and respect. His hair was black and straight, as were his
eyebrows, though they had a slightly downward slant,
shadowing eyes that were surprisingly light.

Angie's pulse was fluttering wildly as she forced herself to walk toward him. She knew intuitively this man
wouldn't be fooled by anything. It made her feel intensely vulnerable. Even her legs felt shaky and doubts
flooded her mind. Would the preparation she'd done for
this interview be enough to satisfy him? It seemed all
too possible his judgment would be based on standards
she knew nothing about.

*   *   *

Taylor Maguire absorbed the stunning impact of her as she wove around the tables between them, her purposeful approach obliterating any doubt as to her identity.

Angie Cordell… teacher…applying for the position of governess…his mind reluctantly acknowledged the unwelcome facts even as his body reacted to a sexuality that thumped into his heart, sent a surge of blood to his loins and stirred urges that made him wish this meeting was in a far different situation.

If *she* had walked into the bar last night…

He'd had his choice of a number of pick-ups—easy sex—sex he needed to settle the fermenting frustration of being celibate too long—yet in the end he'd recoiled from taking it from women who'd held no real attraction apart from the physical release they might give him. Empty sex. He didn't really want that. He wanted…

This woman.

Such lush femininity…a cloud of shiny brown curls bouncing around a soft, beautiful face…skin gleaming like honey satin…an appealing freshness about her lemon dress which somehow accentuated the sensuality of full breasts thrusting against it, the seductive sway of perfectly curved hips, the graceful movement of long legs. Its line of buttons could open all of her to him…if only she wasn't Angie Cordell applying for the impossible position of governess.

Impossible.

No way could he take her.

He struggled to resist the temptation of her, to quell the arousal of instincts he couldn't afford to indulge, to be the man he had to be…*in this situation.*

His eyes were blue, piercingly blue and chillingly cool. Angie barely suppressed a shiver as she came to a halt beside the table he'd chosen. Whatever assessment he'd made while she approached was obviously not warmly positive. Nor was he about to turn on any superficial charm. A smile would have to be won from this man. Unlike Brian, who gave them freely to everyone.

"Miss Cordell…" He offered his hand. "…Good of you to come." His voice was deep and pleasant and as strongly male as the rest of him.

"Thank you for giving me your time, Mr. Maguire," she replied, determined to hang on to an air of confidence no matter how much he rattled her.

The handclasp was brief, over before Angie could even register what his touch felt like. Cool and controlled, she thought, watching him direct the play; gesturing her to the chair opposite his, summoning a waitress, inquiring what refreshment Angie would like, efficiently disposing of the order, everything settled within the space of a minute or two, including himself.

He sat across the table from her, focusing intently on her eyes. The typed sheets of her résumé were on a clipboard, lying on the chair adjacent to his, but he didn't glance at them, probably having gleaned all the information he wanted. Angie felt he was now fitting her to the facts he'd read.

"Why do you want this job, Miss Cordell?" he asked as smoothly as a highly sharpened knife, slicing through to the key concern behind her application.

Angie rolled out her prepared answer. "I've always wondered about life in the outback. This will give me first-hand experience."

A sardonic gleam appeared in his eyes. "I don't run a tourist operation. Giralang is a working cattle station. The view is unchanging and the activities could be considered boringly repetitive."

"Not to you, Mr. Maguire," she said with certainty, sensing he would treat a gush of positive aspects from her with contempt.

"No, not to me," he agreed, his mouth curling in ironic appreciation of her counter-thrust. "I was born to it. I see it differently."

She nodded. "I'd like to see it through the eyes of those who live there."

He could hardly contest that desire, Angie thought, her spirit fired by his antagonistic approach. Why was he being so negative? Had he taken one look at her and decided she was unsuitable?

She would not give in to such a superficial judgment. It wasn't fair. If Mr. Taylor Maguire thought he could arbitrarily dismiss her from his list without a proper hearing, he could think again. She was fed up with not being listened to, having her needs dismissed as irrelevant. For a stranger to do it...this rock of a man...on top of Brian's capricious habit of ignoring what she said...

"Have you ever lived in the country, Miss Cordell?"

She could feel his prejudice and railed against it, even as she pitched her voice to appealing reason. "No. But I once knew someone whose life changed very much for the better after working for six months on an outback station. What he said about it has always stuck with me. I'd like to know for myself how it is."

Funny how she'd instantly thought of Trav Logan when she'd read about the advertisement for a governess. She'd been mad about him in her troubled teen years, drawn to the excitement of his wild reckless energy. A magistrate had given him the option of six months on an outback station or the same time in a correctional institution. Trav had chosen the wide open spaces and it had completely changed the direction of his life. He'd gone jackerooing after that, saying the city was stuffed and the real challenges were outback.

Trav...thriving on the edge of danger. Brian did the same, trading on the floor of the stock exchange. The link suddenly raised a disturbing thought. Was she compulsively attracted to men who liked living dangerously?

"The contract is for a year, Miss Cordell," Taylor Maguire reminded her with a quiet but forceful emphasis, snapping her attention back to him. "A year is a long time. Especially for a city person, used to having entertainment on tap."

He wasn't going to beat her on that rap, either. "I've never been short on commitment, Mr. Maguire. When I take on a job, I see it through."

"Very commendable. However, there is a difference between doing a job and being happy in it."

"I like children. I enjoy teaching."

"Then why give it up for what is basically a supervisory position?"

"I don't consider it would be giving it up and I'm sure your children would benefit from the expertise I can bring to extending the lessons given on school of the air."

Angie could barely contain the anger burning through her. He'd read the résumé she'd given to the employment agency. If he'd considered her overqualified for the job, why grant her an interview? He had to know she could offer more to his children than a minder, so why was he backing off? Would it do any good to confront him with his unreasonable attitude, attack rather than defend?

He was regarding her thoughtfully. Maybe she was getting through to him. It was probably best to let him pursue his own agenda first before trying more active persuasion. Angie waited for the next question, resisting the temptation to break the testing silence.

The waitress returned with their coffees, cappuccino for her, short black for him. Angie stirred in a spoonful of sugar. Taylor Maguire left his unsweetened. Not for him a ready kick of energy, not even sugar. She thought of Brian's growing cocaine habit, his excuses for it and the broken promises that trailed in its wake, and fervently wished she had never become involved with him.

The basic truth was she wanted out—out of her whole life as it currently stood—and if she didn't convince this man to take her into a different world with its own in-built support system, she would have to face up to some other kind of drastic move. Shifting house wasn't enough. Brian didn't want to accept it was over for her and sometimes she was scared he never would.

She replaced the spoon on the saucer and sat back, gesturing her readiness to continue the interview. The coffee would be too hot to drink just yet and the need to win Taylor Maguire's approval had an added urgency. A compelling urgency.

She wished his blue eyes weren't so piercing.

"You're a trained teacher with five years of classroom experience," he started again, picking up on the résumé she'd sent to the employment agency.

"That's correct."

"I imagine you earn very good money, Miss Cordell, much more than a governess."

"The cost of living in the city is high." Especially over the years of trying to fit into the trendy lifestyle favoured by Brian's social circle. Most of his friends came from wealthy backgrounds and seemed to have money to burn. She'd once thought herself lucky to be welcomed into their privileged world. She'd been blinded by the glamour of it but her eyes were wide open now. "I won't be losing, Mr. Maguire," she said with certainty.

He frowned. "You've weighed all this?"

"Yes."

Free meals, free accommodation, nothing to spend her wage on, no fashion stakes to uphold…she'd probably end up financially ahead. Not that it mattered. She was after peace of mind, not economic improvement.

She could see her lack of doubt had unsettled him, disrupting his line of argumentation. It prompted a wry little smile from her. "Some things can't be measured in money, Mr. Maguire."

"Enlighten me," he invited.

"Experience."

The sceptical gleam winked out. He returned her smile, though it was more a twitch of his mouth than an actual smile. "The cost of experience can be very dear, but I take it a smaller income is not an issue to you."

"I have no cause to quarrel with it. As I understand, from the employment agency, the salary you're offering is more than the usual for a governess."

Something dark and foreboding flickered in his eyes. "Perhaps you should have asked yourself why, Miss Cordell."

The drawled words didn't carry a threat, more a touch of self-derision, yet they stirred an unease. "I prefer information to indulging in guessing games," she said cautiously. "I'd like to hear from you what the situation entails for me."

He shrugged, visibly relaxing before answering her. "There are three children on the station who require lesson supervision. You would be used to handling many more so that wouldn't present a problem to you."

"They're not *your* children, Mr. Maguire?"

"Only one. My son, Hamish. He's seven years old."

"Most of my teaching has been with seven-year-olds."

Another wisp of a smile with a twist. "That fact did draw my interest, Miss Cordell."

So what was turning it off? What problems did he see in her taking up the position? "Does your son have learning difficulties?" she probed.

"No. He learns whatever he wants to very quickly," he said dryly.

"A case of not wanting to?" Angie queried.

"Let's say he's become very selective in hearing what's said to him. He lost his mother last year. She was piloting a small Cessna. An engine caught fire and it crashed," he stated, his delivery matter-of-fact, strained of all emotion.

"I'm sorry," Angie murmured with sincere sympathy. "Losing a parent is always disturbing to a child."

Losing a wife was no picnic, either. Grief could bring people together or drive them apart. She couldn't see Taylor Maguire sharing his grief with anyone. He would bear it alone. Which probably meant the child had felt shut out and even more bereft of parental love and care.

"It hasn't been easy for him," he admitted. "And I doubt Hamish will welcome you. He may even perceive you as trying to take his mother's place."

"I can only assure you I would be sensitive to your son's feelings, Mr. Maguire. Given the chance, I would try everything I could to win his trust and confidence."

She meant it. It would give her a real sense of purpose, over and above the educational one. To do something meaningful, to turn something bad around, to make a caring difference to a child…for the first time she felt a positive eagerness toward the job, rather than seeing it as a personal means of escape.

"Unfortunately, Miss Cordell, others would see it the same way."

Her mind still fixed on the emotional hurt of a little boy, Angie didn't catch his father's drift. "I beg your pardon?"

"I'm a widower. You're a very attractive woman. I presume you're unattached or you wouldn't have applied for this position. Your résumé gives your age at twenty-seven, a time when most women have either formed a permanent relationship or are looking for one."

Angie was flabbergasted by the implication. "You think I'm out to catch you?" she spluttered.

He shrugged. "I'm merely telling you what you'd be walking into. We'd be living under the same roof. With others there, as well, but that won't stop the gossip. Gossip is rife in the outback, Miss Cordell. The chat radio session is prime entertainment."

"Well, firstly let me assure you I'm not a desperate female out to ensnare a man, Mr. Maguire," Angie bit out in a flare of resentment. "Not you nor anyone else. In fact you could say men are very low on my priority list at the moment."

"Then you shouldn't be moving into a man's world, Miss Cordell, because you will inevitably draw their attention."

Like Brian's? Everything within her recoiled from a repetition of what she'd been going through. "I trust I'd be under your protection." No one would pit themselves against *his* strength, she thought, hugging the sense of security it gave.

His eyes hardened. "If you stir trouble, I can't guarantee absolute protection."

It's not my fault, she wanted to cry. A desolate hopelessness swept through her as she realised why the interview was taking this course. "So that's the problem. You took one look at me and decided I'd be too much trouble."

"It's a possibility I'd be foolish to ignore," he conceded.

Frustrated by a view she couldn't disprove, Angie searched for a way around it. She shook her head. "I'm neither a flirt nor a tease, but I guess I can't expect you to take my word for it." And it was impossible to change her physical appearance. She looked at him in bleak appeal. "I hope you won't ignore what I can give."

"I am taking that into consideration, Miss Cordell," he assured her. "I felt it was only fair to warn you of matters you might not have considered."

True enough. She had thought more of getting away than what she was going to. "Thank you. I appreciate it," she forced out, momentarily wishing she was dead.

She leaned forward to pick up her cup of coffee, needing to calm herself and reassess where she was now.

In all fairness to him, the live-in situation was a tricky one, given his newly single status. He looked to be in his mid-thirties, the owner of a vast cattle station, certainly not unattractive physically. Most people would consider him "a catch." He wasn't to know she was immune to any man's appeal right now.

On the other side of the scales, it was surely natural for him to want the best for his child, which was why he'd chosen to interview her. A sympathetic teacher with absolutely no sex appeal would not have presented the potential problems he saw with her. Somehow Angie had to defuse them, diminishing the negatives and accentuating the positives.

She drank the coffee and set the cup down again. He hadn't touched his. She glanced up to find him watching her, his eyes narrowed, thoughts shielded. Had he already made up his mind or did her chance at the job still hang in the balance? Impossible to tell. She had to strike at what was most important to him.

"Would gossip worry you?" she asked. Somehow she couldn't believe it of him. Idle talk would be water off a duck's back to this man.

"The woman is usually the target. Especially a newcomer." His eyebrows rose in challenge. "Do you have a thick hide?"

"You're talking of people I don't know, whose opinion wouldn't count with me. As long as I'm fine within myself about what I'm doing, and I would be," she added with conviction, "what other people speculate about wouldn't hurt."

"Not many people achieve such self-containment, Miss Cordell," he said quietly.

You have, she thought, and wondered what had driven him inside himself. Did the outback breed such men, demanding a self-reliance that absorbed adversity and moved on past it?

"I can only tell you how it is with me," she answered, clinging to simple dignity. "I'm at a point in my life where I'm not looking to others to make something of it for me. I need time for myself."

He made no comment. He observed her keenly and she sensed his curiosity, but he chose not to pursue such a personal issue, perhaps wary of crossing the line of non-involvement.

"I am good with children," she went on. "This past

year I had a class of fifteen pupils who'd dropped behind their year's standard of learning because of various behavioural problems and physical disabilities. Most of them I was able to help make the grade, and the others at least had a happier year at school. The headmaster would confirm that appraisal if you'd like to call on him. The telephone number is in my résumé.''

He nodded. ''Is there anything else you'd like to tell me, Miss Cordell?''

He was winding up the interview. Panic fluttered through her. Had she said enough? Still his face gave nothing away. Desperate to leave him with a strong impression of her capabilities, Angie pressed one more point.

'I think I'd understand your son, Mr. Maguire. I was an only child myself. My father died when I was eight. My mother when I was fourteen. I know the sense of…of displacement…very well.''

He frowned. ''I don't believe my son feels *displaced.*''

''No?'' Wrong move! She tried to recover. ''Well, maybe you've given him a strong sense of belonging. I simply meant I'm familiar with loss.''

Which was probably why she had found it so difficult to leave Brian after two and a half years of close intimacy. The need for a loving relationship eroded common sense. It had felt good…for quite a long while. But the bad had become too bad and she hated what it did to her.

''I really want this job, Mr. Maguire,'' she blurted out, unable to stop the raw plea which had to be visible in her eyes.

''I'll keep that in mind, Miss Cordell.'' He rose to his feet, signalling the end of her time with him. ''I appreciate your presentation and the thought you've given to it.''

Cool politeness. Nothing more.

Angie's heart sank as she stood up. ''Thank you for listening to me.''

He nodded. ''I have other applicants to interview after lunch. I'll let you know my decision this evening if that's convenient to you.''

''Yes. Thank you.''

He held out his hand. No encouraging smile. No warmth in his grasp. A brief, formal leave-taking.

Yet Angie felt his eyes boring into her as she walked away and her heart pounded with a flurry of complex feelings. She wished she had his strength. She didn't want to leave him, to have to face her own life again, alone and unprotected. Her mind cried out... *Don't let me go. I need this chance.* But he didn't call after her and she forced her legs to keep walking.

This evening, he'd said. Another seven or eight hours.

Then she'd know.

CHAPTER TWO

THE heat hit her again on her exit from the hotel. Angie wandered aimlessly down the mall, drained of the energy to grasp any purpose now the interview was over. A long afternoon of waiting stretched ahead of her. She had to fill it in somehow.

Best to get out of the heat, she told herself, but didn't feel like going home to an empty apartment. The two other teachers who shared it were still away on vacation, leaving her with no ready company to provide distraction. Watching the telephone would not make it ring before this evening and she doubted she could concentrate on a book.

She could treat herself to lunch somewhere, then take in a movie.

Entertainment on tap.

Angie halted, frowning, as Taylor Maguire's words sat almost accusingly in her mind. A movie would be more an escape from her thoughts than an entertainment, she argued. Especially today. But there would be no ready escapes from anything in the outback.

If she got the job.

Was she really prepared for a day-after-day sameness that could prove boring?

Yes, she answered emphatically, as long as she felt safe. And she would on Taylor Maguire's property. No one would buck his authority. She was sure of it. And she would be free of Brian. Boredom was a small price to pay for the removal of the stress he was causing her.

If she didn't get the job...no, she didn't want to think about that until she had to. Uncaring how her behaviour could be judged, she bought a newspaper, found an air-conditioned café, ordered a Thai chicken salad, and read what movies were on while she tried to enjoy her lunch, reflecting that chicken would probably be a rare dish on a beef cattle station.

The many awards won by a recent British film persuaded her it should hold her interest, so she chose it as the best possible time-filler. Despite its glowing reputation, Angie had difficulty in following its story, which was told in innumerable flashbacks and with so many characters she couldn't get engaged with any of them. She found herself recoiling from the obsessive passion of the male lead and walked out. There was certainly no entertainment in watching a man who pursued his own desire without a care about hurting others.

The heat outside was worse. The movie had depressed her instead of distracting her and since there seemed no point in doing anything else, she caught a bus home. She felt like a limp rag by the time she let herself into the apartment. Nevertheless, it was almost five o'clock so most of the afternoon had gone.

She stripped off, took a long tepid shower, pulled on a pair of shorts and a loose singlet top, made herself a cool drink with plenty of ice and switched on the television. More entertainment, she thought ironically, as a family quiz show clicked onto the screen. She found it better than the movie, her mind harmlessly engaged in giving answers to the questions asked.

The six o'clock news was just coming on when the telephone rang. Angie leapt from her chair in a rush of nervous agitation, not having expected the call so early. Her thumb fumbled over the Off button on the remote control, finally cutting off the noise from the television so she could concentrate on whatever was said to her. She almost tripped over herself in racing to the kitchen where the telephone was installed on the wall. Pressing a hand to her thumping heart and trying to catch her breath at the same time, she lifted the receiver to her ear, hoping to hear what she desperately wanted to hear.

"Hello. Angie Cordell speaking…"

"Hi, babe!"

Instant deflation.

"I made a big killing on the floor today," Brian crowed. "Got to celebrate and who better with than you! I'm on my way right now so you've got about twenty minutes to pretty yourself up for a night on the town."

"No, Brian!" she cried in vehement protest, then in a frantic rush, "I'm busy. I can't go out. I won't. You've got to stop doing this."

The phone was dead.

Angie closed her eyes and took several deep breaths, trying to quell the onsurge of panic. She gritted her teeth in fierce determination. Brian was not going to do this to her. It had to stop.

She dialled his mobile telephone number, hoping to put him off coming. Nothing. He'd switched the power off. Which meant she would have to confront him face to face. Another argument. Angie slammed the receiver down in sheer frustration, then started to tremble.

She hated this. Hated it, hated it, hated it. Hugging herself tightly to stop the shakes, she walked through the living room, down the hallway to her bedroom, then back to the kitchen, repeating the well-worn track over and over again as she tried to settle the rage and fear in her mind.

She couldn't leave the apartment, not before the call

from Taylor Maguire. Besides, even if she did, Brian would probably sit in his car, waiting for her to come back. It only made matters worse, making her feel hunted.

If she didn't get this job, she would have to go to the police and get a restraining order against him. Though she didn't really believe that would work, either. Brian was so clever, with charm enough to fool anybody. He would make her out to be neurotic, someone who needed help. And she did!

Best not to answer the doorbell when he came, she decided. He couldn't know she hadn't gone out since his call. She didn't care if he sat in his car, waiting all night. He had no right to keep forcing himself into her life. Talking to him did no good and she especially didn't want the hassle of an argument when Taylor Maguire's call might come in the middle of it.

Though what if the telephone rang while Brian was at the door? He would hear if she answered it, yet she couldn't not answer. She'd told Taylor Maguire she would be in. Appearing unreliable would not go down well. He might change his mind. He might not give her the job anyway but she didn't want to torpedo what chance she had at getting it.

No point in stressing out about it, she told herself. She had no control over what Taylor Maguire did but Brian could be shut out. At least physically. The television was off. She had to remember not to switch any lights on. It wouldn't be dark for another hour or so. With any luck, Brian would go away, none the wiser she'd been here all the time.

Angie retreated to the kitchen and stayed there. She thought of preparing herself a meal. Her churning stomach denied any interest in it. She ate a bowl of strawberry ice-cream. Slowly. It was something to do while she waited.

At six twenty-five the doorbell rang.

Angie stood absolutely still though her heart hammered in her ears. She watched the seconds ticking around on the kitchen clock. The thin hand had only completed a half circle when the doorbell rang again, given several sharp twists this time. She looked at the telephone, willing it to stay silent. Two minutes went by.

Had he gone? Would he cruise around in his car, trying to spot her in the street, then come back to check the apartment again? She didn't dare look out a window in case he was watching. Three more minutes passed. Angie was just beginning to breathe easily when the doorbell pealed again.

Her hands clenched. Every nerve in her body screamed a protest at the continued torment. It took enormous willpower to hold control, remaining still and silent, doing absolutely nothing that might reveal her presence. The distinct, metallic sound of a key sliding into the door lock froze her mind in horror and delivered a painful kick to her heart. Disbelief warred with reality as she heard the door open.

"Angie?"

It was definitely Brian. But how had he obtained a key to her apartment?

The door closed.

He was inside.

No escape from him. No point in skulking in the kitchen. He was bound to find her sooner or later. Angie waited for outrage over his invasion of her privacy to quell the sickening fear in her stomach. It didn't work. Nothing was going to work. In blind desperation she charged into the living room to confront him. He'd actually picked up the remote control for the television, apparently prepared to make himself right at home.

"Put that down, Brian!" she commanded through clenched teeth.

He was startled to see her at first but smug satisfaction quickly superseded the surprise. "In a sulk, are we? Playing hard to get?"

She didn't need outrage. Hatred burned through her. Brian Slater might be as handsome as the devil himself with his Byronic black curls, magnetic dark eyes and a smile loaded with charisma, but Angie no longer felt the slightest attraction to him. He'd worn those feelings away with his demonic moods and self-centredness. And she was not going to play his games, not now or ever!

"Just reinforcing the *no* I gave you on the phone," she shot at him. "And don't tell me you didn't hear."

He gestured at her skimpy, casual clothes. "You're obviously doing nothing else tonight. Silly to cut off your nose to spite your face, Angie."

"It's over, Brian. Find someone else to celebrate your successes with."

He grinned at her, blithely ignoring her claim and advice. "No drugs, I promise. I've been a very good boy. The least you can do is reward me."

"How did you get the key you let yourself in with?"

He laughed. "Same old place. When you were living with me you always kept a spare key in a little magnetised tin under the fuse box. Saved you from being locked out, remember?"

Stupid to have kept the same habit. She held out her hand. "Give it to me, Brian."

"I'll put it back for you."

"Just give it to me. It's mine."

He huffed exaggerated patience and handed it over. "Now can we be reasonable?" he appealed, pouring on the charm. "I was merely coming in to wait for you. We did share an apartment for years, Angie."

"That doesn't give you any claim on this one. Or on me. Would you please leave now?"

He threw up his hands. "I just got here."

"I didn't invite you."

"Angie…" Indulgent cajoling. He lowered his hands to reach out to her as he stepped forward. "…I want to share with you. We can have a happy evening together."

"No!" She backed off, lifting her own hands to ward him away. "I've told you, Brian. I don't want to pick up our relationship again."

"You said we could be friends."

The glitter in his eyes spelled trouble but Angie refused to give in, no matter what! "That's not working out for me," she stated vehemently.

"You're truly being absurd, babe. I know there's no one else."

The telephone rang.

"Isn't there?" she threw at him to give him pause for thought, then whirled into the kitchen, hoping he would give her a breathing space in which to answer the call all her hopes were hanging on. Desperate hopes. She snatched up the receiver, darting a fearful glance at Brian who'd taken up a watchful position, leaning against the doorjamb, his eyes gloatingly confident that she couldn't get away from him.

"Hello. Angie Cordell speaking," she almost gabbled in her haste.

"Taylor Maguire, Miss Cordell." His deep voice seemed to touch a chord of sanity in a situation fraught with danger.

"Yes?" she quickly encouraged, afraid of being interrupted.

"Once again thank you for your time. I'm sorry to disappoint you, Miss Cordell, but I've decided on another applicant."

Her heart fluttered and sank. For a moment, her mind was quite blank. Then the instinct for survival tore into it. She turned her back on Brian and drove a bright lilt into her voice.

"How nice! Thank you, Taylor. Do come right on over. I'd love to see you tonight."

Silence on the other end of the line. A bubble of hysteria bounced around Angie's brain. The man would think her stark raving mad. Not that it mattered. Since he hadn't served the one critical purpose he could have served, Angie had no compunction in using him to get her out of the corner she was in. Even though it was all pretence.

She tinkled a light flirtatious laugh. "Mmmh...sounds great! It's been so hot today, I sure could do with some cooling down. I'll get my things ready to go. See you soon."

She replaced the receiver and pasted satisfaction on her face as she turned to Brian. "A man I met recently," she informed him. "A man I'm interested in, Brian. So will you please leave now?"

His face looked tight and pinched. His eyes glared fury. For a moment she thought he was teetering on the edge of physically attacking her and it was all she could do to hold a relaxed pose.

"We'll see," he said darkly, and to her intense relief, wheeled away from her and strode out of the apartment, slamming the door after him.

Angie sagged against the kitchen cupboards, blessing

the opportune call that had saved her this time. The misery of her failure to get the job would undoubtedly hit her later, but right now, she could only be grateful she was rid of a horribly threatening situation. Then suddenly remembering the security chain she ran to the door and put it on. If Brian had taken the spare key before tonight and made a copy of it, at least he couldn't get past the chain. If he tried, she would call the police.

It struck her that he wouldn't have walked in here tonight if he hadn't known her flatmates were away. There were no witnesses to what he'd done. He could swear she had invited him in. Her word against his. He was so damned clever with everything he did. And she was alone. No one to back her up for another week. If Taylor Maguire hadn't called tonight…if she hadn't thought fast enough to make him an expected witness…

Angie shuddered. Tears welled into her eyes. Her chest ached from the tension, the awful, helpless feeling of fighting a force that couldn't be reasoned with. She pushed away from the door and tottered to her bedroom, wishing it was a safe refuge, knowing it offered only temporary respite.

We'll see… She shuddered again at the dark threat in those words. Brian was sure to be out there waiting, watching to see the man who was supposed to be coming. When no one turned up…

Angie crawled onto the bed and hugged a pillow as she surrendered to a storm of weeping, unbearably pressured by what was happening to her, the rage and fear and frustration clogging her life, leaving her no room to move on to something better. The chance she'd hoped for with Taylor Maguire was gone. She had to leave here…go somewhere else…anywhere else. Job or no job, she had to get on a train or plane tomorrow and move as far away from Brian as she could. It was the only answer.

The tears kept falling, an endless well of them, grief for her own foolishness in falling for the charismatic attractions of a man who couldn't be trusted. Even before the drug-taking had distorted the darker side of his personality, there had been lies and risk-taking that went beyond easy acceptance. She had been mad to stay with him so long, to think she could change him or even influence him. Brian Slater was a law unto himself and no one was going to stop him from doing what he wanted.

The bedroom was gathering dark shadows with evening closing in. She listlessly supposed she should put on the lights, at least maintain the fiction she was expecting a visitor. Probably futile. Brian would be watching. He'd know. Though someone might arrive to call on another occupant of the apartment block. She might be lucky enough to benefit from a coincidence.

Fired by the need to capitalise on any possible mistake Brian could make, Angie scrambled off the bed and raced through the apartment, switching on lights. Breathless, her heart pumping madly, she was heading for the bathroom to wash her sticky face when the doorbell rang, almost making her jump out of her skin. She stood stock-still, trying to gather the shreds of her strength to meet this new onslaught of emotional tension.

No sound of a key sliding into the lock.

Angie forced herself to backtrack, to watch the front door, to listen for any activity on the other side of it.

The bell rang again.

She started to shake. It was a repetition of Brian's earlier call. But the chain would hold, she assured herself. Even if he had another key, he couldn't break the chain.

A thunderous knocking, then a voice, deep and loud and determined. "Miss Cordell, if you don't open this door, I'll be calling the police to effect an entry."

Sheer disbelief held her stunned.

There was no mistaking that voice.

Taylor Maguire had come to her rescue.

CHAPTER THREE

ANGIE didn't pause to ask why a virtual stranger would care about her, care enough to investigate the strange response she'd made to his call. She thought only of Taylor Maguire's strength as she rushed to the door, strength she could lean on tonight, strength that could keep Brian away if he tried to intrude again.

She pushed the chain out of its slot and wrenched the door open wide, driven by an urgency to get the man she needed inside quickly in case Brian was following and forced a confrontation that would put her in a bad light. "It was so good of you to come," she babbled, gesturing an invitation to enter, her gaze darting past him to check if Brian was loitering on the stairs either way.

"Miss Cordell..."

He hadn't moved. He was frowning at her.

"Please..." she begged. "If you'd just come in for a while..."

He stepped past her without another word. She slammed the door shut and slotted in the security chain as fast as she could. Only then did reaction catch up with her and she leaned against the closed door, hit by the shock wave of sudden release from her torment. Safe... her mind wept with the relief of it...safe because Taylor Maguire had heard a call for help and answered it.

She gulped in a lungful of air and turned herself around to face her saviour. He was standing quite close but her eyes had difficulty in getting him into clear focus. His image wavered, swam. "Thank you," she choked out. Then her knees buckled and she was sliding down the door.

He caught her before she completely collapsed on the floor. With seemingly effortless ease he scooped her up and cradled her against his chest. Angie didn't try to struggle. She closed her eyes over the wet glaze that had distorted her vision and limply gave in to the comforting sense of being enveloped in strength.

He carried her. She couldn't even bring herself to care where. He set her down on the squashy leather sofa in the living room. Angie sank into it as his arms slid away. She wished she could sink into oblivion. It was a shaming situation. Taylor Maguire had seen her as potential trouble and he was right. She was. But she was still glad he'd come.

She heard him leave her side and panic swirled again. "Don't go!" The cry ripped from her throat as she hoisted herself up.

"Stay there! Rest!" he commanded, a figure of indomitable authority, taking charge. In a softer tone, he added, "I'll be back in a moment. You need a drink. And a facecloth."

Angie subsided, railing at her own weakness. Her judgment was hopelessly awry. This was the kind of man who took care of things, not the kind to walk away. All the same, she couldn't just lie here like dead weight and impose on his kindness. She had to think of what to do next.

Pulling herself together was the first step. There was no time to waste if she was to get away from Brian tonight. She couldn't expect Taylor Maguire to stay here with her but he could take her with him when he left, dropping her off at a hotel where she would feel safe until tomorrow. She swung her legs off the sofa and pushed herself into a sitting position, hunching over and taking deep breaths to ward off a cloud of dizziness.

The man of action returned. He didn't criticise her movement. He didn't chat. A glass of water was thrust into her hand. She drank it. He took the glass and offered her a damp washer. She wiped her face and hands, finding it refreshing.

"Thanks," she said huskily, offering him a rueful smile. "Sorry I'm such a mess. I should be offering you something."

"No need. When you feel up to it, you can tell me what's been going on here. It will help clear the air. In every sense."

Exuding efficient and stabilising purpose, he stepped over to the dining table, pulled out a chair, set it down close to her and sat, determined on putting himself in the picture.

Angie had to concede he deserved to know what he'd walked into on her behalf. Most city people wouldn't have involved themselves at all and she couldn't really blame them. It was easier not to know, not to put themselves in any firing line. This man was of a different breed. She'd known that intuitively from the first moment she saw him. Nevertheless, she was reluctant to confess the full truth. It cast her in a dubious light. She didn't know why Taylor Maguire's opinion of her counted, but it did.

"There was someone here when I rang," he prompted, apparently deciding the sooner she talked, the better.

"Yes. We were lovers once," she blurted out. Impossible to skate over that if the situation was to make sense and she needed his sympathy. "I left him because

I couldn't trust him any more. He does drugs. He denies it now but his behaviour…'' She shook her head, knowing no one could have the understanding she did. ''I won't go back to him and he won't let go.''

''What happened tonight?''

''He called to say he was taking me out. I said no but he came anyway. I had to wait in for your call but I pretended I wasn't here. I didn't answer the doorbell. He found where I'd left a spare key to the apartment and let himself in.''

''You didn't have the security chain on?''

She flushed at the stupid oversight. ''I didn't think. Normally I would. I was distracted…worrying about your call…and the job.'' In anguished embarrassment she rushed on. ''It just didn't occur to me he'd go that far. Maybe he knew my flatmates were away so he wouldn't be sprung by anyone other than me. Usually he waits outside in his car.''

A beetling frown. ''Is he there now?''

''Did you see a black Porsche in the street when you arrived?''

The frown deepened. ''Yes, I did.''

''That's him. Waiting to see if someone turned up. It was only the threat of you coming that got him out. He's careful about witnesses.''

''How long has this stalking been going on?''

Stalking… Angie shuddered at the horrible word. It was all the more horrible because it described so truly what Brian was doing to her.

''Six months,'' she answered bleakly.

''Have you gone to the police about it?''

She shook her head. ''Brian comes from a wealthy family. With political connections. He can slide out of most things.'' Her eyes reflected the bitter irony of her position. "I'm a nobody, Mr. Maguire. Whom do you think they'll believe? Besides, they can't enforce protection. How many times do you hear they can't do anything until a crime is committed?"

He didn't argue. "Brian who?" he asked.

"Slater."

"What's the registration number of his Porsche?"

"Triple zero MIL." She'd answered automatically, then thought it an odd question. "Why?"

"I'll get the police to move him on. At least that much can be accomplished." He stood up, so unflappably self-assured in taking direct and immediate action, it dazed Angie. "Where's your telephone?" he asked, glancing around.

"You…believe me?"

His gaze swept back to her, his piercing blue eyes unshadowed by any doubt. "I generally do believe what I see for myself, Miss Cordell. The phone?"

"On the wall in the kitchen," she answered, still stunned he was prepared to take matters into his own hands with the most minimal briefing. A man accustomed to making judgments and acting on them as fast as need be, she surmised, and wished she knew how he had made his final judgment on the governess applicants. Though it was irrelevant now. What was done was done. But she couldn't help envying the woman who had got the job.

She heard him talking in the kitchen, his voice very firm and controlled, quietly demanding, expecting respect and co-operation. He would undoubtedly get it, too. It was one of the less acceptable truths of life that men were more likely to draw an active response out of officialdom than women. And Taylor Maguire was certainly not any man.

The talking ended. He returned to the living room. "We'll be notified when he leaves," he stated with absolute confidence, no question that Brian *would* be moved on.

"Thank you for your...your intervention. May I ask another favour?"

He raised his eyebrows invitingly.

"When you leave, could I get a lift with you to a hotel? I'd prefer not to stay here tonight."

He studied her for several moments before speaking. "This was why you wanted the governess job," he said quietly.

"The main reason," she acknowledged. "Though everything else I said *was* the truth, Mr. Maguire."

He nodded. She had the impression he was satisfied he had it all slotted into place. "Are you in a fit enough state to pack what you want to take with you?"

"Yes, of course." She pushed up from the sofa and held herself steady, proving she was capable of managing. "It will only take me a few minutes to change my clothes and throw a few things into an overnight bag."

"I meant everything you don't want to leave behind. Best we take it with us so you don't have to return here. I'll book you a room at the Hilton for tonight. Tomorrow we'll fly to Giralang. It means you'll be taking up your position as governess earlier than necessary but it saves you from further harassment and me from another trip."

She gaped at him, scarcely believing her ears. "I thought you'd given the job to someone else."

An ironic smile briefly curled his lips. "The young lady I'd chosen asked me to call after eight o'clock. It's not yet eight. What you could call a fortuitous circumstance, Miss Cordell."

"But you don't want me."

The words fell from her lips and the moment they were spoken she berated herself for looking a gift horse in the mouth. He was handing her the chance she wanted, the chance she needed. Why be so self-defeating as to question it?

For some reason it raised a tension between them that hadn't been there before. On her part, it was a reluctance to accept a position he might begrudge because she wasn't his first choice, yet her whole being yearned to go with him, be with him, stay with him.

She didn't know what conflict he held within himself, but she was aware of it. His eyelids dropped, veiling any expression that might have revealed his feelings. His face was a granite mask. There was an unyielding stiffness to his stance, as though his mind would always impose its will on his body, denying it any natural impulses unless there was mental and physical harmony.

After a nerve-tearing silence, he softly said, "I would never leave any woman in your position, Miss Cordell. Whatever the cost of this decision, I'll pay it."

She flushed, pained by the idea she was costing him anything. "I'm sorry you think I'll be trouble. I'll do my best not to be, Mr. Maguire. And I truly am good with children. You won't lose by taking me, I promise."

"We'll see," he murmured. "You need not sign the contract. You might find a year too long for you."

"You doubt my staying power."

He shrugged. "Let's not labour the point. You need to get away. I'm prepared to take you. How long you stay at Giralang will be a matter of how well it works for all of us. Fair enough?"

"Yes. Thank you."

"Do you need help with suitcases? Boxes?"

"I'll manage." She gave him an ironic smile.

"You've done more than enough for me. Please feel free
to use the phone and do help yourself to any food or
drink in the kitchen."

His eyes suddenly warmed, giving her a funny feeling
in the pit of her stomach. "You have guts, Miss Cordell.
I respect that."

Nerves that had been frayed to breaking point, relaxed
into a sweet melt of pleasure. "I won't let you down,"
she promised him and tore herself away from his strong
presence to go and pack for a new and different life.

Resolution burned through her. Whatever his experience with other city people, she would prove his doubts
about her wrong. Whatever it took, she would adjust to
working on an outback station. Hardship, boredom,
heat…she didn't care about any of the drawbacks.

She wanted to know Taylor Maguire's world.

More than that, she wanted to share it with him.

Taylor heaved a sigh of resignation and moved himself
into the kitchen, vaguely thinking of the telephone calls
he had to make. There was no going back on his decision
now. He'd have to live with it. Somehow.

You don't want me.

The innocence in that statement was a dead-set killer
to the desires she stirred. She didn't want *him* was the
bald truth of it. While he had been consumed with the
tantalising excitement her provocative invitation on the
telephone had aroused—the chance of pursuing an attraction that still had him in its grip—she had been
grasping at any straw to save herself from another man.

Of course he'd known something had to be wrong but
the fact she'd reached out to him on such a personal
level had muddled all sense of logic and fired what was
patently an absurd fantasy—a brief but torrid affair with

her, here in the city before he went home. Bitter irony. *She* certainly didn't have a sexual need crying out to be answered and she'd undoubtedly recoil violently from any suggestion of it from him.

He found himself gripping the edge of the sink. He loosened his hands and looked down at them, remembering the feel of her as he'd carried her to the sofa, the imprint of her breasts squashing against his chest, the silky smoothness of her bare thighs, the warmth of her body, its soft femininity. Despite her obvious distress, it had taken all his willpower to act as he knew he should.

Madness to take her with him to Giralang.

Continual torment.

But what else could he have done?

She'd looked so helpless, so vulnerable, so needful of protection. He could not have walked away from her very real plight, leaving her in danger of being assaulted. Or worse.

It would probably only be for a few weeks, he told himself. A month at most. A woman like Angie Cordell would want to be back in a city, once she'd had time to recover from this traumatising experience. Giralang meant no more than an escape to her. She would see it as a prison soon enough. Just as Trish had. The difference was Angie Cordell was free to move on. And she would.

Hopefully before the men returned to work.

Hopefully before he made a fool of himself, wanting what common sense told him was impossible, impractical and downright dangerous to even contemplate. Any close involvement with her at Giralang would be courting the worst kind of trouble. Fantasy and reality did not mix. He had to keep that very clear in his mind and not allow physical need to have any sway on his behaviour toward her.

His gaze fell on a bowl and spoon in the sink. They were smeared with pink ice-cream or yoghurt. He washed them up, then moved to use the wall telephone. He'd set a course of action. He had to go through with it. It was the only decent thing to do in the circumstances. He could only hope his *indecent* obsession with Angie Cordell would soon ease.

She didn't belong to his world.

She wouldn't want to, once she knew it.

CHAPTER FOUR

IT SEEMED to Angie they had been flying over a sea of red earth for a long time. Only when the altitude of the Piper Comanche dropped did she realise the landscape wasn't entirely barren. There were occasional clumps of scrubby trees, the contorted loops of a creek or river, the silver flash of water tanks that probably fed troughs for wandering stock, lines denoting roads which gave some reassurance of civilisation, albeit extremely remote.

From Brisbane they had headed northwest across Queensland to what was called the Gulf country, lying between the outback mining town of Mt. Isa—the largest silver and lead producer in the world—and the Gulf of Carpentaria. Giralang was situated on the Leichardt River, northeast of the town, and by road, about five hours' journey in a four-wheel drive distant from it. The road was currently impassable due to recent flooding.

Angie's head was swimming with the facts her new employer had related to her over earphones during the flight. Taylor Maguire was not a chatty man and she hadn't liked to engage him in too much conversation since he was piloting a plane which, to her mind, was alarmingly small. However, her curiosity about where she was going to had necessitated some questions so she could be at least mentally prepared for it.

A check of her watch assured her they must be nearing the property, if not already over it. Her mind couldn't really encompass an area of almost three thousand square kilometres, which Taylor had told her was the

43

size of the station on which he ran about thirty thousand cattle, another unimaginable number. Nevertheless, she should soon be able to spot the cluster of buildings which he had described as like a small, self-contained township.

Apart from the homestead, there were cottages for the head stockman, the chief engineer, the men's cook, the gardener, all of whom had wives, a large house for the musterers and jackeroos, the Aborigines' settlement, a store, a butcher's shop, schoolroom, office, equipment sheds.

Forty-eight people were on his payroll, mostly men. Many of them were on leave, at the moment, as it was the wet season, during which the general work of the station eased up. Mustering usually began again in March. Nevertheless, Angie felt life couldn't be too lonely at Giralang since she would be living in a community, albeit an isolated one.

Even within the homestead itself, she would not be alone with Taylor and his son. His widowed aunt, Thelma Winton, ran the household with the help of two Aboriginal women, Gemma and Yvonne. Both the helicopter pilot, Gary Dawson, and the bookkeeper, Leo Pockley, lived in. Angie had memorised these names, hoping to save any awkwardness in greeting them over the first few days. She was resolved on doing her utmost to fit in and learn what was expected of her as quickly as possible.

She glanced surreptitiously at the profile of the man sitting beside her, taking in the high, intelligent forehead, thickly lashed eyes narrowed to the distance ahead, straight-line nose, a mouth that was surprisingly full-lipped, providing a touch of softness on an otherwise hard face, a strongly chiselled chin, slightly jutting as though aggressively defying the arrows of fortune. It was strange how the more she saw him, the more impressively handsome he looked. She judged him to be in his mid-thirties, certainly too young to live the rest of his life without a woman.

A disquietening thought slid into her mind… How did single men in the outback manage their enforced celibacy? The occasional weekend trip to the closest town? Taylor Maguire had certainly seen her as a possible source of trouble to his men. To himself, as well? How far did sexual frustration drive a man? Perhaps, while he'd been in Brisbane… She frowned, inwardly recoiling from the idea, even though she reasoned it was a pragmatic solution to a physical need.

She caught herself glancing down at his strong, muscular thighs, wondering what he'd be like as a lover, and felt an uncomfortable stab of guilt over the speculation. Guilt and shock. She couldn't afford to even begin to think along such lines. It was courting trouble which neither of them wanted.

Besides, he had probably been deeply attached to his wife. With their son, Hamish, being seven now, the relationship had been a long-standing one, harder to let go than hers and Brian's, especially when death didn't offer a choice. There was no such thing as a *clean break,* she realised. Emotions lingered on.

''There it is, straight ahead.''

His deep voice boomed through her earphones, jolting Angie out of her reverie. Her gaze fastened on what looked like an oasis in the middle of a desert, a startling patch of green with large, full-grown trees providing shade for a group of buildings, the biggest of which had Giralang printed across its roof.

"How do you maintain a lawn?" she asked in wonder.

"Sprinkler system from the dam."

"What about drought?" He'd told her the wet season was followed by nine months of dry weather, which seemed a long time without rain.

"We have enough bores to see us through a serious drought," came the matter-of-fact reply.

Artesian bores, tapping into the great underground basin of water which lay beneath the outback, the remnant of an inland sea of ancient times. What would happen if it ever ran out, Angie thought fancifully, or were there endless supplies trapped by the earth?

As they came in to land, she noticed the buildings were set out in a grid pattern—very orderly—and were all painted white with green roofs and trim, and green water tanks attached to them, giving a uniform look that was neat and attractive and denoted a caring pride in the place. The Maguire family had owned Giralang since the last century. It was a hands-on operation and always had been, unlike the many cattle stations owned by pastoral companies and run by managers who came and went. It must make a difference, Angie reasoned. There was always more pride in actual ownership.

She held her breath as the plane touched down on the red clay airstrip but the landing went smoothly and she relaxed as it slowed to a halt, adjacent to a huge shed. Her relief at having arrived safely, however, was mingled with a sense of trepidation over the next step in her introduction to Taylor Maguire's world. A Jeep was being driven out to meet them.

"Hamish and Leo," Taylor said, waving to the occupants.

His son and the bookkeeper. Akubra hats, drawn

down low on their foreheads, shaded their features, making it impossible for Angie to see what they looked like, apart from the obvious of being a man and a boy.

Trying to quell the nervous excitement playing havoc with her insides, Angie followed Taylor out of the cockpit and waited for him to open the door. Her new life would revolve around the boy she was about to meet. It would help enormously if she could make a favourable impression.

She snatched her straw hat up from the seat she'd dropped it on, glad she had thought to leave it out of her packing. Clearly hats were the order of the day. Taylor had not commented on her appearance so she hoped what she had considered a sensible, unobtrusive choice of clothes for the trip would meet general approval.

The almost knee-length fawn shorts had seemed both modest and practical for climbing in and out of a small plane. She wore a fawn and white striped shirt over a white singlet, tying the ends casually at her waist. The white walkers on her feet were definitely activity shoes, nothing fancy about them. She might not look exactly "country" but it was the best she could do with what she had.

The door swung open. Taylor made his exit first, ready to render her assistance if she needed it since it was quite a stretch to the ground and only one step to lessen the distance.

"Have you got the new computer, Dad?"

The eager burst of natural excitement from the boy was an encouraging sign of welcome.

"Yes, it's on board, Hamish," Taylor assured him matter-of-factly. "I'll need a hand with it, Leo."

"Figured you would," came the laconic reply.

There was no move away to hug the child, no gesture of warmth or affection extended to either party. Taylor turned straight to Angie, beckoning her down, and dryly stated, "I've brought the new governess, as well."

No burst of excitement greeted this piece of news. No comment, either. Angie backed out of the plane to a silence that twanged on her every nerve. She pasted a determined smile on her face, planted her feet firmly on the ground, then swung around to meet the appraisals being made of her.

Shock on both faces, old and young.

"Angie, this is Leo Pockley. Leo, Angie Cordell."

The formal introduction jolted the bookkeeper into an acknowledgment, though he threw a look of disbelief at Taylor as he stepped forward to offer his hand. "Pleased to meet you, Miss," he mumbled, using the tipping of his hat in courtesy to evade meeting her eyes. Whether he was hopelessly shy or deeply disconcerted by her appearance, it was impossible to tell.

"Thank you, Leo. And please call me Angie," she said, trying to project warmth as she pressed his hand.

Taylor had told her informality was the general rule of the station, everyone using first names, including the children. She shouldn't feel uncomfortable with it, but Leo Pockley's obvious discomfort with her made her feel as though she was being too forward. He was a short, stocky man, grey-haired, with a deeply grooved face which placed him in his fifties. He ducked his head and stepped back smartly, as though her touch had burnt him.

"And this is Hamish," Taylor went on, apparently unperturbed by the impact she was making.

Angie turned to the boy, her smile still firmly in place. No smile from him. No move toward her. He was tall for his age, and very like his father, though his features were yet to harden and fine, and he was unskilled in guarding his expression. His face had mutiny stamped all over it; jutting chin, compressed lips, hostile distrust glaring from his eyes.

"Say hello to Angie, Hamish." It was a command, softly spoken but a firm command, nonetheless.

It evoked a flash of defiance, the boy's gaze briefly locking with his father's, challenging his dominating authority before visibly resigning himself to it. Angie took the initiative, saving his pride a little in making the greeting easier by stepping forward and holding out her hand to him. "Hello, Hamish."

"Hello," he repeated grudgingly, his eyes hating the trap of a courteous handclasp but unable to completely flout good manners under his father's eye. He left Angie with little doubt of rebellion at a later date, when she was the only supervisor.

Angie didn't try to make conversation with the boy while the men transferred her luggage and the box containing the new computer from the plane to the Jeep. She saw no point in inviting a contentious display of rudeness. Experience had taught her if she stood back and declined to force anything, children's curiosity and desire for attention usually drove them to cross the barriers they themselves had erected. Being ignored got under their skin more effectively than all the coaxing in the world.

Nevertheless, it was hardly a propitious start, Angie thought, hoping Taylor was prepared to be patient, too, and not judge the trouble factor too quickly. He knew she had nowhere else to go. Before they'd left Brisbane this morning, she'd posted a letter of resignation to the headmaster of the school where she had been employed.

Another letter, containing a cheque for a month's rent, had informed her flatmates she had left and they could relet her room to someone else. Her bridges were comprehensively burnt.

Despite the thickness of her hair, her scalp felt as though it was getting burnt, too. The midafternoon heat out here on the airstrip was intense. Definitely hat country, Angie decided, cramming hers on her head. She rolled down her shirt sleeves and buttoned them at her wrist, suddenly seeing the sense of the cover-up, protective clothing worn by the others. It was a relief to get in the Jeep and be moving again.

On the positive side of the ledger, Angie was quite enchanted by the drive up to the homestead. There were not only lawns and trees around the buildings, but a stunning array of bougainvillea, massive cascades of colour; pinks, oranges, scarlets, purples and white. She spotted several banana groves and exotic African tulip trees.

Even more amazing was a satellite dish. They were obviously not technologically backward here. After Taylor's crack about entertainment on tap, she hadn't dared ask about television, but it would seem they did have it. There was no lack of comfort, either. Air-conditioning units were set into the windows of living areas. They might be occupying a primitive world in some senses but this was certainly an oasis of modern civilisation.

When they pulled up in front of the homestead, Angie was more amazed. The house could have graced a luxurious block on beach frontage at the Gold Coast. Double-storeyed, it had a deep veranda on both levels, with bougainvillea draped beautifully over the top railings. Double sliding-glass doors dressed the long frontage, denoting its relatively recent construction, and all doors and windows were gauzed against insects.

Angie reasoned this house must have replaced a much older homestead, which might have been more interesting in a historical sense, but she was not about to complain about being misled about life in the outback. She was only too pleased to have modern amenities.

A wide expanse of lawn and garden was fenced and the Jeep pulled up beside the gate which opened to the path leading to the front entrance of the house. They piled out. Leo Pockley offered to carry in Angie's luggage. Hamish hung back with him. Taylor opened the gate and waved Angie forward. Unbelievably there were old established rosebushes growing along strips of garden on either side of the path.

Angie was in a state of awe as she was ushered into a wide hallway. The cooler air inside the house reminded her to remove her hat. The floor was tiled and there were exotic indoor plants in lovely urns on either side of the front door.

"I'll take you to meet my aunt. She'll show you to your room and see you settled," Taylor informed her as he led her past a staircase and to a huge, splendidly equipped kitchen at the rear of the house.

The warm, friendly smell of freshly baked cookies wafted to her, drawing a natural smile. Two Aboriginal women, one rolling pastry on a marble slab, one at the sink washing dishes, paused in their work, responding with wide grins, their dark eyes sparkling with interest. The third woman in the kitchen froze in the act of opening a can of fruit, her whole body stiffening in shock.

She was tall and spare, iron-grey hair pulled back into a knot, her strong-boned face holding the sag of age well though she looked to be in her sixties. Her slacks and long-sleeved shirt gave her a mannish air of authority, more so perhaps because the other women were plump and wearing loose shift dresses. Angie's mind was bombarded with a host of quick impressions, but the overriding one was the almost blank recoil in the grey eyes staring at her.

"Thelma, this is Angie Cordell, our new governess," Taylor dropped into the charged silence.

The grey eyes snapped from Angie to him and their expression clearly questioned his sanity.

Taylor ignored it. "Yvonne… Gemma…" he introduced.

They bobbed their heads, apparently too shy to say anything.

"Yvonne's daughter, Jessie, and Gemma's son, Wayne, will be taking lessons with you," he went on.

"I'm pleased to meet you," Angie said as pleasantly as she could, conscious of waves of disapproval coming from Thelma Winton. "And I look forward to meeting Jessie and Wayne," she pushed out, struggling to remain calm and composed.

"You'll find my Jessie a good girl. Quiet," Yvonne informed proudly.

Gemma laughed. "Not Wayne. That boy can't keep still."

"Boys always tend to be more lively than girls," Angie said warmly, relieved to have some of the ice broken. The lack of any friendly comment from Taylor's aunt, however, was disheartening.

"Leo's taking Angie's luggage upstairs, Thelma," Taylor prompted.

"Yes. Well…" The words were clipped out. The can opener was discarded. A glare at Taylor said *on your head, be it,* then a stiff smile that didn't reach her eyes was directed at Angie. "You must be tired after your long trip. And in need of refreshing yourself."

"Yes, I am," she agreed ruefully, aware that disagreement would be unacceptable. Thelma Winton couldn't get rid of her fast enough, no doubt wanting to give Taylor an earful on his choice of governess.

"Gemma, prepare a tray. A plate of those cookies and a pot of tea. Or do you prefer coffee, Angie?" she rattled out briskly.

"No. Tea will be fine, thank you."

"Milk and sugar?"

"Yes, please."

"Bring the tray upstairs to the room you prepared this morning, Gemma. Yvonne, you supply Taylor with whatever he wants." She swept past the other two women. "Come, my dear, I'll show you where everything is so you can settle in."

Angie looked at Taylor who'd stepped aside to clear a path for his aunt. She caught his gaze and despite the plummeting of her spirits at the less than friendly reception from those she would be living with, she could still sincerely say, "Thank you for everything, Taylor."

He returned a wry little smile, his eyes acknowledging it wasn't easy for her. "I hope it's worth it to you."

She barely had time to nod, having to fall in with his aunt's brisk injunction to, "Come along now." Nevertheless, just that brief exchange made her feel better... the flow of understanding between them.

Taylor Maguire knew where she was coming from. He'd given her the chance she'd wanted, against his better judgment on her suitability for the position—a judgment that was obviously being echoed by those closest to him—and now it was a case of sink or swim on her own. He would be fair but he wouldn't prop her up.

There was no place for molly-coddling in the outback, Angie reasoned, respecting his stance and determined on winning his respect.

Everyone's respect, she added grittily.

Her room was charming, the furnishings mostly green and white with a splash of lemon, creating a light, bright and cheerful environment. She was provided with a double bed, writing desk, bookshelves, a couple of armchairs and a small coffee table, and appropriate lamps for reading or writing. Her luggage was stacked at the end of the bed and a wall-length built-in cupboard offered plenty of storage space. Her own small bathroom was a bonus she wasn't expecting.

"Are there any water restrictions?" she asked, wary of inadvertently earning criticism.

"Not at the moment. We've had good rain so far in this wet season. When the dry comes…well, we'll see." Thelma Winton's dismissive shrug more or less said it was pointless looking that far ahead. The scepticism in her eyes suggested Angie wouldn't last long enough to be worried by water shortage. "Is there anything else you need?"

"No. Thank you. I'm sure I'll be very comfortable here."

A sardonic twitch of the mouth. "Dinner is at seven. I expect you'll want to rest until then. If you need to find me, I'll be in the kitchen."

"Thank you again."

A curt nod. She was already at the door when the sheer weight of the unspoken rejections got the better of Angie's sense of discretion. She had always heard the hospitality of outback people was legendary. The need to know why she was being shut out of it was compelling.

"Mrs. Winton… Thelma…" She found the first name rule difficult to apply in the face of patent disapproval.

The older woman half-turned, one eyebrow raised in impatient inquiry.

Angie took a deep breath and quietly asked, "What's wrong with me?"

It caught her full attention. For a moment Angie thought she saw a flicker of respect before a look of soul-weariness dulled the grey eyes. "This is no place for a city sophisticate," she said flatly. Her gaze mockingly swept Angie from head to foot. "You're stamped with city style. Whatever lure this job had for you…the glamour of a cattle king and his kingdom…it's simply not tenable. I can only hope you won't do too much damage before you decide you've had enough."

"Damage…?" Angie frowned over the word. "I assure you…"

"If Taylor wants to be a fool, I can't stop him," she broke in bitterly. "Just don't take your frustrations with your life here out on the children. Hamish had more than enough of that from his mother."

The shock was Angie's this time. Had Taylor's wife been a city person who'd come to hate being away from it?

Thelma Winton's eyes hardened to grey slate. "I'll see you gone before I'll let that happen again, believe me. The boy deserves better."

Having delivered her baleful warning, Taylor's aunt stepped outside the room and closed the door firmly behind her.

Angie stared at it, realising she'd inherited a legacy of distrust from a dead woman.

Trouble was Taylor's word for it.

A fearful reserve from Leo Pockley.

Hostility from Hamish.

Downright condemnation from Thelma Winton.

The ironic thought came to her… *Welcome to Giralang!*

Nevertheless, there was one big consolation she could hug to herself for both immediate and lasting comfort. Brian Slater wasn't here.

CHAPTER FIVE

THE rain would pelt down any moment now, Taylor thought, glancing at the heaviness of the clouds overhead. He was glad they'd got the helicopter grounded before the downpour started, pleased also they were having a good wet this year. As he and Gary strode up the road from the airstrip, he saw the children racing from the schoolroom to the house, obviously aware of the imminent drenching.

He checked his watch. Just three-thirty. Lessons over for the day. Angie hadn't emerged with the children, he noted, despite the threatening storm. She'd taken to staying in the schoolroom, long after she needed to be there. No joy with Thelma, he supposed. Not that he could blame his aunt for her attitude. There was good reason for it, as well he knew.

"You know, Angie might like a ride in the helicopter," Gary remarked, a lilt of hopeful interest in his voice. "Give her a good view of the place."

Warning bells went off in Taylor's mind. Gary was twenty-seven, a highly skilled helicopter pilot at mustering cattle, earning good money. Of course he'd think he might have a reasonable chance with a woman who'd accepted a governess position.

He was a pleasant, cheerful, happy-go-lucky kind of guy who went out of his way not to hurt anyone. As for looks, nothing objectionable there…sandy hair, lively eyes, open friendly face, an infectious grin, well-muscled body…

57

"She saw it all when I flew her in," Taylor said bruskly, recoiling from the image of any other body but his tangling with Angie Cordell's.

"Yeah. Right. Didn't think of that."

He was thinking of other things, though, getting ready to test his luck.

"Hope you don't mind me asking, Taylor—" Gary gave him a sideways look, loaded with meaning "—but is there something on between you two? I don't want to put my foot in it."

Taylor silently cursed. He should have been ready for it. The question was inevitable, especially with the younger men due back next week. Gary had come in ahead of them, specifically to do a check on the boundary fences and bores, targeting trouble spots for attention. It was only natural he'd want to get in first claim with Angie. If it was viable.

Was it? Taylor wondered. Was she over the bastard who'd been stalking her? She'd been here a month and all that time he'd been aware of a tense reserve in her whenever she was in his company, not inviting nor encouraging an involvement with him.

But the connection *was* there. It didn't matter how much he tried to suppress the attraction he felt, his hormones buzzed in her presence. He suspected hers did, too. Her gaze was averted too carefully from him. The distance she kept so rigidly was charged with awareness.

"Leave her be, Gary," he said decisively.

A huff expressed both disappointment and resignation. "Right you are," came the grudging agreement. "Just wanted to know."

Taylor felt his chest tighten. He shouldn't be giving a *hands off* order. He knew damned well it wasn't for her protection. He'd felt the hit in the groin the moment he laid eyes on her in the Atrium Room of the Brisbane Hilton. Worse in her apartment that night when she'd guilelessly said…*you don't want me.*

He did.

No point in denying it to himself.

Though what the hell he was going to do about it… He'd be a fool to do anything at all after his experience with Trish! Thelma was right about that. It wouldn't work. Not in the long run. But did it have to be the long run?

Angie might be willing to accept a short-term affair. Take it for what it was worth while it was good for them. Was she the kind of woman who took such experiences in her stride? City society seemed to lean that way and she had certainly had one lover. At least when whatever they shared had run its course, she could be assured he wouldn't stalk her like that city scum.

Though this could all be wishful thinking on his part. He didn't know what was going on inside her head. While she gave every appearance of wanting to settle in here and do a good job—she was being extremely conscientious about the latter—might it not all stem from a sense of obligation to him for helping her out of a wretched situation?

She could hate the place—want no ties to it—and pride and gratitude were forcing her to carry on as best she could. The sense of connection to him might be an unwelcome attraction she chose to fight, a complication she didn't need or want. He really should offer to release her from the job instead of thinking how to get release for the desire she stirred.

"She sure is a looker," Gary muttered, lustful admiration in his voice.

Taylor grimaced. Gary was only stating the obvious,

so reprimanding him was ridiculous. Any woman with Angie's attributes was trouble. Every man on the station would probably have fantasies about her. No avoiding that. The only way to defuse worse problems was to put her out of reach.

"Angie's been through a bad experience, Gary," he said, giving him a look of serious intent. "Any ribald comments from the men and you spread the word she is to be treated with the utmost respect. One whiff of sexual harassment and the culprit will be off this station so fast you won't see his dust."

Gary's eyes widened, struck by the force of this admonition. "I'll let 'em know, boss," he said quickly and kept any further thoughts to himself.

Taylor felt a stab of guilt. He didn't have the right to make judgments for Angie. It was quite possible she could find Gary attractive. The interest of a younger man might suit her a lot better than...

No, dammit! It would drive him up the wall watching her with someone else. The chemistry was there for them. He knew it. And if he was going to act on it, it was best done now before the men arrived and started competing for her attention.

A heavy raindrop plopped on the road in front of him, raising steam from the heat of the gravel. Others started hitting the ground with force. "Better sprint for it, Gary," he urged. "I'm going to stop off at the schoolhouse."

"See you later then," he answered, getting a spurt on to beat the rain.

Taylor paused a moment. He was hot and sweaty from the day's long business. So what! he tersely dismissed, edgy with a sudden rise in tension. He only meant to talk to her…get a grasp on how she was feeling about the place…the difficulties she'd faced so far…if she wanted to stay on.

It was time for them to talk.

CHAPTER SIX

THE rain started thundering on the corrugated iron roof. Angie shook her head at the noise. She'd never known rain like it, such consistently hard, drenching downpours, literally battering in their ferocity. The other odd thing was how storms came and went without changing the temperature. Heat was a constant here. It would have been hell to work in this schoolroom without the air conditioner.

A thump on the porch startled her into looking up from her notes, just as the door burst open and Taylor Maguire poured into the room, permeating it with his strong presence, squeezing her heart as though he left it no space to continue its normal, orderly beating. He took off his hat, shook it free of raindrops, hung it on a peg and turned to her, a rueful smile adding its attraction to his air of intense vitality.

"Almost made it," his deep voice hummed at her, making every nerve in her body vibrate with pleasure.

"Closest port in the storm?" she queried, doubting he would actually choose to be alone with her. Why invite trouble? Trouble for both of them!

The comfort zone he had initially evoked with her was long gone, whittled away by an ever-increasing awareness of his almost overpowering masculinity. Whether he sensed the stirring of primitive female instincts in her or not, Angie was extremely conscious of her own supercharged state whenever she was with him. He wasn't entirely relaxed with her, either.

His gaze locked directly onto hers, piercing blue eyes denying her any evasion. "I wanted the opportunity to speak to you out of the earshot of others. This seemed as good a place and time as any."

Apprehension sent pinpricks down her spine. Her mind whirled in panicky embarrassment. Was he aware of how strongly attracted she was to him? Had he sought this private talk to bring it up and dispose of any hopes she might be nursing? A desperate need to keep her feelings for him hidden forced her to maintain the calmest demeanor she could manage.

"Is there some problem?" she asked, pretending total ignorance of any.

He shrugged. "Many, I would think. Though you've kept them to yourself, so I don't really know."

He didn't *know*. The panic receded. Nevertheless, his air of purpose stirred a deep unease which steadily increased as he strolled forward, passing by the children's tables, coming to face her across her desk, propping himself casually on the front edge of it. Angie immediately leaned back in her chair, feeling at a disadvantage, agitated by his closeness. Was it meant to test her reaction to him?

"The question is…" he went on, his eyes relentlessly probing. "…Do you feel you can cope with them or are they wearing you down?"

Angie took a deep breath, struggling to keep calm. There was no signed contract protecting her position. Had he mentally given her a month's trial and this was assessment day? Was he looking for an excuse to remove her from the station before the mustering team arrived next week?

He couldn't point to any trouble she'd made so far because none had arisen. On the other hand, there was only one young man on the station at the moment, Gary Dawson, the helicopter pilot. And *he* had been eyeing her up. Angie had been blandly polite to him, absolutely nothing more. But Gary might have made some comment to Taylor which he'd interpreted as trouble starting.

Resentment stirred, fed by the sense of injustice that had been eating at her ever since Thelma Winton had revealed the prejudice she held, undoubtedly shared by Taylor to some extent. Enough to prevent him from treating her to anything more than the kindly consideration one would offer a guest.

"What problems do you imagine I have?" she asked, deliberately tossing the question back at him. If he wanted to draw some damning information out of her own mouth, he could think again.

A few nerve-tearing moments passed as he weighed the challenge, appraising the golden glitter of the shield she'd pushed over her amber eyes, silently testing it with the strength of his will. She refused to give in.

"How are you finding the schoolwork?" he eventually asked.

"A new and interesting experience. The school of the air sessions are quite marvellous, giving the children the sense of belonging to a larger group and communicating with them. The correspondence sets they do are a good test of what they're learning. It's very satisfying for me to have the time to give plenty of individual attention to each pupil, since I have only three."

Let him find fault with that!

"No problems with the children?"

He meant Hamish, but Angie took her time getting to his troublesome son. "Jessie is a model pupil, diligent in her work, always wanting to please. Wayne is hyperactive, tends to be disruptive, revels in distraction. He needs a bit of carrot on the stick to do his work. I've instigated a system of rewards with him. The computer is the best carrot. He loves playing on it.''

Angie paused, wondering if Hamish had confided anything of what had gone on in the schoolroom to his father. The boy was fiercely self-contained—unnaturally so, in Angie's opinion—she doubted he opened up to anyone. From what she had observed at mealtimes, his relationship with his father was strained, based more on an obedient respect for authority than love.

"Hamish?" Taylor prompted.

It was tricky ground for her. Perhaps a blast of honesty was needed, Angie thought, on the child's behalf, even if it did acknowledge problems Taylor might stack against her.

"Initially he was hostile, belligerent and destructive," she stated bluntly.

"Destructive?" It brought a deep frown.

"On one of the first correspondence sets he scrawled swear words over every sheet. Drew dirty pictures.''

"Why wasn't I told?" The demand was curt and angry.

"Because he was testing me, not you, Taylor. But what you might find of interest is... Hamish expected to be hit for it. He was already ducking as I picked up the papers.''

His face tightened. There was to be no opening up from him on sensitive areas of his life. She knew before he opened his mouth he would make no reply to the implied accusation of previous abuse.

"How did you handle it?" he asked tersely.

"Well, if Hamish wanted to shock or upset me, it didn't work. I went straight for an appeal to his pride. Did he really want to send it in to the correspondence centre with his name on it? Was it how he wanted to present it amongst all the other children's work?''

''What was his response?''

''Defiant at first. By the end of the day, he'd had second thoughts. Since he'd defaced the whole set, I brought up the word processing program on the computer and helped him type out a fresh copy. He did the work and that was that.''

Respect in his eyes. ''He hasn't tried it again?''

''No. We have other little battles. He's very intelligent, constantly challenging.''

''Still hostile?''

''Less so. I don't rise to the bait.''

''You don't find it wearing?''

Angie felt her hackles rising. He was still looking for something to hang on her. ''A teacher's job is always wearing,'' she said pertinently. ''Children can have very complex personalities. I believe it's worth my time, trying to get the best out of them.''

No joy for him in that little speech, Angie thought savagely.

''I notice you stay here long after lessons have ended.''

''Why not? It's my domain. I feel comfortable here.''

''Are you uncomfortable elsewhere?''

Angie silently cursed herself for giving him something to seize on. Though he had to know, had to realise she couldn't feel comfortable in Thelma Winton's kitchen with the chill of disapproval ever constant in the watching grey eyes. The woman didn't bother hiding it.

''I like to wind down from the day,'' she answered. ''I also keep a journal. Writing my thoughts helps to clarify them.''

''A rather lonely occupation,'' he remarked.

"I don't find it so. I enjoy words."

Impasse. He nodded thoughtfully, veiling his eyes. Angie remained tense, waiting for his next line of attack. The top half of his shirt was wet and her gaze was inexorably drawn to where the damp fabric clung to him, delineating the disturbing maleness of his physique, the strongly muscled shoulders, broad chest. Whorls of black hair were flattened against his skin in the opened V of his shirt, just below the base of his neck. She wondered if his chest was matted with them, how it would feel to...

"Do you *want* to ride?"

The soft question startled and confused her, striking as it did through thoughts of sexuality, seeming to hit on the desires she struggled to suppress. Angie felt herself blushing and could barely meet his eyes as the rack of her uncertainties screwed itself up another notch.

"I beg your pardon?" she gabbled out, realising almost instantly he couldn't have been dabbling in sexual innuendo.

"Joe says you're frightened of horses but you're gamely persisting with the riding lessons," Taylor elaborated.

Joe Cameron, the head stockman, whose services as a riding instructor had been offered by his wife, Sue, the first week Angie was here. The school term hadn't been due to begin until February, the children frequently took off on their horses, and Sue had advised if Angie wanted mobility around the station, she'd best learn to ride.

"I'm not exactly frightened. More intimidated," she said defensively. "I've never had anything to do with horses before coming here. Up close they're big, and once I'm in the saddle, it feels a long way from the ground, but I *am* getting used to it."

"You don't have to, Angie," he said quietly.

"I want to," she insisted.

She wanted to ride to the river with the children and not be a total greenhorn in the saddle. It was even more important to her to scratch off the label of "a city person" who had no "country" skills at all.

He measured the set look on her face and murmured, "Pride goes before a fall."

"And determination picks you up again," she retorted.

It evoked a quirky smile. "So it does. I was just wondering if your determination was misplaced. Forcing yourself to do something that goes against your grain is really a waste of energy that could be channelled into a more productive area for you."

"Well, I guess I should be the judge of that," she said, resentment simmering again at his obvious lack of faith in her adjusting to the parameters of this environment. "Did Joe say I was wasting his time?" she asked, wanting to pin down this inquisition.

"No." Another quirky smile. "He admires your guts."

That was a relief. She liked Joe. He was a short, wiry man who'd lived all his forty-something years in the bush, his weathered face and bandy legs testifying that most of them had been spent on a horse. He was patient, good-humoured, always ready to smooth over her mistakes or nervousness with a joke.

"Then have I done something wrong?" she persisted, wishing Taylor would emit a sense of camaraderie instead of holding an impenetrable reserve.

"Not at all," he assured her. "I would say a lot of things right. You seem to be fitting into our little community very well. I've heard only good things about you.''

"They're nice people," she said sincerely. Only the Maguire family kept her shut out of their hearts. Everyone else had been kind and helpful, offering open hospitality and happy to give her the benefit of their experience.

"Yes," he agreed. "Though I appreciate it's taken considerable effort from you. It is a world away from what you're used to."

The control Angie had been exerting over her feelings snapped. He wasn't as blatant as his aunt in his prejudice against her but she'd felt it coming through every word he'd spoken and she didn't deserve any of it. Her frustrations boiled over and the words flew out with almost violent vehemence.

"Don't judge me by your wife!"

It hit him full-on, like a slap in the face. His jaw jerked. A flicker of some dark emotion destroyed the steady power of his probing gaze. Compelled now to drive her point home and goaded beyond endurance by judgments that were not relevant to her, Angie slammed her hands on the desk and stood up, leaning forward in a burst of turbulent aggression.

"No two people are the same. Everyone's life is shaped differently. If you don't know that, you're a man of very limited vision. So I come from the city as your wife did! That doesn't stop me from being an individual in my own right, and I'm fed up with being dumped on because of a hangover from your marriage."

She straightened up, proudly defiant, furiously angry with the situation. "I'm *me*. Angie Cordell. And it's time you took the blinkers off your eyes, Taylor Maguire."

Then she whirled away from him, too agitated by the explosive expulsion of her emotions to keep facing him.

The storm outside hadn't yet eased. There was nowhere to go. She stopped at the window, staring blindly at the torrential rain beating the ground, her arms hugging her midriff to hold in the churning mire of her insides. The thundering on the roof was almost deafening but it wasn't as loud as the silence behind her. Her skin crawled with her awareness of it, the risk she'd taken, the outcome pending.

She told herself she didn't care. He hadn't been openly honest with her about the situation she was walking into. While she was still grateful to him for getting her away from Brian, that was in the past now, and this was what she was living with, and she didn't regret blowing the lid off the truth. Taylor wasn't being fair to her. Neither was his aunt, nor his son. Though she didn't blame the boy for the sins of his parents.

She hated the thought of his wife.

It hurt. It hurt to be put in the same box as her. Dismissed and rejected and loaded with her crimes, whatever they were. It just wasn't fair! She'd lived too long with unfairness from Brian and she simply wasn't up to copping any more of it.

"Apart from telling you when and how she died, I haven't mentioned my wife." The quiet words held a note of perplexity.

"Thelma did," she answered flatly.

"I see."

"I guess you could say she spelled out what you didn't."

"I'm sorry. I didn't realise…"

"At least it made sense of the interview for me."

No comment.

"You want me to go, don't you? You've given me a month's respite and now you want me to leave and channel my energies somewhere else."

"I didn't say that, Angie."

"You were working your way around it." Bitterness at his tactics spewed the suspicion. "Do you have your first choice of governess waiting in the wings?"

"No. I said I'd give you a chance."

"Have you?" She swung around to face him with it. "Have you really, Taylor?"

He hadn't moved. He didn't move now except to make a gesture of appeasement. "Angie, I was merely trying to ascertain how you felt, after being here for a month."

"Then let me tell you your cynicism was shining through every word."

He frowned, shook his head. "I didn't mean to hurt you." The blue eyes fastened on hers with devastating sincerity. "I truly did not come in here to take you down or suggest you leave."

Her heart jiggled painfully. He might be speaking the truth but the judgments were still there, the judgments that ruled his attitude toward her, that kept her shut out of his life, denied any real sharing with him, denied his confidence and trust. She didn't know why it meant so much to her but it did. It did. And the need to fight for justice from him was as much a raging torrent inside her as the rain outside.

"Have I let you down in any shape or form?" she fired at him.

"No. You've exceeded my expectations," he conceded softly.

"Have I caused any trouble?"

An ironic twist. "You've been a model of decorum, Angie."

"Leo Pockley came from the city." He'd told her he'd been a computer programmer who'd worked for the one company for twenty-five years, only to be retrenched at fifty, too old to be easily employable again in that field. Widowed, his children settled in their own careers, he'd made a new life for himself as the bookkeeper on Giralang. "He loves it here," she stated pointedly.

"He feels useful again, Angie."

"But he's fitted in."

"Yes."

"I'm told some of your jackeroos come from the city, too. They soon adjust to the life."

"It's what they want to do. You were escaping, Angie…not coming to…running away from. There's a difference."

"So what?" she fiercely retaliated, her arms flying out to punctuate her argument. "You know perfectly well a city person can adjust to the outback, can fit in and like it. We're not all the same. It's because I'm a woman that you're all cockeyed about it." Then with reckless disregard to what she stirred in him, she demanded, "Do I look like your wife?"

"No!" His face twisted with hatred and he came off the desk in an explosive rejection of the suggestion, his hand slicing the air in agitated dismissal. "You don't know what you're talking about."

"Well, I'll tell you this, Taylor Maguire," she shot back at him. "You don't know me. You haven't even tried to know me. And until you do, your judgments of me aren't worth anything!"

"Aren't they?" he snapped. "What are yours worth, Angie?"

His eyes blazed at her as he moved with fast, efficient intent, skirting the tables to make straight for where she stood by the window. Angie had a vivid impression of power, danger, emotions unleashed and fiercely encompassing her. It pumped her heart faster. She stared at him, unable to look away, unable to speak, her throat constricting, her mind buzzing with the mad excitement of having broken his control, and a wild shoot of joy and longing went through her, making her tingle with anticipation.

She felt a great shifting violent force, gathering momentum as he moved nearer, and she had a sense of chaos let loose and didn't care. She revelled in it. The noise of the rain receded, as though they were being sucked into a whirling vacuum where only she and he existed. Then he was right in front of her, dominating everything, scooping her against him, and she was not just looking at him but absorbing him with all her senses.

She felt the strength in the arms locking her to him, the rock-hardness of his body, smelled—almost tasted— the outback land that owned him, the heat, the sweat, the steamy rain, the aggressive maleness that took it all in its stride. The only sound she heard was his breathing, heavy and strangely intimate this close to her, his chest rising and falling against her breasts. Otherwise stillness, except for his eyes exploring hers with the intensity of raw need reaching out, wanting it reflected.

She didn't know what he saw. The frustration, the hurt, the jealousy, the fear, the thwarted desires... Every turbulent emotion that had contributed to this moment were all centred deep inside her, yet swamping them was a physical thing, a huge vibrant overwhelming rush of sexuality, more powerful than she had ever experienced.

In slow motion it seemed, he bent his head and began

to kiss her, carefully at first, then slightly harder, his tongue feathering her lips, pushing past them. She quivered with pleasure, her response instant, instinctively encouraging. He seized on it, his mouth possessing hers in a storm of erotic passion, and Angie closed her eyes and gave herself up to a swarm of sensation.

She felt it in every part of her, a kiss like no other she had ever known, as though it formed a stream that flowed into every corner of her body, every hidden place. She felt it bursting through her head, pouring down her throat, tingling in her breasts, swirling around her heart, throbbing through her pelvis, racing down her legs.

Her arms were around his neck, hands clutching his head to hers. She felt him cup her buttocks, urging her, moulding her closer to him, exulted in the desire coursing through him, the sheer physical strength of it, and the heat, the aching hunger it aroused in her. His hands dropped to her thighs, dragging on them, gathering up the fabric of her skirt. Then suddenly they stilled. He broke the kiss. He gripped her hips and set her back from him.

Angie moaned at the abruptness of his withdrawal, opened her eyes in anguished protest, and found him staring at her, looking shocked, almost disbelieving. She stared back at him, too dazed to wonder what he was thinking. Her whole body felt strange, shaken. Her legs ached. Her head was light, dizzy.

He dragged in a deep breath. It shuddered out. Angie wasn't sure she was breathing at all. Her eyes clung to his, needing him to make sense of what had happened. She saw his shock overtaken by conscious decision, and the fierce desire to carry the decision through.

"I want to know you, Angie," he said gruffly, his

deep voice echoing through her mind, drawing its ragged edges into some coherency. "I take it you want to know me."

"Yes." The word slipped out, heedless of what it admitted and what it might lead to.

He lifted a hand to her cheek as though saluting her honesty. "Tonight then. If I stay here now, I'll want more of you and we have to stop. I don't have anything with me."

She looked her incomprehension.

"Protection." He stroked her cheek with seductive tenderness. His mouth tilted in a wry smile. "I trust you don't want to get pregnant."

"Oh!" A rush of blood to her head cleared the daze of stupidity. The realisation of what he was saying, what he was suggesting, stunned her anew. It was true. She might not have stopped him if he hadn't pulled back. But to assume she was willing to carry on with it tonight...did he only mean *know* in the biblical sense?

"I've been down that path," he explained soberly. "I won't risk it again. I got my son out of it but the marriage was hell."

She tore her mind off her own dilemma. It was important to hear what he was telling her, make sense of it, make sense of how it related to what they'd just experienced. The connection clicked loud and clear. No protection. A spontaneous sexual encounter...

"Your wife was pregnant when you married?"

"Yes."

It was being out of control that had appalled him. A hard lesson learnt? "Was that the only reason you married?" she asked.

He grimaced. "I couldn't bear the thought of my child being aborted."

"So you paid the price."

He nodded. "Though I did hope we could make a go of it. God knows I tried."

Logic, Angie thought, was amazingly easy to apply to something outside what she herself was feeling. His wife was in the past now. But the past cast a shadow, she reminded herself, even before he spoke the words that spelled it out to her.

"This…what we want from each other…" His eyes pierced her with his warning. "…Don't put a price on it, Angie. You'd better think about that. You can still change your mind. I'll respect whatever decision you make."

He tapped her cheek, stepped back, walked to the door, collected his hat from the peg, and left the school-room without a backward glance.

He'll get wet, she thought, then realised the rain had stopped.

The storm was over.

At least…the storm outside was.

CHAPTER SEVEN

TAYLOR'S mind bounced between wild exhilaration and cautious fear as he headed up to the house from the school. He'd never been turned on so fast and so far in his life as he had been just now with Angie Cordell! The night Hamish had been conceived, he and Trish had been partying for hours—too much to drink leading to stupid carelessness. With Angie... He shook his head...he had no explanation for almost losing all sense of where he was with her.

He wanted her, sure! He'd been thinking about it for a month. A lot of pent-up feeling there. With her, too. Maybe it was just the release of it that had made it so...so intense. Hell! He'd been on the verge of coming, just kissing her. And he ached from pulling back from it. He hadn't been in such a state since his teens.

Why, for God's sake? Was it the long drought of any sexual excitement in his marriage? One burst of it and he was like a boy again, driven beyond any common sense, impatient for more? It had been like spontaneous combustion. And he was still burning.

Tonight!

He half-groaned at the crassness of that suggestion. It was so damned bald, Angie would probably back off from it. Sheer physical need had blown his brain.

It was so long since he'd had good sex he was starved for it, but *tonight* was probably getting in too deep too soon with Angie. In more senses than one, he thought with savage irony. Though it didn't change what he felt. Or what she felt, for that matter.

Could she handle the kind of straight deal he'd put to her? Some women preferred to let things happen rather than be faced with a definite decision. On the other hand, what point was there in pretending? The desire was mutual. No doubt about that. Why not be honest about it? He wanted honesty.

Which brought him up with a jolt, reminded of Angie's accusation he'd been less than honest in keeping things from her. It was true. Yet he hadn't really expected her to stay when he'd first brought her here. He'd been more or less waiting for her to concede it was the wrong place for her. He still wasn't sure it would prove right, despite her insistent arguments.

Nevertheless, he should have a word with his son. To Taylor's mind, there was a big difference between a negative attitude and downright nastiness. Dirty nastiness at that. The boy needed some straightening out. He'd talk to Thelma, too. Angie deserved a fair go from both of them.

He frowned over the other disturbing revelation arising from their conversation. If Trish had dished out physical abuse, he wanted to know about it. He hated the idea of Hamish keeping it to himself, suffering in silence, perhaps being threatened with more punishment if he told. It could explain the withdrawal into himself the past two years, the flashes of hostility.

He reached the veranda, took off his wet boots, then padded down the hallway to the kitchen in search of his son. Only Thelma and her two helpers were there. "Seen Hamish?" he asked, knowing the children would have come here to stuff their faces with cake or cookies after school.

"You'll probably find him in Leo's office," Thelma answered. "They went off together after the rain. Failing that..." She shrugged.

"Thanks."

Taylor nodded and left. The raising of sensitive issues with Thelma would best wait until after dinner when Yvonne and Gemma had gone.

He walked back down the hallway, past the staircase and opened the door to the office which was handily situated at the front of the house with glass doors to the veranda for easy access from outside. Leo and Hamish were both seated in front of the new computer, man and boy enthralled with its capabilities. They hadn't heard the door open.

Taylor paused, reflecting on what Angie had said about Leo fitting in and loving the life here. There was far more to it than using his computer skills. He'd quickly become a grandfather figure to Hamish, the two of them developing a very real bond of affection.

Trish had resented it but Taylor didn't, seeing it as a special relationship which their own families couldn't provide. Trish's parents lived in Brisbane and his were gone, his mother dying at thirty from breast cancer, undetected until it was too late to save her, his father losing his life in a flood ten years ago.

Leo was good with Hamish, always willing to give him time and lend a sympathetic ear to his needs and wants, obliging where he could. He'd won the boy's trust, something Taylor feared he had lost somewhere in the final mess of his marriage. If so, he needed to earn it again. He just didn't know how to reach past the wall his son had built around himself.

He closed the door, alerting them both to his intrusion.

They looked at him, Leo's expression openly enquiring, Hamish's closed and wary.

"Sorry to interrupt but I want to have a talk with Hamish. Would you mind leaving us for a while, Leo?"

"No problem." He turned to the boy. "Don't touch. We'll pick up on this later if you still want to."

"Okay," he sighed, his face reflecting reluctant resignation.

Once the older man had gone, Taylor took the chair he had vacated, wanting to establish a relaxed rapport. "So how's it going at school?" he asked lightly.

Eyes still wary. "Did you ask her?"

"Do you mean Angie?"

He nodded.

"I asked if she was managing okay."

"What did she say?"

"No problems. Said she found it all interesting. Do you like working with her, Hamish?"

He shrugged, relaxing a little, more assured now that Angie hadn't lodged any complaints about him. "She's not too bad," he said off-handedly.

"I've noticed you haven't been exactly friendly toward her. It's hard to come to a new place, not knowing anyone. Like when you go to Brisbane. It's easier if people are nice to you and make you feel welcome."

"That doesn't make you like it," he argued. "I don't like being in Brisbane."

"Do you think Angie doesn't like it here?"

He frowned. "I don't know. I thought she'd hate it. Like Mum. But she doesn't seem to," he added grudgingly, then more darkly. "Not yet, anyway."

"Why like Mum, Hamish?" Taylor asked quietly.

"She looks like her."

"No, she doesn't."

'She wears things like Mum. And she's pretty.''

''There's a lot of pretty women who wear fashionable clothes. Inside they're all different,'' Taylor explained, newly conscious of the truth Angie had spoken. ''Haven't you seen any differences, Hamish?''

''Maybe,'' he mumbled.

''There must be some,'' Taylor prompted.

''Well, she doesn't get mad at things,'' he slowly conceded. ''And you can tell she likes Jessie. She doesn't put her down or anything.''

Like Trish, he thought, who'd clung to a racist streak, despite all his arguing against it.

''And she doesn't send Wayne out, even when he acts up a bit.'' This evoked a rather smug smile. ''So he's stuck with doing his work. Like me. No getting out of it.''

''Sounds like Angie's doing a good job as your governess.''

''I guess.'' Another shrug.

''You shouldn't judge Angie by your mum, Hamish. It's not fair.''

''Guess not,'' he said uncomfortably.

''What did your mum do that you think Angie will do?'' Taylor pressed softly.

Hard accusing eyes. ''You know.''

''No, I don't.''

''She hit you, too. And screamed and yelled. I heard her.''

Dear God! He'd had no idea Hamish had been aware of Trish's tantrums. They'd gone on behind closed doors, mostly in their bedroom, well after he should have been asleep. There'd been the occasional bitter sniping from her in front of Hamish, but on the whole, Taylor had thought he'd kept their son reasonably shielded from the worst of it. Instead, he'd been subjected to it, too, obviously when Taylor wasn't around to stop it.

"Why didn't you tell me, Hamish?"

"You let her do it to you and you didn't do anything."

It wasn't the same! Yet what boy didn't try to be like his father, following the same code of behaviour? Taylor's heart bled for the child who'd tried to act like a man, faced with hysterical unreason and no clear path out of it.

"So you just took it and kept quiet," he murmured sympathetically.

Hamish nodded, his eyes full of the misery he'd kept to himself.

"I'm sorry, son. I didn't know she was like that with you. A man doesn't hit a woman, but I would have insisted she leave us and go back to Brisbane to live if I'd known she was hitting you."

"She would have made me go with her," he blurted out.

"I wouldn't have allowed it, Hamish."

"She said she would…and she tried to…the day she crashed the plane." Tears welled into his eyes. "She tried to make me go with her but I broke away from her and I ran and hid so she couldn't find me. She was yelling and screaming she'd get me from you anyway 'cause she was my mother."

"No…" It was more a groan than a denial.

The tears spilled over. "I'm glad she died," he said fiercely. "I wanted her to go and never come back. When she flew off I wished she'd just keep on flying to the other side of the world and get…get lost…and…" He choked. His face began to crumple.

And Taylor felt the guilt his son had carried this past

year, on top of all his stoic suffering, the fears and insecurity, and without a moment's hesitation, he reached out and lifted his child onto his lap, cuddling him close, rocking him and soothing him as a storm of tears gave release to some of the burden he'd carried.

"It's okay, son," Taylor murmured. "It's not wrong to feel that way when there's been so much hurt. But *you* didn't make her die, Hamish. It just happened. It could have been me in the plane. Or Gary. Whoever took it up that day would have crashed. None of us knew about the fault in the engine."

"But I got my wish," he sobbed.

"No, you didn't. You wished she'd fly to the other side of the world. You didn't wish the plane to crash," Taylor assured him. "You didn't really want your mum to die. You just wanted the bad things to stop."

Hamish bobbed his head.

Encouraged, Taylor went on, speaking feelings he himself had carried, the relief and guilt and grief of Trish's death. "You're glad the bad part is over, that's all. But Hamish, I know you're just as sad as I am that it ended with Mum dying. It would have been much better if we could have changed what was happening with all of us and made everything much happier for her. I'm sorry I couldn't do that for you, son. I just didn't know how…"

Irreconcilable differences. Everything he'd tried…the bargains he'd made…the compromises…all futile. There'd been no hope left at the end.

"It wasn't your fault, Hamish, Mum getting angry and hitting out. She was very unhappy inside herself. She needed help that we couldn't give her. She wasn't always like that…"

How far back did his son remember? When had the

abuse started? Two years...three? He was too distressed to be questioned. Taylor reasoned the more recent memories probably blotted out the better earlier ones.

"She got sick in her head, Hamish," Taylor tried to explain. "It was like all her thoughts and feelings got in a messy tangle and she couldn't unravel them. But in her heart she loved you. And I know in your heart, you loved her. She was your mum, no matter what. And you have to forgive the bad things because she didn't really mean to do them to you. She just couldn't help herself. She'd want you to remember the nice things about her. So try to do that, Hamish. It will make you feel better, too."

The sobs gradually quietened into the occasional hiccup. Hamish lifted a woebegone face from Taylor's damp shirt, his eyes still pleading for more reassurance. "Can Grandma and Grandpa Hayward take me away from you, Dad?"

So that was why he'd refused to go on every trip to Brisbane since Trish had died. It wasn't only the past that needed to be set to rest. The future held its bogeymen, as well.

"No, they can't, Hamish," he said firmly. "This is your home. Even if I died, this is your home with Thelma and Leo and everyone else who lives on this station. It will be your home as long as you want it to be."

"But you're not going to die, are you, Dad?" he asked anxiously.

"Not for a long time, I hope." He smiled to give his son confidence. "I expect to hang around until at least you take over the working of Giralang. If that's what you want to do."

A smile broke through. "Course I do. I'm going to be just like you."

"Hey now…" He tapped his son's chin. "Haven't I just finished telling you no two people are the same? I reckon you'll have to be a lot smarter than me at running this place with things changing all the time. I had to get Leo in to help me with the computer."

Hamish grinned. "Leo says I'm a natural at it."

"Well, there you go. Just don't get so wrapped up in computers you forget about people though." Taylor gave him a serious man-to-man look. "You know what it's like to be treated unfairly. Don't do it to others, son."

He sobered, a flicker of shame in his eyes. "You mean…like Angie."

"I mean everyone. Give them a fair go until you know for certain they're not worthy of it. Okay?"

"What if they turn out bad?"

"Then come and talk to me about it and we'll figure out how best to act. I guess you and I…we should have talked about Mum. I'm really sorry about that, Hamish. Is there anything else you want to ask about her?"

Encouraged to open up, Hamish sought relief from many secret worries and Taylor talked to his son for a long time, re-establishing confidence in their relationship, confidence and an assurance of love that could not be broken.

It occurred to him he had Angie to thank for ripping the scales off his eyes, forcing him to look beyond the surface of things. She was a very smart woman. He shouldn't forget she'd been hurt, too. As much as he wanted her, it ill behove him to ignore her emotional scars. Stupid to make simplistic assumptions. Above all, he had to be fair to her.

CHAPTER EIGHT

ANGIE lingered under the shower, hoping the beat of hot water would wash some of her physical tension away. In another forty minutes or so she'd be sitting down at the dinner table with Taylor Maguire. She had to have her mind sorted out before then. He'd be looking for signals from her.

Tonight…

Could she?

She wanted to…wanted to follow her instincts and believe it would all turn out right in the end, that the intimate sexual connection would lead to sharing all the other important areas, and they would find themselves in soul-warming harmony with each other. She wanted that to happen so badly…to have a truly good relationship, supportive of each other, caring, happy.

But getting in so deeply, right from the start, was a heart-on-the-line risk. How good was her judgment of any man, having made such a terrible mistake with Brian? In fact, might she not be feeling so strongly about Taylor because he belonged to what seemed like a solidly set permanence here at Giralang, a steady continuance that she found deeply attractive, almost compellingly so, given the lack of any secure roots in her life?

She saw no caprice in his character. She was certain he would stick to any commitment he gave. There was a very real sense of security in those two convictions. Yet there was no security about tonight. If she went his way, she would get the chance to really know him. If she backed off, would he pursue knowing her on other levels? He might interpret it as a lack of honesty on her part, a holding off to get more out of him. In which case, he would probably retreat to non-involvement and she would lose any chance of getting closer to him.

The last thing she wanted was to drive him away. She simply didn't know how far he would carry *respecting her decision*. She certainly didn't want *no* to mean *no* to everything between them.

Caution or blind trust...which was her enemy in this situation? What if Taylor only wanted sexual gratification? The sex between them might be wonderful but Angie knew she'd need more than that, and if nothing more was forthcoming...well, she could always leave. There was no contract between them. No commitment.

Don't put a price on it.

Taylor's warning played around her mind as she switched off the shower taps and proceeded to dry herself. He had scars from his marriage. *God knows I tried*—the words carried more than disillusionment, almost a helpless despair, indicating a deeper level of emotional scarring than she'd sustained from her relationship with Brian. The involvement of a child had to make anything bad even more damaging.

For all her arguments, the *city* tag would not be easily wiped from his mind. Harsh lessons left harsh imprints. After her experience with Brian, anyone wearing a *drug* tag wouldn't get easy entrance into her life. It was impossible to rely on them. Not to mention how scary it could all become.

She shuddered, the spectre of Brian's frightening disregard of her wishes still a close horror. So different from Taylor's, *I'll respect whatever decision you make.*

Taylor had treated her with respect all along. Even this afternoon she couldn't complain he hadn't listened to her. He'd been reasonable about everything. Except in kissing her. And that had gone beyond any reasonable expectation.

Attraction, desire, need...

Angie sighed as she drew on her silk wraparound, suddenly very conscious of her body and the loving it wanted. Loving, not just sex, she reminded herself, tying the belt tightly, trying to ward off temptation though it still persisted, tormenting her with its promises of pleasure and the fulfilment of hopes.

She walked quickly to the built-in cupboard in her bedroom and was in the process of choosing fresh clothes when there was a knock on her door. A firm knock. Her heart skipped several beats. He couldn't be coming to her now, she thought wildly, not before dinner. There wasn't time to...she blushed at the track her mind was taking, the track her body was wantonly responding to.

She moved into action to settle the issue, opening the door only wide enough to identify her visitor and hiding her state of undress behind it. Her head swam at the sight of Taylor, dominating the space so...so *physically*. His gaze instantly caught hers and held it, the blue eyes surprisingly warm and soft.

"I just wanted to thank you...for Hamish," he said, the deep timbre of his voice thrumming through her.

Angie was thrown into confusion. Taylor's son had completely slid from her mind. Yet the boy had to be important to him. More important than she was. She frowned, trying to get her wits in order. Taylor had not yet changed his clothes for dinner. He could have been talking to the boy. Her rather blunt appraisal of Hamish this afternoon might have had some effect.

"Would you like to explain that, Taylor?" she asked, sensing it was centred on things which had been kept from her.

He winced, his eyes darkening for a moment. "I guess I should. But for you…" A long, feeling sigh. "May I come in for a minute, Angie?"

A minute that could be critical to her understanding of this family. His mood would change if she said she wasn't properly dressed. The decision that caution was her enemy was instantaneous. However reckless it might be in the circumstances, she wanted—needed—to know what was on his mind. She pulled the door back to let him in and closed it after him to ensure privacy.

He'd taken only a few steps inside when she swung around. Any further movement was instantly arrested. He stared at her, his gaze fastening on the spill of curls from the rubber band she'd used to lift her hair on top of her head for her shower. Damp tendrils dangled around her face and neck and his attention was slowly drawn to them, dragging his gaze down, down to the thin silk wrap, wound revealingly around the nakedness underneath, the tightly tied belt adding emphasis to the full thrust of her breasts and the curve of her hips.

Angie hadn't imagined his preoccupation with his son would be obliterated so swiftly. She stood in helpless thrall to the intense focus on her, feeling the raw burst of desire building from it, her body reacting with a will of its own, her skin tingling, her nipples puckering into hard nubs, pushing against the silk, a hot moistness gathering between her thighs.

His head jerked a little as he wrenched his gaze up. Colour slashed across his cheekbones. His eyes wavered

over hers. "I'm sorry. I didn't realise you were..." His
hand lifted in an agitated gesture.

"I'd like to hear about Hamish," she blurted out, cutting through his embarrassment, anxious not to have him
retreat. A deep breath. A visible reconcentration of his
thoughts. Control regrasped. He nodded and moved
away from her, crossing the room to the double glass
doors that led out to the veranda. Angie had opened the
curtains earlier. He stood looking out for several nerve-
tearing moments. She saw his shoulders square. Then he
half-turned, giving her face a long, searching look.

Angie had stayed by the door, incapable of any movement as her mind leapt through flaming hoops without
getting anywhere. Impossible to discern *his* thought
processes. All she knew was the wanting was even more
alive than it had been this afternoon, as though having
been sparked into tangible expression, it had caught fire
and taken hold.

"Strange..." he said musingly "...if I'd brought
home the governess I'd decided upon, instead of you,
I'd probably be none the wiser about my son and what
he's been feeling all this time. Before and after his
mother's death."

Acutely aware of revelations hovering, Angie kept
completely still, refraining from any prompting comment
in case it deflected Taylor's train of thought.

"It was you...looking like Trish...and having the experience to be perceptive about children's behaviour."

Her restraint cracked, pain at his first observation driving her to rebut his words. "You said I didn't look like
your wife."

He shook his head. "You don't. It's a certain
style...class..."

The *city* tag!

"…And as Hamish put it…pretty." An ironic smile. "A boy's understatement. You are quite stunningly beautiful."

Her heart pumped chaotically, sending a tide of hot blood up her neck, flooding her cheeks with it. Brian had tossed such words at her. She had mostly dismissed them as glib flattery, ego-boosting at the time, pleasing to hear, yet not really real to her. She wanted them to be true from Taylor Maguire…at least, what *his* eyes saw, even though it wasn't true.

He expelled a deep sigh. "You were right about Hamish having been hit. I didn't know. Trish was…unstable…the last couple of years before she died. I thought it was centred on me but Hamish was also a focus of it."

Thelma knew, Angie thought. Or at least suspected it. Why hadn't Taylor's aunt spoken to him about it? Non-interference could be carried too far when a child was being abused. Though maybe if there was no escape route, interference could make matters worse. Sometimes there was no easy solution.

"Anyway, that's why you've been a target for hostility from him, Angie," Taylor said apologetically. "He's been carrying a lot of trauma around inside him. I hope it's been straightened out now. As well as it can be at this stage. He's not a bad kid…"

"I didn't say he was, Taylor," she put in quietly. "I think he'll be a fine boy, given the right direction and support."

"Yes."

For a moment she had a glimpse of the pride and love invested in his son. It touched her heart. She had no doubt he was a good, caring father, one who could be depended upon to do his best by his child. He must have been going through such hell with his wife and trying to keep it from his son, he'd probably been grateful for Hamish's withdrawal, not understanding what it meant.

Then he looked at her with an intoxicating blend of respect and admiration. "You're a good teacher, Angie."

Teacher—another tag.

"It is my profession," she reminded him dryly.

He shook his head. "You have a fine touch with children. It's a gift, not a job."

"Not so much a gift as knowledge and empathy," she corrected him, giving in to the urge to tell him about herself, wanting him to know more of the person beneath the tags he was placing on her. "I was hell on wheels to most of my teachers. When it comes to troubled kids, there's not much I didn't go through myself. It wasn't until my aunt got hold of me in my teens that I reformed and got direction. So I guess you could say I've been there. It gives me an advantage."

He frowned. "You did mention about your parents dying when you were young. I'd forgotten it."

"Not important to you. You'd already decided against me."

"Bad judgment." He gave her a conciliatory smile. "I can't thank you enough for steering me into drawing Hamish out. We settled a lot of bad stuff."

She smiled back. "Consider it a favour returned. You saved me from a lot of bad stuff."

For some reason the comment disturbed him. The tension, which had eased slightly, came screaming back. Angie saw his hand clench. He seemed to be struggling with some decision, not liking it, forcing himself into it. He shifted, facing her full-on, his expression set in determination, yet his eyes warring with it as they fastened on hers, probing with an urgent intensity.

"Angie…perhaps I was…impetuous…this afternoon."

His voice was strained and she could feel the rigid restraint he was holding, the deliberate containment of any show of desire for her. Her heart sank. If he was intent on negating it, burying it, backtracking to his previous neutral position, he must have set his mind against a close involvement with her, caution winning over wanting.

"It hasn't been long since your…uh…unhappy entanglement with the guy in Brisbane," he went on, clearly having difficulty in pushing his argument, given his earlier fervour for almost instant intimacy.

No…her mind screamed. He'd been there that last night with Brian. He had to know there couldn't be a shred of feeling left for a man who had persecuted her. The affair was dead. Every bit as dead as his marriage must have been at the end.

"It's been seven months since I finished with Brian," she stated flatly. "And it wasn't good before that. If you're suggesting I might be on some rebound kick where anybody else would look good to me, I'd take that as an insult to my intelligence."

He looked pained.

He must want an out, Angie concluded, feeling sick with disappointment. She dredged up the dignity to help him end it gracefully. "If you want an excuse to put distance between us again, Taylor, that one doesn't wash. Why not simply be honest with me?" Her mouth twisted with irony. "I'll respect your decision."

He stared at her. She could almost see the wavering in his mind. Again his hands clenched as though reinforcing a control he found difficult to sustain. Angie fiercely willed it to break. They could have something good together. She felt it so strongly. If only he would let it happen.

"I don't feel right about taking advantage of…well, of your being here, employed by me," he said, the words tightly measured for serious impact.

Understanding swept in and almost buckled her knees with relief. A man of honour would hate the accusation of exploitation. He wanted free choice. She had to make him understand she did not view the situation as any kind of exploitation.

"I have a mind of my own, Taylor," she said quietly.

"Yes. Yes, of course you do." Relief. A wisp of a smile, both apologetic and appealing. "So what does your mind say, Angie?"

It didn't feel right to prevaricate. She'd made a firm stand. Her stomach contracted as the choice pulsed through her mind…caution or trust. It was a big choice. Yet, in a way, there was no choice at all.

"I want you," she said.

It was the truth, overriding everything else.

His mouth slowly widened into a smile of dazzling delight. "Honesty," he said, and laughed as he came toward her, released from restraint, his pleasure in her so evident, a cocktail of sheer joy fizzed through Angie.

Any sensible thought was beyond her. She simply feasted her eyes on him—this strong outback man who was beautiful to her—the embodiment of values and virtues that struck deep chords in her, important chords. Nothing else seemed to matter. She wanted, above all else, to share a sense of unity with him.

He stopped in front of her, and still smiling, reached out and tucked a stray curl behind her ear. "You are a remarkable woman, Angie Cordell,'' he said softly, his eyes simmering with his desire. ''Shall we pick this up after dinner?''

''If you want,'' she almost croaked, her throat having gone completely dry from the heat sweeping through her.

''I want.''

The murmured words had an intensity that seemed to thump into her heart, throb through her bloodstream. His fingertips trailed slowly down her throat, raising an exquisite sensitivity. They followed the edge of her wrap, nudging it aside, making room for the slide of his palm, skin against skin, hard flesh moving over soft, caressing the swell of her breast, travelling around it, under it, his thumb gently circling the aureole, teasing her nipple into more excitement.

Angie was totally mesmerised by the sensation of his touch, and all the time his eyes were locked on hers, sharing the mental intimacy of what he was doing, the silence between them heightening the flow of feeling. It was like doors being opened onto something entirely new, intensely seductive yet infinitely dangerous. This was the first step together, he leading, she willing, and soon there would be another step and another, and where they would go was impossible to tell, but retreat was no longer thinkable.

''I want to taste you,'' he said huskily. ''All through dinner, I'll be thinking of tasting you. I hope you'll be wanting to taste me, too.''

Then his hand was gone.

And he was gone.

And Angie was left to dress for dinner.

CHAPTER NINE

"ANGIE, would you mind serving the coffee in the TV room?" Thelma placed the tray on the table for Angie to take, and without waiting for her assent, shot a steely look at Taylor. "I'd like a word with you in the kitchen, Taylor."

Uncompromising demand. Thelma was on the warpath about something. "Sure!" he answered, quelling his impatience to have Angie to himself again. He rose from the dinner table, everyone else following suit.

"Great bread and butter pudding, Thelma!" Gary said appreciatively.

"Yes," Leo agreed. "Love those caramelised bananas, too."

"I'm sorry I was too full to eat much of it," Angie said ruefully, helping to collect the plates.

Thelma snorted at the excuse. "Watching your figure, no doubt," she remarked with a baleful look that swung from Angie to Taylor as she took the plates. She nodded at him, reinforcing the earlier demand, then marched off to the kitchen.

"I'll carry that tray for you, Angie," Gary said, swooping on it before she could demur. He grinned at her, taking away the sourness of Thelma's comment with his good humour.

She returned a smile. "Thanks, Gary."

He and Leo left for the TV room. Taylor stayed Angie from following, laying a hand lightly on her arm. He felt the slight tremor of nervous excitement and knew it had

96

robbed her of appetite. He'd felt the same way, forcing himself to eat the meal he was served while being totally unable to concentrate on it, his gaze continually straying to Angie's lovely face, the soft sensuality of her mouth, her golden-honey skin, the button-through orange dress that made his fingers itch to open it and free the delectable body it covered.

She lifted her gaze to his, the molten gold of her eyes swimming with vulnerability. "Thelma doesn't like me, Taylor," she murmured.

"She doesn't know you," he answered.

"Do you?" It was a searching challenge.

"Give me time. I won't be long with Thelma."

She sighed, offered him a wry smile, then pulled away, trailing after the others to perform the task allotted to her.

He watched her go; the cascade of curls around her shoulders, the seductive curve of her back, the sway of her hips. It was difficult to wrench his mind off the sheer allure of her femininity, but there was more than the physical to the attraction Angie Cordell exerted on him. Her challenge about knowing her raised his awareness of how few facts he actually did know about her life.

Somehow they didn't seem to matter. He liked the way her mind worked, the directness she applied to talking. There was no fluffing around with her. She made communication easy. He liked how she handled Hamish and the other children. He liked the quiet dignity with which she went about her life here, the respect she'd given to everyone on Giralang. He liked the person he had observed, the person she had shown him. It all added to his wanting her, fuel to the desire she'd stirred from the start.

He wanted the woman. All of her.

And she wanted him.

But he had to deal with Thelma first.

As he headed for the kitchen he reflected that he'd meant to talk to Thelma about her attitude to Angie. It was best done now. The bee in her bonnet needed its sting removed. He hoped his talk with Hamish would have positive results where Angie was concerned. God knew hostility was hard to live with. Who knew that better than he?

Angie had asked for a fair chance.

She had more than earned it.

Taylor smiled, thinking of the peaceful look on Hamish's face when he'd gone into his bedroom to say goodnight before coming down to dinner. The boy had already been asleep, emotional exhaustion probably taking its toll. At least his worries had been lifted. Tomorrow should be a happier day for him.

Thelma was at the sink, washing up, when he entered the kitchen. Taylor picked up a dish towel and joined her there. "What's the problem?" he asked, eyeing her grimly set face.

"You know perfectly well what the problem is, Taylor, and I'd advise you to put a stop to it before it's too late," she answered tersely. She paused in her washing to give him a meaning look. "You could have cut the air with a knife between you and Angie Cordell at dinner. I might be old but I can still see what's going on under my nose. And you can bet your boots Gary and Leo could, too. None of us are fools!"

"So?" Taylor tossed back non-committally.

Her eyes flashed furious frustration. "You want to make the same mistake again?"

"Angie isn't like Trish, Thelma," he stated coolly.

"And if you climbed down from your prejudice, you might see that for yourself."

"Prejudice!" she snorted and plunged her hands into the soapy water again, washing with unnecessary vigour. "I'm applying good old horse sense, Taylor. Once bitten, twice shy. If you want to sow oats, go to town. Getting into bed with Angie Cordell will only bring you grief."

"I don't think so."

She shook her head, agitated by what she clearly saw as madness. "You've only known her a month. At least give it more time."

"I don't want to."

Apart from his own urgent needs, it was now a matter of trust with Angie. He'd wanted honesty. He'd got it. What kind of man would he be to back off from her now?

Thelma slammed a plate into the dish rack and glared at him. "For God's sake! Think of the boy! You can't do this to him again, Taylor."

His heart contracted at the thought there'd been more abuse than he'd been told. "Do what, Thelma?" he asked quietly.

"Get into a relationship that will do him more harm. Trish tore that boy apart with her tantrums about leaving here and taking him with her. He used to sneak off as much as he could to keep out of her way. And he's doing the same with Angie Cordell."

Taylor breathed more easily. He picked up the plates in the rack and dried them as he answered his aunt. "I sorted that out with Hamish this afternoon. Like you, he was judging Angie on her appearance, not her character. I've made him understand how unfair that is," he added pointedly.

Thelma turned to him in exasperation. "The fact remains she is *not bred* to this life. Since you obviously feel the need for a woman, why in heaven's name, don't you pick on someone suitable? Someone who'll be a proper partner for you. It's not as if you're lacking in attraction. Diane Westlake is keen on you for one, and she'd fit in well here."

He grimaced. "Diane's a kid, Thelma."

"She's twenty-three. More than old enough for marriage in this country. Take another look at her."

"I've seen her recently enough."

She'd flown her father's plane in several times since Trish's death, supposedly neighbourly calls since the Westlake Station was only a hundred kilometres to the west of Giralang. He was aware she was sizing him up with future possibilities in mind, keeping it low key in respect for a mourning period. He hadn't wanted anything to do with a woman after Trish.

Until he'd met Angie.

"Diane Westlake would make you a good wife," Thelma muttered, banging some crockery together as she went back to washing.

Taylor gritted his teeth. "I'm not looking at marriage."

"You're just going to let Angie Cordell get her hooks in."

The jeering retort tightened his jaw further. "Angie's not like that."

"Every woman is like that with a man she wants."

"You're living in another era, Thelma."

"Human nature doesn't change."

"You're right!" he snapped, angered by the persistent blast of negativity. "I'm a man who's supposedly in his prime and I'd forgotten what it was like to be turned on by a woman. I've felt like a neuter for so damned long, it's like I've suddenly been given a new lease of life. So don't ask me to turn my back on it, Thelma. I'm human and I want to feel everything that being human entails. Including the pleasure of a woman I want."

She swung to him, her face pained, her eyes anguished. "Taylor…"

"No! You've said enough! Too damned much, in fact. I'd be obliged if you'd keep your less-than-happy remarks about Angie to yourself from now on."

He tossed the dishcloth onto the workbench beside the sink and strode out of the kitchen, sick to death of *horse sense*. Maybe he *was* being a fool to plunge into an affair with Angie. He didn't damned well care! A man only had one lifetime. He was thirty-five years old and never before had he felt the high adrenalin charge Angie Cordell gave him. What's more, he might never feel it again. If he didn't follow it through he'd be a fool.

Besides which, he wasn't a total idiot. He planned to use protection. Angie understood the score. They were merely going to explore where this could go for them. Commitment could come later if they both wanted it. But nothing was going to stop him from seizing the moment and riding it for all it was worth.

He opened the door to the TV room and saw only Gary and Leo. "Where's Angie?" he asked, his sense of urgency heightened by the argument with Thelma.

"She didn't stay," Leo answered.

Gary grinned at him. "Wasn't interested in the program."

Taylor nodded and left, uncaring what they thought. He glanced in the lounge room, then the office on the off chance she had gone there to wait for him. Having drawn a blank, he took the stairs two at a time, his heart hammering, worried by the thought Angie might have sought the privacy of her bedroom for other reasons than wanting to be alone with him.

Her door was shut. No inviting crack of light to beckon him in. Taylor hesitated over knocking. Could she have had second thoughts because of Thelma's obvious disapproval? It didn't fit the strength of mind she'd shown. Though as her earlier challenge had pointed out, he didn't know everything about her.

All the same, he couldn't believe she'd shut him out without a word. The darkness had to mean she wasn't in her room. It was quite possible she'd gone for a walk. Physical exercise was always good for working off tension.

He moved on to his own room, striding through it to the door leading onto the veranda. From this upper level of the house, a scan of the immediate grounds might pick up where she was. He stepped out, catching a glimpse of her further down the veranda, standing by the railing, her face lifted to the stars.

He paused, struck by her air of aloneness. It raised a flurry of thoughts…no one for her to run to from that bastard in Brisbane. Parents long gone. What had happened to the aunt from her teens? Someone judgmental like Thelma?

Alone…cut off from her former life.

How much had it meant to her?

What did *he* mean to her?

Then she turned her head and looked his way, the slide of the door having penetrated her consciousness, or maybe simply sensing his presence. She didn't speak, didn't move, yet the concentration of her gaze on him was more arousing than any invitation.

Taylor forgot everything…except how much he wanted her.

CHAPTER TEN

SEEING him instantly dispelled Angie's sense of loneliness. The brightness of the stars was just as instantly forgotten. It was as though the whole universe didn't hold a candle to Taylor Maguire. He walked toward her, a warm living force, a magnet she couldn't resist, a field of energy that inexorably drew on hers, fueling feelings she was powerless to control.

The emotions that had been churning through her—fear of the unknown, rage against fate for delivering her into yet another set of difficult circumstances, sadness over the misery inflicted through conflicts of interest—suddenly seemed superfluous, ephemeral, meaningless things. This man was a basic, vital reality, impossible to ignore or set aside.

She felt every part of her springing with excitement as he closed the dark distance between them, looming nearer and nearer, filling her vision, his face a tantalising mixture of shadow and light, the glow of his eyes an unwavering constant, transmitting a need that would not be denied.

He reached her and with barely a pause, took her hand and slowly lifted it, carrying it to his lips. He held her gaze with hypnotic intensity as he kissed her palm, tasted it, his tongue moving down her lifelines as though probing them for intimate knowledge, then sweeping the softer, fleshier pad at the base of her thumb. It gave her the most extraordinary sensation, as though her hand was a precious receptacle and he was pouring his life essence into it, through it, infiltrating her entire body with it.

Drawn to seek more of him, she turned to lift her other hand to his face, touching the hard, smooth planes of it, her fingers grazing over his skin, wanting to feel the man inside, needing to reach into him as deeply as he was reaching into her. She felt a muscle in his jaw contract, a reaction, a response to her instinctive quest. His eyes suddenly blazed with a searing hunger.

"Yes..." The word exploded from his lips as he lowered her palm, pressing it over the thumping beat of his heart. "I can't bear it. I can't bear it any longer." Raw words, cracking through long-held self-containment. "Come with me."

He captured her other hand and pulled her after him along the veranda, and the night pulsed with danger as she followed in his footsteps, his urgency tearing through her, compelling her on. His door was still open. He took her into the dark cavern of his bedroom and the throb of secret privacies kicked through Angie's heart, the fear of unleashed sexuality beating through the powerful promise of more revelations.

"Touch me now," he commanded, drawing her hands to the hot breadth of his chest, already bare, his shirt unbuttoned and pulled apart. "Touch me wherever you want."

She responded more to the desperate longing in his voice than her own desire, though both drew her into pleasuring him as he directed...blindly, in the ink-blackness of the room, stroking, softly exploring, suddenly revelling in the strange intimacy of it. His flesh felt so alive, rippling with muscles as he dragged off his shirt. Her fingers found his nipples and teased them as he'd teased hers, exulting in her power to excite when she heard him groan.

Her nerves leapt at the snap of the waist stud on his jeans, the rip of his zipper. Her mind registered the point of no return but she couldn't stop touching him, the bunched muscles in his shoulders as he bent to pull off the rest of his clothes, the cords running up his neck, the sheer maleness of his back.

Then he was standing upright again and she knew he was completely naked now, knew he was wholly accessible to her touch, vulnerable to it, and the power he was giving her was intensely moving and daunting. It was the power to hurt, to reject, and it implied a level of trust that squeezed her heart.

The barriers were gone, discarded, and the challenge of acceptance was placed upon her. Her response would measure her wanting for him. No lies. No deception. Naked truth. Primitive, but oh so tangible evidence of her desire to take this journey with him.

Rightly or wrongly, it made Angie feel incredibly special, and her fingers tingled with tenderness as she caressed him, caring for him, wanting him to know and feel he was special to her. Because he was. And this first time would never come again and what she did now was important. It was sexual. It was erotic. It was also an act of love, of giving what was needed and wanted, of reaching out and touching on the most basic terms of all.

He unbuttoned her dress. In a strange way it was like a ceremony, the slow peeling away of her clothes, the touching, the thrall of being exquisitely sensitised, his hands so seductively gentle on her, erotically knowing yet unhurried, savouring every part of her, revelling in every quiver of response. The only sound was their breathing and the darkness added mystery, heightening the sense of discovery, banishing any shame, focusing everything on touch and feeling.

Her mind blurred between fantasy and reality. She lost all sense of past and future. This wasn't so much Taylor and Angie, but man and woman meeting in a time and space that had nothing to do with anything else. It was as though this was a beginning in a world which was yet to know the light of day, the birth of a new life, stirring into consciousness, becoming more and more aware, the fascination of searching, the awe of finding, the sweet satisfaction of knowing.

And when he drew her against him and kissed her, the escalation of feeling was so intense, she needed the lock of his arms around her to hold it in, needed the support of his body as he moved her with him. He lowered her onto a bed and she lay there in helpless abandonment to the kisses he rained on her, spreading rivulets of heat through her as he tasted all he wanted to taste, shaping her breasts to his mouth, piercing her with pleasure as he sucked on them, his hands stroking her stomach, parting her legs, his lips trailing hotly, sensually after them, his tongue circling her navel, circling down, down, finding the folds of her sex, nudging them aside, probing until he found what he wanted, what she was dying for him to find, and he was kissing her there, and she couldn't stop herself from thrusting at him softly, achingly hungry for the ultimate fulfilment of the need screaming through every nerve now.

He went on and on, seemingly exulting in the taste of her womanhood, revelling in the freedom to satisfy his hunger for it, sending sharp, leaping streaks of desire through her, the pleasure of it unfurling, driving her toward climax. She felt the circling tide growing, felt the melting start, and she didn't want it like this, not with him outside her, not sharing in it. She writhed away from him, crying out, "No, please. I want you with me."

She heaved herself up to pull at him, to bring him over her, needing to feel all of him joining with her. She'd forgotten protection but he hadn't. He deftly applied it then settled on her very gently, calming her, holding her poised on the edge of anticipation as he guided himself on the inward journey she craved.

"Be still now! Be still," he commanded, his voice strained with the effort to control, and she knew he didn't want it to be over quickly, knew he didn't want any moment of this experience with her to escape him, knew he'd been holding himself back to ensure he missed nothing.

She tried to hold still, concentrating fiercely on the feel of him as he entered her, but it was so slowly her muscles convulsed around him, begging for more, drawing on him, urgent and insistent and needful. He pushed further, filling her, filling her beautifully, exquisitely, as he went on and on, sliding carefully. She curved and grew around him, making way, welcoming, feeling him become part of her, she part of him as he gradually sank all of himself into her.

There he remained long enough to kiss her, taking her mouth with his so tenderly Angie almost wept from the sheer emotion of it, the deep togetherness it reinforced, the caring in the knowing of it, the welling of pleasure in the sharing, the bonding of their bodies into one.

Then he moved, moving her with him as he worked a rhythm that revelled in discovery, pushing new boundaries, reaching for more and more sensation, driving, thrusting, a wild friction of heat, of pulsing flesh, spreading inwards and outwards, building great fronds of pleasure that bloomed with spangles and sunbursts, invading her arms and legs. She felt her strength ebbing, felt suspended in helplessness as he came into her harder, faster, stronger, and she climbed higher and higher with each beat, until the beat turned into rolls of sweet chaos and she yielded everything up to him as she floated on waves of ecstatic wonder.

Then she felt him come, too, the deep long throbbing of him, the spasms of release, heard his groan at the ultimate expenditure of self and his sigh in the triumphant satisfaction of it. She opened her eyes and looked at him as he lifted himself up from her, saw the solid silhouette of his head thrown back, raised upward, and sensed the sheer glory of their coming together running through him. When he sank down beside her, he gathered up her limp body, nestling it against his, her head on his shoulder, and he kissed her hair and cradled her close, making her feel valued and cherished.

Neither of them spoke. Somehow the silence kept all they had felt safely cocooned, and the darkness provided a comforting blanket, preserving the warmth and the intimacy. But it was only physical intimacy, and however much Angie told herself it couldn't have been a better start to their relationship, she wanted to know how much weight it carried in Taylor's mind. Indeed, whether it was all that *was* on his mind.

She had never been made love to so thoroughly. Nor so intensely. The experience was incomparable to anything she had shared with Brian, on an entirely different plane. And it hadn't come from her. It had been *drawn* from her by Taylor, the initiatives he had taken, the mood he had set, the feeling pouring from him.

Why? she wondered. Why had he brought her to his room when hers had been so much closer? Perhaps his own territory had made him feel more in control, yet he had more or less ceded control to her in many ways. It suddenly occurred to her they were lying on the bed he had shared with his wife. It was a disquieting thought. Was all of this part of some drive to exorcise memories of his marriage? Bad memories? What had gone on—or not gone on—in this bed with his wife?

"Thank you."

The soft murmur was barely a puff of breath through her hair, yet it instantly touched Angie's train of thought, stirring her to ask, "What for?"

"For being you." She could hear the smile in his voice, felt his deep satisfaction, but it didn't tell her anything she didn't know.

"Would you like to explain that in terms I can pin down a bit?" she lightly invited.

He laughed, a rich rumble of pleasure. Then he shifted, easing her onto her back as he propped himself up on his elbow. He gently stroked her face, raking the tumbled curls away from it. "You came with me all the way." His tone carried a soft lilt of surprise mixed with warm appreciation. "No questioning. No baulking at anything. Not even a hesitation. Not once did I feel you weren't in tune with me."

Angie frowned over his answer. Did he think she would go to bed with someone she didn't feel in tune with? What point would there be in it? "I did say I wanted you, Taylor," she softly reminded him.

"Yes. But there are many shades of wanting. And many motives behind it."

"You were…testing me?" She recoiled from the idea even as she expressed it.

He shook his head. "I was being totally selfish, doing whatever I wanted."

She laughed, relieved and amused by his claim.

"You're not a selfish lover. Believe me, I know what that's like." She thought of many nights with Brian when she had lain awake, unsatisfied, after he had taken his pleasure and fallen asleep.

"Have you had many lovers?" he asked curiously, no hint of judgment in his voice.

"No. Only two. One in my rebellious teen years. Then no one else until Brian. Whom I thought was all I wanted in a man," she added with bitter irony.

He trailed his hand down her throat and made idly erotic circles around her breasts, spreading tingles of excitement again. "I can understand why he didn't want to lose you," he murmured, as though her body answered everything he wanted.

Angie was impelled to a fierce rebuttal. "Then he shouldn't have lied to me. Nor spun out on drugs. Nor rolled into bed with someone else. Maybe I ought to know where you stand on that, Taylor."

"I don't like living with lies." He leaned over and licked one nipple into instant hardness. "Nor have I any need or desire for an artificial high on drugs." He treated the other to the same delicate teasing. "And I remained faithful to Trish throughout our marriage."

It was reassuring to have her judgment affirmed. A commitment, once given by this man, would be honoured. He wasn't looking for easy escapes, not with lies nor with drugs. It simply wasn't in his character. Maybe outback people learnt to ride out the blows of fortune, enduring whatever had to be endured until better times came.

"In fact..." He lifted his head, coming back to his propped position. "...You are the only woman I've been with since Trish." His fingers grazed tantalisingly over her stomach. "The only woman I've wanted to be with."

Angie took it as a compliment and was comforted by it, reassured he wasn't the kind of man who would ever take a woman lightly.

He leaned over and brushed her mouth with his, a soft, sensual kiss, through which he breathed the words, "Stay here. I'll be back in a minute."

Then he rolled away from her, off the bed, and she heard him stride quickly to the other end of the room, open a door, close it. An ensuite bathroom, she assumed, imagining him removing the protective sheath, perhaps getting another, hungry for more sex.

She frowned over that thought, yet it did answer what she'd felt coming from him, and if he'd been celibate for so long... *I can't bear it! I can't bear it any longer!* The words he'd spoken suddenly jangled in her mind like warning bells she should have heeded. If Taylor had simply used her, a willing woman, readily available... Angie couldn't bear it!

She frantically fumbled through the dark for a bedside lamp and found one, switching it on to spread some light on what she needed to know. Darkness might have been the cloak for playing out a sexual fantasy. She needed to see Taylor's face when he came back and she wanted him to see hers. It had to be stamped on his consciousness that she was a real person, as vulnerable to hurt as anyone else.

Agitated by a flood of doubts, she shot her gaze around the room he'd brought her to. No photographs of his wife anywhere. No feminine touches left in place. She was on a king-size bed and the rest of the furniture and furnishings were suited to a male taste, shades of blue and brown, heavy-duty chairs and chest of drawers.

Her pounding heart contracted painfully as the door he'd used was opened. Her breath caught in her throat as Taylor stepped into the bedroom and paused, registering the effect of light, staring at the vision of her sitting upright in his bed. She hadn't thought to cover herself—didn't think now.

The sight of him stunned her into mindless admiration for several moments. Seeing him naked was different to feeling him naked. He had the kind of physique sculpted by Michelangelo, beautifully male, perfectly proportioned, but no way could he be mistaken for a cold work of art. His skin glistened with the heat of life and his body exuded such a powerful energy, Angie was swamped by desire again.

"Was it time...or me, Taylor?" she blurted out, driven to ask before he came to her.

He frowned, lost on the context of the question.

"You had a long, celibate period," she reminded him.

His brow cleared. His eyes glowed at her. "It's you. How can you doubt it?" He shook his head as though she amazed him. "I have had offers, Angie. I just didn't want to take them up. Not enough, anyway."

So she *was* special. Even if it was only in the strength of sexual attraction, she had reached something in him others hadn't. The pressure on her heart lifted and her head almost dizzied with pleasure as he grinned at her.

"I'm glad you turned on the light," he said, moving back to the bed and sprawling across it. He picked up her foot and began playing with her toes, a warm happy twinkle in his eyes. "Now I can have the pleasure of watching you, too."

Angie gave up worrying.

The darkness was gone and this was real enough for her.

To begin with.

CHAPTER ELEVEN

THE plane flew in as Angie and the children were strolling back to the schoolroom after morning tea.

"Westlake's Cessna," Hamish said, identifying it as a familiar visitor to Giralang.

He'd been quite talkative all morning, actually smiling at Angie when she praised his work. Credit for his more favourable disposition toward her probably had to be given to Taylor's straightening-out talk with him yesterday. Nevertheless, she couldn't help feeling pleased. It made everything so much easier with Taylor if his son could like her. Especially after last night.

"Bet it's Diane Westlake coming to see your dad again," Wayne tossed at Hamish, his dark eyes sparkling with mischievous teasing.

Hamish threw him a dirty look. The jut of his chin and tightly clamped mouth denied any further rising to the bait.

Angie was puzzled by his truculence. The two boys usually swapped banter with easy good humour, neither taking offence. Since she knew nothing about the woman mentioned, she had no idea of the purpose for this visit, but Hamish's attitude certainly raised questions. He either didn't like the woman or didn't like her talking to his father.

Jessie, always eager to be helpful, turned a knowing smile to Angie. "My mum reckons Diane Westlake is sweet on Hamish's dad."

"Shut up, Jessie!" Hamish shot at her fiercely.

113

A sense of unease crawled down Angie's spine.

Unabashed, Jessie adopted the superior air of an older girl who knew better than her younger male companions and proceeded to shoot Hamish down. "Then why do you think she's been turning up here so much since your mum died?"

"Yeah...sticking her nose in," Wayne piped up again, jumping on the bandwagon.

"It would join up the two biggest cattle stations in the gulf if they got married," Jessie said importantly.

It was clear to Angie this was a repetition of common gossip and she didn't like it any better than Hamish did.

He rounded on Jessie, blue eyes blazing. "My dad's not going to get married. Ever again," he cried vehemently.

Jessie planted her hands on her hips and defied him. "Did *he* tell you that?"

"You just shut up, Jessie Gates."

"See?" she jeered. "*You* don't know."

"That's enough, Jessie," Angie cut in firmly. "You don't know, either, and it's none of your business anyway." She forced an appealing smile. "Let's drop it, shall we?"

Jessie huffed, crestfallen at having been rebuked. Wayne shoved his hands in his pockets and whistled at the sky. Hamish kicked up gravel from the drive as he walked on, head lowered in dark brooding.

Angie had much food for thought herself and she didn't like any of it. While she accepted there were no promises attached to this affair with Taylor, the intimacies and confidences of last night had led her to believe there was a good chance of forging the kind of relationship she'd dreamed about, with a firm foundation of understanding between them, a sharing of values, and the deep feelings aroused and cemented by their instinctive and strong desire for each other. Was she hopelessly fooling herself? Did Taylor just want his bed warmed while he considered a future with Diane Westlake?

Her buoyant spirits punctured, Angie found it difficult to concentrate on supervising the children's work over the next two sessions. Fortunately, the school of the air schedule had Jessie's class on first, Year 5 Library, and she didn't need help. The boys settled quietly into their story-writing, though Angie noticed Hamish's pen didn't move much. He was clearly disturbed.

Certainly the idea of having a stepmother didn't appeal to him, which was understandable, having suffered abuse from his natural mother. However, he might very well view any woman who got close to Taylor as a threat he didn't want to live with. In which case, Angie's position as his governess would quickly become untenable if her closeness to Taylor continued as she wanted it to, and it couldn't stay completely hidden for long, no matter how discreet they were.

She had hoped to establish a comfortable rapport with the boy, given time. With this in mind, she had agreed with Taylor on sensible discretion with their relationship, since Hamish had yet to learn to like her and no good could come out of shaking his newly built sense of security. Now, however, Angie found herself fighting with the suspicion that Taylor might have more motives for discretion.

Did Diane Westlake play a part in his thinking?

Obviously *she* didn't wear a city tag and at least some of the people on Giralang saw an advantageous match in the making if Taylor was inclined that way. Angie tried to reassure herself with Taylor's claim he hadn't wanted any of the women on offer. But maybe Diane

Westlake hadn't offered herself yet, respecting a normal period of mourning while indicating a personal interest if he wanted to pursue it when he was ready.

It would surely be in his mind to make a sensible marriage next time. *If* there was to be a next time. Commonality of purpose, a shared lifestyle with no conflicts over it, the natural understanding that came from the same background and upbringing…such factors had to have a positive impact on him where a long-term relationship was concerned. He was certainly wary of sex leading him into marriage. No matter how aroused he was, he was meticulous about protection.

Not that Angie could fault him on it. She certainly didn't want an unplanned pregnancy. Nor had marriage been on her mind. She wouldn't even begin to consider a long future with Taylor at this stage, when so much could go wrong. Brian had taught her a salutory lesson on that score. She would have married him if he'd asked her early on in their relationship and it would have been a huge mistake.

She just wished she had known about Diane Westlake yesterday. The woman might not be important to Taylor at all, but her arrival today certainly pointed up problems Angie hadn't thought through last night. This wasn't the city where a man and a woman could pursue their inclinations without affecting others. This was a tightly knit world where Taylor's business probably was everyone else's business.

Jessie's library session finished. It was followed by a general scripture lesson, listened to by all three children. Angie's mind kept drifting off it, fretting over Diane Westlake's visit to Giralang. Did it mean her staying overnight? For several days? Was such extended hospitality taken for granted in the outback? Surely someone would have spoken about her coming if she had been expected. On the other hand, perhaps she knew she was always welcome.

The lunchbreak came. Wayne and Jessie skipped ahead as they trooped up to the house. Hamish was in no hurry. He walked beside Angie, a closed, belligerent look on his face. She didn't try to talk to him. For once, she was in complete sympathy with his feelings. Their visitor was no more welcome to her as she was to him. It gave them some mutual ground, not that Hamish was aware of it.

Yvonne and Gemma were already handing Jessie and Wayne their share of a pile of roast beef sandwiches when Angie and Hamish arrived in the kitchen. Thelma, probably drawn by their chatter, appeared in the doorway to the dining room.

''Come and say hello to Diane, Hamish,'' she instructed, encouraging him with a benevolent smile. Her eyes were not so warm when she lifted them to Angie but they weren't quite as frosty as usual. ''Would you come, too, Angie? The Westlakes are our closest neighbours and Diane would like to meet you. We'd be pleased if you joined us for lunch.''

''That's very kind. Thank you.''

Neatly trapped for a woman-to-woman appraisal, Angie thought, suspecting Diane had already been given an earful about her from Thelma. There was no doubting whose side Taylor's aunt would be on if a rivalry for his affections was underway. Hamish, however, hung back beside Angie in the meeting that followed, using her as a buffer against any advance on his space by Diane Westlake.

After the formal introduction was politely negotiated, Angie had time to study the younger woman as she tried to engage Hamish in friendly conversation. She *was* younger, early twenties, Angie judged, with an appealing girl-next-door look, no obvious artifice about her. She was naturally pretty, regular features, dark blond hair cut to a short bob, very attractive green eyes.

Her slender figure was sensibly attired in dark blue jeans and a multicoloured check shirt, giving her a down-to-earth look. The shirt, however, was not *country*—Angie's practised eyes recognised designer label— but it would look *country* to a man. Angie made a private bet it wasn't worn to work in. It was worn to be eye-catching and bring out the green in her eyes.

What struck her most was Diane's air of confidence. Age was irrelevant. This woman knew who she was and her place in the world. If there was such a thing as landed gentry in Australia, Diane Westlake belonged to it, born and bred to it, just like Taylor. She was also very much at home at Giralang, betraying none of the uncertainties a sometime guest might have. Angie envied her that. More than ever before, she felt like an outsider looking in on a privileged circle, wanting to be part of it, knowing she wasn't.

After a series of monosyllabic replies from Hamish, Diane graciously let him go to spend the lunch hour with the other children. Then it was Angie's turn to be subjected to questions, couched in a getting-to-know-you format, but the bottom line was very similar to that in the interview with Taylor at the Brisbane Hilton… Why would a city woman, a professional teacher, want to be an outback governess?

Angie doggedly ate her portion of shepherd's pie in between giving answers and sliding in her own questions. Nothing of a deeply personal nature was said by either party. Diane had gone to a boarding school in

Brisbane for her senior school years—Angie knew it to
be a very expensive one—then on to agricultural college
before picking up her life on the home station again.
Having a Cessna plane at her disposal was probably better than a sports car, Angie thought.

"Everyone on the radio line is very curious about
you," Diane commented with a charmingly disarming
smile. "Why don't you join in the chat sessions each
morning?"

Angie returned a rueful smile. "I don't know the people."

"Oh, no one waits on ceremony up here. You just
introduce yourself and natter on."

"It seems…presumptuous. I prefer to meet people
first." Having been warned of the gossip mill by Taylor,
she was not about to feed it, especially not knowing
whom she should be wary of.

"Well, you'll be meeting them all at the picnic races
but that's three months off. It's a great occasion, isn't it,
Thelma?"

A glow of approval from Taylor's aunt. "Diane and
her family organise it all. The picnic races are held at
their station each year and everyone flies in for the event.
Even some city friends come for it," she added meaningly. "Perhaps there's someone you'd like to invite,
Angie."

She deflected the probe for information with another
smile. "Thank you for telling me."

"In the meantime, getting on the radio could help you
find your feet amongst our widespread community,"
Diane suggested.

Angie shrugged it off. "I guess I'm used to finding
my own feet." Her face was aching from smiling.

"But everything must be so strange to you out here," Diane pressed.

"I like learning. Speaking of which, it's time to collect the children for the afternoon lessons."

Angie was grateful for the excuse to get away, feeling she'd been pecked at all through lunch. Perhaps it was her own sense of insecurity colouring everything said, but Diane's facade of friendliness had seemed false to her, false and threatening. There was purpose in this visit all right, and it had nothing to do with trying to help an outsider find her feet in the outback world. Angie could only await developments for the picture to become clearer. Meanwhile, treading carefully seemed her best option.

Hamish looked as miserable as Angie felt when they settled back in the schoolroom. The three children worked on their mathematics sets for the forty minutes, with Angie checking their progress in case they needed help. Wayne claimed most of her attention. He was always restless after lunch. Once the sets were completed, Angie decided to put on one of the Human Resources and Environment videos, which was both entertaining and educational, an easy way to finish off what had turned into a stressful day.

Diane dropped in just as the video ended. "Hi! Hope I'm not interrupting anything important." She cast a bright look around the children who were obviously not hard at work. "Thelma tells me Taylor and Gary are fixing a leaking bore. Number twelve, which is only about seven kilometres away. Want to ride out with me, Angie?"

Much as she would have liked to observe Taylor and Diane together, Angie knew instinctively the other woman meant to put her at a disadvantage. "It's kind of you to ask, but…"

"Oh, the kids can have an early mark for once," she cut in, assuming an authority she had no right to.

"Yeah!" Wayne cheered.

"And I'm sure Gary would enjoy having your company," Diane went on.

The deliberate pairing off of couples put Angie in her place—the underling who could be manoeuvred anyhow Diane wanted. Angie inwardly bristled. She was sorely tempted to say the man she'd slept with last night might prefer to be partnered with her, but she held her tongue. Jolting Diane's overweening confidence would be a hollow victory if it put Hamish offside with her. Besides, it was up to Taylor to spell out where they stood with him.

She forced another aching smile and said, "No, thank you. I'm not really comfortable on a horse yet."

"Oh! Pity!" An apologetic grimace. "I forgot you weren't born in the saddle like the rest of us."

Like hell she had!

The grimace widened to a sweet smile. "I'll see you later then."

The moment the door closed behind her, Wayne started agitating for an early mark anyway. Too depressed to pour out positive energy in a discussion of the video, Angie agreed. He and Jessie whooped happily and shot outside but Hamish stayed in his seat, his gaze fixed intently on Angie.

"Is something wrong, Hamish?" she asked.

"I've seen you riding with Joe," he blurted out, almost accusingly.

"Then you must know I'm still a learner."

"You could have gone with her to see Dad."

It was clear he didn't like the idea of Diane being alone with his father, even though Gary would be there, as well. Angie surmised he saw her more as a possible spoke in the other woman's wheel than someone he'd prefer his father to be with.

"I think Diane meant to gallop, Hamish," she said dryly. "I wouldn't be any good to anyone if I fell off and hurt myself. It would only cause trouble."

He frowned, seeing the sense in her explanation, yet still disliking the situation. Several minutes passed as he pondered the problem. Angie waited patiently, knowing nothing would be gained by hurrying him. The boy had to sort out his own feelings, though she found it interesting and encouraging that some basic trust in her was emerging.

"I reckon you could handle a ride to the river," he said at last. "We could go slow." His blue eyes were suddenly full of adult responsibility. "I'll look after you, Angie. You won't fall with me. I'll ride alongside and take you the safest way."

Her heart leapt at the offer. Whatever Hamish's reasons for it, this was the first crack in his reserve toward her and a chance for Angie to reach out to him on a more personal level. "Thank you, Hamish. I'd really appreciate that," she said warmly.

He grinned, pleased at her agreeing to his plan. "I'll ask Joe to saddle your horse while you get ready to go."

"You mean right now?"

"Sure. Why not? I'll show you all the good spots at the river," he pressed, eagerly rising to his feet.

It had to be more a gesture against Diane than toward her, Angie reasoned, but she was not about to knock back an opportunity to make progress with him. "Okay.

I'll grab some cookies on my way through the kitchen,''
she offered supportively.

''Great!''

They left the schoolroom together, good humour restored as they hurried off to carry through their arrangements. Angie reflected that her riding with Hamish might
be seen as a snub of Diane's prior invitation but there
was quite a difference in the distances, the river being
only three kilometres away. Besides, earning favour with
Hamish was more important to her life here with Taylor
than travelling in Diane Westlake's dust.

As for the man himself...

Angie's chest tightened.

She hoped she wasn't making a huge mistake with
Taylor Maguire. If by word or deed he denied the attraction between them in front of Diane Westlake...well,
it was probably better to be hurt sooner rather than later.

CHAPTER TWELVE

IT WAS quite beautiful by the river. In contrast to the vast plains stretching into seemingly endless distance away from it, the area close to the water was heavily treed, providing pleasant shade from the heat. The rocky banks sloped so gradually, pools were captured in them, favourite places for the local wildlife. Hamish pointed out a tortoise and a water lizard, as well as identifying all the birds they saw.

True to his promise, he'd watched over Angie's handling of her horse on the way out and tethered both horses to a low-hanging branch while he took her for a walk along the river, adopting the role of teacher as he pointed out the many interesting facets of their environment. Angie couldn't fault him as a companion and she was impressed with his knowledge which he accepted as perfectly natural. This was his world and he loved it.

Eventually they sat on a boulder to rest and Angie risked one small probe into his private thoughts. "Thank you for sharing this with me, Hamish. I've been wanting to come out here."

He picked up a stone and lobbed it into the water, watching the ripples from its entry before answering her. "There's a good place for catching fish further up," he said. "I'll show you another day."

"I'd like that."

He nodded, offering nothing more.

After a few silent minutes, Angie glanced at her

watch. "I guess we ought to be starting back. It's almost five o'clock."

"*She'll* be there," he muttered, bending to pick up another stone. It was more an angry toss this time.

"Why don't you like Diane, Hamish?" Angie asked quietly.

He slanted her a knowing look. "You don't like her, either."

Angie couldn't deny it.

"Mum said she was like a crocodile."

It was his first mention of his mother. Angie kept her mouth shut, wary of making a wrong comment.

"I heard her telling Dad," he went on. "Yelling it at him."

"Maybe she didn't mean it," Angie said softly.

He flashed her a dark look. "It's true. Mum said she was lying on the bank waiting for Dad and when she had him in her sights, she'd slide in and gobble him up."

Angie couldn't help thinking it was an apt description of Diane Westlake, but she felt Hamish wanted his fears diminished. "I don't think your father is the kind of man who'd get taken by a crocodile. Doesn't he watch out for them?"

"Yes. But she keeps coming," he added uncertainly. "Like it's her territory."

"Well, maybe your father lets her come because he knows she hasn't got any teeth."

He looked at her, startled for a moment, then broke into a laugh. "She has so got teeth, Angie," he corrected her in very boyish amusement.

"But maybe not ones capable of gobbling him up."

He grinned at her, relieved by this point of view. Angie could only hope it was true, as far as Taylor was concerned.

"Hamish… Angie…"

Their names boomed off the river, instantly turning their heads to the direction of the caller.

"We're just around the bend, Dad," Hamish yelled back.

Angie leapt up from the boulder, surprised that Taylor had followed them here. With Diane?

The clatter of hooves on stones heralded a fast approach. He came into view, seated on a big black horse which he pulled to a halt once he saw Angie and Hamish standing together. His gaze fastened on Angie, quickly scanning her from head to toe. "You're all right?" he asked, as though wanting her reassurance it was so.

"Course she is, Dad," Hamish answered for her. "I've been looking after her."

He looked at his son and his face relaxed into a smile. "That's good, Hamish. Angie is still a bit nervous about riding. I wasn't sure you knew that."

He'd come to check on her. Never mind what Diane had wanted. Angie felt the smile blooming inside her before it burst across her face. "I wasn't nervous coming here. Hamish rode beside me and kept watch all the time."

"Well, accidents can happen," Taylor remarked, his initial tension dissipating as he dismounted with a fluid grace Angie admired and envied. Maybe she could match that someday. Match him in every way.

"Angie's not silly, Dad," Hamish informed him.

It evoked a grin that set Angie's heart pumping overtime. "No, she's not. In fact, she's probably the smartest lady I've ever met." His blue eyes danced warm pleasure in her.

"Yeah. She's real smart," Hamish agreed.

The sound of a plane taking off distracted all three of

them. They looked up, no one saying anything until the Westlake Cessna had zoomed overhead and disappeared beyond the line of trees.

Hamish spoke first. "She's gone," he said in a tone of wonder, then turned questioning eyes to his father. "Did you tell her to go, Dad?"

He frowned. "You never tell a neighbour to go, Hamish. You always extend hospitality to accommodate them as far as you can."

"Yeah, I know." He kicked at the stones underfoot. "It's just that she usually stays."

"I guess she decided not to this time."

Taylor's gaze turned to Angie, piercingly blue, sweeping for any concern provoked by Diane Westlake's visit, determined on wiping it out. Angie stared back at him, her insides quivering with joy. There was no double game being played. This man stood with her.

"Was it 'cause you came out here for Angie?"

Hamish's question jolted them out of their intense absorption in each other. Both of them had momentarily forgotten his presence. Angie's nerves leapt with alarm at the thought they had given themselves away, that the boy had seen or sensed what was happening between them. Certainly there was a speculative look on his face.

"Diane could have many reasons for going home, Hamish," Taylor answered equably. "It's our job to look after our own people. I put that responsibility first. I'm sure Diane understood why I came out here."

"For Angie," Hamish repeated pointedly.

"Yes," his father agreed.

Hamish looked smugly satisfied. He glanced at Angie, his eyes dancing with mischief. "Maybe *you* knocked out the teeth, Angie." He chomped his jaw up and down

in mock gobbling, then laughed as though all the cares
of his world had been lifted from his shoulders.

Taylor was bemused. ''What's this about?''

''Private joke,'' Angie said, smiling in relief. She'd
proved to be a spoke in Diane's wheel! Hamish didn't
mind if his father liked his governess, so long as the
crocodile was de-toothed.

''Yeah. Private joke, Dad,'' he gleefully echoed.
''Good thing I asked Angie to come riding with me.''

Taylor smiled. ''It was a good thought, Hamish, but
we should be heading home now.''

''Okay. I tethered our horses to the old swing tree.''

He set off, his head high, a lively spring in his step,
no kicking at stones.

Angie started to follow.

Taylor caught her hand, wrapping it in his warmth and
sending an electric charge up her arm with an intimate
little squeeze from his long, sensual fingers. His eyes
were lightly quizzical. ''Am I to be let in on the secret?''

She shrugged. ''It should hardly be a secret to you
that Diane Westlake is not one of Hamish's favourite
people.''

He sighed, rolling his eyes in an appeal for understanding. ''Neither were you until today. Now, suddenly,
you're in his good books. Want to tell me why?''

''I seem to be improving upon acquaintance.''

He chuckled, pleased it was so. ''I was worried he
might do some mischief, without meaning you any
harm.''

''I think we're past that. He was aware I was trusting
him and he honoured the trust.''

''Glad to hear it.''

Taylor did not relinquish her hand as they trailed after
Hamish. It made Angie feel secure enough to say,

"Hamish was upset because Jessie repeated some gossip about you and Diane, suggesting a marriage between you was on the cards."

He heaved an exasperated sigh. "That's Thelma's fond notion. I told her last night it wasn't on. Diane is Adam Westlake's daughter and I extend the courtesy due to her. No more, no less, Angie."

Last night!

And Diane turned up today.

Taylor might be blind to the ramifications of that co-incidence but Angie certainly wasn't. Diane may well have played out a "sweetness and light" role with him, holding back her real interest while she surveyed the situation. Once Taylor had shown his caring for the gov-erness, the lady had flown off, retaining her cover of the valued neighbour's daughter. Angie knew she, herself, would sound like a jealous bitch if she gave her reading of the other woman.

Diane must be in a fury of frustration, Angie thought, but she was clever enough to take herself out of any danger of showing it. A crocodile...waiting on the bank...watching for her best chance to pounce...and de-termined not to blow it prematurely.

Taylor had probably dismissed his wife's description as neurotic. God only knew what sly manipulation Diane Westlake had used to damage his marriage further, but Angie had no difficulty in imagining her stirring the pot behind Taylor's back. The resolution needed was not to fall prey to it herself.

Taylor had come to her.

He cared about her.

She had to hang on to that and not let any outside influence affect her belief in it.

Hamish was holding the horses ready to go. Taylor

helped Angie mount hers, his hands spanning her waist, lingering there until he was sure she was steady in the saddle. "I'm truly okay at this, but thanks," she said.

He grinned. "My pleasure."

And she knew he wanted any excuse to touch her.

Hamish's good humour was not at all dimmed by these familiarities. He looked upon Angie with a benevolent glow, his elation at Diane's departure still very much in play. They rode back to the homestead at a leisurely pace, the three of them abreast, Angie in the middle, being looked after by the two Maguires.

Conversation about the work of the day flowed naturally between father and son, though Angie wasn't excluded from it. For the most part she was content to remain quiet, listening to the nuances of their life pattern here, noting their mutual affinity with the land, the importance they placed on maintenance for the successful running of the station, and seeing how much Hamish wanted to be like his father, adopting his attitudes as though they seeped into him, like a process of osmosis.

The two of them were a unit, belonging together as she never had to either of her parents or her aunt. Again she felt the emptiness of floating outside a charmed circle, able to see it, touch it, even taste it. But that wasn't enough. It would never be enough. She yearned to be inside. Especially with this man.

She looked at him, unaware of the naked need in her eyes. He caught her glance. Instantly a blaze of desire ignited, as though it had been simmering below his surface composure all along, waiting only for a spark from her to burst into flame. Angie wrenched her gaze away, feeling the flare of heat racing to her face as her heart pumped faster. She was suddenly conscious of her breasts swelling with excitement, her legs spread apart over the rhythmic movement of the horse, her thighs rubbing against the saddle, her bottom slightly bouncing.

Erotic images blasted any sane thoughts from her mind. Earthy, animal smells assailed her nostrils. She peeked at Taylor's hands, loosely holding the reins; strong, controlling hands, knowing how to touch, how to mould, how to lead her into the mating act with both tenderness and exhilarating power. Her gaze slid to his hard, muscular thighs, so aggressively male, bringing the more intimate part of his manhood vividly to mind.

"I'll look after the horses, Hamish," Taylor said as they approached the gate to the stockyard beside the barn. "You'd best take your saddle into the tack room then race up to the house and wash for dinner. Thelma won't be pleased if you're late."

He wanted time alone with her!

"Angie might need help with her saddle," Hamish commented.

"Thanks, but I really should do it myself. Joe has taught me how, and I want to practise it," she quickly answered, allying herself with Taylor in pressing the boy to leave them.

"Okay." Hamish grinned at her. "You've done really well, Angie. Haven't even looked like falling off."

She smiled back. "You were very patient with me. It made me feel safe."

"As Dad says, it's our job to look after our own people," he proudly declared.

Our own people.

Angie wished that meant more than employees.

The trick was going to be not to disgrace herself when dismounting. There was a weakness coursing through her legs from thinking of what Taylor intended, what she wanted him to do, need and desire brewing an inner meltdown she could barely contain.

Somehow she managed to get her feet safely onto the ground. The next few minutes were virtually a blur. Hamish rushing around, Taylor lifting his own saddle onto the stockyard railing, then helping with hers, opening the gate, yarding the horses.

"See you later, Dad, Angie," Hamish called, taking off on his run to the house.

They waved. Taylor closed the gate, picked up his saddle again, and walked beside Angie to the barn. Without a word, they entered the dimly lit cavernous building and moved to the partitioned section where the riding tack was stored, bridles on hooks, saddles on trestles. The feelings they shared seemed too powerful for speech, as though talk could only be absurdly superficial, detracting from the momentum of reaching safe privacy where expression could take the course they both craved.

As soon as they had unburdened themselves of the riding gear, Taylor swung her toward him. Angie's arms locked around his neck as he swept her body hard against his. Their mouths collided, great breakers of hunger rolling through their kiss, drawing and sucking and crashing with passionate force, a wild urgent plunder that drove them into feverish need.

He backed against the wall, dragging her in between his thighs, kneading her buttocks, pushing them inward, thrusting her closer, moulding her to the rampant hardness of his arousal. She felt as though she was shattering inside, desperate for his strength to hold her together. He plucked her shirt out of her jeans and a hand snaked up the curve of her spine to unclip her bra. The clawing of his fingers shot shivers of sensation over her skin.

His mouth broke from hers. "Angie..." A heated

groan. He spun her around, her back to him. "...I have to touch." His fingers dislodging her loosened bra, sweeping the naked fullness of her breasts, diving down to the waist stud of her jeans, pulling it apart, his other hand on the zipper, then inside her panties, pushing through the soft bush of hair to the intimate fold below, stroking her into hot liquid.

She swayed against him, her head falling back on his shoulder, and his mouth fastened on her neck, the hunger even more raw and needful, his hand roving greedily over her breasts while other fingers were delving into her, her body clenching around them, convulsing, wanting, wanting, wanting...the thick roll of him against her buttocks, muffled by clothes, and her voice crying out, wild and strange as she had not heard it before, "Let me feel you, too..."

She didn't have the strength to do it herself. She was quivering from the bombardment of sensation, and everything within her seemed to be hanging on a pinnacle of anticipation that only the feel of him could satisfy. His arm hooked around her waist, supporting her as he undid his jeans, then pushed hers down, and at last there was the slide of his hard flesh against hers, the delight of its power travelling between her legs, stroking her with its heat, wonderful slippery pleasure, exquisitely tantalising, not enough.

"Please..."

"Angie, I can't." Despair cracking through his voice. "The risk... I wasn't expecting this."

"It's safe... I swear..." Frantic, aching. "...You must..."

She bent forward, leaning on one of the saddles slung over the trestle, reaching through the apex of her thighs for him, pressing, needing, and with a desperate, animal cry he drove into her, filling her, possessing her in urgent, shocking haste, yet her body revelled in it, loved it, exulted in its ability to take and give as the same awesome thrust came again and again, feeling fiercer, hotter, larger, longer, rocking her with ecstatic waves of ever-increasing intensity.

His arms were hugging her, his hands clutching her breasts, his body mounted over hers. She had the erotic image of them riding together, the smell of leather around them, and it was his world they were climbing and she belonged to it with him, indivisibly together, and he was saying her name over and over and everything was pounding until they burst over the peak, climaxing with a sweet violence that flowed and flooded and warmed and soothed. And at the end of it, the hoarse, emotion-laden whisper of, ''Angie...''

Through the swimming mush of her mind drifted a wondrous, beautiful, heart-hugging thought. This territory was hers, not Diane Westlake's. Taylor was holding her locked to him, his mouth pressing kisses on her skin, breathing *her* name, and there was no room at all for a crocodile to pounce.

CHAPTER THIRTEEN

FOR many weeks the men had been mustering from camp to camp, branding, culling, driving the stock in, and today was the big day. The road train had come this morning and loading the selected herd onto it was underway. From here cattle would be taken to Darwin, then shipped to Indonesia. The logistics of organising it all certainly demonstrated how big a business running a station like Giralang was.

Angie had declared time off from school for the duration and she and the three children hung on the stockyard railings, watching what to her was an amazing scene.

Taylor stood high on the fence by the gate, overseeing the drive onto the loading ramp. He was using a two-way radio to keep in constant communication with Joe Cameron, the head stockman. Leo sat on a specially fitted high chair above the last yard, keeping book on each loading.

The cattle were big red Brahman crosses, and their hooves kicked up clouds of red dust as they were relentlessly moved through the yards by the men on their horses, keeping the herd going with electric prodders and plastic tubes, the cattle dogs circling watchfully, ready to round up any straying beast. The occasional breakaway brought heart-kicking excitement, but both men and dogs were incredibly skilful at maintaining control.

The bellowing from the cattle, shouting and swearing from the men, barking from the dogs, all the jostling and tramping provided continual movement and noise on a scale that bombarded every sense, stamping an indelible reality of what this outback life encompassed; its danger, its vitality, its challenge, the sweat and the heat and the dust, the sheer bigness of it all, dwarfing anything Angie had known before.

It made a city existence feel unreal, as though people only played with toys there, surrounding themselves with manufactured objects, having lost touch with basic nature. Values were placed on things that were meaningless to people bred to this land. It was suddenly very clear to Angie why they held such a reserve about city people. The gap was so great. She understood it now. She could see it, feel it, and she knew she would never feel quite right in a city again.

There was something about all this that went soul-deep. She had heard the outback spoken of as a vast emptiness, but there was substance here, solid substance that emitted a sense of constancy. It wouldn't change overnight. It couldn't be taken away. It represented life in its most primal state and it remained true to its nature. Somehow these qualities soothed the uncertainties that had plagued Angie most of her life. She didn't feel displaced. Being here felt good. Right.

In the four months she'd been at Giralang, she couldn't recall ever being bored. There was so much to learn, all of it of interest to her. Taylor, of course, was so inextricably bound up in the place, it was impossible to separate him from it, which, Angie realised, had its influence on her. All the same, she truly did feel she could live out the rest of her life here…with him.

The tantalising question was…would he want her to?

Today he looked very much the cattle king he was, standing tall above the melee, dominating it with his authority. Yet he wasn't an arrogant dictator driven by a sense of power or ego, simply a man who saw what had to be done and did it, who shouldered responsibility and didn't shirk from doing anything he expected of his men, which earned both their liking and respect. They all said Giralang was a good station to work on.

Angie knew why. It was the quality of leadership Taylor gave them; caring, fair and firm. In her teaching experience, it was always the principal who set the tone of the school, making a remarkable difference to how well it operated. So much depended upon the man in control. The men instinctively trusted Taylor.

She had, too, the night he'd rescued her from Brian. She'd entrusted him with much more of herself since then and not been disappointed anywhere along the line. He had learnt to trust her, too, even putting the contraception issue aside once she assured him she was on the pill. Yet she did not really know what he felt for her, beyond the physical intimacy they shared. She suspected the failure of his marriage still haunted him. He seemed content to be sexually satisfied, living each day as it came with her, not looking any further.

"I'm starving," Wayne declared with feeling. "Must be lunchtime. Let's go get something to eat."

He was off the railings before Jessie began to scramble down after him. "Wayne, we don't have to go up to the homestead kitchen," she called in the big-sisterly, bossy tone she tended to use with the boys. "Our mums are helping the men's cook today. They're getting stuff ready for the barbecue tonight."

His face lit up. "Yeah. We could pinch some of that."

"I didn't mean..." Jessie huffed in annoyance. Wayne had already taken to his heels and she ran to catch up with him.

Hamish hadn't budged. He grinned at Angie. "Wayne will get a cuff around his ears from Bill if he's not careful."

The men's cook didn't take kindly to a disorderly taking of the food he prepared. He used to be in the army and he kept strict account of everything. Angie grinned back. "Serve him right. I think we'd better keep out of Bill's way and go up to the house for our lunch. Or would you rather stay here and I'll bring some sandwiches back for you?"

"No. I could do with a long drink. Get the dust out of my mouth."

"Me, too."

Taylor's head turned sharply toward them as they climbed down from their perch on the railings, his gaze catching Angie's with an alertness that made her realise he'd been aware of her presence all along, despite his concentration on the work in hand.

"Lunch!" she yelled, pointing up to the house.

He nodded and waved them on, quickly returning his attention to where it was needed. Just one glance, re-affirming the close connection between them, and it put a happy spring into her step. She smiled at Hamish, glad he didn't seem to mind the obvious friendship she had with Taylor.

"I suppose someone will feed your father and the men sometime."

"Bill sends out lunch-packs. They all eat on the go today, then have a huge feed up tonight at the barbecue." His eyes sparkled with anticipation. "It's always a great night, Angie."

"It's a great day."

He laughed then cocked a measuring look at her. "You really like it here, don't you?"

"Yes."

"Is it 'cause of Dad?"

"He's part of it," she answered honestly. "I think your father's a great man."

"He looks happy with you," came the speculative observation, then the rueful comment, "He wasn't happy with my mum."

Angie took a deep breath, acutely aware of sensitive ground. "I'm sorry it was like that, Hamish," she said quietly.

"It was 'cause she wasn't happy here," he returned matter-of-factly.

"I guess it strikes people differently."

"Yeah. Dad said you were different. And you are. I'm glad you came to Giralang, Angie. It's been real good."

"It's been good for me, too."

"Are you going to stay?"

"As long as your father will let me."

He nodded with an air of satisfaction. "I reckon Dad will keep you. When he's happy with someone he always tries to keep them on Giralang. It makes everything work better."

A very simple equation in Hamish's mind, but not quite so simple in Angie's. Nevertheless, the boy's acceptance of her as a good part of their lives was heartwarming. His linking her with his mother carried less certain connotations. Did he sense how intimate she was with Taylor, or was he harking back to his initial hostility toward her? Whatever he was thinking, at least he displayed a far more positive attitude toward her than he had to Diane Westlake.

Whom they hadn't seen since her aborted visit two months ago.

But who would be very much in evidence at the picnic races, only three weeks away now.

Angie suspected Diane was bound to make the festive weekend uncomfortable for her, one way or another, but there was no point in worrying about it. Besides, as long as Taylor supported her, surely other people would respect her position with him.

Thelma was concocting a giant trifle in a huge plastic bowl when Angie and Hamish entered the kitchen after having washed off the dust from their faces and hands in the laundry. They helped themselves to food and drink while Hamish chatted on to his aunt about the cattle drive.

Thelma rarely directed conversation at Angie. She wasn't exactly rude but Angie was well aware the older woman hadn't thawed in her attitude toward her. If anything, it was more frosty. The *city woman* tag had probably been updated to *loose city woman* since she and Taylor had become lovers.

"Come on, Angie. Let's get back," Hamish said eagerly, refuelled for the afternoon. He grinned at his aunt. "She doesn't want to miss anything."

"I daresay it is a novelty for her," came the sardonic comment, her grey eyes flicking a derisive dismissal of any lasting interest by Angie in station business.

Her policy of non-confrontation with Taylor's aunt suddenly wore very thin. Usually Angie let such comments slide past her, believing only time would show the older woman they had no sting or power. Somehow today was different. She wanted to correct the judgment Thelma kept making.

"You go ahead, Hamish," she said with an encouraging smile. "I have a couple of things to do before I leave the house."

"Okay," he agreed obligingly. "Don't be long though."

"I won't."

Angie waited until he was out of earshot, then quietly asked, "Why do you want to drive me away, Thelma? What harm am I doing?"

The older woman stopped sprinkling coconut over the trifle and eyed her with steely dislike. "You've got your honeyed claws into both Taylor and Hamish and it will rip them apart when you decide you've had enough."

"I don't think I'll ever have enough."

Thelma snorted. "Sex doesn't cover everything, however good it is."

"No, but it doesn't have to. I like what's here, Thelma."

Icy scepticism. "The novelty will wear off. As it did with Trish."

"She didn't love Taylor," Angie said with certainty.

A sneer of contempt. "You city people fall in and out of love so many times the divorce courts can't keep up with you."

"I'm not talking about a fleeting physical attraction, Thelma. I love Taylor for the man he is...honest and trustworthy and strong and dependable and caring. To me he's not a glamorous cattle king. He's a king amongst men, towering over everyone else in the qualities that mean most to me. And I know this land and the demands it makes on him is an integral part of what he is, and it answers what I've been seeking all my life."

For once, the older woman was stumped for a reply, arrested by the passionate conviction in Angie's words.

A sad irony twisted her mouth as Angie added, "It won't be me who cries 'enough,' Thelma. It will be Taylor. If he wants to."

Silence. Nothing but a blank stare from the older woman.

Angie turned away and left the kitchen, not knowing if anything she said had sunk home or met an impenetrable shield. Perhaps she had spoken out prematurely and only time could prove whatever Thelma needed proven. It was probably impossible for anyone else to look into her own heart and see the truth.

But she knew it. She had never known anything so clearly. And much, much later that day, after the cattle had all been loaded and the road train had departed, and everyone on the station had dispersed to their various habitats to clean up for the barbecue, Angie's deep hunger for the man she loved led her straight into his bathroom where the shower was spilling down at full power, full heat.

He didn't hear her enter. Through the steamed-up glass door she could see his back was turned to her, his head tilted to the streaming water, fingers raking shampoo suds from his hair. Angie had already showered but she couldn't wait for him to finish. She discarded her clothes, opened the shower door and stepped in with him, sliding her arms around his waist, pushing her fingers down over his flat stomach, tangling with him intimately, yearningly as she gently rubbed her body against his.

He went utterly still, as though he was holding his breath, focusing all of himself on the sensations she aroused. She felt the power of him surging under her touch, rising, hardening, becoming fully erect and she revelled in the feeling of owning him, if only this much. She kissed his back and murmured, "I thought you were wonderful today, holding control over all that frazzling activity."

His breath whooshed out and he turned, smiling. "Is this my reward?"

She smiled back through the water. "I've been watching you and wanting you for hours."

"Days, weeks, months, years," he said huskily, lifting her, holding her against him as she sank slowly, exultantly, down to meet and engulf the eager shaft of his manhood, easing onto it with exquisitely felt anticipation.

He pressed her back against the wall, bracing himself to start thrusting, but he kissed her first, a long drowning kiss that made her feel both languid and frantic, loving it but desperate for more of him, hungry for all he could give her. She flexed and pushed at him, driving for the motion she wanted, needed, and he responded wildly, rearing back and plunging forward, lifting her and letting her fall to a pounding rhythm, her body slithering against the wall, water cascading around them, the steam of heat and flesh a hot erotic mist, his hands kneading her buttocks, and inside her, the sweet building of peaks of pleasure, higher, sharper, and the yielding depths within grasping for the utmost pinnacle, and there it was, a glorious, triumphant fusion of giving to each other, possessing each other, sharing and belonging.

"You're the one who's wonderful, Angie," he whispered, kissing her in a rain of fervour.

And as she slowly floated down from heaven, she touched his face and said, "I hope you always think that, Taylor."

"How could I not?" he answered, his eyes so intense they seemed to tunnel into her soul. "You're the best thing that ever happened to me, Angie."

Then love me, she silently begged. *Love me and never let me go.*

But he eased her onto her feet and washed away the aftermath of their lovemaking, tenderly, thoroughly, then dried them both, and while still together, they were apart again, without the words Angie desperately wanted to hear being spoken.

The hunger in her heart throbbed on.

CHAPTER FOURTEEN

THE barbecue was in full swing; hearty appetites being satisfied, everyone in a relaxed, happy mood, joking, laughing, pleased that the work of the day had been achieved without any mishap and all set to party until exhaustion set in. Taylor enjoyed the lively camaraderie of such nights as this...the whole Giralang family celebrating together, their teamwork and unity of purpose understood and appreciated as an integral part of their lives. As natural as breathing.

Did Angie comprehend how deep it went?

Was she herself affected by it, or did her interest have more the collective delight of a keen observer being subjected to a new experience?

Taylor wished he knew. They'd been sharing their meal with Joe and Sue Cameron, the head stockman and his wife having become firm friends with Angie. Taylor watched the lovely vivacity of her face as she chatted to Sue, sharing her impressions of the day. There was no doubt she'd been caught up in the excitement of it, and awed by the skills involved in loading the herd onto the road train.

Something about it had moved her to come to him in the shower. He wasn't sure what. Only that it had been urgent and strongly primitive, as much of the sex between them was, but he'd always felt that came mainly from him with Angie being carried along with it. Yet this time...strange the feeling it had given him, being locked in her embrace while she took possession of him.

The sense of wanting from her had been so strong, and though intensely exciting for him, he wasn't sure he'd answered it for her.

She gave him such incredible pleasure, the *whys* for it had hardly seemed to matter. It happened and he was grateful she'd come into his life. She offered—gave— all the good feelings he'd ever imagined possible between a man and woman, companionably as well as sexually. Now, suddenly, the *whys* had taken on more importance. He wanted to keep Angie with him.

"Hey, Angie!" It was Chris Roland, one of the young jackeroos strolling past to get second helpings at the barbecue. He gave her a wide grin. "You got a taste of cattle dust today."

She laughed. "I sure did."

"We got every one of 'em in without injury," he crowed.

"I thought all you men were incredibly brave and clever," she said, glowing with admiration.

"Just doin' our job," Chris manfully downplayed, but Taylor noticed every lad amongst them looked smugly pleased with themselves and took on an extra swagger as they moved on.

"We'll make an outback woman of you yet, Angie," Joe teased, having already chalked up the credit of making a horsewoman of her.

"That, Joe, would be my proudest moment," she answered, and the golden shine of her amber eyes moved directly to Taylor.

His heart kicked. Did she mean it? Or did she simply have the knack of saying the right thing at the right time to make people feel good?

She'd only been here four months. It wasn't long

enough to make a clear-cut judgment on such a vast lifestyle change. Was it?

He tried to quell the wild hope running through his veins. All this was new to her, new and different, safely distant from the unhappy associations Slater must have left her with.

But she *was* happy here. He couldn't be mistaken about that. Happy with him and everyone else, except Thelma who remained stiff-necked with prejudice, though less than usual tonight. The party seemed to have loosened her up a bit.

The children, especially Hamish, had blossomed with new confidence. As a governess, Angie was unquestionably the best he could have employed. And true to her own word, she wasn't a flirt or a tease. There wasn't a man on the station who didn't like and respect her. The women, too.

She had a very appealing common touch that generated friendly responses, whereas Trish...well, Trish had tended to put everyone's backs up with her air of condescension and expecting special respect as the boss's wife—respect she'd never earned as a person in her own right.

But then Trish had never tried to fit in here, never cared enough to try, not for herself, nor for him, nor their son, and the initial pleasure of queening it over everyone had proved empty all too soon. Angie *did* fit in, though whether this was the instinctive reaction of a chameleon who'd been hurt in too many moves and was intent on avoiding all trouble, or a natural response to the life here, Taylor wasn't sure.

"Angie..." Hamish ran up, urgently eager. "Come on, quick. Bill's uncovering the second earth oven with more potatoes and stuff. You missed the first one."

She leapt up from the bench seat. "Right! Excuse me, people. Got to go and see this."

Hamish grabbed her hand and they were off together, their mutual pleasure in the show-and-tell exercise evident. Taylor grinned after them. It was great to see his son being a natural boy again and he deeply appreciated the way Angie promoted it in him.

Sue stood up, collecting their plates. "Anyone for seconds?"

"Might have another baked potato, love," Joe answered. "With the trimmings."

"What about you, Taylor?"

He shook his head. "I'll hold on for sweets, thanks, Sue."

She left them, giving Joe a speaking look before she turned away. Taylor wondered what message she was transmitting to her husband. Joe cleared his throat, an ominous sign. It invariably heralded touchy business. Taylor cocked his eyebrow, inviting his head stockman's confidence. As usual, Joe was not about to be hurried into coming to the point.

"Reckon you've got a good thing going with Angie, Taylor," he started.

"That I have, Joe," he agreed warmly.

"The men think she's a bit of all right. They'd do anything for her, you know."

"I'm glad they feel that."

Joe nodded a few times. "Kids are happy with her."

"Yes, they are."

"So are the women. Even though Angie's city bred, they reckon she's got her heart in the right place."

Taylor nodded. He didn't need to be told Angie had a good heart. She was more than fair in her dealings, caring, giving, and very perceptive and considerate of others' feelings. She never asked too much of anyone, was always ready to oblige reasonable requests, and seemed content within herself. All in all, she was a very special person, to him a unique woman he would hate to lose.

Not just because of the sex. *She* made that wonderful...the person she was inside, the woman who complemented the man in him. Perhaps his instincts had somehow picked that up from their very first meeting at the Brisbane Hilton. The feelings she aroused then had been coloured by his own physical frustrations, but she'd been touching him in other ways long before he'd taken her to bed with him...her intelligence, her honesty, her enterprise, her courage.

The attraction was long past skin-deep. He suspected it always had been, though he hadn't allowed himself to dwell on it, upholding a barrier of caution against the uncertainty of a future with her. He wished he could set the uncertainty aside.

Proud to be an outback woman...fact or fantasy?

Maybe Angie had a need to fit in. A desperate need. Her pleas at the interview had held a desperate edge. He'd thought he understood it when he found out about Slater, but there could have been other underlying factors driving her, as well, a seeking for something that had always eluded her, perhaps a sense of identity she'd never found.

Was there an overwhelming need to belong to someone or somewhere? A person and place she could call her own? Any person, any place, as long as they gave her a sense of belonging?

He kept coming back to the electric moment in the shower when she'd claimed possession of him, and then her desperate desire for his possession.

Was *he* the man Angie wanted…or did he *represent* something she wanted?

Did it matter…as long as she stayed with him?

"Picnic races coming up soon," Joe said, cutting into Taylor's private reverie.

"Mmm…a good break for the men."

"Yeah. There's a couple of horses they want to enter. Reckon they'd have a chance of winning."

"Arrange it then, Joe."

"Will do. No worries. 'Cept Angie."

Taylor frowned. "What's Angie got to do with it?"

Joe eyed him directly. "Angie will be coming with us, won't she?"

"Of course."

"Well, you know how women talk," Joe said meaningly.

Gossip was a fact of life. The thought of Angie being wounded by it twisted his gut. "What are you getting at, Joe?" he asked sharply, determined on straightening out the situation in no uncertain terms.

Joe's grimace held apologetic appeal. "Just don't like the idea of Angie getting hurt. Sue reckons Diane Westlake will be gunning for her. Diane…she can come over as sweet as pie but Sue says she's damned good at sticking the knife in and giving it a sly twist. Thought you should know so you can watch out."

Diane! The singular accusation of bitchy malice jolted him. It instantly raised a string of uncomfortable memories. "Trish used to say that but I never saw it myself," he commented, troubled that he should have given more weight to Trish's venomous reaction to Diane instead of dismissing it as neurotic nonsense. Joe's wife was one of the most down-to-earth women Taylor knew. He couldn't dismiss her opinion lightly.

"Sue says men can be right blind about such things," Joe followed up, nodding his head, accepting his wife's words as undoubted truth. "Wouldn't be good if Diane made Angie feel bad, Taylor."

Behind his back! That's what Trish had always claimed. It had seemed so alien to the face Diane presented to him, still did, but he wasn't about to risk being wrong about it. Especially since she had shown interest in him since Trish had died. If Diane thought Angie was spiking her chances at the marriage Thelma was in favour of…and that raised questions about Diane's last visit…like what had gone on behind his back then?

Hamish had taken Angie out riding…the sudden sympathy between them…nothing said to him, but Diane flying off before she had to face him and Angie together. Sly…he didn't like it. He didn't like it one bit. His relationship with Angie meant too much to let Diane sour it in any way.

"I appreciate the advice, Joe."

"Hope I'm not speaking out of turn."

"Not at all. A timely warning never goes astray. Give my thanks to Sue."

The two women were on their way back. Taylor felt a surge of turbulent emotion as he watched Angie coming toward him, so warmly beautiful and infinitely desirable, yet what stirred him most was the memory of how vulnerable she had looked the night he'd rescued her from Slater. He didn't want anyone to hurt her. Ever again. And by God, he'd protect her with all that he was!

CHAPTER FIFTEEN

ANGIE couldn't help feeling a little apprehensive over what kind of welcome she would receive at the picnic races, being a newcomer, a governess from the city who didn't know the ropes, and commonly known to be connected to Taylor Maguire in more than an employee sense. She didn't doubt she would have the ready support of everyone from Giralang, with the possible exception of Thelma, but Diane Westlake could prove a snake in the grass, if not a crocodile.

Within hours of arriving at the Westlake Station, her fears appeared to be groundless. Diane was all charm and warm hospitality in her greeting, more than backed up by her father who was brimming with good humour and clearly on very friendly terms with Taylor, welcoming him with a huge grin and a vigorous handshake. He was a big barrel-chested man with a voice to match.

"I hear your men have brought a couple of promising nags," he boomed.

"Could give yours a run for their money," Taylor replied, his eyes twinkling.

Adam laughed and ran an appreciative eye over Angie, winking at her as he said, "Taylor's a dark horse but he sure knows how to pick a fine filly." It was a compliment, plain and simple, no hint of anything but admiration in his eyes.

"Angie Cordell, Adam," Taylor introduced.

"A pleasure to meet you, Angie." A warm handclasp. "Diane tells me you're from the city. There'll be other city folk coming in for the weekend. Hope they won't make you homesick.''

"Not a chance," Angie assured him, and everyone else within earshot. "I love being here."

"No place like it," he said proudly. He looked askance at his daughter. "Though I don't suppose your hotshot financier will agree."

"You never know, Dad," Diane said archly, her eyes flashing some indefinable challenge at Angie. Somehow it seemed both sly and smug, as though she nursed a secret which both amused her and made her feel superior.

Adam rolled his eyes in mock chagrin. "She's got herself a city boyfriend. Diane, who was born in the saddle. Can you make sense of that for me, Taylor?"

Tit for tat? Angie wondered. Wanting to show Taylor he was a fool, trying to mix oil with water?

"Well, Adam, there could always be an outback man under the city clothes, trying to get out," Taylor answered dryly, curving an arm around Angie's shoulders, drawing her into sharing a smile with him. "I've had my prejudice beaten into the dust by the way Angie's taken to the life. She's a constant marvel to me."

Her heart turned over. His vivid blue eyes were warm and loving, no doubts at all. Diane and her city boyfriend were nothing to him. Totally irrelevant. And in an instant, the worry Diane had stirred disappeared and a surge of happiness lifted her spirits. It didn't matter what anyone else thought as long as Taylor wanted her at his side.

So it continued that first afternoon with everyone they met, Taylor holding her close, smoothly performing introductions, subtly impressing the fact she was his woman and very much part of the life at Giralang, not someone to be condescended to as a temporary figure from the city. It was like being handed a golden passport to acceptance, removing all grounds for discord or reservation. Each meeting turned into a happy exchange of news, everyone taking it for granted she understood what they were talking about. She was one of them.

The legendary outback hospitality was here in abundance, no frills or pretensions, a carefree friendly open warmth that soaked into Angie and spread a wonderfully festive atmosphere. Fifteen cattle stations had set up elaborate camps along the river bank, tents for sleeping quarters, marquees to house the eating tables and enough supplies of food and drink to satisfy the fierce appetites forged over a week of competitive fun.

In a way it was like Christmas in the middle of the year. Power generators attached to each camp ran deep freezers filled with enough turkey, steak and ham to feed an army, and at every marquee they were offered champagne, rum, whisky or beer. It was a time of reunion, of commiseration on bad luck, celebration of good fortune, and the general pleasure of congenial company with mutual interests. Angie was swept up in it all and loved every minute of it, loved even more the sense of belonging Taylor gave her.

Many people had arrived up to ten days beforehand, including most of the men from Giralang, bringing their horses and supervising their training for the races, trucking in the equipment and setting up camp, getting everything ready for the big week. A three-deep tier of tents were lined up with military precision, a procession of billowing canvas and guy ropes stretching from either side of the main hospitality marquee which was run by the Westlake Station and centred to face the arena where the main festival activity took place.

It wasn't all horse-racing. Most of the fun was centred around the children. A schoolroom was set up by itinerant teachers who gave the school of the air children a taste of lessons in a real classroom situation, plus the opportunity of learning how to mix and play with those whom they only knew from their voices on the radio. Angie was involved in this, along with the other governesses and mothers who supervised their children at home.

Best of all though were the games organised for the children. They played a loose form of cricket, touch football, tug-of-war, tunnel ball—all team games that frequently involved their parents and a great deal of barracking and excitement. They laughed themselves silly over novelty events like the father and son three-legged race. When mothers were required as partners, Hamish insisted Angie stand in with him, and Taylor stood on the sidelines cheering them on.

Angie couldn't remember ever having such a happy time. She was occasionally aware of Diane swanning around in the background, playing gracious hostess, but nothing the other woman said or did intruded on Angie's sense of well-being. The days rolled by, gathering a momentum toward the big races at the weekend, one of Giralang's horses emerging as a favourite to take out the main event, stirring great pride and joy amongst the men.

Angie saw the plane fly in on Friday morning and thought it was probably bringing the city visitors, but she didn't really relate them to herself. She'd moved a long way from having anything in common with them. Diane was welcome to her new boyfriend. Angie even wished her joy of him.

The schoolroom packed up that morning, the teachers having established a wonderful camaraderie amongst the children which would undoubtedly boost their enjoyment in the answer sessions on school of the air, the familiarity from this week still fresh in their minds so they could easily fit faces to voices. For Angie, meeting the mothers and other governesses had wiped out her reluctance to join in the radio chat sessions. She eagerly looked forward to keeping their acquaintance going.

The stroll back to the Giralang camp for lunch was interrupted several times by new friends calling out to her and Hamish. As they passed the Westlake marquee, a hail from Diane caused no stab of unease. The unfailing support by both Taylor and Hamish had given Angie a confidence and security the other woman couldn't shake. She turned, a smile of inquiry flashing forth.

It froze on her face.

The crocodile was back. Two crocodiles, their teeth bared in readiness to mash Angie in their jaws. It was the second one who caused her heart to cramp and shot icicles down her spine… Diane's city boyfriend…the hotshot financier…none other than Brian Slater!

She felt the blood draining from her face, had the sickening sensation of the ground shifting under her feet. No place was safe anymore. The oppression she thought she had escaped pressed in on her again…the lies, the twisted thinking, the refusal to accept rejection, the sheer perverseness of his pursuit of her, the frightening persistence insidiously eating away at her freedom, trapping her in a web of devious plays that reduced her to a quivering mess of vulnerability.

Brian…Diane…two of a kind, she realised, pursuing their quarry with self-centred relentlessness, but the insight did no good. She stood like a mesmerised rabbit as they bore down on her, disbelief mixing with horror at the sheer malice of what couldn't be a coincidence.

The knowingness in Diane's eyes…her smug pleasure in it…the glitter of triumph in Brian's…his satisfaction in it…somehow they'd got together and planned this meeting, each for their own ends. Angie knew it in her gut, which was twisting into nauseous knots.

"Angie?" Hamish, sensing something wrong, stepped back to take her hand and stand with her.

It was no comfort. No protection, either. She couldn't even bring herself to glance at him. She couldn't tear her eyes off the approach of the two crocodiles, feeling the menace in every step they took toward her, struggling to raise a mental shield against the coming attack, to suppress the fear of the damage they wanted to wreak.

"Brian tells me you know each other," Diane opened up, her voice dripping with mock innocence.

"Angie…" Brian spread his arms as though he expected her to fall into them. "…Who'd have thought you'd be hiding out here?" His eyes exulted in having found her.

"Angie's not hiding," Hamish growled like a guard dog whose instincts were obviously registering something dangerous and hostile.

Brian laughed, his easy charm drawn into instant play. "I only meant she left Brisbane so abruptly we didn't have time to say goodbye…" He lifted his indulgent smile from Hamish to her. "…Did we, darling?"

It goaded her to answer, "I said goodbye, Brian. More than once. You chose not to listen."

"Well, we all make choices we regret," he returned smoothly.

"I don't regret mine," she bit out, clenching her teeth against his oily suggestiveness.

Diane came in with a smarmy warning. "Early days

yet, Angie. I always think it's rather short-sighted to burn bridges.''

''What opinion do you have on someone who keeps trying to build a bridge to nowhere?'' Angie flashed at her, anger flooding over the fear.

Diane shrugged, her eyes derisively belittling Angie's point as she answered, ''I guess it's all in one's sense of vision. I have a long view of things myself.''

Angie suddenly had no doubt Trish had suffered from Diane's *long view.*

''Besides, life is full of surprises,'' Brian said with another megawatt smile.

Orchestrated by him, Angie thought bitterly.

''I know I'm going to be vastly entertained by this outback weekend,'' he went on. ''Especially with you here, Angie.''

''Angie's with me and Dad,'' Hamish piped up belligerently.

''Oh, Hamish!'' Diane laughed dismissively. ''A governess isn't on duty all the time. School's over now and she's free to do as she wants.''

''Angie likes being with us,'' he retorted stubbornly. ''We're going to lunch now.'' He tugged at her hand.

The reinforced link with Taylor's son pulled Angie out of the futile compulsion to face the obsessive drive of these two destructive people. Argument won nothing from them. Common sense would never prevail. No stand would alter anything. There was only one course to take, the one Brian had driven her to before. Walk away.

''Yes, Hamish. We'll go now,'' she said, the bleakness in her heart making the resolution sound too much like defeat. Which it was, in a way. She simply couldn't beat these people. She had no weapons to use against them. Retreat…escape…but there was no safe place. Not even Giralang. Brian knew now. And he wouldn't let go. Neither would Diane.

"By the way," Diane slid in quickly, her eyes brightly challenging. "Dad wants you and Taylor to join us for lunch, Angie. You will pass on the invitation, won't you?"

"I'm looking forward to having your company," Brian said with relish.

"Dad is expecting you," Diane pressed, closing the trap with equal relish.

Taylor. Her heart ached with need as she walked away with his son. Taylor had saved her once. Maybe he could again.

CHAPTER SIXTEEN

ONE look at Hamish and Angie as they entered the marquee told Taylor something was badly wrong. His conversation with his aunt came to an abrupt halt as alarm kicked through his heart. Angie's face was pale and lifeless, her usual vivacity totally wiped out, all positive energy drained from her body. Hamish was virtually pulling her with him and his expression was fighting mad.

"Diane's got a man with her who upset Angie. And she was mean, too, underneath her crocodile smile," he declared heatedly, defying any correction to his judgment of the situation. "I don't care if she is our neighbour, she's real slimy, Dad. And so's he."

"The city boyfriend?" Taylor asked sharply of Angie, wanting to break through her air of bleak withdrawal.

She looked at him, her beautiful amber eyes glazed with hopelessness and slowly filling with tears. "It's Brian. Brian Slater," she choked out. "Diane brought him to me. She knew." Her head shook in helpless anguish. "She knew."

Even as his stunned mind groped to make sense of what she said, Taylor wrapped Angie in his arms and tried to soothe her distress with comforting caresses. Slater, the devious bastard, finding his way to Angie again. Through Diane, no doubt, but with her connivance? Surely not! "How could Diane have known about him? It must be coincidence, Angie."

160

"No," she sobbed. "I saw it in their eyes. The complicity. I can't think how...unless you told her."

The quiver of betrayal in her broken voice smote his heart. "No," he answered strongly. "I told Diane nothing about Slater. I swear it, Angie."

"About me, then." She lifted tear-washed eyes, searching for answers, however much they hurt. "The day she rode out to you at the leaking bore. You must have said something to lead her to Brian."

He shook his head, raking his memory, certain he'd kept Angie's private business absolutely private. "Not a word pertaining to your life before Giralang," he stated with conviction.

Her head sagged onto his shoulder. "It doesn't matter now," she said listlessly. "It's done. She wants to get rid of me. Somehow she found Brian and she's using him."

It was shock talking, he reasoned, the revival of trauma, the sense of persecution. It was neurotic to think...but hadn't he used that excuse to himself when Trish had ranted about Diane? Don't overlook anything, he cautioned himself. Angie had shown him many times she saw some things more clearly than he did. He had to believe her, protect her, take care she was never victimised again by anyone.

"Is he a bad man, Dad?" Hamish asked.

"Yes. Very bad. But don't worry, Hamish. I won't let him get near Angie again," Taylor vowed, determined on confronting the situation head-on.

"What about Diane?" Hamish's eyes burned with a steadfast belief in her badness, too, not the slightest doubt about Angie's accusation.

Faith and trust in him was obviously hanging in the balance and Taylor was instantly persuaded to give his son the assurance he wanted. ''I'll deal with her, as well.'' Neither of them was about to ignore a source of pain to the woman who had given so much of herself to them.

''Go and fetch Gary and Joe and Bill,'' he commanded, a plan of action forming in his mind. ''I want them on standby.''

''Right!'' his son replied with keen satisfaction, and raced off to do his part.

''I don't understand what's going on,'' Thelma pleaded, her face creased in concern and bewilderment at Angie's breakdown and what was ensuing from it. ''What has this Brian Slater done?''

Angie shuddered. Taylor held her more tightly. ''Angie got involved with him, not realising he was one of those possessive freaks who won't let go. He'd been stalking her for months before the job at Giralang came up. She needed it to get away from him.''

''Oh! So that's why…'' Her face drooped in pained regret and the gaze she turned on Angie was a confused mixture of guilt and sympathy. ''You should have told me, Taylor. I said some harsh things. Made it difficult. Not welcome. Oh, dear!'' She shook her head in self-chastisement. ''I wasn't very friendly. If you'd only told me…''

''Angie wanted to leave it behind her, Thelma.''

''Oh!'' Her hands clapped her face in horror. ''Oh, my God!'' She stared at Taylor, completely stricken. ''Maybe this dreadful situation is my fault. I didn't know it could lead to anything bad.''

''What?'' he snapped.

''Diane mustn't realise what kind of a man he is,'' she excused, clinging to her view of Adam's daughter.

"What part have you played in this, Thelma?" Taylor bored in.

She answered in a fluster. "It's just that…well, the day Diane came to Giralang, she wanted to know everything about Angie. I got out her résumé for the governess job from your filing cabinet and I left Diane with it while I…"

"So she had the information to track Angie's life in Brisbane," Taylor cut in, furious that her confidential papers had been misused.

"I didn't mean any harm," his aunt pleaded.

"Diane does, Thelma. She stuck barbs into Trish and she's trying to do the same to Angie. You'd better take off your rose-coloured glasses where Diane Westlake is concerned. She's no friend of mine."

She was shocked. "Trish?"

"Yes, God help me, I didn't believe her. But I believe Angie, Thelma, and I will not allow Diane to do any more damage to me and mine. Her malicious mischief-making ends here. Can I trust you to stay with Angie and look after her while I take care of this business?"

It jolted his aunt into vigorous loyalty. "Of course you can, Taylor. I won't leave her for a second." She stepped over to gently squeeze Angie's shoulder, a gruff and genuine appeal in her voice as she begged, "Please forgive me, my dear. I've been so very, very wrong."

Angie wearily lifted her head. "You were coming from a different place, Thelma. That's all. It's not your fault."

"Dad…"

Hamish was back with the three men Taylor trusted to get the job done. He held up his hand for them to wait then gently cupped Angie's face, drawing her gaze to his, wanting her to see, to know and trust his strength of purpose, his resolve to keep her safe. He tenderly stroked the tear stains from her cheeks as he spoke with all the latent force of his will.

"One hour at most, Angie, and I'll have Slater out of your life again and he'll have no taste for returning. That, I promise you."

She looked agonisingly unsure. "He's with Diane. We're invited to lunch with Adam. And *them*." Her mouth twisted in a travesty of a smile. "To make a meal of me, I guess."

"No. I'll be doing the serving, Angie." The violence he felt toward Slater could barely be contained, but Angie needed control from him. Iron control. "You stay here with Thelma. Don't move from this marquee until I return. Will you promise me to sit tight?"

Still the fear of everything going wrong—Slater sliding out of trouble—Diane backing him up. "Adam's our host, Taylor. And Brian has connections."

"Adam's my friend. He'll support me. And the outback has its own set of connections. It will be all right, believe me, Angie," he assured her, projecting the power he knew he could wield on this, his own ground. "I'll put some of my men on watch here so you'll feel protected. Okay?"

She bit her lip and nodded, too sick at heart to offer any more argument. She needed proof and Taylor needed action. He sat her down at a table in the back corner of the marquee and left her to Thelma's kindly fussing, knowing his aunt would do everything in her power to make amends for her faulty judgment.

A group of his jackeroos were standing just outside. He signalled Hamish and the others to join him there. "Chris…" he addressed the lad who always glowed under a smile from Angie. "There's a nasty city guy who's

intent on making Angie's life miserable. Hamish will
stay with you and point him out if he comes this way.
You guys keep a watch out, will you, while I straighten
this out with Adam Westlake?''

''I'll punch his lights out if he comes anywhere near,''
Chris growled.

Satisfied Angie was well guarded, Taylor proceeded
to the Westlake marquee, outlining his plan to his three
trusty lieutenants and what he required of each of
them…Bill's bull strength and army training to intimidate, Joe's canny ability to see any attack or escape coming and foil it, Gary to fly the plane. Staunch support
was readily given. They took up a stand by the bar in
the hospitality marquee as Taylor made his way to the
table where Adam was hosting a group of guests for
lunch.

He had no difficulty picking out Brian Slater.
Whatever other city guests had arrived were obviously
being entertained elsewhere. Apart from Adam, Diane
and her *city boyfriend*, there were three other station
owners and their wives—all well-known to Taylor—and
two empty chairs, presumably for him and Angie and
predictably placed opposite Diane and Slater.

Adam saw him coming and hailed him heartily.
''Taylor, at last. We've been waiting for you. Where's
Angie?''

''Don't tell me she's not with you,'' Diane chided
prettily. ''I asked her especially.''

''Yes. Angie told me how well you planned the invitation, Diane,'' he stated coldly, icy blue eyes slicing
through her deceit. He gripped the back of the chair designated for him and remained pointedly standing as he
addressed his old friend. ''I'm sorry, Adam. I will not
sit down with the man your daughter has brought here.

Nor will I suffer his presence in any company close to me. I am holding this chair to stop myself from tearing him apart here and now.''

It stopped the buzz of bonhomie dead. Eyes turned from him to Slater in an appalled silence. Brian Slater's sangfroid was almost admirable, except Taylor felt the sliminess of it, just as Hamish had. The glossy handsome city slicker relaxed back in his chair, a quirky half-smile on his face as though prepared to be amused by Taylor's making an utter fool of himself.

Superficially he was quite a star, tanned and lean and dressed with casual elegance in designer country wear. His black hair was styled long enough to provide a romantic frame of waves and curls for finely sculpted features. His dark eyes gleamed with sharply intelligent calculation. The onus of proof was on Taylor and the sense that Slater was used to winning—confident of it—oozed from him. It made Taylor's skin crawl as he finally appreciated what Angie had been up against.

''Good God, man!'' Adam expostulated. ''What's he done?''

Taylor eyed Slater with contempt. ''He's a spoilt to the bone, rich city kid, riding the fast lane, snorting cocaine, and believing he can have anything he wants, never mind the rights of others.''

Slater's smooth brow wrinkled in mock bewilderment. ''This is quite outrageous.'' His voice was calm, aimed at soothing ruffled feathers. ''I've never even met you until this minute.''

''You're also a psychopathic liar,'' Taylor declared with steely conviction. ''Angie has given me chapter and verse on you, Slater.''

''Oh, Angie.'' He waved a weary dismissal. ''Diane will tell you I was nothing but polite to her. To me,

Angie Cordell was just a chick I lived with for a while…''

First mistake. Angie had won a lot of liking and respect amongst the station folk this week. There was a subtle stiffening around the table as Slater continued referring to her with an insulting edge of contempt.

"She took it hard when I dumped her. I thought she'd be over it by now. I tried to be friendly…''

"Like continually invading her life after she'd walked out of the relationship with you, having suffered too much of your abuse to ever want to be with you again,'' Taylor mocked savagely. "Like filling her with dread at what you'd do next as you stalked her, month after month, ignoring her rejections, overriding her objections, laying siege to her apartment.''

Slater rolled his eyes in a show of pained disbelief. "Angie told you that?'' He shook his head and sighed. "I shall really have to consider suing her for slander if she goes on blackening my character like this. I assure you, the woman must be unstable…''

Second mistake. No one who'd met Angie would consider her unstable.

"Taylor, Brian comes from a highly reputable family,'' Diane put in with a touching air of wounded pride.

"A family who's been shovelling his sins under the carpet for years. Not to mention paying them off,'' he lashed at her.

"You only have Angie's word for all this,'' she defended.

"You're wrong, Diane. You told him Angie would be here, didn't you?''

She hesitated, faced with his absolute certainty.

"Her name might have come up. I talked about many of the people who'd be here.''

"All of them strangers to Slater except Angie. You must have had quite a conversation about her."

"Well, it was a coincidence, Brian's knowing her," she defended, realising vagueness wasn't going to work.

"And your meeting him—the one man who'd plagued her life and sanity—and bringing him here to do it again…that a coincidence, too, Diane?"

"I don't know what you're implying," she blustered.

"Better drop it, Diane. Drop it all," he warned bitingly. "Because I'm a witness to what Slater did to Angie, and I don't imagine anyone here thinks I'm unstable."

"A witness!" Slater squawked incredulously. "That's totally impossible. There was nothing to witness."

Taylor stared right through his charade of innocence. "I called Angie about the governess job the night you caught her alone and vulnerable. I was the man on the other end of the phone line when Angie used me as a bluff to get you out of her apartment. Which you'd entered by stealing her spare key and using it, despite her repeated refusals to see you again. Home invasion it's called, Slater. Violation of her rights."

"She obviously made up that story," he scoffed.

"Because of her rather obscure cry for help on the phone, I came to her apartment that night, Slater. At first she pretended she wasn't in. When I indentified myself, she hauled me inside in a frenzy of fear, then literally collapsed in a nervous heap, speechless, completely traumatised because you were still outside waiting for her, waiting to pounce again once you were confident of an all clear."

"This is a totally distorted interpretation of…"

"I saw you out there, Slater. I watched you waiting

to do what you wanted, to take more and more from Angie.''

He sneered. ''You're repeating what *she* fed you and it's not the truth.''

Taylor's fingernails dug into the wooden frame of the chair. His hands itched to close around Slater's neck and squeeze the truth out of him. Nevertheless, he knew his best course was to keep ramming it down his throat. And convincing everyone else of it.

''You can't talk your way out of this one, Slater. I was there. I saw the state Angie was in. No one could play-act that. I was the one who calmed her down and gave her an escape from you, the one who phoned the police to move you on so I could remove her as cleanly as possible from your victimisation.''

''There is a very simple explanation for my presence there that night,'' he drawled with strained patience.

''Yes,'' Taylor agreed. ''Angie had no family to help her, the women she shared the apartment with were away, and she had no one to turn to because the general run of people run scared of standing up to a wealthy, well-connected psychopath like you, and you thought you could get away with what you were doing.''

The oily scum leaned forward in reasoning appeal. ''I tell you, she is hopelessly neurotic about our relationship.''

''You don't have a relationship with her anymore, Slater. And Angie has gained a family. Everyone on Giralang is her family. In fact, she now belongs to the whole outback family, none of whom gives a damn about your influential city connections. So you have no-where to move except out of here with no return ticket. You came to hurt one of our own, to show her there was no escape from you.''

"Oh, this is absurd!" he cried, openly vexed now, glancing around for support.

There was none. Even Diane had turned her face away, wise enough to recognise which side her bread was buttered.

Taylor held up his hand to signal his men forward. He turned to Adam who sat stony-faced, deeply disgusted at having been deceived in Diane's special guest. "Mind if we borrow the Jeep outside, Adam? It will make a quick trip to the airstrip and Gary will fly Slater out if you have no objection."

"Key's in the ignition," he said in strong affirmation of Taylor's arrangements.

Gary, Joe and Bill moved around to crowd Slater's chair. He looked at them as though he couldn't believe what was happening.

"You have no right..." he began blustering.

"You're the one who has no rights here," Taylor corrected him.

No one raised a murmur of protest on his behalf. He glared at Diane. "You said these people were civilised."

"Provided *you're* civilised," Taylor said pointedly, "my men will give you courteous escort onto a flight from Mount Isa to Brisbane."

Slater rose to his feet, adopting an air of outraged dignity. "You and that deranged woman will be hearing from my solicitor."

"Make one more move against Angie and I will personally feed you to a crocodile," Taylor bit out, the violence he'd restrained shimmering with unmistakable intent. "Don't ever make the mistake of thinking I'll fight to your rules and rights, Slater. Out here we have our own. And the first rule is survival. We shoot mad beasts. We shoot diseased ones. I happen to feel a bullet is too clean for you."

"You're talking murder, man." There was a very satisfying catch of fear in Slater's voice. He looked wildly around the table. "In front of witnesses, too."

"Didn't hear a thing," Adam declared.

"Taylor's talking about cattle, Adam," one of the other station owners blandly informed him.

"Yeah...culling trouble," another affirmed.

"Got to shoot venomous snakes," one of the wives remarked. "Did it myself the other day."

The line of support was unquestionable. Taylor gave it a moment to sink in then smiled his own satisfaction. It was a smile that promised deadly attrition.

"I'd strongly advise you never to step foot in the gulf country again, Slater. It's not unknown for city people to be taken by crocodiles. Through their ignorance of survival rules."

He nodded to Bill who immediately took over. "If you'll come this way, sir, we shall facilitate your departure." It was said with the military aplomb he'd never lost.

Slater glared at him, measured the beefy arms and shoulders of the men's cook, and decided to effect an exit on his own two feet. "I have belongings in my tent," he stated angrily.

"We'll collect them on the way," Joe said with an obliging air.

There were no farewells. As the escort moved their responsibility out of the marquee, Taylor started to follow, wanting to check there was no last-minute resistance from Slater.

Adam's chair scraped back. "I'll see him off, too," he said gruffly. He stood up and paused, frowning at his daughter. "Bad judgment, Diane. Don't be taken in so damned easily in future."

"I'm sorry, Dad," she said meekly, eyes cast down, a flush of shame—or suppressed fury—burning her cheeks. "He really fooled me."

"Better sort yourself out, girl," Adam admonished, "and put this behind you."

She nodded in humble submission.

Taylor wondered if the lowered lids veiled her frustration with the outcome of this last piece of malice, then dismissed the speculation as irrelevant. He'd pulled her fangs and delivered a warning she'd respect if she had any sense. Humiliation did not suit her. Besides which, Diane was first and foremost a survivor. Taylor was confident the warning would be heeded.

Adam clapped his shoulder as he joined him to see Slater loaded into the Jeep and taken away. "Got to thank you for that, Taylor. Wouldn't want my daughter any further involved with such a snake. Saved us a bundle of trouble, I reckon."

"He's poison all right," Taylor agreed, barely refraining from telling Adam his daughter was tarred with a similar brush, but hopefully, the shock of this dangerous misfire with Slater would serve as a sobering lesson to her, and no good would come of alienating a man who'd always been a staunch friend to him. Family invariably held first loyalty. Criticism of his daughter would not be welcomed. "Thanks for your ready support, Adam," he said warmly. "I appreciate it. And so will Angie."

"She all right?" he asked in quick concern.

"She will be." He nodded to the Jeep. "With him gone."

Gary was behind the wheel. Slater was jammed between Joe and Bill on the back seat and there was noth-

ing smooth about him now. He looked as if he was in a
hard place and sweating over it. Gary saluted Taylor, a
silent assurance this business would be finished as arranged, then drove off on the first leg of returning Brian
Slater to *his* family and connections who were more than
welcome to him.

Taylor turned and offered his hand to Adam, "Thanks
again, my friend."

"Pleasure." Adam's clasp was strong. "Mind you
bring Angie to the dance tonight. We'll all make her feel
at home."

Taylor nodded, hoping it would be true in a very deep
sense, and Angie would always feel at home with him,
his family and his friends. "I must get back to her now.
Sorry about lunch."

Adam grinned. "Well, Diane might have to choke it
down but you've given me a better appetite for it. Didn't
like that city slicker even before you blasted him."

Satisfied their understanding was solid enough to hold
their friendship together, Taylor took his leave, anxious
to clear Angie's fears, then perhaps settle some of his
own.

He wanted—needed—some time alone with her. It
had been such a busy, crowded week. He'd meant to
wait until they were back at Giralang before opening up
on the issues burning in his heart but the double-
barrelled encounter with Brian Slater had brought them
to the surface in a searing rush. He knew what had
driven Angie into his life. He had to know what had
kept her in his arms.

And if she wanted to stay there for the rest of her life.

CHAPTER SEVENTEEN

TAYLOR had done it again. The wonder of it clung to Angie's mind, making the ride along the river bank a rosy haze. Her horse automatically followed his, picking their way toward a private picnic spot away from the camp. Taylor knew where he was going. She didn't care, as long as it was with him.

Occasionally she glanced at the sky, the amazing image of the plane flying Brian away vividly implanted in her memory. The blue expanse above, stretching from horizon to horizon, remained clear of any man-made object. Brian was gone. Never to return, Taylor had assured her.

Incredibly, they'd all taken her side—Taylor, Hamish, Thelma, everyone from Giralang, the friends she'd made throwing a protective ring around her, actively resolving her problem, the outback people standing firm in support of her, believing in her, caring about her, even Adam Westlake going so far as to castigate his daughter for her association with Brian. Never had she thought—nor imagined—this could happen to her.

It wouldn't have in the city. People simply didn't connect into a solid, all-encompassing network in an urban environment. This had to be something very special to the outback, and that something special had been given to her by the man riding beside her. Taylor Maguire. *He* had drawn her into his circle of belonging—the charmed circle—and she now belonged to it, too...one of them.

Angie marvelled at the turning point in her life that

had brought her to the man who answered everything for her. She remembered her first impressions; his aura of strength, the sense of endurance that defied anything to beat him, a man of action. All true, she thought, then quickly added compassion and caring. She doubted any other person would have come to her rescue as he had the night he'd called her in Brisbane. Then changing his mind about the job, for her sake. Now this...

Angie looked at him, her heart swelling with love.

He caught her gaze and smiled inquiringly. "Will here do?"

"Yes." Yes to anything with him, she thought.

They dismounted and tethered their horses to a log. Taylor laid a ground rug on a sandy stretch under the trees overhanging the river. The lunch-sized cool box Thelma had packed contained ham rolls, apples and cans of lemonade—simple fare but very welcome. The ride and the relief of being freed from Brian again had re-awakened Angie's appetite.

She and Taylor sat facing the soothing flow of water, munching away in a companionable silence. It wasn't until the food and drink were consumed that either of them felt like talking. Angie was content simply to be and Taylor appeared immersed in his own thoughts.

"Feeling better?" he finally asked, his clear blue eyes holding some inner tension as they scanned her face and took in her relaxed posture.

"On top of the world again," she assured him, a warm, tingly feeling spreading through her at his concern. "Thanks to you."

His mouth twisted self-mockingly. "It was as much for myself as it was for you, Angie. I want you to be happy here because I want you to stay with me. Which, in a very personal sense, makes me little different to Slater.''

''No! You're not like him at all,'' Angie protested. ''Believe me, I know.''

He shook his head. ''I don't want to let you go, either. I understand his compulsion to keep you. I doubt there'll ever be another woman to match what you give me and I'll always be grateful for having known you…however briefly…in the span of my life.''

Fear fluttered through her heart. Was he about to say her time with him was up? But why? What had she done wrong?

''You must have thought of Giralang as a safe place,'' he went on, his eyes searching hers, watching intently for the reflection of the truths he believed he was speaking. ''I think you embraced the life there because it was one life you could have with relative peace of mind.''

Her brain raced, clutching at other reasons she could put to him, anything to stave off the decision she felt coming. He paused and it took an effort of will not to rush in with argument, to wait and hear more of what he was thinking. To her intense relief, her silence prompted him to expand on how he saw her situation.

''Now I've made it even safer. Perhaps more attractive because of it. But it's not the only safe place in the world for you, Angie. I know Slater has stirred bad memories again.'' There was a flash of contempt in his eyes as he added, ''but I doubt he'll be moving away from the protection of his connections in Brisbane for a long time to come.''

She didn't doubt it, either. Brian would have been shaken to the core to find himself unsupported and totally isolated amongst a crowd of hostile people.

''Adelaide is a nice city. So is Perth,'' Taylor suggested quietly. "I'm sure they'd be every bit as safe as the outback. And I've seen how quickly you can adapt, Angie. You could make a new life for yourself in either place."

Her heart sank. It was the city prejudice again. Though perhaps it was less a prejudice than a worry about the future. It wasn't only her future at stake here, but his and Hamish's, as well. If the tie between them was to be broken, his reasoning obviously pointed to its being better done before expectations deepened. Hamish already wanted to hang on to her. And Taylor?

He sat with his knees up, forearms resting on them, hands linked between them, not reaching out to her with touch. He looked relaxed but she could feel the restraint he was imposing on himself, the determination not to use physical persuasion in this decision-making. Yet there was an aching appeal in the eyes holding hers.

"I need to know where you really want to be, Angie," he said bluntly. "I need a sense of direction from you. And it must be an honest one. You do see that, don't you?"

"Yes," she whispered, her throat constricting with an emotional awareness of how much depended on her reply.

Her initial fear was baseless. Taylor didn't want her to go. He just didn't feel it was fair to press her to stay if it wasn't truly right for her, so he was clearing the way for her to choose. With Brian's effect on her fresh on his mind, Taylor could not—would not—go down the same path, however much he wanted to keep her with him.

But how to convince him there wasn't any question in *her* mind? Angie was acutely conscious of this being another turning point, the most critical one of her life

because what she most wanted was hanging on it. She
was almost frightened to begin. Tension coursed through
her, squeezing her heart into pounding painfully. There
seemed no other course but to risk everything now. He'd
asked for honesty. Angie knew she needed it, too.

"Do you love me, Taylor?"

The vulnerable yearning in her eyes seemed to be reflected in his.

"Yes," he answered simply.

"And I love you," she replied with soul-deep fervour.
"You don't think it's enough to hold us together?"

Anguished uncertainty looked back at her. "I don't
know, Angie. My life…everything I've lived for…is
tied up with Giralang. I can't take it out of me. Not for
anyone. I'm asking…can it be…is it…more than a safe
place to you?"

Angie knew a straighforward, "Yes," would not suf-
fice. Taylor's doubts went too deep to be easily erased.
She had to make him understand why the truth was the
truth before he would fully accept it.

"It's good to feel safe," she answered slowly. "It's
good to be free of the shackles of fear because it allows
you to see what's around you and get it in a perspective
that isn't distorted. You remember the interview at the
Hilton?"

He nodded.

"I told you then I wasn't looking to others to make
something of my life for me. I needed time for myself."

"Healing time," he murmured.

"No. More than that. Time to sort out what had real
meaning to me. What was important to my life. Apart
from being free of Brian."

He pondered her words for several moments before

asking, "Have you come up with any answers that satisfy you?"

She smiled. "All of them, I think."

His responding smile was less sure. It appealed for her confidence. "I'd like to hear them."

She took a deep breath. "It might not be easy for you to relate to. Our backgrounds are very different, Taylor."

"Try me," he encouraged.

Somehow she had to *make* him understand. He probably wouldn't believe her answers otherwise. She averted her gaze, desperate to appear in control of herself. On impulse she leaned forward and picked up a handful of the sandy red earth around them and used it as a focus for Taylor's attention.

"See how this isn't packed solid? It trickles through my fingers, nothing holding it together. That's what my life felt like before I came to Giralang. Not just with Brian. All of it since my dad died. He was shot, trying to foil a robbery in a bank. I lost everything then."

"Surely your mother…"

"Mum couldn't hold herself together. She needed someone to lean on. She drifted through a string of boyfriends who took up most of her time. I became what's called a latch-key kid, more or less looking after myself."

She shot him a derisive look. "You think of the city as a place of entertainment, full of people to provide it. To me, it's rarely been anything but lonely. I think cities are the loneliest places in the world. No one has the time to get to know you as they do out here. They don't really want to know and they don't really care about you."

She heard the passion rising in her voice as she pleaded, "Do you think I want to go back to that when I've felt the kind of community life you have out here?

The caring and the sharing? The looking after each other?''

He frowned, seriously assessing her point. ''Some people can find it claustrophobic after a while, Angie, everyone knowing each other's business.''

He was thinking of Trish again! Angie had to swallow a surge of bitter resentment for the woman who had blighted his life and left a legacy of shadows that had to be fought. The anger of being misjudged shook her voice as she cried out against it.

''I craved the blanket of acceptance you call claustrophobic. I went looking for it while my mother sought the kind of love she wanted. The friends I had from conventional families weren't allowed out at night so I found other friends from similar situations to my own. I ran wild for years, looking for what you've had all your life…a place to be…with people who shared it…even though it was a life I hated!''

It moved him. He gestured an apology, his expression pained by her pain. ''Angie, I'm sorry. You needn't dig up these memories for me. If you're sure this life is what you want…''

''But *you're* not sure and I can't bear your doubting me,'' she protested, her heart aching with the need for his belief. ''It'll go on if you don't hear me now. If you don't understand…''

''Then tell me,'' he invited softly, caringly.

Tears blurred her ears. She fiercely blinked them back, swallowed hard, and forced herself on. ''By the time I was fourteen I'd joined up with a local gang led by a guy called Trav Logan. There was a kind of sympathy between us. We clicked. He watched out for me and kept me out of the bad stuff. But he had a record of trouble with the police and when the guys in the gang raided a warehouse of electrical goods he got caught. So I lost him, too. But at least something good happened to him. The judge gave him a choice of six months on an outback station—it was a special program—or time in a correctional institution.''

''So he was your friend who found what he wanted in the outback,'' Taylor murmured, remembering what she'd told him all those months ago.

''Yes,'' she replied quickly, relieved he had listened to her then and was trying to put it together now. ''Having come here myself, I understand why he felt what he did about it,'' she pressed earnestly. ''It's much bigger than the city and life takes on a different scale. It has a vast, intricate pattern to it with challenges that have to be met, yet there's the sense it's never going to change on you. The pattern will stay the same, no matter what.''

''And that's important to you?'' Taylor gently probed.

''I think for both Trav and me, it's like the solid foundation that had eluded us until we experienced this. You were brought up with it so it's always been there for you, a constant you take for granted. We didn't have constants. The things in our lives kept shifting, even as we clung to what seemed like some kind of solidarity. A gang. A sometime mother...''

Taylor winced. ''I remember you saying your mother died when you were fourteen.''

The anguish of that terrible time flooded out of her memory and she jerked her gaze away from his, staring blindly at the river for several moments as she struggled for calm. The flow of the water soothed her inner agitation and gradually caught her attention. It moved endlessly in one direction. There never was a backward flow, she reflected. None with death, either.

She *had* to move forward, giving Taylor the direction

he needed, the understanding of where she'd come from so he could go forward with her. No looking back. No *going* back. They could make a future together if he would only put the past to rest.

With regathered resolution, she explained, ''Mum had gone to a party where they smoked marijuana. About two o'clock in the morning, she went pillion-riding on a motorbike. It crashed at high speed and she was killed.''

Her flat recitation produced a heavy silence, loaded with the emptiness left by her mother's death. Her own bleak sadness was echoed in Taylor's voice when he finally remarked, ''I guess that removed your last bit of security.''

She turned to him on a fierce roll of emotion. ''I hate drugs. I hate what they do to people. I like it that we're free of all that out here. And the air is clean. You see all the stars at night. You don't know how lucky you are, Taylor. Whatever struggles you have are *with* nature, not against it.''

''I see what you mean, Angie,'' he said comfortingly. ''It always feels good to leave the city pollution behind and…''

''No. It's more than that. Much more,'' she cried. ''There's the belonging, Taylor. You don't know how wonderful it is to belong. To really feel it after not having it. When Mum died, my aunt—Dad's older sister— took me in, doing her moral duty with an iron fist in a respectable glove. There was no love dispensed. Only discipline. And once I was through teacher's college and had a teaching post, she couldn't wash her hands of me fast enough.''

''She told you unequivocally there was no going back

to her?'' he questioned, horrified that any family member would be so ruthless in dispossessing her.

Angie grimaced at the truth he found so unpalatable. But truth was truth. "Not for anything," she told him flatly. "She made that clear. Though God knows I earned my keep with her. If she'd only shown…just a little affection."

The realisation of her aloneness was starkly visual in his eyes. At least he understood that much now. Angie heaved a desolate sigh and tried to explain more.

"I swear I did my best to fit in, Taylor. She was a spinster, very much set in her own ways. It just wasn't right for her or for me." She pleaded another difficult truth. "Any more than it was right with Brian, though I fooled myself into believing it could be. I think I was starved for someone to love me. I kept on trying to make the connection with him work until I realised it never would."

Taylor startled her by reaching over and taking her hand, interweaving her fingers with his. The intensity in his eyes caused her heart to catapult around her chest. "Does our connection work, Angie?" he asked softly. "Or are you trying hard again?"

"I never had to try," she answered, her nerves almost unbearably strained by the desperate desire to convince him. "I felt the connection from the beginning. When the interview for the governess ended, I didn't want to leave you. It wasn't because of Brian. It was *you*, Taylor. I felt instinctively you had what I needed. Then later, that night, I never had a doubt about going with you. The trust was automatically there. The trust and the overwhelming wish, simply to be with you."

"You had the same pull on me, Angie, though I tried to deny it," he said ruefully.

"Because I was a city woman?"

"Yes. Though I realise now you didn't belong anywhere. You hadn't yet found a place to call home."

Tears pricked her eyes at his understanding. "You are the place, Taylor. You and Giralang are one. To love you is to love what made you what you are. I've found my home…" The tears welled and spilled "…If you love me," she finished huskily.

"Love you…" He moved so fast, Angie was caught breathless as he lowered her to the rug and leaned over her, tenderly trapping her beneath him, his eyes eloquently begging her forgiveness for his doubts. "You've just saved me from the hell of imagining a life without you. I love you so much, Angie, it was killing me to even consider you might want to leave."

"Oh, Taylor…" More tears welled. "I would die inside without you."

"Don't cry, my darling." He frantically kissed the wet streaks from her eyes. "I can't bear for you to feel hurt."

She wound her arms around his neck. "Just love me. Love me and all the hurt will go away."

"Angie…" It was the warm breath of love, caressing her skin, seeping into her heart. His kiss said it more truly, pouring all the passion of his feeling through her, the loving and cherishing and yearning to be one with her. "Angie…will you marry me? Have children with me?"

"Yes…" She held him tight, revelling in the power and strength of him, the stability and solidity he offered her, promised her, gave her. "Yes, Taylor, yes!"

No past…only the future…a future together stretching forward to span the rest of their lives…and the promise of it…the commitment to it…throbbed through the heat of the afternoon as they made love to each other on the bank of a river that kept flowing onward, a force of nature feeding its life-giving water to the timeless land of the outback.

Hamish grinned as he watched his father and Angie circling the dance floor, their solo waltz clapped by everyone who'd come to the picnic races. Angie looked real pretty in her red dress and his dad was whirling her around, both of them laughing like they were bubbling with happiness.

"You said your dad was never going to get married again," Jessie complained, put out because she'd had no warning of the announcement that had just been made.

Hamish, who had been hugging the secret for hours, turned a smug face to her. "*You* said he was going to marry Diane Westlake."

Jessie huffed. "Well, he *is* going to get married anyhow."

"He's got to so everything will be right," Hamish informed her cheerfully. "Angie said we're going to have a big family so there'll always be Maguires at Giralang. I'll have a whole gang of brothers and sisters and they'll be looking up to me as the leader."

"You mean more kids?" Wayne frowned disapproval. "We'll be kicked off the computer to give them a turn, Hamish."

"Nah… Dad's got to keep updating computers. We'll put them on an old one to play with, Wayne."

"Yeah…" He grinned with relish. "We can show 'em a thing or two."

"*I'll* be watching," Jessie said archly.

Wayne gave her a dark look. "Better tell Angie you

only want brothers, Hamish. Girls just want to mess up everything.''

''Angie doesn't mess up,'' Hamish pointed out.

''Yeah, well, she's different.''

Different…she sure was, Hamish thought, watching his father and Angie dancing together. She'd made a big difference to everything. And it was good seeing her so happy with his dad. Her eyes were all sparkly, like she had stars in them.

He wondered if she knew what Giralang meant. It was something he could tell her now she was going to stay forever. She'd like knowing it was an old Aboriginal word from a long time ago, before even the first Maguire came to the gulf country. As far back as anyone could remember their home had been called Giralang.

It meant…the place of stars.

Always had been.

Always would be.

THE OUTBACK
NURSE

by

Carol Marinelli

Carol Marinelli recently filled in a form where she was asked for her job title and was thrilled, after all these years, to be able to put down her answer as writer. Then it asked what Carol did for relaxation and after chewing her pen for a moment Carol put down the truth – writing. The third question asked – what are your hobbies? Well, not wanting to look obsessed or, worse still, boring, she crossed the fingers on her free hand and answered swimming and tennis, but, given that the chlorine in the pool does terrible things to her highlights and the closest she's got to a tennis racket in the last couple of years is watching the Australian Open – I'm sure you can guess the real answer!

Don't miss Carol Marinelli's new novels available from Medical and Modern Romance™ in the summer

For Dad, with love always

CHAPTER ONE

'BUT there must be some other work—anything?' Olivia fought for control, trying to keep the note of panic from her voice.

'Ms Morrell, we have plenty of work on our books, particularly for someone with your casualty experience. However, as you've said you will only consider a live-in position, it makes things very difficult. Even the large teaching hospitals are cutting back on their living accommodation—the agency nurses just don't get a look-in.'

Olivia nodded. She had heard it all before. This was the fifth agency she had tried and the only one that had actually come up with a job—a live-in position nursing a recently disabled gentleman in Melbourne. The work in itself didn't worry her, but in her present emotional state Olivia doubted if she would be much good at bolstering the young man's spirits.

'Well, thank you for your time.' Olivia stood up, smoothing her smart grey skirt. Trying to blink back the ever-threatening tears, she reached for her bag. 'If anything comes in, you will let me know?'

Miss Lever looked up from the files she was half-heartedly flicking through. Suddenly she felt sorry for Olivia for despite the designer clothes, immaculate hair and make-up she obviously wasn't as together as she first appeared.

'Just a moment.' Miss Lever tapped the keyboard of her computer. 'I'm sure this won't remotely interest you, but I did receive an e-mail today from our New South Wales office. It would seem they're having trouble filling a particular vacancy. It is live-in, but I can't imagine....' Her voice trailed off as she printed off the particulars.

'Tell me about it,' Olivia said sitting down sharply. Surely there must be a job for her.

'The position is for a charge nurse with advanced nursing skills to work in general practice.'

'It sounds perfect.' Olivia nodded enthusiastically.

'I think you'd better let me fill you in a bit before you go getting too excited. The practice is in Kirrijong—have you heard of it?'

Olivia nodded. 'Vaguely. It's way out in the bush, isn't it?'

'That's an understatement. It's very pretty apparently, but also very isolated. The practice covers a vast area and the surrounding townships. But when I say "surrounding", you could hardly say they're close by. Kirrijong isn't close to anything. They're actually in the process of building a small cottage hospital to service the area, which is due for completion in three to six months. The position is available until then, but if you like it...' Miss Lever gave a cynical smile '...I'm sure they'd be delighted to keep you on.'

She looked over at Olivia, expecting to see a look of horror on the well-made-up face. This was, after all, no modern city surgery. Instead, she was surprised to see Olivia closely reading the e-mail, her face full of interest. Perhaps she would get her commission after all. 'You did your midwifery training in England, I see, as well as your general training.'

'Yes, but I came straight out to Australia afterwards, and I've been in Casualty ever since. Apart from the odd surprise delivery in the department, I haven't practised.'

Miss Lever shrugged. 'They only say midwifery training desirable. You're more than qualified and, anyway, they're desperate.'

'What do you mean?'

'Well…' Miss Lever shuffled uncomfortably in her seat. 'Look, I'm not aware of your circumstances and, of course, it's none of my business, though it does appear you need a live-in job in a hurry.'

Olivia blushed. Was it that obvious how desperate she was?

'I just feel I should emphasise this is not the sort of job you're used to. Apart from your regular hours, you will be expected to help out in emergencies at any given time. It's an extremely busy surgery, with a large, complicated patient list. A lot of procedures that in the city would be done in a hospital are undertaken there.'

'Would I be the only nurse in the practice?'

'Yes, and if there's a seriously ill patient there will be no cardiac arrest team to bleep, no surgeons waiting scrubbed up in Theatre. Just you and the good doctor until the road or air ambulance arrives, and that can take a long time.' She paused a moment, before continuing, 'I ought to tell you that by all accounts Dr Clemson isn't the most pleasant of personalities.'

'In what way?'

Miss Lever leant over her desk and lowered her voice. 'Well, according to the last two girls sent there—who, incidentally, only managed two weeks between them—Dr Clemson is recently widowed and extremely bitter. He's supposedly very moody and demanding.'

Olivia let out a sigh of relief. For a moment she had thought Miss Lever was going to say he had made a pass at the other nurses. The very last thing she needed right now was to be stuck in the middle of nowhere with an elderly doctor and his roving hands.

'That doesn't worry you?'

'I've had more than my share of moody, difficult doctors, I can assure you. I'm not going to collapse in a heap if he barks at me. I can give as good as I get. As long as Dr Clemson can cope with that, I can manage his tantrums.'

Miss Lever looked at Olivia's determined face and the fiery red hair. She had no doubt she could.

'You sound as if you don't want me to take the position,' Olivia added.

'On the contrary…' Miss Lever smiled '…I just want to be sure you know what you're letting yourself in for. I'm not too keen on being on the receiving end of the formidable Dr Clemson's temper if I send someone unsuitable. I actually think you'll do very well—you've got a marvellous résumé. Three years in charge of such a busy casualty department must prepare you for just about any eventuality.'

'Just about,' Olivia agreed.

'Look, why don't I go and rustle up some coffee and leave you on your own for a few minutes to think it over?'

'Thank you, I'd appreciate that.'

Miss Lever walked to the door and, turning to ask how Olivia took her coffee, thought better of it, seeing her brimming eyes as she fished in her bag for a handkerchief. Closing the door quietly behind her, she shook her head. It was most unlike Miss Lever to put someone off a job—usually she was just interested in the commission. But there was something about Ms Morrell, a vulnerability behind that rather brittle exterior that made you not want to add to her troubles. She obviously had enough already.

Olivia leant back in the chair glad to be alone. Under normal circumstances she'd have had hysterics at the thought of a job out in the bush, with only a bitter old doctor as her colleague. But, then, who'd have thought, she reflected, she'd ever be in this situation, practically begging for a job? Sister Olivia Morrell, always so immaculate and in control. How happy she had been—a job she'd loved, Unit Manager in the emergency department at Melbourne

City Hospital, wonderful friends and, to cap it all, engaged to Jeremy Forster, Surgical Registrar, dashing, successful and good-looking.

Closing her eyes for a second, Olivia flashed back to the fateful day when Jessica, a dear friend and trusted colleague, had come into her office and asked for a private talk. How clearly she remembered the disbelief and horror as Jessica had gently told her that Jeremy was having an affair with his intern, Lydia Colletti.

At first Olivia had thought it must have been some sort of sick joke, a ghastly mistake, but, seeing the pain in her friend's eyes, she'd known she'd been hearing the truth. Looking back, it all seemed so obvious. Jeremy's mood swings, the exhaustion, the constant criticism. She had put it all down to the pressure of his work. He was due for a promotion soon to junior consultant and the competition was stiff. If they could just get through this, she had reasoned, surely he would be happier?

To add insult to injury, despite knowing the long hours and close proximity Jeremy shared with Lydia, she had never once felt threatened. She had trusted him. What a fool, what a stupid trusting fool.

Painfully, Olivia recalled their final row. She had confronted him, of course, and he'd sung like a bird, telling her in all too great a detail her faults, but Olivia had refused to take the blame for his infidelity.

'How could you do this Jeremy? How could you make love to her and then me?' she demanded, but Jeremy was unrepentant.

'Oh, come on, Olivia, when did we last make love? Our sex life is practically non-existent.'

'And that's supposed to be my fault?' she shouted, her anger welling to the surface. 'It's you who's always too tired or too busy. And now I know why, don't I? You were too damned exhausted after being with Lydia!'

'Well, at least she enjoys it Olivia. With you it's like making love to a skeleton, and about as lively.' He spat the words at her, his guilt and desire to end the discussion making him brutal.

Until finally, exhausted and reeling, all that was left to do was to throw a few hastily grabbed items into a bag and get out with as much dignity as she could muster, desperate to put some space between them.

It seemed that everyone except her had known about the affair. She couldn't go back to face the sympathetic stares and embarrassed silences. The only solution was to hand in her notice, which unfortunately meant surrendering the city apartment she leased from the hospital. Jessica's spare room provided a welcome haven but they both knew it was only temporary.

'Sorry I've been so long.' Miss Lever placed a cup and saucer on the desk in front of her and Olivia forced a smile, suddenly remembering where she was.

'I took the liberty of ringing Dr Clemson and telling him about you. You are still interested, I hope?'

Olivia nodded.

'Good. He was very keen.'

Olivia took a deep breath. 'How soon would he want me to start?'

'How soon can you get there?'

Hauling her suitcases off the train onto the platform, Olivia noticed she was the only passenger getting off at Kirrijong. In fact, the train only passed through once a day. Not for the first time, it hit her just how isolated she was. Gradually the city and suburbs had faded into endless bush, the lush green grass paling into sunburnt straw, acre after acre of dry cracked land. She had heard how the drought and dry winter had affected the farmers but, seeing for herself the parched bush and emaciated livestock, it made her realise the drought was far more than just a news bulletin or a page in the newspaper. Times were really tough here.

'G'day there, I'll get these. You must be Sister Morrell,' a friendly, sun-battered face greeted her, his eyes squinting in the setting sun. 'Jeez, how many cases have you got?'

Olivia blushed. It did seem a bit excessive, yet most of her clothes were still back at home. Throwing caution to the wind, Olivia had sold the car Jeremy had bought her as an engagement present, freeing up some cash. Jeremy would be furious. Blowing some money on a wardrobe more suited to the bush than her designer Melbourne gear had been a good tonic, at least for an afternoon.

Olivia was slightly taken back by the warmth of the man's welcome, having expected, from Miss Lever's description, a far more aloof greeting. Judging him to be in his mid-fifties, wearing dirty jeans and faded checked shirt, with a battered akubra shielding his face, Dr Clemson certainly didn't look the ogre Miss Lever had predicted. 'It's a pleasure to meet you, Dr Clemson.' She offered her hand, startled when he started to laugh.

'Youse didn't think I was the doctor? I can't wait to tell the missus. I'm Dougie, Dougie Kendall. My wife Ruby is Clem's housekeeper. I do a few odd jobs around the place, help out with the land.' He started to laugh again.

Olivia seethed. Did he really find it so funny? It was an obvious mistake. 'Well, Mr Kendall,' she said evenly, 'it's a pleasure to meet you.' It wouldn't do to get the locals offside quite so early.

Climbing into his dusty ute, Olivia winced as Dougie carelessly threw her expensive suitcases in the back. All the windows were wound down, forcing her to shout responses to Dougie's continual chatter. He pointed out the various residences as he hurtled the ute at breakneck speed along the dry, dusty road.

'That there belongs to the Hunts, a beaut family. Just had

a baby, a little fella, so no doubt youse'll be seeing them soon. And the land from now till the crossroads belongs to the Rosses.'

Olivia looked at the vast acreage and huge brick residence, far more formal than the weatherboard homes they had passed.

'They own a lot of land—mind, not as much as the doctor. Their daughter Charlotte is a model, well, that's what she calls herself anyway, I could think of a few other things.' He looked over at her, awaiting a response, but Olivia didn't rise to the bait. She wasn't interested in gossip. 'Charlotte's forever flitting in and out. One minute London the next Italy. She's supposed to be living in Sydney, but manages to put in an appearance here often enough and grace us with her presence. She's out with the doctor tonight—that's why he couldn't meet you.'

'Really?' Despite her earlier disinterest, Olivia sat up, suddenly intrigued. How rude. Surely he could have taken a night off from romancing someone young enough to be his daughter to welcome a new colleague.

'It's no business of mine, but she's a bit touched.' Dougie tapped his head and laughed. 'Clem wanted to come and meet youse himself but Charlotte rang with yet another "emergency" and of course he ends up running off to sort her out. Charlotte's a bit of a drama queen, if you know what I mean.'

Olivia knew what he meant all right. Wasn't that Lydia's game? Playing the helpless female, waiting for Jeremy to dash to her rescue. Olivia swallowed hard. While she had been bending over backwards to make their relationship work he had been rushing around comforting Lydia for every trivial hiccup or imagined problem that came her way.

'We're coming up to the surgery now.'

Night seemed to have fallen in a moment, with no dusk

to ease it in. Through the darkness Olivia could make out a huge rambling federation-style house with an array of plants hanging from the turned veranda posts. Dougie drove slowly past, the ute crunching on the gravel driveway. 'That's the doctor's house. The front of it is the surgery and he lives in the back part—it's pretty big.' He drove on for a couple more minutes and brought the truck to a halt. 'This is you.' He gestured to a pretty weatherboard with a huge veranda. The same array of hanging plants and terracotta pots adorned the entry and a wicker rocking chair sat idle in the front.

'Just for me?'

'Yep, all yours. My wife will be in through the week to take care of the cleaning and laundry. She'll show youse the ropes better than I can.'

'There's really no need. I can manage my own cleaning. I'm quite capable—'

'Sister,' he interrupted, 'youse'll be busy enough without running around doing housework. Anyway, don't be doing me missus out of a job.' He spoke roughly but his eyes were smiling.

'Oh, well, if you put it like that,' Olivia replied.

Dougie brought in her luggage as Olivia inspected 'home', her shoes echoing on the gorgeous jarrah polished floorboards that ran the length of the house. The lounge was inviting with two soft cream sofas littered with scatter cushions and a huge cream rug adding warmth to the cold floor. Someone thoughtful had arranged a bowl of burgundy proteas on the heavy wooden coffee-table. A huge open fireplace caught her eye. Olivia doubted whether she'd need it for, though dark outside, the air still hung heavy and warm.

'There's some red gum chopped. Ruby will set a fire up for you tomorrow. It still being spring, we get the odd chilly evening, though not for much longer. There's a fan heater in the kitchen cupboard, youse'll need that in the morning to take the chill off.'

Olivia smiled. 'It's a lovely house, beautifully decorated.'

'That was Kathy's work.'

'Kathy?' Olivia questioned.

'Yep, Kathy—Clem's wife, or rather late wife. She loved decorating. Spent weeks on this place, painting, stencilling, finding bits of furniture here and there.'

He spoke in the same casual manner but Olivia could hear the emotion in his voice.

'Anyway…' he gestured to the kitchen '…there's plenty in the fridge and cupboards to get you started. Ruby will be over in the morning to take you to the surgery. We don't want you feeling awkward on your first day.'

'Thank you, that's very kind.'

Dougie waved his hand dismissively. 'No worries. I'll leave youse to get settled in but, mind, if you need anything there's our number by the phone in the kitchen.' With a cheery wave he was off.

Olivia noticed he didn't even close the front door, just the flyscreen. This obviously wasn't the city, but old habits died hard. Olivia closed the door and turned the catch. A pang of homesickness hit her but, determined not to feel sorry for herself, she set about unpacking, until finally, with every last thing put away, she put the suitcases into the study wardrobe. This was home for now.

Peering in the fridge, Olivia smiled. There was enough food to last a month—a dozen eggs, bacon as thick as steak, milk, cheese. The pantry was just as well stocked. Tackling the Aga, Olivia put the kettle on. She'd earned a cup of tea and then she'd go straight to bed. The day seemed to have caught up with her all of a sudden.

A sharp knock on the door made her jump. Glancing at the clock, she saw it was edging on ten. Tentatively she opened the heavy door. Leaving the flyscreen closed, she peered at the large figure outlined in the darkness, trying to sound assured. 'Can I help you?'

'Olivia?'

'You are…' she said questioningly.

'Jake Clemson, but everyone calls me Clem.'

Olivia blushed, fumbling with the catch. 'Please, come in.' He was her new boss and she was treating him like some madman from the bush.

'I didn't mean to scare you.' He shook her hand firmly. 'Welcome to Kirrijong.'

Olivia smiled, taken aback not only by the unexpected friendliness but also by his appearance. Why had she assumed he'd be older? The man standing before her must only be in his thirties. She had imagined some austere, elderly doctor in tweeds. Jake Clemson, standing well over six feet, with battered jeans and an equally well-worn denim shirt, certainly didn't fit the image she'd had of him. His dark curly hair needed a good cut—he looked more like an overgrown medical student than a GP.

'I had hoped to meet you myself, but something came up.'

Olivia shrugged. If she had been expecting an apology or even an explanation she obviously wasn't going to get one. 'No problem. Mr Kendall was very helpful.'

'Dougie's a great bloke. I knew he'd take care of you.' He peered over her shoulder into the living room. 'Time for a quick chat?'

Olivia blushed again, suddenly feeling very rude. 'Of course. Come through—this way.' It was his house. As if he wouldn't know where the lounge was she thought feeling silly, but he just smiled.

'If I know Dougie and Ruby, there'll be a few stubbies in the fridge. Do you fancy one?'

Nodding, she followed him into the kitchen as he casually opened the fridge and helped himself to the beer.

Opening two stubbies, he made his way back to the living room. Obviously, if she wanted a glass she'd better get it herself!

'So how do you feel about coming to work here?' he asked in a deep, confident voice with only a hint of an Australian accent.

Olivia busied herself pouring the beer and managing to spill most of it. 'I'm really looking forward to it,' she lied. She could hardly tell him she was having a full-on panic attack and wondering what on earth had possessed her. 'The agency gave me quite an extensive brief. It all sounds very interesting, though I wish I had a bit more midwifery experience.'

He stared at her, taking in her slender frame and long red hair. The cheerful, confident voice belied her body language. Those huge green eyes were looking everywhere but at him, and her long hands were clutching that glass so tightly he half expected it to shatter. 'Ms' Morrell obviously wasn't as confident as she would have him believe.

'There is a lot of obstetrics here, but don't worry about that for now. I'll hold your hand, so to speak, for the first few weeks, and if I'm not around for some reason you can always call on Iris Sawyer. She used to be the practice nurse up until a couple of years ago. Iris is retired now, and happily so, but she doesn't mind missing a game of bowls to help out now and then, and her experience with the locals is invaluable.'

Olivia nodded, reassured by the confidence in his voice.

'Your résumé is rather impressive. I see you worked under Tony Dean in your last job. He gave you a glowing reference. I know him well. We're old friends.'

'You are?' Just the fact that this huge, daunting man was a friend of her beloved Mr Dean, the senior consultant in her former casualty department, made him somehow seem much less intimidating.

'Yes. Tony Dean was a junior consultant in Sydney when I was a mere intern. Later, our paths crossed again when I went back as a paediatric registrar. That would be five or six years ago. He moved on to Melbourne and I came here, but we still keep in touch. He's an amazing man as well as a fine doctor, but you don't need me to tell you that. Many times I've rung him for advice about a patient, or had them flown there by the air ambulance. I've probably spoken to you on the phone at some time.'

He smiled. It was a nice smile, genuine. Olivia managed to sneak a proper look. Judging by his qualifications, he'd have to be at least in his mid-thirties, but he appeared younger. He was undeniably handsome in a rugged sort of way. Unruly dark curls framed a tanned face with just a smattering of freckles over the bridge of his nose. She had been right first time—he really did look like an overgrown medical student.

'How long did you work there? I know it's in your résumé, but I can't remember offhand.'

'Five years, three as Unit Manager. I'd just left all my family behind in England, so I was feeling horribly homesick and foreign.'

'Had you been to Australia before?'

Olivia nodded. 'Yes but just on a working holiday, which is when I met my…' Olivia hesitated. 'My ex-fiancé. He was an intern then. Anyway,' Olivia added hastily, because the last thing she wanted to talk about was Jeremy, 'Mr Dean started within a couple of weeks of me. We were the "new kids on the block" together.'

'Why did you leave?' His question was direct and he watched as her shoulders stiffened, her hands yet again tightening convulsively around the glass.

'Personal reasons,' she answered stiffly.

Thankfully, he thought better than to push it—there

would be time for that later. Instead, he explained her new position.

'A contrast to Casualty, but there are a lot of similarities. As well as the usual coughs, colds and blood pressures, we're up against whatever they present themselves with at any hour of the day or night. From heart attacks to major farming accidents, we're the front line. You need to keep your wits about you. They breed them tough out here and they don't like a fuss. It takes a lot of skill to read between the lines. What may appear quite trivial can often be far more serious. Most tend to play down their symptoms.' He noticed her suppress a yawn.

'I'm not boring you, I hope?' he asked sharply.

Olivia sat upright, taken back by the first glimpse of him being anything other than friendly. 'Of course not.'

Clem stood up, and Olivia reluctantly admired his athletic build. 'You must be tired. You've had a long journey and it's almost midnight. I seem to think everyone else keeps my ridiculous hours. I'll let you get some sleep and I'll see you in the morning, Livvy.'

'It's Olivia, not Livvy,' she corrected him, following him to the door. 'And thank you for coming over, Dr Clemson. I'm looking forward to getting started.'

'Good. Hopefully you'll enjoy working here. And it's Clem, remember?'

Olivia suddenly felt embarrassed at how prudish she must have sounded, but she hated her name being shortened.

She watched him depart in long deliberate strides.

'Watch out for Betty and Ruby. Don't believe a word they say about me,' he shouted jokingly over his shoulder as he disappeared into the night.

As Olivia closed the door and firmly locked it, Clem rolled his eyes heavenwards. She wouldn't last five minutes. She was obviously well qualified and extremely intelligent, but she was as jumpy as a cat, and he somehow couldn't imagine her on a search and rescue. Sure, she looked stunning, he thought reluctantly then checked himself. She was probably anorexic—you didn't get a figure like that on three good meals a day.

CHAPTER TWO

OLIVIA awoke an hour before her alarm, determined to get the day off to a good start. Dougie had been right—the house was freezing. Reluctant to light a fire, instead she pulled on a pair of socks and a large jumper over her skimpy silk nightie and turned on the tiny fan heater. Jeremy would have had a heart attack if he could have seen her. Not sure how or where she'd get lunch, Olivia took advantage of the well-stocked fridge and prepared an enormous breakfast of bacon, eggs and wild mushrooms.

Mopping up the creamy yolk with a third slice of toast, she tried to decide what to wear for her first day. The usual white uniform seemed so formal, and according to the forecast it was going to be too hot for trousers. Settling on a pair of navy culottes, teamed with a white blouse and navy jacket, Olivia finally felt happy with her selection—smart but casual. She was nervous. What if the patients hated her?

With shaking hands, somehow she managed to put on her make-up, carefully trying to create a natural look. It had been a standing joke between herself and Jessica, the effort Olivia took over her appearance.

'Honestly, Olivia, you look smarter coming off duty than I do going on,' she'd often joked and Olivia would laugh back.

But her appearance was important to her. It had mattered so much to Jeremy that eventually it had rubbed off. Somehow she felt so much more confident with her 'face' on. After smoothing the wild mass of Titian ringlets into a chic French roll, she was finally satisfied.

'G'day. It's only me, Ruby.'

Olivia walked into the hall and watched as a huge woman burst through the front door. She had a mass of keys in her hand, as well as an array of brushes, a bucket and mop.

'Here let me help you with that,' Olivia offered.

'I'm right.' Ruby deposited her burdens on the hall floor. 'So you're Livvy? Dougie said you were a beaut, he wasn't wrong. I'll fix us a nice cup of tea before I get started. Youse must be feeling a touch nervous but, no worries, I'll take youse over and introduce you to everyone.'

Ruby was truly amazing to watch. Without even pausing for breath, she had taken Olivia's arm and seated her at the kitchen table then proceeded to fill the kettle.

'How are you finding it—a bit bewildering?'

'Just a bit,' Olivia conceded.

'Oh, we're a strange lot, that's for sure. The other nurses took one look and ran. Didn't even see the week out.' She eyed Olivia carefully.

'Well, I'm here for a lot longer than that, I can assure you,' Olivia responded with more conviction than she felt.

'Yep, I reckon you are. But a word of advice from an old chook who's been around the yard a while.' She leant over the kitchen bench and, despite the fact there was only the two of them, spoke in a theatrical whisper. 'Don't go letting the doctor upset you. Clem's bark is far worse than his bite.'

Although curious, Olivia felt she really shouldn't be discussing her employer.

'He seems very nice,' she answered noncommittally, though she secretly hoped Ruby would elaborate. Olivia didn't have to wait long!

'Oh he's golden. He snaps and snarls now and then but I just picture him as a spotty young teenager. I don't tell him that, mind, I just say ''Yes, Clem, no, Clem,'' and wait for his mood to pass—it soon does.'

'Everyone has their off days.'

'Of course, but he's got worse. It's to be expected, mind, with all he's been through. He's far too busy, and now with this new hospital and everything. I just don't know how he does it. He's always had a temper, but since Kathy passed on…' She blew her nose loudly on a hanky she'd fished from somewhere in her very ample bosom. 'Tragic, there's no other word for it.'

Olivia looked on, fascinated. This woman never stopped talking though she was busy all the while. The breakfast dishes were now washed and back in their various cupboards and the bench had been wiped down.

'It must be difficult for him,' Olivia agreed. 'He's very young to be a widower.'

'Whoever said only the good die young wasn't wrong. A real living angel was Kathy. And he's not coping. I don't care how many times he tells me he's all right—I know he's not.'

Olivia tried to steer the conversation. It really was getting too personal. 'I hear it's very busy at the surgery.'

'Tragic,' Ruby muttered, then, blowing her nose again, she stuffed the hanky back into her cleavage. 'Oh, the surgery's busy all right. Far too much work for the one doctor. It will be great when we get the hospital. A lot of the locals are opposed to it but they'll soon come round. They're just scared of change, and they'll be wary of you, too,' she added, 'with that English accent and your city ways. But youse'll soon win them over.'

'I hope so,' Olivia answered glumly.

'Of course you will,' Ruby reassured her. 'Now, come on, sweetie, we can't be here gossiping all day. You don't want to go making a bad impression.'

Walking over to the surgery, Ruby linked her arm through Olivia's. Really, Ruby was getting more maternal by the minute. Of course, just to add to Olivia's nerves, the waiting room was full. As they entered the chattering stopped and Olivia felt every face turn to her. Smiling tentatively, painfully aware of a deep blush spreading over her cheeks, she wanted to turn and run. Sitting at the desk was a middle-aged, harassed-looking woman with frizzy grey hair that had never seen conditioner.

'Thank goodness you're here,' she said as a welcome. 'I'll just let the doctor know.'

'Now, just settle a minute, Betty.' Ruby blocked her desk. 'There's always time for an introduction. This is Sister Olivia Morrell and, Sister, this is Betty. She's the receptionist here and chief cook and bottle-washer.'

'Isn't that a fact?' muttered Betty. 'I'm sorry, Sister. It's lovely to meet you, and not a moment too soon—the place is fit to burst as usual. Clem's needed over at the Hudsons. Apparently the old boy had another turn,' she added in low tones to a very attentive Ruby.

Olivia was sure that Betty shouldn't be discussing the patients with the housekeeper, but she was obviously in for a few surprises. The bush telegraph would appear somewhat similar to the hospital grapevine, and that took some beating. Even the switchboard staff had apparently known about Jeremy and Lydia.

'Anyway,' said Betty with a smile, 'we'll get there.' She nodded as a young woman came out of what appeared to be the consulting room. 'I'll take you through to Clem.'

As Olivia walked in, she noticed how much smarter Clem looked than on their first meeting. He was wearing beige trousers and a navy sports jacket, and a tie was sitting awkwardly on his thick neck. His black curls were smoother and she caught a whiff of cologne as he stood up and once again shook her hand warmly.

'Good morning, Livvy. It's good to have you on board.'

Olivia winced but Clem didn't notice.

'I did want to take some time to show you around but, as you can see from the waiting room, we're pretty full on.'

'That's all right, I'll manage,' she replied in what she hoped was an enthusiastic voice.

'Good girl.'

Olivia winced again as he nodded appreciatively. She didn't have to be a genius to see that Clem wasn't particularly politically correct.

'I'm sorry to throw you in at the deep end but I see from your résumé that you can suture, which is an absolute luxury for me. I've never had a nurse here that can stitch and, frankly, I've never had the time to teach them.'

'As long as the wound is examined by you before and after I suture, that's fine.'

Clem nodded dismissively. 'Well, in the treatment room I've got Alex Taylor. He's gashed his hand on some barbed wire while mending a fence. I've had a look and there doesn't appear to be any nerve or tendon damage, but the wound in itself is quite jagged and dirty and will need a lot of cleaning and debriding. If you could get started on him, that would be a great help. Buzz me when you're finished or if you've any concerns.'

'Right…' Olivia hesitated. 'I'll get started, then.'

'Good. He also needs a tetanus shot,' Clem added, more as an afterthought, then, picking up his fountain pen, started to write on a patient's file in a huge, untidy scrawl. Olivia stood there, not sure where to go. He hadn't exactly given her a guided tour of the place.

'Was there anything else?' he asked, without bothering to look up.

'Er, no,' she replied hesitantly. He obviously wasn't going to hold her hand. Perhaps Betty could show her where the treatment room and the equipment was. But back in the waiting room Betty was looking even more harassed than before. The phone was ringing incessantly, while she tried to force an uncooperative piece of paper into the fax machine. Oh, well, she'd just have to find her own way.

Alex was infinitely patient.

'No worries, Sister,' he said, adding reassuringly a little later, 'Take your time, Sister, I'm in no hurry.'

Olivia bustled about, trying to find suture packs and local anaesthetic. Finally, with her trolley laid out and her hands scrubbed, she was ready to start.

'Right, Alex, I'm with you now.'

'Right you are, Sister.' The elderly man nodded.

Olivia examined the wound carefully. Clem was right. It was indeed a nasty cut, very deep with untidy jagged edges and very dirty. After waiting for the local anaesthetic she had injected to take effect, Olivia once again inspected the wound, this time more thoroughly. The tendon and its sheath were visible, but thankfully intact.

'Alex, everything looks all right in there. I'm just going to give it a good clean and then I'll stitch it up. You shouldn't feel any pain, but if it does start to hurt you be sure and tell me.'

'Very good, Sister.'

Olivia was quite sure he wouldn't. Alex hadn't even let out a murmur while she'd injected the anaesthetic. 'Dr Clemson said you were repairing a fence?'

'Yep. The sheep were getting out and wandering off. I was gonna wait for me grandson to fix it, but he's away at uni till the holidays and I can't be doing chasing the stupid things. I'm too old for that.' He went on to tell Olivia about his farm and how his grandson was studying agriculture. She encouraged the conversation to take Alex's mind off his hand. Anyway, it was interesting to hear what he had to say.

'He's forever coming back from uni, full of new ideas and notions about what he wants to do with the land.'

'And does that worry you?'

''Struth, no,' Alex answered firmly. 'I'm all for progress.
Mind, I'm too set in me ways to be changing things myself.
But as for the young fella, he can do what he likes as far
as I'm concerned. Farming's big business now it's a sci-
ence.' He laughed. 'It'll all be his one day and I'm just
glad he wants it. Not many young folk stay now. You just
look at Clem. He wanted to stay in the city and carry on
his work with the children.'

'But he came back,' Olivia ventured, curious despite herself at the insight into her boss. She had finished cleaning
the hand and debriding the dead tissue. Aligning the edges,
she started to suture.

'Old Dr Clemson—Clem's father—went to pieces after
his wife died. His health started to fail. Clem came back to
help out. He's a good sort, not like his brother Joshua—he
didn't even make it in time for his own mother's funeral.
Anyway, then the old fella died, God rest him. By then,
though, young Clem had fallen in love with Kathy, and she
would never have considered leaving here. She loved
Kirrijong and it loved her.' Alex winced slightly and Olivia
wasn't sure whether it was from pain or emotion.

'Is that sore, Alex? The anaesthetic is starting to wear
off, but I'm just about finished now.'

'I'm all right,' he said, then continued his tale. 'Kathy
belonged here, and for a while so did Clem.'

'What do you mean?'

'Well, he's busy with building the hospital and he's flat
out here, but I don't reckon his heart's in it. I know he's
grieving and I reckon the place has just got too many painful memories for him. I reckon we'll be lucky if he stays.'

Olivia's eyes suddenly misted over. Poor Clem. She
knew all about painful memories and being alone. But if
Jeremy had died? To totally lose someone… She wondered
how Clem even managed to get up in the morning. At that
moment she heard Clem walk into the room. He stood over

her as she tied the last knot, surveying her work. The bitter tang of his cologne was a heady contrast to the chlorhexidine solution she was using on Alex's wound. Acutely aware of his closeness, her hand trembled slightly as she snipped the silk thread. Clem let out a low whistle and shook his head.

'You've made a rod for your own back Livvy. I couldn't have done a better job myself. You'll be doing all the suturing now. Right you are, then, Alex. Keep it clean and dry, and I'll see you again in a week. Here's a script for some antibiotics—that's a nasty cut and we don't want it getting infected. Any problems in the meantime and you're to come straight back.'

Alex rolled up his sleeve as Olivia approached with his tetanus shot. 'Right you are, Clem.' He got up from the trolley and added, 'I hope you don't go scaring this one off—she's a diamond.'

Olivia blushed but Clem laughed.

'I'll try not to.' He shook Alex's good hand and reminded him once again to return if needed.

'Bye, then, Sister. Thanks very much.'

'No, thank you Alex, for being so patient.' She smiled warmly at him and hoped all her patients would be as pleasant.

The rest of the morning passed in a whirl of dressings, recording ECGs and taking blood. An old lady eyed Olivia dubiously as she sat her down and produced a tourniquet.

'Clem normally takes my blood. I've got very difficult veins, you know.'

Taking a deep breath, Olivia forced a smile and assured the woman she knew what she was doing, adding, 'Dr Clemson is so busy this morning he didn't want to keep you sitting around, waiting for him, when you've probably got far better things to do.'

This seemed to appease her and grudgingly the woman offered her arm. Thankfully the needle went straight in.

Finally the last of the patients had been dealt with. Despite this, Betty still had to shepherd out a group of ladies from the waiting room who were conducting an impromptu mothers' meeting. Firmly closing the door, Betty let out an exaggerated sigh. 'They'll be wanting me to serve them tea and biscuits next. Come on, Sister, it's time for lunch.'

Leading Olivia through the surgery to the private part of the house she took her into the lounge room. Again, it was beautifully furnished, the walls lined with books, heavy drapes blocking out the harsh midday sun. Kathy must have used her talents in here as well. In one of the huge jade leather chairs, which clashed ravishingly with the dark crimson rug, sat a fat ginger cat. In the other chair, looking equally relaxed, sat Clem. His tie loosened, he was working his way through a large pile of sandwiches.

'Come in, come in. Ruby's done us proud as always—help yourself,' he said, offering her a plate. 'Don't wait to be asked or there won't be anything left. Isn't that right, Betty?'

Always conscious of eating in front of strangers and still full from her large breakfast, Olivia picked gingerly at a huge roast beef sandwich Betty had cheerfully put on her plate.

'Coffee, Sister?'

'Thank you, Betty, and, please, it's Olivia, remember.'

'Cream and sugar, Sister?' she asked, completely ignoring her request.

Didn't anybody here use the right name?

'No, just black will be fine.'

Clem raised his eyebrows. 'I'd suggest you tuck in, Livvy, we've got a busy afternoon ahead of us. I don't know what time we'll finish.'

'But I had a huge breakfast,' Olivia protested, then, seeing the expression on their faces, she hastily took a bite.

A talk show was on television, wives confronting their husbands' mistresses. That was all she needed.

Betty was lecturing her on the benefits of thermal underwear for night calls. 'It can be cold at night if you have to go out in a hurry,' she said, looking disapprovingly at Olivia's skinny legs. A psychologist on the television show was banging on about how wives often let themselves go after they got married. Jeremy had certainly accused her of that and they hadn't even made it up the aisle!

'I'm quite sure Olivia wouldn't be seen dead in thermals. Isn't that right?' Clem teased.

Olivia thought glumly of the small fortune she had spent on sexy underwear in an attempt to resuscitate her and Jeremy's dying sex life. All to no avail. 'Dr Clemson— Clem,' Olivia said curtly, 'as friendly as you've all been, I'm sure you wouldn't expect me to discuss my underwear—or was there something in my job description I didn't read?'

Betty coughed nervously; the television blared out the merits of keeping an air of mystery in the bedroom. Clem merely threw his head back and laughed loudly.

'Good for you. We're far too familiar here. Come on, we've got work to do.' And picking up the half-eaten sandwich left on her plate, he took a huge bite. Olivia watched distastefully and stood up.

'And if I'm not being too personal,' Clem said with more than a hint of sarcasm, 'may I suggest you go and put on some sunscreen and a hat? Half my house calls seem to be done in the middle of a field. Some insect repellent might be useful, too.'

Outside, he handed her the keys to a large black four-wheel-drive.

'This is yours, but I'll drive today, give you a chance to

get your bearings. Just put the petrol on my account at the garage.'

'Wonderful.' That was a relief. She had been beginning to wonder if 'transport provided' might mean a bus pass.

'Before we head off I'll just show you the set-up.' He opened the back door. 'As you can see, I've got all the back seats down. It's better to keep it like that so if the need arises you can transfer someone supine. There's a camp-bed mattress rolled up in the corner there, with a pillow and some blankets.' He opened up a large medical emergency box. 'I'll run through the box. Pay attention— you don't know when you might need it.'

Olivia bristled. She was only too aware of the importance of the equipment Clem was showing her—he hardly needed to tell her to listen.

'All the usual emergency drugs and intravenous solutions, all clearly labelled—giving sets, needles, syringes.' He took out each piece of equipment in turn, gave her a short lecture on its use and then replaced it. Olivia stood there, silently fuming. While she appreciated him showing her the contents, he was talking to her as if she were a first-year nursing student. 'An intubation kit,' Clem stated as he held up a plastic box clearly marked INTUBATION KIT.

'Is it?'

Clem chose to ignore her, instead painstakingly going through the various tube sizes and the appropriate ages they would be used on. Olivia automatically picked up the laryngoscope and checked that the bulb was working—it would be no fun attempting to put an intubation tube down an unconscious patient's throat if the light didn't work.

'There's spare bulbs here, but check it weekly. Have you ever intubated a patient before?' Clem enquired.

'Yes, several, but only in a controlled setting. Mr Dean insisted his senior nursing staff knew how, just in case. Anyway, it helps assisting doctors if you've done it yourself.' She thought for a moment. 'But I've never intubated anyone without supervision.' Clem heard the note of tension creep into her voice.

'And hopefully you won't have to. You can always bag them until help arrives, but who knows what can happen? At least you know your way around the kit. You can have a go, that's got to be better than doing nothing and watching someone die.' Olivia nodded glumly, not for the first time wondering just what she had taken on.

'Now the defibrillator. It's pretty standard, you can run a three-channel ECG off this model—'

'I've used that type before,' Olivia interrupted.

'Here's the on-off switch,' Clem continued, blatantly ignoring her again. 'Keep it plugged in overnight to charge it, but just run the cord through the Jeep window into the garage wall. Are you listening? I hope you're taking all this in,' he snapped rudely.

'I've used a defibrillator before—this model, in fact. I know what I'm doing.'

'I'm sure you do,' he said through gritted teeth, 'but when I ring you at one in the morning to come and assist me in an emergency, I need to be sure you know exactly where all the equipment is and how it works. It's no good you driving off in a hurry and leaving the bloody defibrillator still charging on the garage floor.'

'Obviously not,' Olivia retorted. She was nervous enough about her new responsibilities, without him treating her like the village idiot. 'I'm grateful to you for showing me things, but I really don't need a total re-train. If I don't know or understand something then I'll ask.' She stood there resolutely, staring defiantly into his angry, haughty face, awaiting his wrath, but it never came.

'Well, just make sure you do,' he said after what seemed an age. Turning his large back on her, he deftly replaced the equipment.

With her face burning, Olivia made her way to the passenger seat. She knew she had been right to stand up to him. He had to treat her, if not as an equal, at least with some respect.

Climbing into the driver's seat, he started the ignition. 'We'll go the back way. It's a short cut but don't use it till you're comfortable with the Jeep.' And without looking over once, he gave her a run-down on their first patient. 'The first port of call is the Jean Hunt, for her postnatal check. She's just had her fourth baby. A son after three daughters…young Sam. He's six weeks old now.' Clem skilfully guided the car around the tight bends.

'Oh, yes,' Olivia recalled. 'Dougie mentioned them. They must be thrilled.'

'Not exactly,' Clem replied grimly. 'Everyone's thrilled except Mum.'

'Oh, dear.'

Clem finally glanced over at her, realising she understood the situation.

'Exactly.'

Olivia remembered only too well the tearful mums on the maternity ward, trying desperately to appear happy to relatives and wondering why on earth they'd been feeling so miserable and unable to cope.

Clem continued, 'After an extremely long and exhausting labour with a difficult posterior presentation, young Master Hunt entered the world quite healthy, screaming his head off, and he hasn't stopped since. A complete contrast to the girls, who were the most placid little sheilas you could imagine. Alicia, the youngest, actually had to be woken for her feeds for the first couple of months. Not only does Jean have a husband and three other children to cope with, she's also dealing with a never-ending stream of well-wishers bringing little blue gifts and telling her how delighted she must be feeling.'

'Poor thing,' Olivia sympathised. 'How's his weight?'

'Borderline. He's gaining, but not as much as I'd like.'

Olivia thought for a moment.

'Could he have reflux?' she suggested.

Clem shrugged. 'I really don't think so, though I have considered it. I've seen a lot of reflux babies but Sam just doesn't quite fit the picture. I think it's more Jean.'

'Is she breastfeeding?'

'Trying to, but I'm going to suggest she puts him on the bottle today.'

Olivia couldn't believe what she was hearing. How behind was this place? Everyone knew you encouraged breastfeeding.

He looked over again. 'What's wrong, you don't approve?' Clem parked the car and turned around to face her.

She looked at him properly for the first time, and realised just how attractive he really was. 'It's not a question of whether I approve or not. I was taught to promote breastfeeding, that's all. To give in after such a short time seems strange to me.'

'Look, I do see your point. Breast is best and all that, but only if it's working. When it isn't, the bottle is fantastic.'

Olivia opened her mouth to argue but he cut her short.

'There's no breastfeeding mothers' support group here, no lactation consultant to call in, just the help you and I can offer. You may have only done a morning here, but you can surely see how stretched we are.' He held up his hand to silence her as she again attempted to put her point. 'Let me finish, then you can have your say.'

Olivia snapped her mouth closed and folded her arms.

'I've been round nearly every day since Sam was born, but there's not much more I can do. He's healthy, he's just hungry. For whatever reason, breastfeeding just isn't working this time. Anyway, Jean's far more experienced than you or I—after all, she's successfully fed three children. It's a bit like taking snow to the Eskimos, offering her advice on her feeding technique.'

Olivia grudgingly nodded.

'And as chauvinistic as it may sound to a liberated young woman like yourself, Mr Hunt will be back from a hard day's work at the farm this evening. He'll want to come back to a tidy house and a meal. It doesn't mean he loves her any less than the sensitive twenty-first century men you may mix with, it's just the way it is here. And I can tell you now that Jean isn't going to take a stand for sisterhood and to heck with routine.'

Olivia digested his speech. She actually understood far more than he realised. She herself had desperately wanted to start a family as soon as they'd got married. But as with their elusive wedding date, Jeremy had wanted to wait, for what she hadn't been quite sure. The thought of Jeremy coming home to a messy house, a crying baby and a hysterical mother made her realise he wasn't the modern, liberated man he liked to think he was. Taking her silence as dissent Clem went further.

'I could prescribe anti-depressants or tell her to hang in there till things improve, but I'm not prepared to do that, at least not this early in the piece. That's not the kind of medicine I practise.'

And despite the fact she had indeed only worked a morning with him, Olivia knew that already. It was obvious from the adoration of his patients that he was a wonderful caring doctor. Still, she wasn't prepared to give in that easily. 'I still think you should go in there with an open mind,' she said defiantly, but, watching his face darken, wished she'd held her tongue. She probably wouldn't last the week out, like her predecessors.

'May I suggest something?' Clem said slowly.

'Of course.' Olivia nodded weakly. Perhaps he was going to tell her to remember her place.

'Maybe it should be *you* that goes in to the house with an open mind. In fact, why don't you decide what Jean should do?' he suggested.

'And if I don't come down on your side, you'll simply override me,' she retorted.

Clem shook his head. 'You don't know me very well. Of course, I could override you but I won't. It's your call.' He picked up his doctor's bag, effectively ending the conversation, and got out of the vehicle. Striding to the front door, Olivia had to half run to keep up with him. Knocking firmly, he turned. 'Remember, an open mind.'

Jean Hunt opened the door still in her dressing-gown, her hair unbrushed, her eyes red and swollen from crying.

'Oh, Clem, I'm so glad you're here. He's been screaming all morning.' She ushered them through to the family room, apologising for the mess. The house was in chaos. Toys littered the floor and piles of washing lay over the chairs and sofa. The morning's breakfast dishes were still on the breakfast bar. 'Please, sit down,' she said to Olivia, removing a pile of nappies.

Clem peered into the crib. 'He's asleep now.'

'Yes, but it won't last.' Her eyes brimmed. 'Can I get you a cup of tea?'

Clem turned to Olivia. Taking her cue, she jumped up.

'I'll sort out the tea. Why don't you let Clem examine you while Sam is asleep?'

Clem nodded appreciatively.

'He'll be awake before you know it. Six weeks old and he's hardly slept for more than two hours at a time. The girls were so easy—I just don't know what it is I'm doing wrong. Brian's so thrilled at having a boy, he just doesn't understand...' Jean's voice broke and her shoulders shook with emotion.

Clem, towering over her, put his arms around her heaving shoulders and spoke softly. 'Come on, Jean. Let's go through to the bedroom and I'll do your postnatal check, then we'll sit down over a nice cuppa and try to sort something out.' Gently he led her away.

After switching on the kettle, Olivia hastily did the breakfast dishes and wiped down the benches. The family room wasn't dirty, just untidy. She put the toys back into their box and started to sort out the laundry, folding the nappies into a neat pile and placing the rest into the groaning ironing basket. The place looked a lot better, and by the time Clem retuned she had made the tea.

'Jean's just getting dressed.' He raised his eyebrows 'You've been busy.'

Jean was eternally grateful. 'Sister, you didn't have to do that.'

'No problem, Jean. I'm glad to help.'

While they drank their tea, Jean, in a faltering voice, told them her problems. 'If I could just get a decent sleep and the house in order I'd be all right, but Sam takes for ever to feed. Then, when I finally get him off, no sooner have I put him down than he's awake and screaming again. I'm at my wits end.' She ran her fingers through her unwashed hair.

'Does Sam have any long sleeps at all?' Clem asked.

'Sometimes, at about five, which is useless for me. The girls are home from school then, wanting their tea, and then Brian gets in. As the girls go off to bed up gets the little fella, and that's me for the rest of the night, trying to keep him quiet so that Brian can get a good sleep.'

'Could Brian get up to him for a couple of nights, at the weekend perhaps so you could get a break?' Olivia volunteered. 'Perhaps if you expressed some milk?'

Jean shook her head. 'He's up at five a.m. to go to the

farm. It's the same at weekends—the cows still need milking. I can't expect him to be awake at night with the kids.'

Olivia finally realised the woman's predicament. Just then Sam stirred and let out a piercing cry, which made them all jump. It was amazing just how much noise a small baby could make. Clem picked up the infant as Jean started to weep.

'What's wrong with him, Clem?'

'Put him to your breast, Jean, and let me see you feed him.' Olivia spoke calmly, and Clem handed Sam to his mother. The irate baby arched his back and butted against Jean's breast, searching frantically for and finding her nipple. He latched on and mercifully relaxed. Making little whimpering noises, he suckled hungrily.

'Very good, Jean, you're doing wonderfully,' Clem encouraged. 'Just try and relax.' At that point Sam let out a furious wail and the angry protest started again.

Jean was just about at breaking point. 'What's wrong with him?' she screamed above the ear-splitting shrieks of her son.

Olivia walked over and gently took the baby from the distraught woman. The baby snuffled against her. Olivia felt his hot, angry little face against hers, breathing in the familiar baby smell. Rocking Sam, gently trying to soothe him, she contemplated Jean's situation. For all her knowledge and training she had no real experience. Here was a woman who had borne four babies to her nil. She had a husband and children to care for and a house she was proud of. The well-rehearsed platitudes of 'persevere' and 'things will get better' seemed woefully inadequate. Olivia could see what was wrong. Jean had plenty of milk but she wasn't letting down, probably because she was too tense. Appearances mattered, and to tell this woman to ignore the housework and concentrate on the baby, to get a take-away and not worry about dinner, would be like speaking a for-

eign language. Heck, there wasn't a burger bar for two
hundred kilometres.

Clem watched Olivia closely as she rocked the baby.
Sam rooted hopefully and, finding her finger, sucked hungrily, but again there came the same wail of frustration.

'He's hungry, Jean,' Olivia said.

'He can't be. I fed him just an hour ago. You saw me
just try—that's not what he wants.'

Olivia gently but firmly explained about the letdown re-
flex. 'It's automatic in some women, as it was for you with
the girls. But anxiety, tension, lack of sleep—any one of
these can affect it. It's a vicious circle. The more Sam cries,
the harder it is for you to relax and for your milk to get
through. Have you considered trying him with some formula?'

'But breast milk's best—everyone says so,' Jean protested.

'A contented mum and baby are what's important. Anyway, giving him a bottle now doesn't automatically mean
you have to give up on breastfeeding. Perhaps after a couple of feeds and a good sleep you'll be ready to do battle
again. You could maybe give him a bottle at night and
concentrate on breastfeeding in the day. There are lots of
options. Even if he does end up on the bottle, you've given
Sam your colostrum in the first few days, which is full of
antibodies, and he's had six weeks on the breast. You've
done very well.'

'What do you think?' Jean turned to Clem.

'I totally agree with Livvy.' He stood up. 'I've got some
formula samples in the car. Why don't you make him up
a bottle and we'll see how he goes?'

Half an hour later a much happier Jean cuddled her satisfied son. Young Master Sam made contented little noises.

'Feeling better now?' Clem enquired.

'Much, but I'm a bit disappointed.'

'Well, don't be,' Olivia said firmly. 'Like I said, it might be a different ball game tomorrow. But whatever you do, don't go getting stressed—just enjoy each other.'

'Thanks ever so.' She looked over at Olivia. 'You've both been wonderful.'

'We haven't finished yet.' Clem darted outside and returned with a huge casserole pot. 'Ruby's forever trying to fatten me up. There's more than enough here to feed the family, Jean.' He took Sam from her and put him gently into the crib. 'Now, the place is tidier, the baby's asleep and dinner's taken care off. You get to bed.'

'I should get some ironing done,' Jean protested, but Olivia quickly jumped in.

'Don't you dare.' She shooed her down the hall.

'I wouldn't argue with Sister Morrell if I were you, Jean. I've a feeling she'd win. Now, off to bed, Doctor's orders. We'll see ourselves out.'

Back in the car Clem praised her. 'You did a great job in there.'

'Only because I listened to you first,' Olivia admitted. 'I shudder to think of the mess I'd have made if you hadn't forewarned me.'

'I think you're being a bit hard on yourself,' he said kindly. 'We'll need to keep a close eye on Jean, make sure things are improving—she's on a short fuse at the moment. Let me know if you're worried about her.' He turned and smiled. 'It's good having you on board, Livvy.'

As she opened her mouth to correct him he started the engine. Oh, what was the point? She might just as well get used to it.

The rest of the afternoon passed quickly. In each home they were made welcome. Despite Clem's sometimes brutal honesty and arrogant assumptions, it was obvious the patients all adored him. Everywhere they went the patients insisted on making a cup of tea. As if he hadn't had a drink all day, Clem gratefully accepted and listened as they chatted. Finally, armed with a bag of lemons and some lamingtons, they had finished the rounds.

'For a day's work well done, I'll buy you dinner. It's time for you to visit the local hotel.'

'But we can't. I'm in my work clothes,' Olivia wailed. The thought of having to talk to him socially terrified her.

'I'm not intending to get you drunk, I can assure you, but it's nearly seven already and I'm sure you're about as keen to cook dinner as I am.'

Driving into the main street, he parked and escorted her straight into a bistro. Gorgeous smells wafted from the kitchen and Olivia realised how hungry she really was. Again Clem was greeted like a long-lost friend.

'G'day there. The usual, Clem? And what about the young lady?'

'An orange juice, please.'

Clem remembered his manners and introduced her. 'This is Olivia Morrell, the new sister at the practice.'

'Pleased to meet you, Livvy,' the landlord greeted her cheerfully. Casually holding her elbow, Clem led her over to a table by the window and went back to the bar to fetch their drinks. Olivia gazed out of the window at the miles of land stretched out before her. The road continued far into the horizon. It was magnificent. She wished she were here with Jeremy. It had been so long since they'd been away together or even out for a meal, just the two of them. There had always been work, or a function to attend. Perhaps if she'd insisted, or just gone ahead and booked a weekend away, maybe they could somehow have prevented the mess they were in.

'Daydreaming?'

Olivia jumped as Clem placed their drinks on the table. 'I was just admiring the view.'

'Yes it's pretty spectacular,' he agreed. 'As are the pies

here. I took the liberty of ordering for you. They do the best steak pie I've ever tasted.'

'Sounds marvellous.'

Conversation was surprisingly easy. He was very good company, with a wicked, cynical sense of humour. Olivia felt herself start to relax as he told her tales of the locals. The pie, as promised, was spectacular, the sauce rich and spicy. Mopping her plate with a second bread roll, she felt Clem staring at her.

'What?' she said, hastily putting down her roll.

'Nothing. I'm just glad you're enjoying the food,' he remarked.

'And why shouldn't I be? It's delicious.'

Clem surprised himself at how much pleasure he took in watching her unwind. For the first time since they'd met she was actually looking at him for more than ten seconds when he spoke. The constant fiddling with her earrings or hair had stopped. He decided to broach a question he had been wondering about. 'You said last night your "ex-fiancé". Was the break-up very recent?' Those stunning green eyes frantically looked over to the bar as if in a silent plea for help, her hand immediately shooting up to her earrings.

'Yes.' Olivia replied reluctantly.

'Were you engaged for long?'

'We were together five years, engaged for two.'

Clem let out a low whistle. 'Ouch,' he said simply, and took a drink of his beer. For a second she thought the conversation was over but he wasn't letting her off so easily.

'He's not exactly a fast mover. Why weren't you married?' he probed.

Olivia sighed, wishing he would just drop it. 'We were happy the way we were, there wasn't any need to rush,' she stated, bringing out the old platitudes she had used on her friends and parents so many times in the past.

'Rubbish,' Clem said rudely. 'I have a theory about couples in long engagements and so far I've always been right.' He paused. 'Do you want to hear it?'

'Not particularly, but I've a feeling I'm going to.'

Clem grinned and continued. 'One is desperate for the commitment, the other is holding out, but both pretend a long engagement is what they want. It's the same with couples who live together—there's always one holding back. Am I right?'

He was, of course, damn him, but she certainly wasn't going to let him know as much.

'Actually, no, you're not. Jeremy's been under a lot of pressure recently. We were waiting till he made consultant. There wasn't time to concentrate on a wedding as well.'

'Well, I'd have made time,' Clem insisted. 'I'd have snapped you up years ago.'

It was an innocent statement, made entirely in the context of the conversation, but for some reason Olivia felt herself start to blush. Clem didn't seem to notice.

'So what does he think about you being out here?'

'He doesn't know.'

'You're not some fugitive on the missing persons list, are you?' The tone of his voice made her look up and she was relieved to see he was smiling.

'He's a bit too busy with his new girlfriend, I would think, to be looking for me.'

Clem took a long drink of his beer. 'So one call from Jeremy and I could lose the only decent nurse this town has seen in months.'

'I'm more responsible than that,' Olivia retorted quickly. 'I'm not just some puppy dog that can be summoned. I've accepted the job and I'm aware of my obligations.'

'Whoa.' He raised his hands.

'Anyway,' she continued, 'as I've only been here a day, aren't you judging me rather hastily?'

'On the contrary. I believe in first impressions, though I must admit I was wrong about your eating habits.'

Olivia gave him a questioning look but he didn't elaborate.

'Kathy always said I knew at a glance...' He took a hasty sip of his drink and then in a soft voice he continued, 'Kathy was my wife. She died,' he said simply. Now it was his turn to avoid her gaze.

'I heard. I'm so sorry. How long ago?'

'It will be two years in a few months, but the way it feels it might just as well have been yesterday.' He drained his glass. 'Hold onto your heart, Livvy, because you only get hurt in the end. I sometimes wonder if the pleasure of being in love is worth the pain.' He gave her a rueful smile. 'Listen to us two lonely hearts getting maudlin.' The carefree shift in his tone did nothing to disguise the sadness hanging in the air. 'Can I get you another drink?'

Olivia reached for her purse. 'No, it's my turn. I'm going to have a coffee.' Like her, he obviously didn't want to talk about his loss. The difference was, she was too polite to push it. 'Can I get you one?'

Clem shook his head.

'Another beer, then, or a cup of tea perhaps?' she offered.

'Olivia, sit down a moment. There's something I must tell you,' Clem said in a serious voice. She tentatively sat down. What on earth could it be?

'You must promise not to tell any of the patients this. If it were to get out, so many people would be offended.'

Olivia nodded nervously. Whatever was he going to say? She'd only known him five minutes.

He leant over the table, taking her hand and drawing her nearer, looking around to make sure nobody could hear. Leaning forward, she listened intently.

'I hate tea. Absolutely loathe the stuff, and every day I'm forced to drink gallons.'

'What?' Olivia looked up at him, startled. Was that it? Throwing his head back, he started to laugh, so loudly, in fact, that a few of their fellow diners turned around, smiling, to see what was so funny. Unperturbed, he carried on until finally she joined in. It had been so long since she'd truly laughed and, what's more, she marvelled, it felt wonderful.

CHAPTER THREE

SITTING at her kitchen table, Olivia attempted to pen a reply to Jessica's letter. A niggling sore throat which had been troubling her for a couple of days seemed to have come out in force. Pulling a face as she downed some soluble aspirin, Olivia reread Jessica's letter. Although apparently still full on with Lydia, Jeremy was pestering Jessica to find out where Olivia had moved to. She took some solace when she read how awful he was looking—black rings under his eyes, unironed shirts, creased suits and snapping at everyone. Which was most unlike Jeremy, who saved his mood swings for the home front. At work he was calm, unruffled and totally pleasant to one and all.

Perhaps he was actually missing her, realising what a terrible mistake he'd made. What if he did get in touch? Could she take him back after all he'd put her through? Olivia knew the answer should be no, yet a part of her couldn't let go. He had been her first real relationship, her first and only lover. The reason she had left her family and friends in England and travelled to the other side of the world. Letting go just wasn't that easy.

She had been in Kirrijong a month now. The locals were starting to accept her. Alex had returned to have his sutures removed, bringing her a bunch of proteas and several bottles of home-made tomato sauce. Her fridge and pantry groaned with the weight of home-made wines and chutneys, nectarines and lemons. They waved as she passed in her black Jeep and had started to make appointments to see her without Clem. It felt good to be liked and wanted. Yet each night she crept into the huge wooden bed and, while hating herself for being so weak, longed to feel Jeremy's arms around her, ached for the warmth of human touch.

It was Wednesday and she wasn't due on duty till eleven. Normally Olivia arrived early anyway, there was always more than enough work to do, but she had allowed herself the luxury of a lie-in and the chance to catch up on some letters. She hadn't been feeling herself at all lately. Initially Olivia had assumed it had been the pressure she was under, but now, with this niggling throat and persistent headaches, she began to suspect she was coming down with the same flu that seemed to be sweeping the rest of the town. Yelping as she noticed the clock edging past ten-thirty, Olivia dressed quickly. The morning had caught up with her.

Breezing into the surgery bang on eleven, she smiled confidently at the now mostly familiar faces.

'Morning, Betty. Are these for me?' Picking up a pile of patients' files, she started to flick through them.

'Yes. One's for stitching—he's out the back. And there's an ECG that needs doing—Clem wants it done as soon as you arrive. And a word of warning—he's not in the sunniest of moods this morning.'

Olivia raised her eyebrows. So she was finally going to see the legendary dark side of the good Dr Clemson.

'He came in like a bear with a sore head this morning and then, to make matters worse, her ladyship arrived.'

'Her ladyship?' Olivia enquired, not having a clue whom Betty was talking about.

'Oh you haven't had the pleasure of meeting his lady friend, Charlotte, have you?'

'His lady friend?' Olivia recalled the first night she had arrived in Kirrijong, when Clem had failed to meet her. Funny, although she'd heard what Dougie had said, by the way Clem had spoken about Kathy she'd just assumed there was no one else. Anyway, it didn't matter to her who he went out with, of course it didn't, Olivia thought firmly. She was just surprised, that's all.

'If you can call her a lady.' Betty lowered her voice. 'What he sees in her I'll never—' She coughed suddenly and started to shuffle some papers. 'Speak of the devil.'

Clem held open his door and Olivia felt her jaw drop for there, walking out of his office and looking completely out of place in a doctor's surgery in the middle of the bush, was six feet in heels of absolute drop-dead gorgeous sophistication.

Dressed in an immaculate white suit, her skirt at mid-thigh revealing the longest bronze legs imaginable, Charlotte Ross sauntered over to the desk, tossing her raven black mane. There was arrogance about her, an air of superiority, that, Olivia guessed, came when you were that beautiful. She looked straight through Olivia and Betty and picked up the telephone, barking orders at Dougie who doubled as the local taxi. She shook a cigarette out of her packet. Olivia felt her temper rise. Surely she wasn't going to light up here? Charlotte obviously had some discretion, though, and put the cigarette back in the pack.

'Thanks, Clemmie, I'll see you this afternoon,' she purred in a voice quite different from the one she'd used on Dougie.

Clem nodded. 'Fine. I'll see you then,' he answered. Charlotte had obviously done nothing to cheer him up, judging by the murderous expression on his face.

Catching sight of Olivia still standing there, holding the patients' files, he turned to her. 'So you finally managed to get here, then?' he barked.

'I beg your pardon?'

'You're late,' Clem announced to the waiting room.

'Sister's been here a good ten minutes...' Betty soothed.

'She's getting you to make excuses for her now, is she?' he demanded of poor Betty.

Olivia couldn't believe what she was hearing. She looked around the now silent waiting room at the expectant faces. 'If I might have a word in your office, Dr Clemson,' she said in as steady voice as she could manage, given the circumstances.

'I'm too busy, and so are you. You've already kept the patients waiting quite long enough as it is. I'll deal with you later.' And disappearing into his office, he left Olivia quite literally shaking with rage.

A deep, throbbing voice with the hint of a fake American accent broke the silence. 'I'm going to wait in the lounge. Call me when my taxi arrives,' Charlotte ordered. Tossing her hair again, she waltzed out of the surgery, though not before she'd managed to smirk at Olivia.

Fuming, Olivia got through the rest of the morning. How dare he talk to her like that, let alone in front of the patients? The atmosphere progressively worsened as the day continued, with Clem barking orders and constantly buzzing her on the intercom. 'Do this. Fetch that. Where are the results for this patient?' Olivia did as she was told, for the time being. The last thing she wanted was another scene in front of the patients. It was fruitless, as well as unprofessional.

'But if he thinks he's getting away with it he's wrong. As soon as surgery is over I'll let him know exactly what I think of his behaviour.'

'You'll just make things worse. Let it pass, he'll settle down soon,' Betty pleaded.

Finally the last patient had been dealt with. Olivia made herself a cup of coffee and took a half-hearted bite of an apple. Sitting at her desk, she started to write up her notes. It seemed that no matter what you did in nursing these days it produced a never-ending pile of paperwork to be completed. A shadow over her file told her Clem was standing at the desk, but she didn't look up. She certainly wasn't going to make an apology easy for him.

'I would have thought you'd had plenty of time to eat this morning, judging by how late you were.'

Well, she evidently wasn't going to get an apology. Olivia looked up from her notes. Clem's face looked down at her, so hostile she could hardly believe the change, but she refused to be intimidated. 'I most certainly was not late this morning. I was due to start at eleven, which I did. It's now two forty-five and I'm working through my break.'

'How very noble,' he said sarcastically.

That really was the limit. So she had been warned of his black unreasonable moods. So he was up to his neck in work. So the man was a widower. If he thought she was going to scuttle into the corner and hide like Betty, he was wrong. She'd had enough of irrational mood swings from Jeremy to last her a lifetime. She certainly didn't need it from him. 'No, Dr Clemson, it isn't noble, merely necessary. The files have to be written up and I have to eat. I am human after all, although judging by the way you treated me this morning I doubt you either noticed or cared.' She watched his face darken with rage. If he'd been angry before, he was really mad now.

'And what exactly,' he said menacingly, sitting down opposite her, 'is it that you don't like about my behaviour?'

Olivia took a deep breath. Oh, well, she might as well let him have it. She obviously wasn't going to be here for much longer. 'I don't like being spoken to like a naughty child, particularly in front of the patients. If you have a problem with my work, discuss it with me in your office. I also don't like you taking your beastly temper out on me.'

'Anything else?' he snapped.

'Yes, actually, there is.' She was gaining momentum now. 'I most definitely don't appreciate being told I'm late for work, or you implying that I'm taking excessive breaks, when the truth is I'm working way over the hours you specified in my contract. I don't mind working late, every night if necessary. I don't mind coming in early. However, if I'm due to start work at eleven and I have no indication that you need me earlier, don't get angry with me for not being here. I'm not a mind-reader.' Her temper had bubbled to the surface.

'Well, that's obvious,' he replied. 'Because if you could read my mind you'd be ringing up the unions, claiming unfair dismissal. I hadn't realised you were so militant, Sister.'

Olivia stood up. She'd had enough of this ridiculous conversation. 'Are you sacking me, doctor? Because if you are just say so and I'll be straight out of here.'

Clem got up. Despite her height, he was still a good head taller than she was. Olivia stood there, her face defiant. He wasn't going to intimidate her.

'That would seem to be your standard answer to any criticism or confrontation. But where are you going to run to this time? You've exhausted Victoria and New South Wales. Perhaps you should cross the border and see how you go in Queensland—until the next time someone pulls you up, that is. Still, there's always the Northern Territory.'

He was poisonous. That was the utter limit. How dare he drag her personal life into this? How dared he make such unjust assumptions about her? Stunned by his contemptuous remarks, she stood there, her face white, literally shaking with rage. What on earth could she say to that? He opened his mouth to speak but Olivia found her voice.

'Don't.' She put her hands up in front of her. 'Don't you *ever* speak to me like that again.' And something in her voice told him he'd totally overstepped the mark.

'Livvy...'

She shook her head. Whatever he was going to say, she

didn't want to hear it. There were no excuses to justify that outburst.

'Just get on with your work. I'm going on a house call, you can page me if you need me. I don't know how long I'll be.' The contempt in his voice had gone but his arrogance remained. Refusing to look at him, she stood there quite still as he haughtily left the surgery.

Only when the door had safely slammed behind him did Olivia promptly burst into tears. Clem's dramatic exit was ruined somewhat when he had to return to retrieve his car keys. Seeing her sitting at the desk, weeping, a huge wave of guilt swept over him. To have reduced this proud, troubled woman to tears gave him no pleasure. His apology was genuine and heartfelt.

'I've made you cry. I'm sorry.'

It was Olivia's turn to be difficult. 'Don't give yourself the credit.'

'I can be so pig-headed at times. I really didn't mean it.' He handed her a tissue from the box on the desk, which she accepted with a sniff.

'I'm not crying about you. I've come up against far more arrogant doctors than you in my time.'

'I'll try to take that as a compliment.'

Olivia managed a faint smile.

'If it's not just me that's upset you, who has?' The gentleness in his voice touched her. He sat on the desk, putting a tender hand on her shoulder, troubled by how fragile she felt. 'I know I'm not your favourite person after today's episode but I'm here if you want to talk.'

Olivia felt her anger evaporate. She so badly wanted to talk, to share, and Clem did seem genuine in his interest. Perhaps a man's opinion would offer some insight.

'A friend wrote this morning. It would appear that the object of Jeremy's desire still isn't me.' Clem didn't respond and she continued tentatively, 'I took some refuge in the fact that he looks awful, hoping that perhaps he's missing me after all. But who am I kidding? It's probably all the sex that's exhausting him.'

He smiled down at her, not moving his arm. 'What's she like?'

Olivia tried to describe Lydia objectively, fighting back the image of the scarlet woman with six-inch nails and a cleavage to die for. 'Well, I'd like to call her a bimbo, but she's actually very clever. She's his intern. Jeremy's a surgical registrar,' she explained. 'She's also very...' Olivia hesitated '...pretty. All boobs and behind, blonde hair, baby blue eyes.

'I never saw it coming,' she went on. 'Lydia's the antithesis of what Jeremy usually likes. She's scatty, disorganised, but apparently she made him feel "needed".'

'Not exactly the "burn your bra" type, then?' Clem said dryly, and Olivia managed a shaky smile.

'She makes me feel like a frigid spinster, yet I was the one engaged to him.'

'You're hardly relegated to the desperate and dateless pile yet,' Clem reasoned. 'You're gorgeous.'

'Jeremy didn't seem to think so.'

'Jeremy sounds like an idiot,' he stated, but feeling her body tense under his hand he realised he was on the wrong track.

'He's just confused,' Olivia said defensively.

'Maybe, but he doesn't have the right to hurt you like this.'

'He's hurting, too.'

Clem doubted this. He had met more Jeremys in his career than he cared to remember. So pumped up by the instant adoration and authority a white coat gave them, they actually felt they deserved their affairs. It didn't matter who got hurt in the process, just as long as they got what they assumed was their right. And in this case Olivia was the victim.

Clem's face hardened and his grip involuntarily tightened on her shoulder. For Jeremy to have reduced this strong, eloquent woman to tears and self-doubt made him churn inside. He hoped Jeremy got what he deserved. Olivia wriggled away uncomfortably. 'I'm fine now. Thank you for listening.' The mask was back on, her guard up.

'Look, Olivia, I'm always here if you want to talk.'

Olivia shook her head and blew her nose loudly.

Cursing himself for his poor handling of the situation, he remained seated and tried to revive the conversation, determined to be less antagonistic. 'Why don't I come over tonight and we can talk properly?'

Olivia shook her head. 'No, but thanks, anyway. I'll be all right now.' She picked up her pen. The conversation was over. Clem hesitated, as if about to say something. Olivia's pen paused over the file, his hand moved to her face and, picking up a loose curl that had escaped, he smoothed it behind her ear. The seemingly innocent gesture caught her completely unawares.

'I'm not taking no for an answer. I'll bring dessert.'

He left the surgery, this time closing the door gently behind him. Olivia sat there, stunned. How on earth had that just happened? A few moments ago he had been the second most loathsome man to walk this earth and now she was having dinner with him. Putting her hand up to her face where he had touched her, she felt her burning cheeks, then, firmly shaking her head, she set back to work.

Finally the last of the files had been written up, and after packing her bag with various bandages, dressing packs and solutions Olivia headed into town to make her own house calls. There were only a couple of dressings that needed doing and one postnatal visit. Which should, she reasoned,

leave her with plenty of time to have a long bath and prepare a nice dinner for herself and Clem.

It was a pleasant drive into town, and Olivia took her
time. Approaching an old Queenslander-style home, she admired the immaculate garden with an abundance of flowers
that had obviously been lovingly tended. An elderly woman
on the veranda waved to her as she passed and Olivia cheerfully waved back, relishing the laid-back friendliness of this
tiny slice of Australia. But the woman kept on waving and,
just giving herself time to indicate, Olivia swerved the Jeep
and bought it to a hasty halt. Jumping down, the hot afternoon sun's glare made it impossible to see the woman.
Holding her hand up to shield her eyes, Olivia called out.

'Is everything all right?'

The elderly woman came into focus. Breathless from
running, her lined face was full of concern. 'I thought you
were the doctor. I saw the Jeep,' she gasped. 'I've been
trying to call him. It's Harry—he's got these chest pains. I
called an ambulance, he's really crook. Please, help.'

In no time Olivia helped the lady into the passenger seat
and, executing a hasty U-turn, crunched the gears and sped
the short distance up the drive and back to the house. The
journey was all it took to glean that the lady was called
Narelle and was Harry's wife. Coming to a sharp halt,
Olivia was tempted to go in first and assess the situation,
but she kept a cool head and instead quickly opened up the
back of the Jeep, grabbing the emergency pack. Despite its
considerable weight, she ran into the house.

The drapes were pulled and after the brightness of outside it took a couple of seconds till she could see in the
cool dark room, but one look at the elderly man's grey,
sweaty face was all she needed to know the trouble he was
in. Slumped in a large armchair, he was obviously in a lot
of pain. Olivia turned on the oxygen cylinder, her moist

palms making it difficult to turn the lever. Gently she placed an oxygen mask over his face.

'Harry, I'm Olivia Morrell, Clem's nursing sister. Show me where the pain is.'

A shaking hand came up to the centre of his chest.

'And does it go anywhere else?' He shook his head. Realising it would be too much exertion for him to speak, she addressed Narelle as she hastily attached the cardiac monitor. 'When did the pains start?'

'About half an hour ago. He was just pottering in the garden. I told him it was too hot to be out there.'

'Has he ever had anything like this before?'

Narelle shook her head. 'Nothing. He's as strong as a mallee bull is our Harry.'

'No angina, high blood pressure, breathing problems, diabetes?' Olivia ran through a list of various medical complaints.

'Nothing. He just has a flu shot once a year.'

'How old is Harry, and is he allergic to anything you know of?'

'Sixty-eight and, no, he's not allergic to anything.'

Olivia scribbled down Clem's mobile number. 'Narelle, try Clem on this number.'

'I have been. I got it from the answering machine at the surgery but he's out of range. I left a message with his paging service. I've been trying to get hold of Betty but she's not home.'

So she really was on her own.

'It's his heart, isn't it, Sister? Oh, God, he's not going to die, is he?' Narelle started to panic, her voice rising to a crescendo, and Olivia knew she had to keep her calm. Any upset would only further distress Harry.

'Get me a small glass of water. I'm going to give Harry some aspirin.' The simple instruction was all it took to stop the woman's mounting hysteria, and she dutifully nodded.

But before Narelle even had time to turn for the kitchen the situation suddenly intensified as Harry's condition deteriorated rapidly. His eyes rolled back into his head and he slumped further into the chair. Deftly Olivia felt for his carotid pulse. Unable to palpate it, she glanced over at the monitor, which confirmed her fear—Harry had gone into cardiac arrest. Olivia gave him a hefty thump on the chest in a bid to kick-start his heart.

'Narelle, help me get him onto the floor,' she ordered, but Narelle was completely hysterical. There was no point in trying to calm her down. That would have taken time and that was what she was fighting against. Dragging him down to the floor by herself, trying to block out Narelle's desperate screams, Olivia worked quickly but methodically.

Having hastily attached the ambu-bag to the oxygen, she inserted the small curved tube that would keep Harry's airway open and enable her to give him the essential oxygen he so desperately needed. Then she rhythmically pumped his chest. Her cardiac massage was practised and effective, even managing to stop Narelle in her tracks as the regular bleeping of Harry's heart emitted from the monitor. But as soon as Olivia stopped, so too did Harry's heart, reverting instead to the chaotic and ineffective fibrillation that showed up as an erratic, squiggly line on the monitor. If Harry were to survive he needed more advanced lifesaving measures. Tearing open the defibrillator pads with her teeth as she systematically bagged him, Olivia charged the monitor and placed the pads on his chest.

Narelle was now all over Harry, shaking his limp shoulders, kissing his grey cheeks, begging him not to die.

'Narelle, stand back. I need to shock him.' Despite the firmness of her tone and the obvious direness of the situation, Narelle ignored her pleas, and Olivia was left with no choice but to physically drag the hysterical woman off her dying husband and practically throw her onto the couch.

She left Narelle there, sobbing piteously, as she applied the paddles and shocked her patient. The squiggly line remained. Olivia gave him a couple more breaths of oxygen and massaged his chest as she waited for the defibrillator to recharge to a higher setting. Shocking him for a second time, she held her breath and watched the monitor.

Her natural nursing instinct meant that her desire for this stranger to live was heartfelt and genuine, but the thought of being left alone with Narelle and a body if the resuscitation was unsuccessful was also on her mind as she watched the flat line on the monitor with mounting trepidation. But just as Olivia was about to recommence her resuscitation, the monitor flickered as it picked up Harry's heartbeat again. It was slow and irregular at first, but gained in momentum until his output was good and he had started to groan and thrash about, disorientated and in obvious pain. Olivia replaced the ambu-bag with an oxygen mask and lowered her face to his.

'It's all right, Harry,' she said in his ear, her tone gentle and soothing. 'Your heart went into a funny rhythm, but it's beating normally now. I need you to lie very still.'

Harry nodded faintly while Narelle, noticeably calmer but in shock, muttered something about going to fetch water.

Olivia reached for her mobile. She didn't have any choice. Her hands were shaking so much she could hardly manage the tiny keys, but luckily she got straight through.

'Melbourne City Hospital.'

Olivia swallowed hard. 'This is Sister Olivia Morrell.'

'Sister Morrell, it's good to hear—'

'I'm out bush with a critically ill patient. I need some urgent medical advice. Can you put me straight through to Tony Dean?' It was an instruction, not a question and for once Switchboard didn't argue. In an instant she heard Tony Dean's welcomely efficient voice.

'Olivia, where are you?'

She relayed her address with the help of a much calmer Narelle.

'I've got a sixty-eight-year-old man, no previous. Half an hour of chest pain. His ECG showed ST elevation. He went into a VF arrest. I've shocked him twice, and got him back, but…' Olivia glanced over to the monitor, alarmed at the sudden irregularity of his heart rhythm. 'He's throwing off a lot of ectopics. His heart rate's around 45. I'm worried he's going to arrest again. I'm trying to get hold of Clem, his GP, and an ambulance has been called, but that could take ages.'

'You're working for Jake Clemson?'

To Olivia the question seemed entirely irrelevant, but she knew Tony Dean too well to make a smart reply. He wouldn't be wasting time with niceties. 'Yes.'

'Well, that means you'll have everything you need in an emergency pack.'

'But I can't just go ahead and give him drugs without—'

'Yes, you can. This is a life-threatening situation and you're liaising with an emergency consultant.' He spoke very clearly and Olivia knew without a doubt that Tony Dean would face head on any medical legal consequences that might arise and would defend her to the hilt.

'Give him a bolus dose of lignocaine—that will help with the ectopics—and start a sodium bicarbonate infusion. He needs some morphine for pain. You know what you're doing, Olivia. You know the scene, and you've done it a thousand times. Just pretend you're in Casualty with a very incompetent junior doctor and you have to tell them what to do.'

And that was exactly what she did—and it worked. Suddenly she was in complete control, running the show. Looking down at Harry, she gave him a wink. 'You're going to be all right now.' And when Harry managed the tiniest wink back Olivia just knew that he really was.

Tony Dean stayed on the phone, organising the air ambulance from his end, leaving Olivia free to deal with her patient. When the road ambulance arrived she confidently said farewell to Tony, knowing Harry was in the best hands now. The crew worked efficiently alongside Olivia, ensuring Harry was pain-free and stabilising him for his transfer to the base hospital. Through it all Narelle held Harry's hand, whispering words of love and encouragement. Betty had arrived and was outside awaiting the air ambulance. The entire place, in fact, was a picture of quiet efficiency when Clem burst in, somewhat breathless.

'I came as soon as I heard.'

Picking up the ECG tracing, he squeezed the old man's hand.

'G'day there, Harry. What's been going on?' he asked Olivia.

'A myocardial infarction.' Clem nodded and Olivia continued, 'He arrested about five minutes after I got here. I shocked him twice and he reverted to sinus rhythm but he was throwing off a lot of ectopics. I liaised with Tony Dean as I couldn't get hold of you. I gave him a bolus of lignocaine, 5 mg of morphine and a sodium bicarbonate infusion. The ambualnce officers also gave—'

'Anything for nausea?' Clem interrupted.

'Some Maxolon, and I—'

Again Clem interrupted her. 'Good. I'll arrange an air ambulance.'

'It's on its way. They should be here soon.'

'We should give him some aspirin.'

'He's had that.'

For a second Olivia was worried she might be in trouble. Tony Dean, she had no doubt, would back her, but Clem?

He was an unknown entity. But the appreciative smile that crept onto his worried face answered her nagging doubts.

'I didn't need to rush, then, did I, Harry? Livvy had it all under control. It looks like you've been in the best of hands.'

'She's been marvellous,' Narelle enthused. 'Sister, I'm so sorry. I was no help. I just panicked when I saw him like that, I didn't know what to do. Sister had to drag me off him,' she explained to an attentive Clem.

'The air ambulance is in sight,' Betty shrieked from the doorway, destroying in an instant the calm aura that had prevailed. The flurry of activity continued until Harry was safely on his way to the coronary care unit at the base hospital and his niece had arrived to drive Narelle there.

'All in a day's work,' Olivia reflected, as she packed up her box and carefully disposed of the needles and syringes she had used into the small yellow sharps container. Afternoon rounds still had to be done and any earlier intentions of a gourmet meal soon disappeared once she finally made it home and surveyed her fridge.

Not for the first time since arriving at Kirrijong Olivia yearned for the convenience of a local take-away or even a decent deli. She hadn't arrived home till six-thirty and, as it was Ruby's day off, by the time she'd had a quick tidy up it was nudging seven. How she longed to throw a ready-made lasagne in the oven and spend an hour in the bath and put on some make-up. Instead, she hastily browned some mince and threw in some of Alex Taylor's home-made tomato sauce, praying that it would be as good as Alex had promised.

Gargling with asprin for the fourth time that day, she pondered whether to get Clem to take a look at her throat. Perhaps she needed antibiotics.

A quick shower and she faced the mirror. The usually

sleek red hair had curled from the shower steam and framed her flushed face in a wild mass of Titian ringlets.

'What am I doing?' With a jolt she realised she was treating this more like a date than a simple meal between two colleagues. The aspirin wasn't helping much. Her cheeks were burning and every bone in her body ached. Resting her hot face against the cool, smooth mirror, she started to calm down. So maybe she did fancy him, just a bit, and who could blame her? He was undeniably good-looking and working so closely...

'Stop it, stop it,' she reprimanded herself. Hadn't that been one of Jeremy's excuses? She was just being stupid. Anyway, who needed the complications? 'Not me, that's for sure,' she reminded herself firmly. He was her boss, no more, and anyway hadn't she vowed she was off men?

For the first time in years she left off her make-up and pulled on some denim shorts and a plain T-shirt. She certainly didn't want him to think she'd made any effort. If only Olivia had known that when Clem arrived, bringing with him a bottle of red wine and a tub of wickedly fattening double chocolate chip ice cream, his startled expression wasn't, as she assumed, one of disapproval.

Instead, as she opened the door he caught his breath in amazement at the stark contrast to the sophisticated, glamorous woman he was becoming so used to. The sheer natural beauty that radiated from her was truly terrifying; she looked about eighteen. The gorgeous riot of curls that fell in a wild tangled mass onto her slender shoulders gave a warm glow to her face. Without make-up her features were so much more delicate. Clem very nearly flung the ice cream and wine at Olivia and beat a hasty retreat to the safety of his own house. How, he tried to fathom, could he not have noticed how truly beautiful she was?

But he didn't run. He marched through in his usual arrogant way, muttering something about the 'bloody moz-

zies', and started poking about her kitchen drawers, trying
to locate the corkscrew. Olivia added the pasta to the boil-
ing water and busied herself stirring the sauce and cutting
up some bread. Finally, just as the small talk had run out,
the pasta was ready, and with the aid of a couple of glasses
of wine the conversation started to flow. Of course, they
talked shop. Olivia noticed how Clem's face lit up when
he spoke about children. Many times she had marvelled at
his skill to calm the most terrified child or distressed baby.

'I called in on Jean Hunt today. Young Sam is going
great guns. She's still breastfeeding, with the odd bottle in
the evening. Jean's singing your praises. You should call
in, you won't recognise her. Perhaps you could do Sam's
twelve-week assessment.'

'I will.' She nodded. Gradually he was handing over
more and more to her and she revelled in it. She was already doing the weekly antenatal clinic and was thrilled to
be using her midwifery skills, awaiting with anticipation
the next delivery, which he had agreed would be hers.
Despite her earlier trepidation, she wasn't nervous at the
prospect. She couldn't have asked for a better assistant than
Clem—he was a paediatrician after all. 'Don't you miss it?
Paeds, I mean.'

'Definitely. There's something so rewarding about looking after children. They're so amazingly resilient and up-
lifting. Even the sickest ones manage to give you something
back—a smile, a picture. You're never lonely when you're
on the kids' ward.'

He spoke with such passion Olivia couldn't help but
probe further. 'Have you ever thought about taking it up
again?'

'I think about it every day,' he answered with simple
honesty.

'Then why don't you?' It sounded straightforward

enough, but Clem stared at his plate and then looked up at her with a smile she was sure was false.

'Isn't that the six-million-dollar question?'

They moved through to the lounge for dessert. Olivia felt very decadent. Any meal at Jeremy's had always been eaten at the table so as not to mark the furniture. So instilled was this into her, even now she ate her morning toast alone there. Scraping the tub, he offered her the last of the ice cream. Olivia declined. 'No, you have it.'

He shook his head. 'I couldn't eat another thing. That was fabulous, Livvy. Is there no end to your talents?'

'Well, actually,' Olivia confessed, 'I can't take credit for dinner. The pasta is courtesy of Mrs Genobile for dressing her varicose ulcer and the sauce is from Alex for suturing his hand.'

Clem laughed. 'The patients have really taken to you.'

'I've taken to them,' she said honestly. 'The patients here are a lot more appreciative on the whole than the ones in Casualty. Mind you, when you're not waiting six hours on a hard trolley to be seen perhaps it's easier to be gracious.'

'I admitted I missed paeds, now it's your turn. Do you miss it?'

Olivia thought back to her work in Casualty. The team-work, the comradeship. No matter how busy or how tragic the situation there was always time for each other, whether it was a sympathetic chat or a sudden burst of zany hysterics to lighten the mood. It seemed a world away and suddenly she was hit with such a huge wave of homesickness it threatened to drown her. She wondered if she'd ever be amongst them again. She nodded. 'I miss it a lot. That's not to say I'm not happy here,' she added hastily. He was her boss after all. 'But, like you, I think I'd found my niche, career-wise that is. But Jeremy…' Her voice trailed off, not wanting to bring him up again. She was tired of trying to defend him to Clem.

'Go on,' he insisted.

'I'm sorry I keep going back to Jeremy. You'll think I'm using you as an unpaid counsellor.'

He brushed aside her apologies. 'Talk to me, Livvy, I mean really talk. It might do you some good to let it out.'

'I don't want to sound pathetic.'

Looking into his meditative eyes, Olivia felt hypnotised. He had a way of looking at her that somehow seemed to bring her usual barriers of reservation crashing down, and amazingly she felt herself start to open up.

'There's really not much to tell. The same old story—I loved him and thought he loved me. Then I found out he was seeing someone else. He's living with her now. That was the one thing I held back on. Sure I stayed there more often than not, but I wouldn't move in with him. Not until we were married. Maybe I should have.' Olivia shifted uncomfortably, unaccustomed to sharing such intimacies. 'You surely can't want to hear this. You've enough problems without mine.'

'Let me be the judge of that.'

So she told him, well, bits. Choking on the words as she recounted some of the crueller things Jeremy had said to her, things she could hardly even repeat to herself. And he listened—not judging, not criticising, just listened—and topped up her wineglass, and for the second time in their short history he gave her a tissue.

'The strangest part was right at the end, after he'd said every hurtful thing imaginable and I'd handed in my notice and moved into Jessica's. He did a complete about-turn and asked me to come back to him. To start again and forgive and forget.'

'And what did you say?'

'Nothing. I took this job.'

'Were you scared you might relent?' His insight was amazing. Olivia nodded.

'Five years is a long time, and we really did have some good times. I didn't get engaged lightly. To me it was a heartfelt commitment. Part of me doesn't want to throw it all away. Maybe he has changed and learnt his lesson. Perhaps I should give him another chance. But part of me thinks he's blown it. I don't think I could ever really forgive him, ever really trust him again. It's over.'

Clem took her hands. 'Livvy, I hear you when you say it's over, but reading between the lines I can't help thinking you're considering taking him back. I'm sure if it's what you really want then you'll get back with Jeremy, but think hard. You know the saying, "Be careful what you wish for, it may come true." Yes, he might say he's changed and he might mean it for a while. But if he's serious about getting you back, what's he doing, living with Lydia? Shouldn't he be doing his damnedest to show you he's changed?' Clem's face was only inches away, his voice lulling her.

'That's what my mum says, but he really isn't as bad as I've made him out to be,' Olivia replied, suddenly defensive. 'I'm hardly objective, a woman scorned and all that.' She laughed bitterly.

'All I know,' he said gently, still holding her slender hands, 'is that when I had Kathy here, no matter what the circumstances, my main concern above all else was her. Love is about trust. It should make you feel secure, happy and content. Love should make you feel loved. It would have never even entered my head to look at another woman no matter what our problems, and we had our share, I can assure you. But we were a team.'

Olivia saw his eyes mist over and his beautiful full mouth fight for control. She wanted to comfort him but she didn't know how, scared that if she put her arms around his shoulders he might think she was coming on to him. Damn Jeremy, she thought. He had left her so twisted and screwed up she didn't even know how to respond to a friend in anguish.

'Does time heal at all?' she asked. And they knew her question was meant for them both.

'Well, "they" tell me it does. And sure, I'm not the wreck I was in the first few months after Kathy died. There's an old retired doctor in the next town, Dr Humphreys, and there's many a time he had to take over as I was in too much of a state to carry on. But gradually I pulled myself together and, apart from the occasional lapse, I'm in control or appear to be. But not an hour goes by when I don't think of her. Yesterday I went into the basement to find something and I found an old jumper of hers. I could still smell her…' His voice broke. 'Every night I get into bed and there's a huge space where Kathy should be.' His hands covered his face and Olivia was sure she could see the glimmer of tears between his fingers. 'She was too young, Livvy, she shouldn't be dead.'

Olivia sat there frozen, scared to speak in case she started crying, scared to touch him and, more alarmingly, scared of the feelings he stirred in her. In a stilted voice to hide the wave of emotion she felt, she searched for an answer to his dilemma. 'Have you considered moving away, starting afresh, getting away from all the memories?' Olivia felt a jolt inside—the thought of him leaving horrified her. Taking a gulp of wine, she forced herself to focus on the conversation and try to ignore the sudden shift in her feelings towards him. She would analyse them later.

'Well, there's a can of worms.'

'What do you mean?'

'My father's dream was that I'd take over from him as the town GP. Between my brother Joshua and me, I was the safer bet. While Joshua was off backpacking around Asia, calling himself a photographer, I was up to my neck in medical books. It was all I ever intended to do. But after medical school I did my hospital internship and I literally fell in love with paediatrics.

'I was doing very well. I'd just completed my exams and had been made registrar when Mum died suddenly and Dad literally fell to pieces. A case of history repeating itself. I came back to help out and that's when I fell in love with Kathy. Dad just faded away, he died of a broken heart. Kathy never wanted to leave here, but that's another story.'

He stopped talking suddenly and took a long drink. 'I think that's quite enough about me for one night and as for you, young lady, you look as if you're about to drop. Are you sure you're feeling all right?'

Olivia sensed there was a lot more he wasn't telling her. 'Oh, I'll be fine. Just a bit of a sore throat.' That was an understatement. Her throat was killing her.

'I think you'd better get off to bed—doctor's orders.'

'Oh, well, in that case...' She smiled and stood up. Their eyes met and held. Olivia caught her breath, watching transfixed she saw his pupils dilate as his face moved towards her. She could feel his rough chin, feel his mouth on hers. It wasn't a long kiss, just a gentle, unrushed, goodnight kiss, but it held promise and a passion Olivia was scared to interpret. She swayed slightly. Clem caught her wrist.

'Hey, you're really not well.'

'I just stood up too quickly.' She tried to catch her breath, wondering if she'd misread the kiss for he was talking quite normally, apparently unaware of the effect he'd had on her.

'Why don't you take tomorrow off?'

Olivia shook her head. 'I'll be fine, honest.'

'Well, at the very least have a lie-in. Come in a bit later—we'll manage.'

'I couldn't do that. I've got this frightful boss, you see. You just wouldn't believe the fuss he makes if—'

'Hey, hey.' He laughed. 'I really am sorry about this

morning. I can't promise it won't happen again, though, but I will try. I don't ever want to make a promise to you and break it. I always keep my word.'

She knew he was talking more about Jeremy than this morning's incident, and the strangest thing of all, considering her total distrust in men, was that she really believed him.

'I'm sure you do,' Olivia replied.

He moved towards her again, all the time gazing deeply into her eyes. This time there was no mistaking his intention. He was going to kiss her properly. She could feel her pulse pounding in her temples as his warm hands tenderly cupped her face, igniting a passion that, however unexpected, was welcomely received.

But before his full, sensual lips met hers the urgent sound of his pager rudely interrupted the sensual spontaneity of the moment. Its incessant tones took a few moments to register and Olivia opened her eyes abruptly, shaken by what had taken place. Trembling, she sat down as he picked up the phone and punched in a number.

'Do you know what time it is?' The abruptness of his voice made her look up. Clem never spoke to his patients like that, only his staff, she thought cynically. 'Look, Charlotte, it's been a long day. I'm tired.' He looked over at Olivia and rolled his eyes.

Olivia managed a small smile but her mind was whirring. Charlotte. She'd forgotten about her, and now here she was, trying to get hold of Clem at eleven o'clock at night. They must be an item after all. Feelings of shame swept over her. Had she inadvertently been doing to Charlotte what Lydia had done to her?

Clem dropped the phone back into the cradle. 'Look, I'm sorry. I'm going to have to rush off.'

'Nothing serious, I hope?' She was fishing now, secretly

hoping—and feeling cruel for doing so—that his answer would indicate that Charlotte was unwell—a patient.

'No. Just some personal business,' he answered evasively. 'Thanks for dinner.'

There was her answer.

Her composure completely restored, Olivia stood up. 'It was my pleasure. Goodnight, Clem. See you at work.'

The intimacy had faded in an instant.

As he got to the door he turned. 'Look after that throat,' he said, and then he was gone.

Closing the door behind him, Olivia let out a sigh. That had been far too close for comfort. If Charlotte hadn't rung when she had who knew what could have happened.

Taking a couple more aspirin, Olivia crawled into bed. For a moment she closed her eyes and allowed herself the luxury of remembering the feeling of being held in Clem's arms. It had been so long since she had felt wanted. So long since a man had looked at her with lust instead of loathing, compassion instead of contempt.

'No!' She banged her fists on the bed. Clem would be with Charlotte by now. Men—they were all as bad as each other, and she wouldn't let herself forget it again. As far as she was concerned, this night simply hadn't happened.

Turning off the light, she finally drifted off into an uneasy sleep.

CHAPTER FOUR

HAD Olivia been even remotely worried about facing Clem she didn't have time to dwell on it, for the bedside phone awoke her from a restless sleep in the early hours. Fumbling, she picked up the receiver. Knowing the call would be work-related, it forced her mind to concentrate as she flicked on the bedside lamp.

'Livvy, it's Clem. I know I said the next one would be yours but it happened in rather a rush.'

Instantly she was awake, reaching for her pen and notebook in case he was going to give her an address, as she tried to make sense of what he was saying.

'Did I wake you?' he barked.

She glanced at the bedside clock. 'Well, it is two in the morning. Is everything all right?'

'Helen Moffat just delivered, three weeks before her due date,' he explained. 'It was very quick. The baby seemed fine at first, but now I'm just a bit concerned. She's not holding her temperature and her blood sugar is a bit low. I don't want to overreact and get an ambulance, but I do think we ought to keep a closer eye on her. Could you open up the surgery and set up the incubator? I'll bring her over.'

'Sure. I'll be right there.'

Jumping out of bed, Olivia dressed quickly. She might as well put on her uniform as she was obviously going to be there a while. Pulling a comb through her hair, now even more wild and curly, she twisted it into a knot and expertly tied it on her head. She brushed her teeth, put on a slick of lipstick and ran the short distance to the surgery.

The incubator only needed plugging in, as it was always

made up and ready for any such emergency. Clem had said the baby's blood sugar was low so she prepared a paediatric burette and had a flask of dextrose in case the infant needed an infusion.

There was no doubt that the treatment room was impeccably equipped. In fact, many of the monitors here were more up to date than the ones she had used in Casualty. Olivia knew Clem fought tooth and nail to ensure his patients were given the best health care, despite the fact there was no hospital within easy access.

Sure, the town got behind him and arranged fund-raisers for various pieces of equipment, but from what she had seen and heard, a lot came from Clem's own pocket. He was undoubtedly on a good salary—the sheer volume of patients and procedures he undertook assured that—but he certainly didn't rest on his laurels. Instead, he pumped a lot back into the practice and on nights like this it showed.

Unsure if the mother would be coming, Olivia turned down the most comfortable of the patient trolleys and put on the fan heater, despite the warmth of the night.

Her throat was hurting in earnest now. Opening the drug cupboard she took out some aspirin and swallowed them without water.

'Caught you red-handed!'

Olivia swung round, aghast. Surely Clem didn't think she was stealing drugs? He stood in the doorway, dressed in the same clothes he had left her house in, carrying the newborn wrapped in a huge bundle of blankets.

'They're aspirin,' she said tersely, holding out the silver wrapping for him to inspect, then colouring when she saw Clem was laughing.

'Don't be so paranoid,' he teased, then in a more concerned voice added, 'Is that throat of yours no better?'

'It's nothing for you to worry about, though I had better put on a mask—this little lady has enough to contend with without my germs. Where's Helen?' Tying the paper mask, she walked over. Clem had a slightly euphoric manner about him, which at first she put down to too much Charlotte. But remembering her time on a labour ward, she realised with disquieting relief that his mood was more likely to be elevated from the delivery.

'At home. I gave her pethidine, not realising this little lady was going to make such a rapid entrance. She had a good cuddle with the babe while I stitched her, but I think she deserves to sleep it off in bed rather than on one of our hard trolleys.' Clem grinned as she peered into the swag of blankets. 'Livvy, at this ungodly hour anyone else would be wearing jeans and an inside-out T-shirt, yet you manage to look as if you're ready for a day's work. Do you sleep in your uniform?'

'I like to look smart. It's better for the patients,' she replied primly.

'Well, as your patient's only an hour old, I'm sure she'd forgive you if you weren't looking your best. I bet under that mask you're wearing lipstick.'

He was right, of course, but she wasn't going to let him know. 'Don't be silly,' she chided, lowering her eyes, glad the mask was covering her face. She really was useless at lying.

'Well, say hello to Kirrijong's newest resident. Isn't she gorgeous?' Gently he placed the baby in the incubator and unwrapped her. She really was a beautiful baby with an angry look about her pink face which seemed to say, Would you please just leave me alone?

'She's a bit jittery,' Olivia observed.

'It was a very quick labour. I think she's a bit stunned, and she's not very big. Five and a half pounds,' he added. Olivia tried to convert the figures in her head as she pricked the baby's heel to measure her blood sugar. 'Don't make me feel old,' Clem winced. 'Two and a half kilos.'

'That's better.'

'What's her sugar now? I gave her some dextrose back at the house.'

'Four.'

'Fine. We'll check it again in an hour.'

Olivia checked the baby's temperature with the scanner. 'Her temp's still a bit low.'

Clem nodded. 'I'm sure she's fine, though. A few hours' rest in the incubator will do it. We'll check her obs hourly. If she doesn't hold her temp and sugar I'll get her admitted, but I don't think there's any need at this stage. She doesn't need any more glucose for now but we'll push the feeds. There's some sachets of formula and bottles here.' He looked over at her. 'And before you tell me off, Mrs Moffat has already had a nurse and is coming over to feed the baby first thing in the morning. It would seem she's as keen on breastfeeding as you are.'

'I wasn't going to say anything,' Olivia retorted.

'I know. I'm only playing. Why don't you go back to bed, grab a couple of hours while you can?'

Olivia shook her head. 'No. Why don't you? I'll be fine. I'm up now anyway. I'd never get back to sleep.'

He was about to argue, but the thought of bed was far too tempting. 'Are you sure? We could take it in shifts. If I'm back by six you could go home, have a rest and then start a bit later.'

Olivia nodded, for a moment tempted to remind him of yesterday's temper tantrum, but she knew he felt awful enough already, without her rubbing it in.

'You're a godsend, but call me if you're at all concerned. I'm only down the hall.'

Preparing the bottles, Olivia tried not to dwell on the fact that Clem was lying on a bed only a matter of metres away. While it was very reassuring medically speaking, Olivia tried to ignore the pleasantly disturbing feelings the thought evoked. Resolutely she turned her mind away—that was one path she was definitely not going to be taking. Instead, she focused all her attention on the new baby, which was definitely far safer.

Olivia really didn't mind staying up. Making herself a cup of coffee, she settled into the reclining armchair they often used for older patients who were having a dressing and couldn't make it onto the trolley.

She had done her midwifery training at twenty-one, but more for a feather in her cap than any great vocational yearning. It had certainly come in useful on the odd occasion, but at that young age the agony of birth, the swollen breasts and hormone-induced tearful moods had seemed so alien.

Now, however, as her biological clock had started to tick more loudly, she could appreciate so much more what it was all about. Despite her aversion to the labour and post-natal wards, she had always loved the nursery. Loved looking at the tiny newborns, sucking on their fat fists, with nothing to worry about except their next feed, their whole lives ahead of them.

She recognised, too, that adrenaline rush Clem had obviously had from the delivery. Bringing a new life into the world. There was nothing more intimate or magical than that. Maybe it was something she could think about. Perhaps she could do a refresher course and this time around really enjoy midwifery.

She had checked the baby's obs and given her a feed by the time Clem came back, his black hair tousled and his clothes rumpled. 'Thanks for that, I really needed a sleep. How has she been?'

'Good. Her sugar was just on three. I've given her a bottle and her temperature's normal. She seems fine, but the feeds exhausted her. Were Helen's dates right? She's acting just like premmie.'

'I'm sure that's it. Mrs Moffat didn't want to go to the base hospital for a scan so I had to go by her dates. I think the baby's probably more likely thirty-five or -six weeks, than thirty-seven weeks gestation. She's just going to need a lot of small, frequent feeds and be kept warm. We'll keep an eye on her for the rest of the morning, and if she has any further episodes I'll get her admitted.'

'Do you want a coffee?' Olivia offered.

'I'll get it. You go and grab some shut-eye. Don't bother coming in till ten.'

'But you'll need to shower and change. Who'll watch her?' Olivia asked.

'I'll get Betty to come in early, she can keep an eye out. It's not as if the baby's very sick. Rest assured, if there are any problems Betty won't hesitate to pull me out of the shower. She's done it before.'

Olivia raised her eyebrows. 'Now, there's a picture I don't want to dwell on—Betty dragging you out of the shower!'

Clem laughed. 'Betty didn't seem to mind, though I was rather embarrassed, I have to admit. Not because Betty saw me naked, more in the sure knowledge that the whole of Kirrijong would hear about it in all too graphic detail.'

Olivia laughed with him. 'I'll be off, then.' She hesitated for a second. Her body ached for her bed, yet a part of her was reluctant to leave the cosiness of the temporary nursery and Clem in this good humour. Still, what else could she do? There was no reason for her to stay. No logical one anyway.

Her morning shower did nothing to refresh her, but despite feeling awful Olivia dragged herself to work. Her throat felt like sandpaper and every joint in her body ached. She didn't want Clem thinking she was being slack or, more to the point, she didn't want him thinking she was remotely affected by the events of the night before. She needn't have worried. His pleasant mood had evaporated and the night's happenings were evidently history. And that's the way you want it, she reminded herself firmly.

Baby Moffat was fine and slept peacefully. The surgery was unusually quiet and the morning dragged on endlessly, broken only by the occasional blood test and the baby's obs and feeds. Olivia took the opportunity to attack the chaotic cupboards in the treatment room and attempt to get them into some sort of order, but her heart wasn't really in it. Finally, at eleven, Clem checked the baby over and allowed her to go home to her parents, with strict instructions and regular home visits.

Listlessly Olivia washed down the incubator and prepared it for its next customer.

'Are you sure youse should be here?' Betty enquired gently.

'I'm fine,' Olivia replied with more conviction than she felt.

Betty bustled about, tidying magazines and watering the wilting plants. 'Fine, my foot. Youse should be in your bed. I can go and tell Clem—he'll understand. He's very good if his staff need a sickie.'

'No, don't,' Olivia replied, a little too sharply. Betty raised a quizzical eyebrow. 'I'll speak to him myself. I might give afternoon rounds a miss, and catch up tomorrow.'

'Well, if you're sure. I'm finished for the day but it's no problem for me to tell him before I go.'

'No,' Olivia replied firmly. 'You go home, have a good afternoon.'

As Betty fetched her bag Charlotte appeared, just as beautiful as the day before. Olivia flushed, unable to meet the other woman's eyes.

'Can I help you?'

Charlotte almost imperceptibly screwed up her tiny nose. Olivia was positive that she'd had a nose job.

'Where's Clem?' Charlotte asked Betty, completely ignoring Olivia.

'He's in the study,' Betty answered tartly.

Charlotte flounced off, leaving behind a heavy scent of expensive perfume, but as she got to the doorway she turned around and for the first time finally addressed Olivia. 'You could fetch Clem and I some coffee.' And with that she strode off, leaving Olivia standing open-mouthed, staring at her very trim departing backside.

'Ooh, she brings out the worse in me, that one. I dunno what the doctor sees in her,' Betty fumed.

'She and Clem are an item, then?' Olivia had to know.

'It would seem so. Nothing official, like. But she's forever ringing him up and dropping in, and I know they go out when she's in town. They used to date before Clem started courting young Kathy. She must be turning in her grave now that vamp's back on the scene. Not that it's any of my business who he sees, but I tell youse this much— the day she moves in I resign. The thought of seeing that sour face every morning would put me off me cornflakes.'

'But she's very beautiful.' Olivia didn't want Betty to even get a hint that she could be remotely interested in Clem.

'No, sweetie, beauty is from within and that one is as hard as nails. The grief of losing Kathy has turned him if he can't see what a nasty piece of work she is.' And muttering furiously, she bustled off.

Olivia was glad to see the back of her. While she could happily listen for hours on end to Ruby's endless tales and scandals, there was something about Betty's incessant gossiping that irritated her.

Olivia knocked at the study door. Clem looked up surprised when he saw her carrying in the laden tray.

'You didn't have to do that. You're not the housekeeper.'

Charlotte didn't say anything, just sat there puffing on her cigarette.

'You look awful,' Clem stated bluntly.

'Thanks very much,' Olivia muttered.

'Let me take a look at you. We'll go down to the surgery.'

'There really isn't any need. If it's all right, though, I'd rather go home. I've no urgent house calls, and you said you wanted to check on baby Moffat yourself. I can catch up tomorrow.'

'We'll see how you are first. I really think you ought to let me take a look at your throat.'

'I'd rather just go home,' Olivia answered firmly, aware of Charlotte's exaggerated yawn.

'Very well. But go straight to bed and if you feel any worse I want you to call me.'

Olivia nodded and thankfully left the stuffy confines of the study.

Emptying the contents of her handbag onto the bedroom floor, Olivia, with a thermometer under her tongue, searched frantically for some aspirin. 'Some nurse you are,' she muttered to herself. It was no use. She would have to go back to the surgery and get some, but the thought of facing Charlotte and Clem together unnerved her. The chemist's was only a fifteen-minute drive. If she left now she could be there and back in bed within half an hour. Looking at the thermometer, she was alarmed to see how high her temperature was. Oh, well, there was nothing else for it. Grabbing her purse and keys from the floor, she ran out to the Jeep.

Olivia decided to take the short cut Clem had shown her when she'd first arrived. It was along an unsealed road and would eventually take her out at the turning for town. That way, at least Clem wouldn't see her driving off. She was supposed to be sick after all.

'This is ridiculous,' she scolded herself as the four-wheel-drive bumped along the rough terrain. 'Behaving like some fugitive when I'm only nipping out for some aspirin.' A nagging voice told her she was in no fit state to be driving but she didn't realise it was the fever that was making her act so rashly. Clinging to the wheel, she wished she'd taken the main road. Clem had managed to make it look so easy, but in her present state she wasn't up to advanced driving skills.

Suddenly the vehicle spluttered, jolting a couple of times, and then stopped. Frantically she turned the key in the ignition—nothing. With mounting panic she pumped her foot on the accelerator—still nothing.

'Damn, damn,' Olivia cursed as she checked the fuel gauge. It read empty. She let out a small wail of horror. Of all the stupid things to have done. She had always been so meticulous. What was happening to her? First running out of aspirin, now petrol—and here of all places. She pictured her mobile telephone lying useless on the floor at home, along with the rest of her handbag contents. Gripping the steering-wheel, she fought to regain control. 'Don't panic,' she told herself firmly. 'Think.' It was no big deal. She could walk to the garage. It couldn't be that far.

Getting out of the vehicle, Olivia eyed the endless road ahead. There was no way she could walk it—that would take for ever and in her present state she simply wasn't up to it. Perhaps she should just wait. Surely someone would come along soon. But who? Clem had said that practically no one used this road. What if she were to cut through the bush? That would take ages off the journey and would bring her onto the main road. She couldn't just sit here and do nothing. Olivia tentatively stepped off the road and into the scrub. It wasn't that dense and if she just kept heading in the right direction she would be there in no time. Once on the main road someone would give her a lift.

Purposefully she walked, ducking branches, the eerie silence broken only by her own breathing and the snapping of twigs as she stepped on them. Suddenly something warm brushed her leg and Olivia let out a scream. A possum, which had been happily feasting on some berries until she had disturbed him, stood there frozen with fear. For a second he stared at Olivia with terrified eyes and then shot up the nearest tree. The incident was over in seconds, but it was all it took to unnerve her, and in that instant she lost her bearings.

For a few minutes she wandered in circles, frantically trying to find a familiar landmark, something she recognised, but it was useless. Finally, overwhelmed and exhausted, Olivia's legs gave way and she lay on the rough forest floor. How could she have been so stupid? She was really in trouble now. Who was going to find her? No one even knew she was out here. Clem thought she was safely tucked up in bed. Even if he did somehow notice that she was gone, he was hardly going to come out looking for her, let alone here.

Her face was burning, her throat so swollen she could hardly swallow. Olivia could hear the kookaburra's laughing in the treetops. Laughing at her for being so silly to think she might get Jeremy back, laughing at the stupid city girl who had got herself well and truly lost.

The hours limped by and finally her eyes grew too heavy to keep open, the urge to sleep, just for a little while, tempting. Perhaps she would wake up with renewed energy and start again. But she resisted the urge, terrified of waking up only to still be here. As night drew in, though, too scared to stay awake and listen to the animals' shrieking, Olivia gave in to temptation and let sleep wash over her.

How long she lay there she wasn't sure, but the sound of footsteps woke her. 'Over here,' she croaked, terrified her voice would desert her and she might be missed. A torch shone brightly in her face, making her put her hands up to shield her eyes from the sudden light.

'What the hell are you playing at, you bloody idiot?' There was no mistaking Clem's angry voice.

She felt so ill and cold, and totally, utterly, humiliated. 'I'm sorry, I didn't feel well,' was all she could manage to rasp.

'So you drove off into the middle of nowhere and went for a bush walk?' Clem demanded.

Her head was spinning, sweat drenching her. 'I went to get some aspirin.' Olivia tried feebly to explain.

Clem, relief and fear making him shout, realised this wasn't the time to be reprimanding her. This woman was sick. 'It doesn't matter now,' he said more gently. 'Come on, Livvy, let's get you home.'

And suddenly it all hit her. Whether it was because of her raging temperature, or the weeks of agony Jeremy had put her through, or a deep-rooted longing for her family in England, a huge surge of loneliness and desperation hit her like a bolt of lightning and she let down the guard she had fought so hard to keep up. 'What home?' she croaked. 'I haven't got a home. Nobody wants me.'

'Hush now.' Clem cradled her in his arms. 'Things will seem better soon.' He stroked her sodden hair, drenched with sweat, and rocked her gently. Feeling his strong arms around her and the solid weight of his body, for a moment Olivia leant against him, breathing in his familiar scent, allowing herself to be comforted. Gradually the panic in her subsided.

'I'm sorry. I'm fine now,' she gasped, mortified at Clem seeing her like this.

'You're anything but fine.' He fiddled around with a two-way radio and gave some garbled message about locating and retrieving. With horror Olivia realised he was talking about her. There was a search party out after her.

'I ran out of petrol,' she attempted again to explain.

Clem shook his head. 'You never, ever leave your vehicle. If Laura Genobile hadn't been out riding and seen the Jeep, who knows what could have happened to you?' Seeing her sitting there utterly defeated, the anger in Clem, borne from fear, evaporated and he scooped her up in his arms. 'I'll lecture you later.'

She insisted on trying to walk and he half dragged her through the bush, but her legs were too weak and soon gave way. Clem lifted her up and with no strength left to argue, there was no choice other than to let him carry her what was, in fact, just a short distance to his car. Laying her on the back seat, he gently lifted her head and gave her a drink of water and then drove her back home.

Dougie and Ruby were waiting anxiously, and ran out to meet them as Clem carried her into her house. 'Oh, Livvy, where on earth have you been? We've been so worried,' came Ruby's anxious voice as she hovered nervously, while Clem gently lowered her onto the bed.

'She just popped out to get some aspirin,' Clem replied dryly, but the sarcasm in his voice wasn't wasted on Olivia. 'I'm just going to examine her. Perhaps you could find a nightdress, Ruby.'

Olivia sat up, determined to retrieve her dignity and horrified at the thought of Ruby holding up one of her skimpy nightdresses for all to see. 'I'd like a bath first if you don't mind.'

Clem sighed. 'How did I guess that you'd have to argue?' He sounded irritated. 'Very well. Ruby, perhaps you could run a bath, not too warm, and then help her into bed. I'll get my bag and a couple of things from the surgery, then I want to examine her properly.'

After her bath Olivia sat lamely on the edge of the bed, wrapped in a huge towel. The exertion had completely depleted any remaining strength she might have had. Ruby peeled away the towel and Olivia attempted to cover her naked breasts with her arms.

'This is no time for modesty,' Ruby fussed.

Even in her semi-delirious state she managed to feel a glimmer of horror as Ruby lifted her arms and dressed her in a huge, gaudy, pink and purple floral nightdress. 'Where did that come from?' she croaked.

'I prepared your room. Your nightdresses wouldn't cover a sparrow. I didn't want youse feeling embarrassed in front of Clem so I fetched a few of mine—there's some more in your top drawer.' Ruby rubbed Olivia's hair dry vigorously with the towel. 'Right, sweetie, into bed with you.'

Thankfully, she slipped her aching body between the cool crisp sheets and laid her burning head on the soft pillows. She knew she must look an absolute fright, but for the first time in her adult life she couldn't have cared less about her appearance. Remembering her earlier hysterics, Olivia lowered her eyes in embarrassment as Clem entered the room.

'That's better.' He smiled. 'Thank you, Ruby. Perhaps you could make Livvy a warm, milky drink with a bit of sugar. Dougie has just gone to sort out the Jeep.'

'I've put everyone to so much trouble. I'm so sorry.'

'There, there, sweetie.' Ruby's fat hand held Olivia's slender one. 'Don't go getting upset. We're just all glad you're safe. You had us so worried.' Closing the door as she left, Olivia held her breath as Clem walked over to her, sure he was going to scold her, but he didn't say a word. Popping a thermometer into her mouth, he picked up her slim wrist and took her pulse. Olivia glanced up shyly at him.

'One of Ruby's passion-killers?' he said, looking at the

fluorescent gown that smothered her. The sudden unexpected humour caught Olivia by surprise and a small smile flickered over her pale lips. The thermometer wobbled. Taking it out of her mouth, he glanced at it but she couldn't read his expression. Gently he felt her neck. 'When did you start to feel unwell?'

Olivia thought for moment. 'Well, I've been under the weather for a while. I put it down to stress and a new job, but over the last few days I've been feeling a lot worse. I think I've got the flu.'

'I'll decide what's wrong with you,' he stated firmly. 'Your glands are huge. Let me have a look at your throat.'

Olivia obediently opened her mouth, wishing Ruby had let her brush her teeth.

'Ugh,' he said. 'No wonder you feel awful. Now, pull up your nightie. I need to examine your abdomen.'

'But I've got a sore throat,' Olivia protested weakly.

'Livvy, I'm a doctor. Would you feel more comfortable if I asked Ruby to come in?' he offered.

'No, of course not.' It wasn't that she didn't trust him, far from it. She was just all too aware of her painfully skinny body. She had always been on the thin side, but since she had broken up with Jeremy the weight had fallen off her.

Clem helped her to sit up and deftly removed the pillow, gently lowering her till she lay flat on the bed. His large hands gently probed her stomach. Olivia lay there, every muscle in her body rigid, mortified at the embarrassment of it all.

'Relax, Livvy, please,' he urged. 'Are you tender there?'

'No.'

'Or there?' He pushed again.

'No,' she lied.

'Livvy, please, relax your muscles—you're making it impossible for me to examine you. How about there?'

Olivia winced slightly. 'No!' Hastily she pulled down the awful nightdress and sat up. 'Look, I'm fine, I tell you. Now, if you'll just give me some aspirin and let me sleep, I'll be all right.'

'No, you won't.' Replacing the pillow, he held her shoulders and gently eased her back. 'It will need to be confirmed by a blood test, but I'm pretty sure you've got glandular fever.'

Olivia relaxed onto the pillow and closed her eyes. In a funny way it was actually a relief. So that's what was wrong with her. At least it explained the exhaustion and lethargy. At least there was a reason for the ever-threatening tears. She wasn't losing her mind after all, just struggling against a nasty viral infection. Clem let her digest the news and then continued. 'I was attempting to examine your abdomen for any enlargement of your liver or spleen. You certainly don't make things easy.'

An awful thought suddenly occurred to Olivia. 'I couldn't have infected any of the patients, could I? What about baby Moffat?'

Clem smiled. 'Unless you've been going around town kissing your patients passionately there's nothing to worry about. And if you have,' he added teasingly, 'we'd better have a long talk.'

Not the patients, just the doctors. She blushed as she remembered the previous night. Thank goodness Clem's pager had gone off when it had. Clem must have read her mind, but it didn't take an Einstein to guess what she was thinking.

'I had it myself when I was a student, so I know how rotten you must be feeling,' he said lightly, but the inference was there—she couldn't have given it to him anyway.

'So, what now?' Olivia asked, but she already knew the answer.

'Bed rest, bed rest and more bed rest, and not just because of the glandular fever. I believe you're emotionally exhausted as well as physically, and until you rest and get your strength back you're going to keep picking up every bug around. I'll move you over to my house, where it will be easier for Ruby and I to keep an eye on you.'

'No,' she answered quickly. 'I'll manage fine here.'

'Are you listening to a word I say, or are you just deliberately being difficult?' Clem asked, exasperated. 'Livvy, you have glandular fever. It isn't going to go away in a couple of days, you need to be looked after properly.'

'I said I'll manage,' Olivia replied with as much strength as she could muster.

'Look.' He appeared to relent. 'If you really can't stand the idea of having me looking after you, then perhaps I could arrange for transport to take you back to Melbourne. Is there someone who can care for you there?' Clem felt cruel, saying this, but it really was the last card he had left up his sleeve to play against this most unwilling patient.

Olivia lay there, defeated. Who, indeed? She couldn't dump herself on Jessica again, and all her other friends had jobs and families—they didn't need an emotional wreck with glandular fever to land on their doorsteps. And Jeremy? That was almost laughable. Perhaps she'd end up sharing a house with him and Lydia. Olivia turned her troubled eyes to Clem and shook her head. If she'd expected a look of sympathy she didn't get one.

'Well, then, it looks as if you're stuck with us. I'll compromise, though. You can stay here on the strict condition that you ring if there's the slightest problem, and that Ruby and I can drop in freely. At the first sign that you're doing too much I'll carry you over to the main house myself. Understood?'

Olivia nodded glumly. She wasn't exactly inundated with options.

'Good. Now, try and get some sleep. I'm going to fetch

some paperwork from home and then I'll be back. I'll be in the lounge all night if you need anything.'

Olivia opened her mouth to object. He couldn't stay here. He had surgery in the morning and she knew he had hardly slept last night. Then, remembering his threat of carrying her over to his house, she thought better than to argue. Clem was quite capable of bundling her up in these blankets and taking her over there right this minute. 'Thanks,' she muttered, though not very graciously.

'Now, is there anything I can get you?'

Shaking her head, she watched as he walked to the bedroom door. 'Clem?'

He turned. She wanted to say thank you, for finding her, for caring. And to say she was sorry for all the trouble. But she was scared she might start to cry. What was it about this man that brought her usually hidden emotions bubbling to the surface? 'Could I have another milky drink?'

He gave her a wide smile. 'Oh, no, what have I done? They say nurses make the worst patients.'

For the next forty-eight hours Olivia's dreams were as erratic as her temperature. Jeremy would appear in bed next to her, his lithe, taut body as beautiful as it always had been, whispering endearments, telling her how much he loved her. She would turn and reach out for him but then the door would open and Lydia would be there, carrying huge syringes and saying, 'Trust me, I'm a doctor.' Her husky voice would fill the room. Panicking, Olivia would reach for Jeremy for reassurance, for help, but he would lie there, laughing.

'How could I not want her, darling? Look at yourself—did you really think I would choose you?'

She would wake up screaming, drenched in sweat, desperately trying to escape the hypodermic that Lydia bore, fighting against them both. Within seconds dear Ruby would appear, as solid as a rock, in a vast dressing-gown, her hair in a net. The room would be flooded with light and Olivia would sob into the huge bosom, wishing Ruby were her mother. 'There, there, sweetie, it was just a dream. No worries, just a horrid dream,' the familiar Aussie voice would say. Ruby would stay with her then, dozing in the chair, and Olivia would lie there listening to Ruby's gentle snoring, praying for the morning so she could say she'd got through another night.

By the fourth night her temperature had long since subsided, yet the nightmares stayed. She awoke at two a.m. gripped with the same panic and fear that had haunted her since Jeremy had gone. Jeremy—where was he? Why wasn't he lying there next to her? And then it dawned on her that she was alone and he was with Lydia. This wasn't a nightmare she was having, this was sheer, living hell.

She longed for her mother, longed for the vast oceans that separated them to miraculously disappear and Mum to be there to somehow make things all right like when she was little, to promise things would seem better in the morning. But her mother was in England, as unattainable as Jeremy. The tears fell then, and she didn't fight them, just let the great shuddering sobs that convulsed her body come, doing nothing to hold them back.

Suddenly the light flicked on and she felt comforting hands massaging her shoulders, gently stroking her hair. 'It's OK, Livvy, let it out.'

Olivia froze. Where was Ruby? This was Clem she was weeping on. Abruptly she turned onto her back, pulling the covers up to her chin. 'I'm all right, it was just a dream.' She could feel his solid weight on the bed next to her, feel the warmth of his leg against hers through the thin sheet. What did it matter that it was Clem? At least it was another human being.

'Come here,' he said softly, and opened his arms to her.

She lifted her body slightly and, unresisting, allowed him to pull her towards him, enveloping her in his embrace. His strong arms wrapped tightly around her fragile frame and he held her securely, rocking her gently as she wept, never admonishing her, not once telling her to calm down, until finally the sobs subsided. Clem eased her back onto the pillows, tenderly wiping away her tears with the corner of the sheet. 'You've been through one hell of a lot, but things will get better.'

'Do you really think so?'

'I know so,' he said with conviction. She searched his face. He seemed so positive, so sure, and she badly wanted to believe him. Even before he moved she sensed his departure. As he stood up she felt the coldness of the sheet against her leg without him there.

'Please, don't go.' The words were out before she could stop them.

'I'm not going anywhere, I'm right here.' And sitting himself in the bedside chair, he leant over and turned out the light. 'Try to get some sleep. I'm here if you need me.'

Aware of his powerful presence, comforted by his regular breathing, gradually she drifted off and had the first peaceful sleep she'd had in weeks.

'Clem said you could have a bath today.'

Olivia winced as Ruby flung open the bedroom curtains. The bright morning sun flooded the rumpled bed. She looked around the room, her eyes coming to rest on the chair where Clem had slept, desperately trying to remember what she had said. How could she have let him see her in that state? How could she have lowered her guard like that? It was as if she'd been to a wild party and had a frightful hangover without the pleasure or excuse of champagne. Burying her head under the sheets Olivia frantically tried to piece together just what she had told him. She could vaguely remember the word Jeremy coming up too many times and a speech about her mother, and then pleading with him not to go.

'Oh, God.'

Ruby was over in a flash. 'Livvy, are you all right? Should I fetch Clem?'

'Oh, no, please, don't.' Even the thought of facing Clem made her blush from her head to her toes. Getting up slowly, Olivia made her way gingerly to the bathroom on legs that felt like jelly. Ruby placed a pile of towels and yet another flannelette creation on the vanity unit.

'I'll be right outside. If youse get dizzy call me straight away.'

'I will, I promise.'

Slowly she lowered herself into the huge enamel tub and wallowed in the luxury of the hot, bubbly water. She massaged conditioner into her hair and lay back, letting the water lap over her body. Deliberately she blocked all thoughts of Jeremy and Clem out of her mind, and just relished the moment.

'C'mon, now, sweetie, you don't want to overdo it.'

Exhausted from her exertions, Olivia sat obediently as Ruby dried her hair a few minutes later. 'I think I've got some cotton pyjamas in the dressing-table drawer,' Olivia ventured, crossing her fingers as Ruby scrabbled through her drawers. Sure enough, there they were, under a pile of lingerie.

'I'll go and fix you some breakfast while you get changed, but no hanging around—pyjamas on and then bed.'

Feebly she ran a comb through her hair and tied it in a high ponytail secured with a white scrunchie. Catching sight of herself in the mirror, she screwed up her face at the pale, drawn reflection that stared back. Realising she must be approaching death not to even want to put on make-up, Olivia acknowledged there were some absolute essentials in life and liberally sprayed her wrists and neck with her favourite perfume. Feeling refreshed but exhausted, gratefully she crawled back into the fresh bed Ruby had made up. She soon bustled in, carrying a tray.

'I've made you some toast and scrambled eggs. Now, there's freshly squeezed orange juice, with just a squirt of lemon. Be sure and drink it all, youse need your vitamin C.'

Olivia looked at the laden tray and felt a huge lump in her throat. Dear Ruby, she had made such an effort. She had even picked some anemones from the garden and arranged them in a tiny vase. 'I'll try.'

'You'll do more than try,' Ruby insisted. 'I used to squeeze the oranges and lemons for poor Kathy—she reckoned that was what got her through the mornings.'

The piece of toast in Olivia's hand dropped to the plate. She stared at the untouched orange juice. She knew it was none of her business, but she just had to know. 'What was she like—Kathy?'

The question stopped Ruby in her tracks. Taking a deep breath, she sat on the bed beside Olivia. For a while she didn't say anything, just stared out of the window, then she finally turned.

'She was the best,' she said in an unusually subdued voice. 'I remember her as a little 'un always smiling. She always loved Clem, long before he even noticed her. I remember when he started to date that Charlotte. Kathy's mum told me she cried the whole night through. Then the next thing I heard they were together and I've never seen a couple happier. They loved each other so much. Not that they were gushing or anything like that. It was just so obvious to everyone. They didn't need to tell you, it just showed in their faces. Clem's never been the same, and I don't think he ever will be. There's this sadness in his eyes, always there. He's always thinking of her.'

'How did she die?'

'Cancer. A wicked disease, it's no respecter of age or beauty.' Ruby wiped away a tear that spilled down her fat, rosy cheeks.

'Was she very beautiful?'

'She was a real beaut, our Kathy. Didn't need make-up, she was beaut inside and out. We all loved her. I used to come and sit with her near the end if Clem had to go to an emergency or when we could persuade him to have a sleep. Not once did she complain or worry about herself, just Clem—how he'd cope, who'd look after him. She never once said, "Why me?"'

Olivia felt the hot tears spill now onto her own cheeks. The two women sat there for a time, both locked in their own private thoughts. Finally Ruby stood up. 'C'mon, Livvy, eat your breakfast now, sweetie. I'll get on.'

Half-heartedly Olivia pushed the toast around her plate. The tears that fell unchecked were for Kathy, the beautiful woman she had never met. Kathy. So cruelly robbed of time, taken for no apparent reason from the people she loved. And they fell for Clem, too. A good man, who didn't deserve this—to be left alone to pick up the pieces without his beautiful wife by his side.

CHAPTER FIVE

GRADUALLY Olivia regained her strength. Ruby, ever diligent, petted and fussed over her like a broody hen, coaxing her to eat the huge meals she prepared, letting her ramble on endlessly and shooing out visitors when she felt it was getting too much.

Not that she had many—a couple of her regular patients dropped in, bearing fruit and chocolates. Iris Sawyer, the retired practice nurse, had been a couple of times, but despite her insistence that the surgery was coping and Olivia should concentrate on getting well, the visits only served to make Olivia feel even more guilty. Iris should be enjoying her retirement, not covering for her. Betty seemed to feel it was her duty to visit daily and fill Olivia in on every last piece of gossip she could glean from the surgery. Olivia found the visits exhausting and was always relieved when Ruby appeared at the bedroom door and suggested Betty join her in the kitchen for a cuppa.

The only person she looked forward to seeing was Clem. He was good company and never demanding. He would sit on the edge of her bed and chat idly about his day or the patients. Sometimes he would bring over the plans for the new hospital, asking her advice on the layout. It was nice to be involved and he always took her suggestions seriously.

'You've just shot our budget for another five grand,' he would say with a laugh as she overhauled the resuscitation area or moved the nurses' station. Other times he would just sit in the armchair and write his notes, the silence never awkward. Sometimes Olivia would drift off to sleep, only stirring when he left as he gently tucked the blankets in around her and put a cool hand on her forehead to check her temperature. He had never told her off about the stupidity of her actions, but she felt a lecture was only a matter of time.

One afternoon as Clem flicked through a medical journal Ruby burst through the bedroom door, her face hidden behind a huge bunch of yellow roses.

'These just arrived for you, Livvy. They must've cost a fortune, there's no florist in town, they had to be sent by courier.' She practically tossed Clem the mail she had collected and then, blatantly indiscreet, hovered by the bed as Olivia, her hands shaking, opened the tiny envelope.

'They're from Jeremy,' she said in an incredulous voice 'How did he know I was sick?'

'That's my fault, I'm afraid.' Ruby at least had the grace to blush. 'He rang a few days ago. He sounded nice and so concerned and I knew how youse was missing him and all.'

'But how did he know I was here?' Olivia asked, bewildered.

'Tony Dean probably told him,' Clem answered logically, without bothering to look up from his mail. 'And I wouldn't be too hard on Ruby. I nearly rang Jeremy myself when you did your disappearing act. You do realise, don't you, that he's on your résumé as your emergency contact?'

Olivia chose to ignore the question and its obvious implications, tears welling in her eyes as she read the card. 'He's coming to see me. He wants to talk.'

'Well, he'd better step on it. If the time his flowers took to get here is anything to go by, you'll be disgustingly healthy and back at work by the time he arrives.' There was no mistaking the harshness in Clem's voice, though all the while he spoke he carried on reading his mail, not even glancing at Olivia or her flowers.

'Don't be like that, Clem. It would have been hard to organise the delivery,' Ruby reasoned, seeing the disappointment flicker in Olivia's eyes.

'I just can't believe he's coming all this way to see me.'

'Neither can I,' Clem replied dryly, then in a gentler tone added, 'Just don't get your hopes up, OK?'

Olivia nodded.

'I'm going for a walk. I'll pop in later this evening.' He stood up and stretched, yawning without bothering to cover his mouth, his untucked shirt lifting with the movement just enough to reveal a glimpse of his muscled stomach. Olivia turned away, suddenly embarrassed.

'You're going already?' She couldn't hide the disappointment in her voice.

'I need some fresh air and I'd better go and check on the builders. There are a few things that need to be sorted—anyway, I expect you've got a bit to think about.' He gestured towards the flowers and then sat down on the bed. His dark eyes turned to her and Olivia felt her pulse rate rise. It was as if he were staring right at her very soul. Shaken, she looked away. Her soul really wasn't up to scrutiny at the moment. 'Please, Livvy, be careful.'

Unable to speak, desperately trying to keep her breathing even, it was all she could do to nod dumbly at him. In that instant she knew beyond a shadow of a doubt that her rising pulse rate and flushed cheeks had nothing to do with the glandular fever. It wasn't only Jeremy she had to be careful about. There was no hiding from it—she felt far more for Clem than she had ever dared admit, a physical attraction so strong she could almost taste it. As he left, gently closing the door behind him, Olivia lay back on the pillow, bewildered and confused at the feelings that coursed through her. The scent of Jeremy's roses seemed to overpower the room, clashing with the lingering musky traces of Clem's aftershave.

'Ignore him, pet. He's in a bad mood because he got a letter from his brother Joshua. He probably wants Clem to send him yet another blank cheque. Youse just enjoy your flowers. He sounds sound like a fine young man, that Jeremy.'

'He had an affair, he's still living with her,' Olivia reminded the elder woman, who had heard the whole story time and again.

'Happen he made a mistake. My Dougie was no angel. Many a tear I shed over his dalliances, but once we were wed, well, he's never looked at another woman,' Ruby said as she tucked in Olivia's bedspread. 'Now, try and get some rest.'

The phone by the bed rang shrilly. Ruby had just gone out.

'Hello.'

'Olivia, darling, is that you?' There was no mistaking the husky voice on the other end.

'Jeremy,' she gasped incredulously. 'I just got your flowers.'

'Sorry I took so long in sending them, but I've been caught up at the hospital.'

In just one short sentence he had incriminated himself. Wasn't his roster always his excuse? If he'd just stayed quiet she could have gone on believing that the flowers had simply been delayed. It was as if a huge alarm bell had sounded in her head.

Be careful, Olivia warned herself, echoing Clem's words from just moments before.

'What can I do for you?' Olivia spoke slowly, playing for time so she could decide how to handle the situation.

'Darling, don't sound so formal. I'm ringing to see how you are, of course. I've been so worried. Tony Dean said you were out bush in Kirrijong of all places, and then I finally track down a number and some old biddy tells me you've got glandular fever. I've been trying to speak to you for ages, but every time I ring some proprietorial bush quack tells me you're resting. I hope they're looking after you all right. Has he checked your liver function and—?'

'I'm being looked after beautifully,' Olivia answered curtly. Far better than you would have, she wanted to add, but she simply wasn't up to a row.

'Oh, well, good. I just wanted to make sure. Some of these country doctors can be a bit old-fashioned—they don't always keep themselves up to date. I just want to know you're getting the correct treatment.'

'Don't be so pompous,' Olivia snapped. How dared he make out Clem was some sort of backwater hick?

'Let's not argue, sweetheart,' he soothed. 'Right now I'm far more interested in finding out when you're coming home.'

Olivia nearly dropped the phone. He was talking as if she might have been delayed at the shops. 'What about Lydia?' She heard his sharp intake of breath.

'You leave her to me, Olivia. I miss you. I was an idiot to ever let you go. I need you, darling.' His voice dropped and slowly, caressingly he whispered endearments, using all the phrases of old that had never failed to win her around.

She lay motionless on the bed, listening, her knuckles white as she gripped the telephone. How did he do it? He had treated her so badly and yet she could feel herself weakening. There was something about his manner, a desperation creeping into his voice that made her think that maybe, just maybe he had changed.

She closed her eyes and for an instant Clem's face flashed into her mind, but she resolutely pushed it away. She mustn't confuse the issue. Clem had Charlotte and, anyway, this was five years of her life they were talking about. Surely that must count for more than some idiotic notion she had only entertained for literally five minutes.

'Are you and Lydia completely finished?' Even before he replied she knew there would be a flood of excuses.

'Darling, she's harder to get rid of than a red wine stain,' he drawled.

'Have you tried salt?' Olivia quipped, but Jeremy wasn't to be deterred.

'Just tell me you're coming home and I'll have her out of here in five minutes flat. She's absolutely obsessed with me, you know. I'm not just making excuses. She pursued me relentlessly, just never let up. I know I should have been stronger, but I was so stressed, what with this interview coming up and us going through a rough patch.'

Her mind whirred. What rough patch? As far as she'd been concerned, there hadn't been any major problems, just the usual dramas Jeremy was so good at creating. No relationship was perfect all of the time. Surely if it had been that serious he should have come to her, tried to work things out, before jumping into bed with Lydia. 'I don't want to hear excuses, Jeremy.'

'Of course you don't. You're not well, I understand that, but things will be better now. We can work this out. Just come back home. I really miss you, darling.'

'It has nothing to do with whether I'm well or not,' Olivia retorted sharply. 'And anyway I've got obligations here.'

'What are you talking about?' Jeremy answered, irritated and somewhat taken back by her refusal. This wasn't going to be as easy as he'd anticipated.

'I've got a job here. I can't just up and leave on a vague promise that you'll get rid of Lydia.' Her voice was rising. How dared he assume she'd drop everything and rush back into his arms?

'What about me?' he wailed like a selfish five-year-old. 'Aren't your obligations to me? I am your fiancé after all.'

'Ex,' Olivia stated resolutely. 'You relinquished your rights when you went to bed with Lydia. Don't try to turn this on me.'

Realising he was on the wrong track, Jeremy changed his tune. 'Olivia, calm down. Please, don't upset yourself. Obviously we can't sort this out in one telephone call, but surely five years together is worth fighting for?' Taking her silence as a positive sign, he continued, 'I was hoping to tell you this over a bottle of champagne but, given the circumstances, I'll tell you now. I know it will cheer you up.'

Olivia lay there, exhausted. What now? Wasn't this enough to be going on with?

'I got it, sweetheart,' he purred into the phone. 'I've been offered the junior consultant position. We're on our way, darling, you and me together. Mr Felix can't wait till you're well enough to go out for a celebratory meal. Things really are changing.'

So that was his plan. Jeremy wanted to dispel any rumours of relationship difficulties to his new boss. And though it would never be said in so many words, wasn't Jeremy now expected to have a wife on his arm at the never-ending round of functions they would have to attend? Was that why he wanted her back? She lay there, not saying a word, just listening to his endless stream of platitudes.

'Don't write us off, Olivia. I made a mistake, sure, but we've had five years together, we can't just let it go. I've been doing a lot of thinking and I've decided you're right. Perhaps it is time to set a date, and then we can start a family, put all this mess behind us.'

He was good. She had to give him that. The sugar to sweeten the bitter pill. Wasn't a baby the one thing she had desperately wanted? But not like this, not a patch job to save a crumbling relationship. She thought of Jean Hunt and how she had fought so hard to keep it all together. What if she had a difficult baby like young Sam? Jeremy would be out the door in a flash.

With every ounce of self-control she could muster, Olivia spoke in clear, even tones. 'Jeremy, the last thing I ever wanted was this "mess", as you call it. It was your doing. Do you really think I'd just come back and marry you after what you've put me through?'

'Olivia, please! Just listen—'

'No, Jeremy, *you* listen. Thank you for the flowers, thank you for ringing up to see how I'm doing, and congratulations on your promotion. Now, if you'll excuse me, I'm very tired.' And leaving him spluttering, she hung up and then promptly removed the telephone receiver from the cradle.

Over the next few weeks Jeremy rang regularly. More often than not Olivia let the answering machine take his calls but she occasionally picked up. To his credit Jeremy did seem genuinely sorry for the pain he had caused and it was obvious that he missed her, but Olivia deliberately kept the conversations light, too exhausted for another confrontation. Clem, on the other hand, became more and more distant. Still kind and considerate, he seemed rather formal. It was as if their brief intimacy had never happened and, indeed, Olivia sometimes wondered if she had imagined the whole thing.

Christmas was looming, but this year it held no excitement for her. It only served to ram home her loneliness. She thought glumly of the hospital balls that she was missing, the parties and celebrations. Ruby bustled into town with Olivia's shopping list and she listlessly wrote a few cards, but that was about as exciting as it got.

Late on one particularly long, boring afternoon Jeremy

rang while Clem was visiting. Instead of politely leaving the room, he stayed and carried on writing his notes. Not to be intimidated, and curious about Clem's reaction, Olivia carried on the conversation but Clem didn't appear remotely fazed. Damn him, Olivia thought. She might just as well have been talking to her mother.

Jeremy, on the other hand, unused to such a friendly audience, carried on chatting. Then, as if sensing another man's presence, for the first time Jeremy began to talk more intimately. His husky tones did nothing for her but, catching Clem's eye, Olivia blushed furiously and started to giggle. Clem rolled his eyes, obviously not remotely impressed by her behaviour. Hastily she concluded the conversation.

'You didn't have to hang up on my account,' Clem said curtly as she replaced the receiver.

'I didn't.'

'How's Jeremy?' he asked dryly.

'He seems fine,' Olivia answered noncommittally.

'And Lydia?'

'What do you mean?' How cruel of him to bring her up Olivia thought.

'Well, not so long ago she was the object of Jeremy's desire and the reason for your misery. I just wondered if she was still on the scene.'

She didn't respond. Maybe the phone call had got to him after all.

'You seem a lot better. I was thinking you could go for a little walk tomorrow. It will do you good to get some fresh air.'

Olivia nodded eagerly. It would be great to get out and blow away some cobwebs. 'When can I go back to work?'

'Easy.' He smiled. 'Let's see how you go tomorrow. There's a nice little track that takes you to a clearing by a creek, it's pretty spectacular. Ruby will give you directions, and mind you listen to them. No short cuts, please.'

Olivia blushed. 'I really am sorry about that.'

'I know, and I hate nagging, but just because it's pretty out there don't be lulled into a false sense of security. Looks can be deceptive. You've escaped a nasty situation once—next time you mightn't be so lucky.'

For a second she wasn't sure if he was talking about Jeremy or the bush.

'Take a mobile just to be sure. Please?' he added as she opened her mouth to protest. Grudgingly she nodded. Considering how her previous expedition had turned out, she was hardly in a position to argue.

Ambling through the bush next day, following Ruby's instructions to the letter, Olivia found the clearing easily. Dear Ruby, she had packed her the most the most spectacular lunch and smothered her in factor fifteen sunscreen and the biggest hat. 'Don't youse go getting heatstroke,' she had warned her, waving her off like an anxious mother.

Her weeks in bed had seen spring give way to summer. It was as if the world had been put on fast forward. Pulling back an overgrown bush, she turned into the clearing and Olivia caught her breath in wonder. A flock of rosellas, startled by the intrusion, flew off momentarily, only to return seconds later and adorn a huge coral gum tree, their green and red feathers decorating the old gum spectacularly, like a native Christmas tree.

A tiny stream, its level low from the unforgiving droughts, trickled by and life blossomed around it, the grass lush and green and dotted with flashes of vibrant colour from wild flowers, the bushes laden with berries, a stark contrast to the sunburnt, barren landscapes that had become so familiar. It was a tiny slice of heaven, and just the place to do some serious thinking.

Hungry from her walk, Olivia tucked into her sandwiches. Gradually the birds, which at first had eyed her so suspiciously, gave in to temptation and tentatively approached the crumbs she threw. Surrounded by beauty, she lay back on the grass, closing her eyes against the bright afternoon sun. Now her mind didn't turn automatically to Jeremy. Instead, it was Clem that filled her senses.

She wrestled with her thoughts, trying to fathom what on earth had happened. It was a question she had been trying to avoid. Clem. Sure, she knew patients often mistook their feeling of gratitude for something else. Was that what had happened to her?

Perhaps it was because he had been there for her and could empathise. He understood where she was coming from, knew how lonely the world felt when you came into an empty house at the end of a hard day. He rolled over in bed at night to reach for Kathy the way she had for Jeremy, only to be confronted by a cold, empty space. He, too, had suffered loss, and one far greater than hers.

But then again he had Charlotte. And that hurt. It hurt far more than she liked to admit, and it had nothing to do with how much she didn't like the woman. Just the thought of him with Charlotte made her stomach churn. Had she felt that with Jeremy and Lydia?

Just a few weeks ago she would have given anything to have had Jeremy begging her to come back. She was flattered by his attentions, of course. Proud of him for making consultant as well. After all, he had worked hard enough for the promotion. But what of his proposal? Wouldn't he now expect her to play the part of the consultant's wife—intimate dinner parties, the tennis-club set? Wouldn't he be even more insistent she give up work, with the incentive of a baby and his promise to be faithful if she complied?

All these things she would have done without question and, no doubt, enjoyed, but his infidelity had not only torn apart their relationship, it had forced her to examine herself. She did deserve better. Of course she was pleased that he hadn't just written them off and their engagement hadn't been a total farce. But what was it that Clem had said? That love should make you happy, content and secure. Jeremy had taken all those things from her. At the moment she didn't know what love felt like. The tears had dried up weeks ago and been replaced by a kind of numbness, a hardness that was alien to her.

Packing up her backpack, she emptied the last of the crumbs onto the grass, grateful to Ruby and Clem for letting her in on such a magical place.

Though Olivia had dreaded it, Christmas in Kirrijong turned out to be the happiest she had spent in Australia.

'I didn't know Jeremy was a horticulturalist,' Clem quipped when he arrived on Christmas morning and saw the red roses which had duly arrived the day before.

'What do you mean?'

'Well, his knowledge of flowers is truly amazing! Yellow and then red roses—how exciting! Good God, Livvy, did you really spend five years with him?'

And for the first time she didn't try to defend Jeremy. Instead, she merely laughed as the flyscreen opened and Ruby and Dougie barged in.

'Happy Christmas!' Ruby gathered her into a bear hug while Dougie struggled in with trays of food.

'Happy Christmas!' Olivia laughed, and it really was.

Ruby had embroidered some cushions and Olivia stared in wonder at the tiny delicate stitching, amazed that she had gone to so much effort. Ruby in turn shrieked with delight when she opened her chocolates and smellies.

'My favourites, Livvy. How did you know?'

'You bought them, remember?' Olivia replied warmly, as Ruby yet again enveloped her in a hug.

Clem bought her a compass and a pack of flares, which raised a few laughs, and a huge bottle of her favourite perfume. 'I saw your supplies were getting low,' he said gruffly. He caught her eye and they shared a tiny smile when he opened the jumper Ruby had bought on Olivia's behalf—garish red and green diamonds emblazoned the front.

'Livvy said for me to get youse a pen but I reckoned that you needed a couple more jumpers for those night calls,' Ruby explained with a beaming smile.

They had a barbie in the garden and much later, when they'd settled down to play Monopoly, all cheating shamelessly, Jeremy's inevitable phone call felt to Olivia more like an intrusion than a welcome diversion.

Finally, when the day had ended and Olivia had fallen exhausted but contented into bed, the only thing that had been missing, she reflected, had been mistletoe.

CHAPTER SIX

'THERE is absolutely no need for this. I'm perfectly well. I just want to go back to work.'

'Livvy, do I really need to remind you that you've had glandular fever? I need to examine you thoroughly before I even consider letting you return,' Clem replied, exasperated.

'Well, I'd rather you didn't.' The words came out too harshly, and instantly Olivia regretted her tone. But better that than let him know how she felt. How could she even begin to explain to this impossibly difficult man, who thought she was completely hung up on Jeremy, that her dreams were, in fact, constantly of him, and there was nothing remotely decent about them? It was as if her mind, jaded from self-control and reasoning by day, by night surfaced and took flight, visiting territories alien and uncharted but full of illicit promise.

She could hardly let him examine her. Apart from everything else she was painfully aware of her body. Never voluptuous, the glandular fever had managed to obliterate most of the few curves she'd possessed. Clem might have already seen her at her absolute worst, but she still had some pride. There was no way she was going to let him see her emaciated body.

Running his fingers through his shock of jet hair, Clem threw his pen down on the desk. 'Livvy, you're impossible but, of course, my opinion doesn't count.' He sighed and looked at her pleadingly but she wouldn't relent. 'Obviously I can't force you to let me examine you, but I can refuse to let you back to work till it's documented you're medically fit.'

Olivia frowned. That was something she hadn't considered.

'Look, old Dr Humphreys is coming to town on Tuesday for a consultation. He still has a few old faithfuls that he visits and I'm sure he'd be happy to see you. In the meantime, if you trust me enough, will you let me take your blood? We can at least check your liver function and if that's normal and Dr Humphreys agrees, you can start work again. Very part time, mind you,' he added sharply, ignoring her eager nodding. 'And at the slightest sign you're overdoing it I'll sign you off for a month, and don't think I won't.'

'Fine. And, no, I won't overdo it.'

Rolling up her sleeve, he picked up her arm, frowning slightly in concern. She had gone from being slender to downright skinny. His long fingers traced a vein, then gently he flicked her almost translucent skin to bring the vein to the surface. His dark curls fell over his forehead and Olivia noticed the tiny lines around his eyes as he squinted, concentrating.

She resisted a sudden urge to run her free hand through his hair. She closed her eyes, but he filled her senses. She could smell his aftershave, hear his regular breathing, feel his body close to her. If she fainted now, at least she could blame it on the needle, she thought, for a brief moment revelling in his closeness. Charlotte, Charlotte, Charlotte, she chanted to herself. It was a mantra she found herself repeating at the most inappropriate moments, like now. This really had to stop.

Clem coughed gruffly. Labelling the bottles, he spoke with his back to her. 'You need to put on some serious weight. I'm going to prescribe you a supplement meal drink. I want you to take it three times a day on top of your regular meals. I'm also going to order an iron screen. I suspect you're anaemic.'

He turned around and suddenly he wasn't the doctor any more. 'You need to look after yourself, Livvy. I mean really look after yourself and not expect too much. This really isn't the time to be trying to sort things out with Jeremy. You need a bit of peace. If he puts too much pressure on just tell him to back off. Don't play games with your health.'

Touched by his concern and confused by her feelings, so scared he might read the desire in her eyes, she purposefully rolled down her sleeve and nodded.

'Don't worry, I'll be fine.' It was safer to dismiss him.

Old Dr Humphreys took her blood pressure and listened to her chest. He must be well over seventy, Olivia thought, and had the concentration span of a two-year-old.

'Well, Dr Clemson was right. You are seriously underweight. How are you feeling?'

'I'm fine,' Olivia replied with more conviction than she felt. 'I'm just horribly bored and desperate to get back to work.'

'I don't know, you young sheilas, always wanting to work. Well, if youse feel well enough I can't see why not. But any worries, I want you to come straight back.' With shaking hands he went through her notes. 'You're a tad anaemic but the supplement will correct that. Your liver function's normal now, which is good. I'll just take a look at your stomach.' The telephone interrupted him. 'No, Dr Clemson will want those results, Betty. No worries, then.' He replaced the receiver. 'Now, where were we? That's right, I was about to look at your throat.'

Olivia didn't bother to correct him. Instead, she obediently opened her mouth as he gave her throat a cursory glance. He really was losing the plot. Just the sort of doctor Jermey had been worried about.

'Well, everything seems in order. I'll arrange another blood test in a month's time to check your iron levels. In the meantime, just take things slowly.'

'I will. Thank you.'

'No worries.'

Leaving the surgery, she walked slap-bang into Clem.

'Everything all right?' he asked.

'Everything's fine. I'll be back at work tomorrow.'

'Why not take the rest of the week off? Start after the weekend. We'll manage.'

'Dr Humphreys said I could start straight back, there really isn't anything to worry about. I'll just do mornings, like we agreed.' Determined to resist his attempts to keep her at home, her voice became more insistent.

'He examined you properly?' Clem demanded, refusing to budge.

Olivia evaded the question. 'Clem, please, you're carrying on like a headless chook.' She darted around him and out of the door. Stopping briefly, she smiled reassuringly. 'I'll see you in the morning.'

For all her efforts to get there, the exhilaration of being back at work soon wore off. If she had been expecting a welcoming committee, or at the very least to be eased into things, she couldn't have been more mistaken. Though the patients were delighted to see her and genuinely concerned about her health, they still wanted to be seen quickly. Clem was at his bloodiest, constantly snapping and downright rude at times, and though Olivia managed to escape most of his wrath, he certainly didn't seem intent on making her first day pleasant.

Olivia spent the afternoon in bed, not waking till the evening, amazed at how exhausted a few hours in the surgery had left her. For a moment she lay there, thinking about Clem. He really was the most complicated man. One moment he was gentle and caring, but he could change like the wind. Part of her was furious at him for treating her poorly on her first day back, while on the other hand she couldn't help but be concerned about his erratic behaviour. These weren't the childish tantrums Jeremy was so good at throwing. Clem's moods seemed to run far deeper. He was a good man, you could just tell. Time and again she had marvelled at his compassion. He never took the easy route to lighten his load.

She thought of baby Moffatt. It would have taken far less effort to have simply called an ambulance and had the baby admitted, and in these days of liability, safer, too. Instead, he had thought of the parents, the strain it would have placed on them, the distance that would have separated them from their newborn and had taken it all on himself. That wasn't the cool, distant man she had seen this morning.

Kathy's death was obviously still affecting him deeply. There was room for compassion and understanding. She hoped Charlotte had what it took to reach him.

Though not hungry, Olivia forced herself to cook some supper and listlessly ate it, knowing she desperately needed to put on some weight. Her clothes were all falling off her and, though never busty, what little she had seemed to be receding at the rate of knots. Taking the revolting meal supplement through to the lounge, Olivia flopped in front of the television and flicked through the channels. There was a good film just starting, a real weepy. Just what she needed. It would do her good to have a real cry over someone else's awful love life.

Just as the film climaxed the doorbell rang. Olivia was in floods of tears, of course. 'Damn.' She went to press the pause button and then remembered it wasn't a video she was watching. Oh, well, she had seen it before and knew it had a happy ending. If only real life was so easy.

There, standing in the doorway was Clem. 'I needed to see you to explain. Your first day back and I behaved appallingly. I've made you cry again after I promised I wouldn't.' He looked completely exhausted and, Olivia guessed rightly, slightly inebriated.

'You didn't make me cry. I was watching a film,' she stated firmly. 'And anyway you didn't promise, you just said you'd try not to. Sit down.' She gestured to the sofa. 'I'll get us some coffee.'

Clem did as he was told but as she turned and headed for the kitchen he reached for her hand, pulling her back to face him. 'I didn't come here for coffee, Livvy. I came to talk. I know I've had a bit too much to drink, and for that I apologise, but I know what I'm saying.' He let go of her hand and for a second she stood there, not sure what to do, uncertain what she might hear, her hand tingling from his touch.

'And what is it you're saying, Clem?' she asked finally. He looked up, his eyes filled with despair and something else she couldn't interpret.

'That I'm worried about you, Livvy, and I don't think Jeremy's very good for you.'

'Well, that's really not for you to decide. But if it makes you feel any better, I had rather worked that one out for myself.'

'Good. You deserve better, like what I had with Kathy. She died two years ago today.'

Putting his face in his hands, Olivia watched, mortified, as a tear slid between his fingers. 'Oh, I didn't realise. I'm so sorry.' So that was what this was all about. His black mood and now this drinking to blot out the pain. She could feel his grief, sense his utter loss. Taking a couple of deep breaths, he composed himself and leant back in the chair, his fingers fiddling aimlessly with the heavy gold band on his wedding ring finger, the pain etched in his strong features so intense it made her want to weep with him.

'I'm so confused. Part of me just wants to lie down with her, but the other part wants to get on with my life. I'm so torn, Livvy.'

Olivia resisted the urge to put her arms around his shoulders and simply cry with him. Maybe it would help but she couldn't be sure.

'I know she would want me to pick up the pieces,' Clem continued. 'She told me so herself. We talked about it once and she said it would break her heart if she thought I was destined to a life of grief and pain alone. I said all the right things, of course. That I'd be all right and she didn't have to worry, but I never thought it would really happen and definitely not so soon. I didn't think I was ready to move on. I certainly wasn't looking for another relationship, then before I knew it…' He was rambling now, but she let him talk without interruption. Better out than in. 'I just feel so damn guilty, and I took it out on everyone, including you. I didn't mean to be so rude. It was just easier today of all days. It's not the day to be making progress.'

Olivia shrugged. 'Perhaps it is. Maybe by talking, by letting things out, you've taken a step in the right direction.'

'I guess so. I've been dreading today and it lived up to my worse expectations. I was thinking about you, and I couldn't bear how I'd behaved, how I'd treated you on your first day back, so I came over to try to explain.'

Her heart went out to him. In the depth of his grief he still had taken the time to come over to apologise and explain his actions. Taking a deep breath, Olivia followed her instincts, battling with her usual reserve. She went over, sitting beside him on the couch. This time she didn't hold back, this time she knew how to respond, and she tenderly put her arms around him as he poured his heart out.

'I just don't know if I'm ready to start again. Part of me is so lonely and it would feel so good to be loved and held, yet part of me says it would be unfaithful to Kathy.'

'Has there been anyone else since Kathy?'' she asked gently. For a moment he didn't answer and she held her breath, terrified she might have intruded too far and equally scared of his answer.

'What do you think?' he answered slowly.

For a moment she sat there quite still. It was a silly question after all. Six feet three, every inch a man. As if he wasn't sleeping with Charlotte. What man wouldn't? So here he was on the anniversary of his wife's death, beating himself up because he'd met someone else. She wanted to scream that Charlotte wasn't good enough, what on earth was he doing with her? But knew she would be speaking out of jealousy. Clem needed a far more objective opinion and, for whatever reason, he had come to her for it.

'Just because you're moving on with your life, it doesn't mean you love Kathy any less. Maybe the time for grieving is over. That doesn't mean you have to forget Kathy. There's enough room in your heart for someone else. Falling in love again doesn't have to detract from the love you shared, and in time you'll work it out.'

She felt him relax against her and she longed to bury her face in his dark hair, to kiss away the pain and tears and somehow make everything all right, but it wasn't her place. All she could do was be there for him.

'You can talk to me, Clem. I'm a friend as well as a colleague, and I hope I always will be. You don't have to bottle things up, it's good to get these things out.' Blindly she continued, almost repeating what he had once said to her and praying she didn't put a foot wrong, ignoring the pain that seared through her as she battled with the image of Clem and Charlotte together in bed.

Feeling his shoulders tense beneath her arm, she knew she must have said the wrong thing.

'You still don't get it, do you?' He read the confusion in her eyes. Shrugging her off, she knew she had lost him. 'Perhaps I will have that coffee after all,' he said flatly. The moment was gone.

Waiting for the kettle to boil, Olivia tried to make sense of the jumbled emotions that coursed through her, and yet despite the confusion her thoughts were amazingly lucid.

Had she fallen in love with Clem? Was it possible to love someone you knew so little about? Sure, she knew Clem was a widower and a kind and caring doctor, and undoubtedly over recent weeks he had become a good friend. But they had never had a relationship, never shared any intimacies bar one kiss, and as intoxicating as it had been to her, it didn't add up to much in the scheme of things.

Yet didn't this man fill her dreams and stir her emotions in a way she had never thought possible? Weren't her feelings amplified around him—a smile, a laugh, a tear, a sob when he was around? Why, he just had to look at her the wrong way and her temper, so usually well in check, would bubble to the surface. With just the faintest brush of his lips she had felt giddy with longing. If Charlotte hadn't paged him that night....

Charlotte! Just thinking her name brought Olivia to her senses. She had no right to even be entertaining such thoughts. And anyway Clem was in the lounge, grieving for Kathy. Even if she could somehow wave a magic wand and make Charlotte disappear, she still had to face the fact that he deeply loved Kathy and always would. Beautiful, forever young Kathy, whose only sin had been to die too soon. How could she ever live up to that?

Carrying the drinks through, she saw Clem sprawled out on the sofa sound asleep. Taking a doona from the blanket box and a pillow from her bed, she tucked them in around him as gently as Clem had done for her countless times during her illness. For a moment she gazed at him, taking in the dark eyelashes fanning his cheeks, his beautiful full lips slightly apart. Lucky, lucky Charlotte. The urge to touch him was irresistible. Tiptoeing forward, she leant over him and gently kissed him on the forehead.

'Goodnight, Clem. Sleep well,' she murmured softly.

He stirred slightly as she crept out. Flicking off the lamp she made her way the short distance to her own room and lay on the bed, concentrating on keeping her breathing even, unable to relax, so conscious of Clem asleep nearby and so scared of what the future held.

It seemed she had only just drifted off when she heard the front door close. Climbing out of bed, she padded through to the lounge. The doona and pillow were now neatly folded on the sofa. Wandering through to the kitchen to make a coffee, Olivia saw a note from Clem on the table. She didn't read it straight away, but forced herself to wait until she was back in bed with a coffee by her side. With a trembling hand she unfolded the paper, wondering what he would have to say in the cold light of day.

'Thanks for listening last night, though I can't recall much of what was said. I don't make a habit of getting drunk and crashing on young women's sofas. (Not recently anyway.) I really think we need to talk.
Clem
P.S. You really ought to keep some aspirin in the house.

Olivia laughed at the last line and then reread the note. Whatever did he want to talk about? He had said it all last night. Clem had needed a friend and confidante and she had been there. Despite his popularity, Clem, Olivia realised, had no one he could really talk to. You couldn't imagine Charlotte talking about anyone but herself for more than five minutes, and at the end of the day, despite their affection for him, every one of Clem's local friends was also his patient.

Olivia realised how lucky she was for, although they were on the other side of the world, her parents were always there when she needed them, if only on the other end of the telephone. Clem's family consisted of his brother, and from what Olivia had heard Joshua wasn't exactly family-orientated. If anyone had had an excuse for drinking too much, Clem had had one last night.

CHAPTER SEVEN

'COULD I get James another drink of water, please?'

'I'm a receptionist, not a waitress,' Betty muttered to Olivia. 'That's the third drink they've asked for. You'd think she'd have given him breakfast before they came.'

'It might be nerves. He's not waiting for me to take his blood, is he?' Olivia enquired, looking over at the woman sitting anxiously with her young son.

'No, he's waiting to see Clem. They haven't even got an appointment. I warned Anne that they'll have to wait ages to be seen and now she's making me suffer, like it's my fault. I've enough work to be going on with, without providing a running buffet.'

Her whining voice seemed particularly grating this morning. Olivia shot her a withering look. 'It's not as if you're rushed off your feet. Clem hasn't even arrived yet,' she pointed out.

'Well, I'm going to ring him if he doesn't come soon. I'm fed up with the patients moaning at me about how long they have to wait, yet as soon as they're speaking to Clem it's all sweetness and light.'

For once Clem was late in. Not that Olivia needed him to start her day as there was an endless queue of patients waiting for various tests and dressings. She couldn't help but feel sorry for Clem when he arrived. The waiting room was packed and, given the fact he had spent a night fully clothed on her sofa, he couldn't be feeling his best. She couldn't be sure, but Olivia thought she caught the faintest hint of a blush on his deadpan face as he bade her good morning.

Betty was at her most irritating, trying to hurry Olivia along and juggle her list. 'Mrs Addy has been waiting an hour for her blood test. Why are you seeing James Gardner first? He's not even on your list.'

'Because he doesn't look at all well,' Olivia replied sharply, leading him through to the treatment room. That was an understatement. He looked as if he was about to pass out. Even if he just lay in a screened-off area till Clem could take a look, at least she could do some obs and keep an eye on him.

Scanning his notes, she saw that James was nearly ten years old and, apart from the usual childhood illnesses, he had always been healthy. Carefully she checked his heart rate and respirations, which were slightly raised. Popping a thermometer into his mouth, she noted that his lips were cracked and he looked dehydrated. 'You're not feeling the best, are you, mate?' She smiled sympathetically at the boy. 'I'll just ask your mum what's been going on.'

He nodded his agreement.

'Mrs Gardner.'

'Please, call me Anne.'

'Anne, how long has James been unwell?'

'A few days. I thought it was some twenty-four-hour bug he'd picked up from school so I kept him home, but he's getting worse. He's at the toilet every five minutes, though I'm not surprised—he's drinking heaps. I think he might have a urine infection. He didn't want to come to the doctor, they get embarrassed at this age.'

Olivia nodded. 'I know. But you're obviously unwell, James. The doctor's used to this sort of thing. It's best to get it sorted.'

'There's something wrong, I know it. I'd never normally turn up without an appointment. Betty was really put out, but I could hardly wake him this morning, Sister.'

'Don't worry about Betty. You're his mum, you know if

your child is sick. I'll just take his blood pressure and I'll get Clem to come and have a look.' And then I'll strangle Betty, Olivia fumed to herself.

'I don't want to jump the queue. I don't mind waiting,' Anne said.

'He needs to be seen,' Olivia said matter-of-factly.

James's temperature was normal but Anne was right—there was definitely something going on. Wrapping the cuff around his arm, Olivia leant forward, subtly smelling his breath as she took his blood pressure. With dismay she knew her hunch was right—there was no mistaking the classic pear drop scent, all too familiar from her years in Casualty.

'James, your blood pressure's fine, but if you don't mind I'm just going to do a finger-prick test to check your blood sugar. It will only sting for a second.'

'No worries,' he mumbled, hardly flinching as she pricked his finger. His mother watched anxiously.

His blood sugar was so high she couldn't get an accurate reading. It was a textbook case of diabetes—the unquenchable thirst, the acetone smell on his breath.

'I'll just go and get Clem.'

Betty was really flustered now. 'Mrs Addy was the first patient here,' she said. Mrs Addy was also her sister-in-law, Betty failed to mention, and obviously expected a few favours.

'I'll see her when I can, not when you tell me,' Olivia snapped, furious with Betty for making the Gardners' wretched morning just that bit harder for them. 'Is Clem with a patient?'

Betty, realising she might have overstepped the mark, adopted a more professional manner. 'He's just finished with a patient, but he's on the phone. I'll buzz him and let him know you're coming.'

Such was her concern for young James, Olivia actually

forgot to be embarrassed as she walked into his office, but when she realised Clem was on the phone to Charlotte, nerves caught up with her.

'Look, Charlotte, I'm really snowed under.' He motioned to Olivia to sit as he attempted to finish the conversation. 'I'll see you tomorrow when you get here, and don't worry.' Clem rolled his eyes upwards. 'OK, we'll sort that out later. Drive carefully.' Putting down the phone, he gave her a rueful smile. 'I bet you're feeling a lot better than I am this morning.'

'Probably,' she replied lightly, 'but I've got a James Gardner in the treatment room who, I can guarantee, is feeling worse than you. He was waiting with his mum to see you, but he looked so awful I took him in the treatment room to do some obs. I noticed his breath smelt of ketones so I took a blood glucose. It's off the scale.' Clem stood up. 'He actually doesn't look too bad, considering just how high his glucose is.'

'What have you told him?'

'Nothing yet. Anne knows he's sick but she seems to think it's a urinary infection. It's going to be a shock.'

'Poor kid.' He shook his head. 'Good pick-up, Livvy.'

For some reason she found it impossible to take a compliment from him. 'Hardly. You'd have to be blind to miss it,' she replied, embarrassed but flattered.

He caught her arm in the doorway. 'Many would have let him wait. You're good at your job, Livvy, good at what you do. Don't sell yourself short.'

Yet again Olivia marvelled at his tact and skill with patients. After examining James thoroughly, he somehow managed to sum up the gravity of the situation to James and Anne without alarming them.

'You definitely need to go to hospital, James. Your sugar's very high and you'll need some treatment to get it back to normal. The medicine you need is called insulin, and for now it has to be given in a drip.' He gave him a wide smile. 'You're going to have to wait for that ride in the helicopter, mate. You're sick, but not that sick. We'll get the treatment started and then Livvy and I will look after you till the ambulance gets here. How does that sound?'

James nodded. He was too sick to care, and hardly batted an eyelid when Clem inserted the intravenous cannula. Anne seemed to feel the pain for him.

'He'll be all right, won't he?' she asked, trying desperately to stay calm in front of her son.

Clem beckoned her over to the door out of earshot of James, who lay half-asleep on the trolley. 'He's going to be fine. But he's going to have a lot to deal with. Once he's stabilised he's still going to need the insulin. Do you know about diabetes?'

Anne nodded. 'My sister has it. She has to inject herself twice a day. Will it be the same for him?' she asked, fighting back the tears.

'Yes,' he replied, and Olivia knew that the truth, however brutal, sometimes just needed to be told. 'And it will be hard for James to accept that,' Clem continued, gently but firmly. 'We're going to have to help him realise his diabetes is completely manageable, and that it isn't going to stop him leading a full and active life. He will be all right,' he reiterated. 'Once in hospital, as well as treating him medically, they'll educate James and you all about diabetes. By the time he comes home he'll be telling me what to do—and I'm only half joking.'

Anne managed a wobbly smile and then started to cry. 'I'm sorry. It's just such a shock.'

'Of course it is,' Clem said gently. 'The ambulance will be despatched from the base hospital—it will probably take a couple of hours. Would you like me to ring Andy for you?'

Anne shook her head. 'No, I'll ring and tell him myself, but thanks, Clem.'

Clem had a word with Betty, now the picture of concern, and she ushered Anne into Clem's room so she could speak to her husband in private.

Walking over to Olivia, he gave a wry smile. 'She thanked me, can you believe it? Hell, this is a lousy job sometimes.'

Olivia didn't say anything—she knew he was right.

'I think we'd better start an insulin infusion here. Ideally I'd like to wait till he's admitted, but as that's going to take a while I think it would be safer to get things under way. Are you happy with that?'

Olivia nodded her consent and set about preparing the insulin in a saline and potassium infusion. In no time everything was under control and Olivia carried on with her other duties while keeping a watchful eye on James. The ambulance took nearly two hours to arrive but James's condition didn't deteriorate—in fact, his sugar started to come down. However, he still needed close observation and it was a relief when he was safely on his way.

Olivia enjoyed being busy. It was actually nice in some ways to have such an acute patient. It was like being back in Casualty, but the morning completely exhausted her. She didn't need to be asked twice when Clem popped his head around the door on his way out to home visits to suggest she leave all the paperwork till later and go home and rest. 'There's nothing here that can't wait. You try and have a sleep this afternoon. Don't forget how sick you've been.'

'I won't.' As he went to leave, Olivia knew she couldn't just let him walk away without checking he was all right. 'Clem.'

He turned in the doorway.

'How do you feel?'

He shrugged slightly. 'Nothing that a good night's sleep won't fix,' he answered, too casually.

Olivia nodded, not wanting to push. 'You know where I am.'

Clem nodded. 'I've really got to go. I've got a house call right on the outskirts and it's going to take me ages to get there. But thanks.' He smiled. 'For everything.'

Boosted by their conversation, Olivia decided to at least sort out the paperwork. Some she could take home and maybe do this evening. Betty was bustling about, straightening magazines, determined to stretch her hours so she could claim overtime. The phone ringing finally gave her something to do, yet she still managed to complain about it. Olivia collected up the last of the files and flung her bag over her shoulder.

'A cup of tea, Sister? Clem just rang. He forgot some tablets so he's on his way back. I thought I'd make a brew.'

Olivia suppressed a smile, thinking of Clem's revelation about hating tea. 'No, thanks, Betty. I'm finished here. I'm going home.'

Even before she heard the frantic banging on the surgery door, some sixth sense told her the sound of running footsteps on the drive were those of someone in real trouble. With lightning speed she ran to the door and undid the bolt. A young man who couldn't have been more than twenty stood there, breathless, his face etched with fear and panic. 'She's in the car. She's having it.'

And Olivia knew this was no first-time father getting over-excited.

Betty let out a moan of horror when she saw the man. 'Young Lorna, but she isn't due for months yet.'

Grabbing a wheelchair from the entrance, Olivia raced over to the car. 'Lorna Hall, is it?'

He nodded. She remembered Lorna from the antenatal

clinic. She hadn't seen her for a while but she'd be no more than twenty-six weeks gestation.

'She's in agony, the contractions just keep coming.'

She could hear the terror in his voice. 'What's your name?'

'Pete.'

'OK, Pete, you just stay calm and follow my instructions.' Olivia steeled herself. Taking a deep breath, she opened the car door. Keeping her voice as calm as possible, she greeted the terrified Lorna and briefly examined her. The forewaters were bulging and Olivia knew that if her waters broke the baby could be here in seconds.

'I want to push,' she screamed.

'Not yet,' Olivia said firmly. That was the last thing she wanted her to do. If she could just get them inside the surgery, at least there she had some equipment. It looked as if this baby was going to need all the help available. She looked anxiously over her shoulder. Where the heck was Betty when you needed her? Then she steadied herself. Betty would do the right thing, of course. She'd be ringing Clem to tell him to step on it.

With Pete's help they managed to get Lorna into the wheelchair and rushed her inside. She was trembling all over, her toes curled with the effort of not pushing. Inside, Betty and Pete lifted Lorna onto the examination couch while Olivia hastily pulled on some gloves. She made a mental note to later praise Betty for her efforts. Not only had she rung Clem but also Iris Sawyer and she had managed to plug in the resuscitation cot and open the emergency delivery pack. Lorna started to scream in earnest and Olivia knew this was it. This baby was coming, ready or not.

'I've got to push.'

'OK, Lorna, just hold on a moment longer.' She turned to Betty.

'Go and get the Doppler. It's on my desk.' Betty shook her head. 'Doppler?' Olivia could hear the apprehension in her voice and knew she had confused her. 'I don't know what you mean.'

Olivia forced a reassuring smile. She knew she had to keep Betty calm. 'I use it in my antenatal clinics. It's like a microphone attached to a speaker, to hear the baby's heart,' she said, and mercifully the penny dropped.

'Oh, yes.' Betty rushed off and returned seconds later.

Olivia squirted some jelly on Lorna's abdomen and, having felt the baby's position, she placed the Doppler and listened for the heartbeat, the microphone magnifying the sound for all to hear. Everyone relaxed for a second as a heartbeat was picked up—everyone, that was, but Olivia. The heartbeat was dangerously slow and dipping lower during the contraction. The baby was in foetal distress and the low rate told Olivia there wasn't much time. This baby needed to be born and quickly.

Slipping an oxygen mask over the young woman's face, Olivia explained in reassuring tones what she was about to do. 'You breathe normally. The extra oxygen you're getting will help your baby. I'm going to break your waters. It won't hurt, I promise. You'll just feel a gush.'

Deftly she grabbed the tiny hook-like instrument and ruptured the membranes, knowing this would expedite the birth. The liquor was stained with meconium, which was normally the baby's first bowel movement after birth. The fact the baby had passed this was another sign it was in danger, and if it were to inhale the meconium at birth it could run into all sorts of problems.

'I've got to push,' Lorna screamed.

Betty took Peter's arm. 'You wait outside, pet.' She led him away.

'No, Betty, Pete should be here.'

Betty turned and looked imploringly at Olivia.

'Lorna needs him,' Olivia said firmly, while nodding in understanding. Things certainly didn't look good, but this was his child and he had every right to be there. Apart from anything else, she needed every pair of hands available. 'Pete, hold Lorna's hand, and get her to follow my instructions.'

He did as he was told and much more, guiding and coaxing his terrified wife, drawing on an inner reserve that people somehow found in times of desperation.

Listening to the baby's heartbeat, this time Olivia knew there was no chance of Clem making it back in time. If she didn't get the baby out it would be too late. For a second she felt panic rise in her. But only for a second. It was as if she were on autopilot, in some ghastly, complicated birth video that she had watched in her midwifery training—except this time she was the co-star and poor Lorna the heroine. She'd broken the waters. Lorna had to do the rest.

For a second Olivia eyed the shiny stainless-steel forceps and thought about what Clem would do if he were here. He would probably use them. After all, if this baby wasn't born quickly it didn't stand a chance. But she didn't have the qualifications or experience, and in the wrong hands they could be lethal. Resolutely she looked away. It was up to her and Mother Nature. Despite the other people in the room, never had she felt more alone.

'Lorna, when the next contraction comes I want you to push as hard as you can, right into your bottom. I want you to really push hard,' Olivia repeated. 'Just concentrate on that, and don't stop till I tell you.'

Lorna nodded, then the pain took over. 'It's coming again.'

'Right, push. Come on, push hard.' They all encouraged her. Pete, oblivious of his wife's nails digging into his forearm, coaxed her, demanding that she keep on pushing.

'I can't,' Lorna screamed.

'Yes, you can, you're doing marvellously. Keep pushing. The harder you push the sooner your baby will be here,' Olivia encouraged, as the tiny head emerged. She swiftly suctioned the tiny nose and mouth so the baby wouldn't inhale the meconium when it took its first breath. Deftly she felt around the baby's neck and with dismay she realised the umbilical cord was wrapped around it.

'Don't push,' Olivia said firmly.

'But I have to.'

'No, Lorna. You mustn't. I want you to blow instead, like you're blowing out a candle. Don't push,' she reiterated, for if Lorna pushed now the cord would tighten around the baby's neck. Pete took over, telling his wife exactly what to do, leaving Olivia free to deal with the baby. Swiftly she grabbed the clamps and clamped and cut the cord. The infant's colour was ghastly.

'Lorna, I want you to push now.'

Lorna flailed exhausted, against the pillow. 'I don't need to, I'm not having a contraction,' she said faintly.

'You still have to push—your baby needs to be born.' For a split second their eyes locked and it was all it took to relay the urgency of the message. With her new maternal instinct Lorna somehow found the strength to push. Her young face purple from the exertion and pain, she pushed for all she was worth and when it was all too much Pete inspired her to push some more.

Olivia delivered the tiny baby and, leaving Betty and Pete to look after Lorna, she glanced at the clock as she rushed over to the resuscitation cot, the tiny form grey and limp in her hands. Laying him down, she again swiftly suctioned his tiny nose and mouth, and with infinite relief she saw him make the tiniest respiratory effort but his breathing was far too slow and irregular. Using her stethoscope, she listened to his heart, alarmed at its slowness. The baby's extreme bradycardia combined with his minimal respiratory effort meant that he wasn't being anywhere near sufficiently oxygenated, and Olivia was left with no choice but to commence a full resuscitation. With the ambu-bag she gently pushed oxygen into his lungs and massaged the tiny chest with her fingers, counting the compressions in her head as she willed the baby to respond.

'Why isn't it crying? Why isn't my baby crying?' Lorna begged, while Pete tried to reassure his wife.

'Sister's doing all she can. It'll all be all right, Clem's here now.'

Olivia didn't have time to acknowledge Clem's arrival but she had never in her life been so pleased to see anyone. He took over the respirations as she continued to massage the chest.

'What was his one-minute Apgar?' asked Clem, referring to the initial assessment Olivia had made of the baby. A score of three or less indicated a gravely ill infant.

'Two.'

'How long's it been?'

Olivia looked at the clock and for a second she thought it had stopped. Had it really only been three minutes since this tiny little boy had come into the world? It felt like an hour. 'Three minutes. Oh, come on, baby, breathe, please.'

Time seemed to take on no meaning as the world ran in slow motion. The baby's heart rate picked up, which meant she could take over the respirations while Clem, with great skill, managed to insert a line into the umbilical cord and administer lifesaving drugs directly into the baby's system.

Suddenly Olivia felt the faintest resistance in the ambu-bag. She saw his rib cage flutter and rise as his lungs expanded on their own. His flaccid limbs started to move, his tiny fists clenching. He started to cry, not the normal, lusty scream of a healthy newborn but a tiny wail like a mewing kitten. But it was a cry nonetheless, and the tension in the room lifted slightly. He was by no means out of the woods but at least they were heading in the right direction.

Olivia attached him to a multitude of monitors as Clem went off to briefly check on Lorna. Gently Olivia stroked the tiny infant's cheek. He might have got off to a lousy start in life but he did have some luck on his side. His GP was a fully qualified paediatrician after all. Clem was back in a moment.

'How's Lorna?'

'Terrified, of course, but Iris is here and she's very good. They heard him cry and I've briefly told them what's going on. I'll explain more when I know myself. Now, let's see how he's doing.' They looked at the array of monitors. 'What did you make his five-minute Apgar?'

'Seven.'

Clem nodded in agreement. 'Which is a good pick-up.' He listened to the newborn's chest. 'He's struggling and his oxygen saturation's low. Put him in a head box and we'll see if they improve.'

Olivia nodded. The baby was using his accessory muscles and grunting with each exhausting breath. He looked like a tiny washed-up frog.

'Betty's ringing the emergency transfer team, but it will be a while till they can get here.'

'Where will he be going?' Olivia asked as she set up the equipment that would enable the baby to receive a higher concentration of oxygen.

'Melbourne or Sydney, wherever there's an intensive care bed.'

Betty appeared and, unable to tear her eyes away from the tiny newborn, relayed her message. 'I've got the emergency transfer team on the line.'

'Thanks, Betty.' Clem nodded to Olivia. 'I'm going to get some much-needed advice from them and then I'll be back, but if there's any change tell Betty to come and get me straight away.'

Olivia nodded without looking up—there really wasn't any time for niceties.

Betty stood there, frozen. 'I've never seen one as small,' she said in a choked voice. 'But he's so perfect.'

One of the monitors was causing Olivia some alarm, and she didn't respond to Betty's comments. The baby's oxygen saturation level, never particularly good, was now starting to fall. She checked the probe attached to his tiny foot and the flow level to the oxygen head box. All the equipment was working perfectly. 'Betty, tell Clem his oxygen saturation has dropped to 80 per cent and is falling.'

'Eighty per cent,' Betty repeated, and rushed off.

Clem returned within a moment. 'The transfer team is mobilising—they've got a bed for him in Sydney. We were just debating whether to intubate yet or wait for them to arrive, but as his sats are falling they said to go ahead now.' A tiny muscle was flickering in his cheek, the only sign that this was causing him any concern. Apart from that detail, he looked as impeccably cool and in control as always. 'Set up an intubation tray, please, Livvy.' He gave her a reassuring smile. 'Don't worry, I did a stint in anaesthetics before I came to practise in the middle of nowhere.'

Olivia smiled in what she hoped was a reassuring manner. Despite Clem's apparent confidence, she knew he must be apprehensive. It was one thing to be competent at emergency anaesthetics, and he would obviously get practice out here, but a baby this tiny was a totally different ball game. Poor Clem. Still, they had no choice.

'Betty, take Pete and Lorna into another room. Stay with them and ask Iris to come in here.' He paused for a moment. 'Actually, you stay here and tell Iris to stay with Lorna. Livvy, move the phone over here. There's an anaesthetist on the line and he's going to talk me through in case I need any help.'

Betty held the receiver to Clem's ear as Olivia assisted Clem with the procedure. Thankfully the intubation went smoothly and in no time the baby was connected to the respirator. Through it all they were guided by the experts in Sydney. Again she realised how well stocked Clem had the surgery. Most of the drugs and equipment that the neonatal doctors recommended they had, and so were able to follow the instructions almost to the letter without having to make do. This baby really was being given every opportunity.

When his condition had stabilised, and on the advice of the transfer team, they wheeled Lorna and Pete in to finally see their baby. Olivia bit hard on her lip, fighting back tears as Lorna, with shaking hands, reached into the portholes and touched her tiny son. Pete held her shoulders as tears streamed down his face.

'It's all right, baby, Mummy's here,' Lorna soothed her son, gazing in wonder at the tiny hands she held, no bigger than her fingernails.

'He looks so tiny,' Pete said in a gruff voice. 'So fragile and helpless.' He stared at the monitors. 'All this equipment?'

'I know the monitors look frightening,' Olivia explained gently, 'but they're all helping him and giving us the information we need. None of them are hurting him.'

'But he was crying before. Why isn't he now? And why has he got that tube down his throat?' Lorna asked shakily.

Clem had already explained what each of the monitors and tubes were for, before he'd bought them to see their son, but obviously in their anguish it had been too much to take in. With infinite gentleness he explained again. 'That tube is helping him to breathe. You're right. He was crying, and he was breathing on his own, which is a very good sign. We chose to do this because his little lungs are too small to cope at the moment and he was getting exhausted. This machine will do the breathing for him and give him a chance to rest.'

'He'll be all right, though? He'll make it, won't he?' Lorna was inconsolable and unfortunately there were no guarantees.

'He's got a long battle ahead of him, but he's going to a great hospital. The emergency transfer team is coming here to get him and I'm constantly in contact with the specialists in Sydney. They'll be here soon. We're doing everything we can.'

'Can I go with him in the helicopter?' Lorna asked.

'That's not up to me, Lorna. The transfer team will have to decide,' Clem answered gently. 'There's not much room on board with all the staff and equipment. It will have to be up to them—they know best.'

Lorna started to cry in earnest, completely overwhelmed. 'He's just so small…'

Clem nodded. 'He's pretty tough, though, and he's made it over the first hurdle. With expert care he'll have the best possible chance.'

Pete cradled his wife in his arms. 'He's got a chance, Lorna. Clem says so. That's enough to be going on with for now. Let's just be grateful for that.'

The wait was interminable but finally the sound of the helicopter heralded the arrival of the emergency team. They wheeled in a huge incubator equipped with everything the baby would need to get him safely to Sydney. Olivia could only stand back and marvel at their skills. They handled the tiny baby so expertly and confidently, attaching him to their equipment, assessing his condition each step of the way.

They were there for well over an hour, ensuring he was completely stable before they transferred him, all the time reassuring his parents. They even took a couple of Polaroid photos, one of the baby and the other of Lorna and Pete next to the incubator, holding their tiny son's hand. Pete's parents arrived as Olivia was helping Lorna, stunned and exhausted, into the helicopter, but there was no time for them to see their newborn grandson. The baby's needs had to take precedence.

'Give these to Pete,' Lorna said in a shaking voice, handing Olivia the Polaroids. 'He can show them the photos.'

Impulsively Olivia reached over and hugged Lorna tightly.

Lorna clung on, grateful for the human touch but completely unaware how out of character this was for Olivia. 'Thank you, Livvy, thank you,' she said tearfully.

As the helicopter left, carrying its precious load, Clem turned to Pete. 'Are your parents going to drive you to Sydney?' Clem asked.

Pete nodded, tears coursing down his cheeks as he gazed at the photos.

'Well, take it steady,' he said, as practical as ever. 'The last thing Lorna needs is for you to be involved in accident. I'll ring the hospital later, see how he's doing.' His voice wavered slightly. 'Chin up, mate.' Clem shook Pete's hand. 'We'll all be thinking of you.'

As they waved off the car, watching it crunch its way down the gravel path to whatever the future held for them, Olivia finally broke down. Clem said nothing, just pulled her into his arms and let her cry. Finally, as the sobs subsided, he lifted her chin to make her look at him. 'Not the ideal first delivery, but you did a fantastic job.'

'If I had just got him out sooner, but the cord—'

'Don't do that to yourself. You did absolutely everything anyone could have done. Any hope he's got is because of you, so don't beat yourself up with what ifs. You gave him a chance.'

Olivia nodded, glad he understood. She knew she couldn't have done anything differently, but she just needed to hear it. His arms still around her, he looked down.

'You look completely done in.'

'It's been an exhausting day.' Olivia wriggled away, suddenly conscious of his embrace. 'Where's Betty?'

'Off to tell the whole town, no doubt. She's a terrible sticky beak.'

Olivia was about to agree, then remembered the wisdom Betty had shown when it had been needed. 'She really helped in there.'

'Why do you think I keep her on? I know she's a lousy receptionist but her heart is in the right place and she does come up trumps when you need her. I'm very choosy about my staff. That's why your predecessors didn't last.'

'Really?' Olivia frowned 'The agency gave the impression they left because…' Her voice trailed off. She could hardly repeat what Miss Lever had said about him.

'Because I was moody and difficult?'

Olivia shuffled uncomfortably. 'Something like that.'

'And is that how you find me?' he enquired.

Olivia thought for a moment.

'Yes,' she answered truthfully. 'Though not in the way I expected. I mean, you're a very good doctor and a wonderful boss…'

'But?'

'But nothing that would make me want to pack up and leave, unless, of course, I didn't want to be here in the first place.'

'Exactly. You've got it in one. A lot of people seem to think they'll come out here for a bit of a holiday and, as you know, it couldn't be further from the truth. At the end of the day, to the people here we're all they've got medically speaking. It's an awesome responsibility.'

'I know, and it terrifies me. I have to remind myself

sometimes that I ran a busy casualty department, and that I'm used to making difficult decisions and I am up to this. But sometimes, like today, I realise that we're alone at the front line. In Casualty there was always someone to confer with, someone's opinion there for the asking. I don't know how you do it. It must get pretty scary sometimes.'

'It does and that's the very reason I only keep good staff. I'd rather struggle on alone than with someone who isn't up to it. Take today. Betty is a receptionist—that's all she's paid for. Sure, I give her a few perks and sometimes I think it's more than she deserves. But just as she's seriously getting on my nerves and I think it's time I put my foot down and had a word, she outshines herself like she did this afternoon. It makes the incessant personal calls and sticky-beaking look rather irrelevant.'

Olivia understood. Betty really had been marvellous.

'So when some young nurse arrives, and straight away asks where the local hotel is, running out the door on the stroke of five and taking the phone off the hook at night, I have no compunction about being as moody and difficult as my reputation allows. You, on the other hand are the complete opposite. We work pretty damn well together.'

Olivia took this all in, touched by his praise but embarrassed as well. 'So why are you still so moody and difficult with me, then?' she teased, shrugging off his compliments.

He didn't answer. Instead, he stared at her for what seemed an eternity. Finally she dragged her eyes away. Clem cleared his throat. 'I don't know about you, but I could do with a stiff drink and I don't fancy fielding questions from concerned locals down at the hotel. Anyway, I want to ring the hospital later see how he's getting on.' He gestured to the private part of the house. 'Will you join me?'

Olivia hesitated, torn. It was certainly tempting to spend the evening with him but, given her feelings, she wasn't sure it was appropriate. But surely a drink with a friend after the afternoon they'd had wasn't unreasonable, and anyway she wanted to be there when he rang the hospital. She looked down at her soiled clothing. 'I'll go home and have a bath and change first. There wasn't exactly time to put on an apron.'

Clem smiled, noticing for the first time the mess she was in. 'Fair enough. I'll wait for you to come over before I ring.'

Olivia nodded. She knew how he felt. Neither wanted to be alone if the news was bad.

CHAPTER EIGHT

UP TO her neck in bubbles, Olivia tortured herself by going over and over the events. Oh, she knew what Clem had said and hoped it was true, but if only she'd had more experience. Was there *anything* she could have done differently?

Getting out the bath, despite a huge fluffy bathrobe and the warm evening, Olivia couldn't stop shaking. She suddenly felt light-headed. Clutching the bedside table, she sat down on the edge of the bed, waiting for the dizziness to pass. Maybe the bath had been too warm, Olivia reasoned as she relived the birth for the umpteenth time. Perhaps there *had been* something more she could have done, and Clem, knowing how hard she had tried and how upset she was, didn't want to make her feel worse. Of course not, she admonished herself. Clem was a wonderful teacher. If there was anything to be learnt from today he would have told her, no matter how hard it might be to hear. Still, an incessant voice kept nagging, maybe she could have done better.

She dressed slowly, pulling on some denim shorts and a white cotton blouse. A niggling pain in her shoulder made putting on her make-up more of a chore than usual, but without it her complexion was so pale, and Clem would only start nagging about her being back at work. The phone started to ring as she picked up her keys and grabbed a bottle from the fridge. The answering machine could get it. She didn't have to explain where she was going to anyone.

Clem greeted her warmly. 'I was starting to think about calling out the search party again.'

'Am I ever going to live that down?' Olivia grinned, offering the bottle she had brought.

'Not if I have any say in it.' He looked at the bottle 'Champagne. Are we celebrating?'

'To toast my first delivery in Kirrijong.' He caught the flash of tears in her eyes. 'It might not have been as I planned, but he deserves to have his head wet. It's still a miracle.'

'Oh, Livvy.' He swept her into his arms. 'Of course it's a miracle. That little tacker has touched us all—he's a fighter. Come on, we'll have a drink and then we'll ring to see how he's doing.'

He led her through to the lounge and sat her down. It was a room she had her lunch in every day and yet by evening light and without Betty it felt completely different. The heavy drapes were drawn and the gentle lighting illuminated the welcoming warmth and intimacy of this beautiful home. As Clem popped the cork he shot her a wary look. 'Your liver function test was normal?'

'Perfectly.'

'I still wish you'd let me check you. Nothing against Dr Humphreys. He was a fine doctor.'

'Was' being the operative word, Olivia thought, but didn't say anything. 'How's the hospital going?'

'Painfully slowly. That's two patients today who really needed it. Of course, Lorna and the baby would have been transferred anyway, but it would be nice to have an anaesthetist and a few more pairs of hands. Not,' he added, handing her a glass of champagne, 'that we didn't cope admirably, but I'm tired of coping, and constantly being on call makes it impossible to relax. Take yesterday. I had to ask Dr Humphreys weeks in advance to cover for me because I knew I'd need a night to myself, what with Kathy's anniversary and everything. Not that I was planning to get plastered, I hasten to add. That rather took care of itself. I really am sorry.'

'Clem, please, don't apologise. There's really no need and, anyway, you really weren't that bad.' She changed the subject. 'So, when do you think it will be up and running?'

'Another couple of months. I'm going to start advertising for staff.'

'Do you think you'll have much luck?'

Clem looked at her thoughtfully. 'There shouldn't be too much trouble. It's a different kettle of fish, recruiting for a country hospital compared to a GP practice. The incentives will be pretty good and there'll be a lot of experience to be gained. At least they won't have to ship every remotely interesting case off to the base hospital. The serious ones will still go to Melbourne or Sydney, but that's pretty standard.' He paused, as if about to say something.

Olivia waited. He had never formally offered her a job there, and she had just assumed that there would be one. Still, it would be nice to be asked. Clem didn't say anything, just reached over and refilled her glass. He obviously had other things on his mind.

She put her hand over the top of the glass and some champagne trickled through her fingers. 'That's plenty, thanks. I haven't had a drink in ages it will go straight to my head.'

Clem stood up. 'A fine host I am. You haven't eaten dinner, and I'm the one insisting you eat regular meals and fatten up. I'll fix us something now.'

'Please, don't. I'm honestly not hungry.'

He ignored her, of course. 'Just wait there. Put on some music, make yourself comfortable.'

He disappeared into the kitchen and Olivia eyed his music collection. It was far more familiar than the highbrow operas Jeremy pretended to listen to, and at least his stereo system looked user-friendly and Clem actually had cassettes. Jeremy's was all CDs and digital everything. It looked like a flight deck in a Boeing 747.

Settling on a hits mix she smiled as he entered.

'Dinner will be twelve minutes, according to the box.' He picked up the cassette holder Olivia had chosen. 'Now there's a blast from the past.'

'It reminds me of my wild youth.'

Clem raised an eyebrow. 'Really, Sister Morrell?'

'No, but I sometimes wish it had been.'

'Well, you sit there and reminisce about what could have been and I'll ring the hospital.'

Olivia nodded. She had been waiting for him to ring but had been too terrified of what the outcome might be to suggest it herself.

He was back within a few moments. 'He's stable.'

She let out a sigh of relief and Clem continued, 'There's been no major dramas since he left us, all his vital signs are as good as can be expected.'

Olivia digested this, but the question that was eating at her had to be asked. 'What about…?' She hesitated, unable to get the words out.

'Brain damage?' He asked the question for her. 'Livvy, you know it's far too soon to even begin to answer that. It could be weeks, months even, before they know.'

Oh, she knew that, knew all the statistics and that brain injury wasn't always immediately apparent, and she knew that there was still a lot to happen that could influence the outcome, but it wasn't enough. She turned her huge green eyes on him. 'But what do you think, Clem? What's your own opinion?'

Clem put down his glass. He knew she felt guilty, and with absolutely no reason. It was just part of the job. If you cared enough you got involved. 'I think,' he said slowly, 'that the little guy and Lorna and Pete have a struggle on their hands. No baby born at twenty-six weeks gestation sails through. If he comes out of this totally unscathed it will be a miracle. But miracles do happen, we saw that today. His one-minute Apgar was awful, but he was resuscitated very effectively and he picked up quickly—that counts for a lot. He looked in pretty good shape for such a premmie by the time the transfer team got here. I think we can be cautiously optimistic, and confident we did all we could and did it well.

'Hell.' Clem stood up suddenly. 'I forgot about the dinner.'

He returned minutes later with a vast pizza. 'I hope you like them crusty.' He laughed as he cut the pizza into generous slices. They knelt at the coffee-table, eating the pizza from the serving plate. Despite her earlier protests, Olivia realised she was hungry after all and tucked in unashamedly. About to reach for her third slice, she felt Clem staring at her.

'What are you staring at? Have I got something on my face?'

'Relax, I was just thinking how other woman must hate you. No matter what you eat, you never gain an ounce.'

'Nerves,' Olivia quipped. 'I'm just a bundle of them. It's probably just as well my life's in such a mess. The day I'm actually content I'll probably pile on the kilos and end up with hips you could—' Suddenly, and she never knew quite how it happened, Clem put a finger up to her lips and she knew the time for talking had ended.

'Livvy, look at me.'

She sat there quite still as he gently lifted her chin and slowly she raised her eyes to meet his. It was like looking in a mirror, seeing the burning desire she felt reflected in his, and she was finally in no doubt her feelings were reciprocated. Her heart was racing, her breathing speeding up, making her breasts rise and fall rapidly. He hadn't even kissed her yet, but the effect of this handsome, sensual man close up was more intoxicating than any champagne.

Sensing her consent, driven by his own desire, Clem moved his face towards her and teasingly showered her face then her neck with tiny butterfly kisses. Her eyes closed, her lips parted, she drowned in her senses, the bitter tang of his aftershave, the sweetness of his lips on her smooth skin.

Finally his mouth found hers and hungrily he kissed her, desperately forcing her lips apart with his tongue. He tasted of champagne and decadence and danger. She could feel the rising current that surged between them, hear their hearts beating in unison, and she revelled in it.

The distance from the living room to the bedroom was quickly negotiated and gently he laid her on the bed, all the time kissing her as if he couldn't bear to let her go. And she didn't want him to. Her ardour rising with each gasping breath, she could feel his hard, muscular body pushing against her slender frame. Instinctively she arched her body towards him, inflaming the fire that burnt between them. Expertly he undid her blouse and gasped as his searching hands encountered the gentle swell of her ripe breasts, a delicious contrast to her slender body.

With a gentle moan he buried his head into the velvet softness of her bosom, his tongue enticing her hardening nipples. One tender hand stroked her neck, while the other slowly, deliberately moved down, and Olivia knew she wanted him to go on, ached for him to go further.

'Are you sure, Livvy?' His eyes locked with hers and she nodded her consent.

'I'm sure,' she murmured, her voice not wavering as she gazed into his eyes. 'What about…?'

Gesturing to the *en suite,* he went to climb out of bed, but she gently pulled him back. 'No. I'll go.'

She darted into the bathroom, grateful for the chance to

gather her thoughts. She wanted that brief moment. Gazing in the mirror at her flushed cheeks and bright eyes, her lips red and full from the weight of his kiss, she knew that she had never been surer of anything in her life. Rummaging through his cabinet, she found the tiny foil packages and, ever the nurse, checked the expiry date on the back. A gurgle of laughter escaped from her lips as she realised that here she was, probably doing the most reckless thing she had ever done in her life, and the pedantic, efficient side of her was checking dates!

Making her way back to the bedroom, she gazed at Clem's outstretched body lying on the bed. Her heart was in her mouth but she couldn't help but gasp in admiration at the sight of him. Taut muscles subtly defined by the gentle bedside lamp. The silky shadow of ebony hair over his broad chest tapering into a fine line along his toned abdomen, edging downwards as if directing her to the very pinnacle of this beautiful man.

For once she had no reservations, no qualms, no self-doubt. Slowly, seductively she made her way to the bed. Kneeling astride him, she bent her head, her Titian curls tumbling onto his chest, her supple lips tenderly, teasingly exploring his torso. Boldly descending his rigid abdomen, relishing his scent, savouring the delicious salty tang of his skin on her lips, aware of her power as a woman.

She heard his sharp intake of breath as her lips moved lower still, teasing him until he could take it no more. In one supple movement Clem sat up, his strong arms engulfing her, laying her down on the rumpled sheets, the need to be inside her surpassing everything.

And then they were one, locked together in a rhythmic embrace that transcended all else, their bodies in blissful unison, driving each other on to a zenith that was as pure as it was magical.

Lying there, their bodies entwined, slowly the world

came back into focus—the ticking of a bedside clock, the ceiling fan delivering a welcoming gentle breeze on her warm, flushed skin. But just as suddenly as their intimacy had ignited it seemed to die. Olivia sensed his detachment even before he said a word.

'Clem?' Her voice was questioning, anxious, and his response did nothing to allay her fears. With a deep sigh he rolled onto his back and gazed at the ceiling, breaking the physical contact.

'Livvy, oh, Livvy.' His voice was deep, thick with emotion. He turned onto his side, propping himself on his elbow, and gently picked up her hand. 'I shouldn't have rushed you.'

Olivia shook her head. 'But you didn't. I thought it was what we both wanted?'

'It was, it is…' But it sounded to Olivia more as if he was trying to convince himself than her.

'Then what's wrong?' she demanded.

'Nothing's wrong, I just think we need to talk. Livvy, I never want you to regret a moment of our time together. I never want to hurt you, and without wanting to sound mercenary I won't let myself be hurt again.'

'What makes you think I'd hurt you?' she asked, bewildered.

He pulled her hand up to his face, his lips gently brushing her slender fingers. 'There was an engagement ring here not so long ago. We've both got so much emotional baggage I just think we should have cleared a few things up first, before we went this far.'

Suddenly she felt stupid. Acutely aware of her exposed breasts, she sat up and grabbed at the bedspread, pulling it around her. Never had she felt more vulnerable.

'There's no need to explain,' she said haughtily. 'I mean, I'm sorry if I forced you.' She knew she was being cruel, but she wasn't feeling very gracious. He had initiated things, he had asked her over and made love to her, and now he was calling a halt, telling her to slow down. Didn't she have any say here?

'Livvy, please, don't get upset. Just let me explain. You know I want you. It's just...'

'Just what?' Her voice was rising now. Olivia swallowed hard a couple of times. She wouldn't lose it here. The day had been bad enough without this. How dare he land this lot on her? 'Just that you thought you were ready, but now you're not sure? Or just, you thought I was? Well, I've got news for you, Clem. Make your mind up a bit earlier next time. I'm not a tap you can just turn on and off, I'm a woman!' In one movement she stood up, grabbing at her carelessly discarded clothes. In an instant he was beside her.

'Livvy, stop it.' His voice was firm without being harsh as he pulled her into his arms, holding her body stiff and unyielding against him. 'God, what did that bastard do to you? All I said was that we needed to talk,' he murmured into her hair, gently stroking her, gradually rekindling the intimacy and tenderness the night had held until finally she relented, relaxing against him, allowing herself to be comforted.

'All I was trying to say,' he repeated gently, 'was that we need to talk.'

'I know, I know.' She buried her face in the warm shelter of his chest. Olivia knew she had overreacted, and she knew he was right—they did need to talk, but not now. Jeremy, Kathy, Charlotte—they all had to be addressed, but surely it could wait?

She nodded, nestling into him. 'I know we do but, please, Clem, not tonight.'

Tenderly he drew her back onto the rumpled bed and back into his arms.

'I'm sorry I upset you,' he said softly. 'My timing can be lousy sometimes.'

'Oh, I don't know about that,' said Olivia huskily, running her long fingers lazily between his muscular thighs, boldly taking him in her hands and guiding him gently towards her. 'Your timing seemed perfect to me.'

Wrapped in his arms she slept so soundly even his pager didn't disturb her. Clem awoke her with a tender kiss.

'What time is it?'

'After one. I just got paged. Elsie Parker's taken a turn for the worse. There's not much I can do but I think it would help the family if I was there.'

Olivia nodded. Elsie Parker was in her late sixties and at the end of a long battle against ovarian cancer. 'Poor things. Is there anything I can do?'

Clem shook his head. 'I don't know how long I'll be. You go back to sleep, you look exhausted.'

'I'm all right, but I think I'd better go home. I don't really fancy waking up to find Ruby trying to make your bed.'

Clem laughed. 'Good point. The minute Ruby finds out, the whole town will know. It would be nice to get used to the idea ourselves first.' He squeezed her thigh through the sheet. 'You don't mind?'

Olivia shook her head 'No, you go.'

'I'll see you home.'

'Clem, I live two minutes away I can get there myself. Go and see how Elsie is doing—she needs you now.'

He smiled appreciatively and gave her a hurried kiss before he left. She lay there for a few moments after he had gone, remembering their love-making, her body tingling just at the memory of his touch, until finally, reluctantly she left the crumpled bed where they had finally found each other.

CHAPTER NINE

A SUDDEN violent spasm in Olivia's stomach awoke her. Retching, she just made it to the bathroom in time, a cold sweat drenching her. Leaning over the sink she rinsed her mouth from the tap and caught sight of herself in the mirror. Her face was pinched and pale, perspiration beading on her forehead, her eyes dark and sunken. She peered at her reflection. Imagine if she had stayed the night at Clem's—it was hardly a face to wake up to.

Gradually the pain eased to a dull ache and she made her way gingerly back to her bed. She looked over at her alarm clock—it was just after five. Surely the pizza would have been all right? It was only a frozen one, and it wasn't even as if she'd had a lot to drink—she hadn't even finished her glass of champagne.

Olivia drifted into an uneasy sleep, only to be awoken what seemed like seconds later by the sound of her alarm. She was no hero and under absolutely any other circumstances there was no way she would have even considered going into work. But given the developments of the previous night, what else could she do?

The thought of ringing Clem and saying she was too sick to come in was incomprehensible. He would misinterpret it as embarrassment or guilt. Their relationship was just too fragile and vulnerable to jeopardise at this tender stage. No. The music had to be faced. It was Friday. If she could just get through the morning then she'd have the whole weekend to recover and, anyway, she'd had far too much sick time already.

The pain in her shoulder made putting on make-up even

more difficult. Slapping on a great deal of foundation and blusher, she managed to look almost normal and made it to the surgery just ten minutes late. Thankfully, there were no patients waiting for her.

Betty greeted her warmly, obviously buoyed by the experience they had shared. 'Have you heard how the baby is? I wanted to ask Clem, but Mr Heath was already waiting and got in first.'

'Clem rang the hospital last night and they said he was stable. I would imagine he'll ring again this morning when he's got a minute. I'm just going to go into the treatment room to catch up on yesterday's files. Would you call if any patients come for me?'

Betty nodded. 'Would you like me to bring you in a coffee?'

She was obviously in the mood for a chat which was the last thing Olivia felt like, but she suddenly felt guilty, remembering how badly she'd needed to go over and over the birth. Betty must be feeling the same.

'Thanks, Betty, that would be lovely. Oh, and, Betty, I meant to thank you yesterday but I never got the chance. Your help was invaluable to me and I'm sure Lorna and Pete would say the same. I know Clem was pleased with you.'

'I did nothing,' replied Betty, blushing to the roots of her hair.

'Of course you did. Your actions bought us some time, which was what we were fighting for. What's this?' she added, pointing to a large jar on Betty's desk.

'I've organised a collection for Lorna and Pete—they'll be struggling, having to stay in Sydney. It's got off to a great start—everyone in the hotel chipped in.' The jar was crammed with notes and coins already, and the baby wasn't even twenty-four hours old.

Olivia felt a huge lump in her throat. Everyone was finding it tough here, the drought was really biting, and yet they still managed to chip in, sure in the knowledge that others were worse off. Only last week they had arranged a huge convoy of trucks to take feed for the cattle up in Queensland, knowing that if they thought they were struggling here, the situation was dire further north. It was just one huge family and Olivia felt privileged to belong. She dug into her purse and added a fifty-dollar note to the collection.

'That's very generous,' Betty said. Olivia gave her a small wink.

'Jeremy can afford it,' she joked, thinking of the car she had sold to get her here.

Betty giggled and even Olivia laughed. Maybe she would make more of an effort with the receptionist.

'We're going to have a working bee next weekend to fix up the house for them. Poor Pete had only got round to buying the paint—they just moved in last week. I know you've been sick and we don't expect you to help with the house, but maybe youse can knit something?'

Olivia nodded weakly. She had never held a knitting needle in her life. 'Of course.' She made a mental note to write to Jessica, and ask her to send a little matinée outfit. She could always tear out the label. A wave of nausea swept over her. 'I'll get started on those notes,' she said weakly, escaping to the treatment room. Betty was far too pleased with the praise to notice Olivia's rapid departure.

As she sat at the desk the words blurred in front of her. This was ridiculous—there was no way she should be at work. Maybe she had overdone things, what with the glandular fever and then all the drama of yesterday. Clem would understand. After all, hadn't he insisted she take it easy and tell him if there were any problems? She would simply tell him that she wasn't feeling well, and be totally professional but friendly. Her plans were to no avail, though. Walking

out into the waiting room, she promptly collided with
Charlotte, who practically shoved Olivia out of the way in
her haste to get to Clem's room.

'I need to see Clem immediately!' she barked at Betty.

'He's in with a patient,' Betty retorted sharply. 'I'll let
him know you're here as soon as he's finished.'

'I don't care if he's in with the Queen of England,'
Charlotte snarled. 'I need to see him this instant.' It took
all of Olivia's tact and even more of Betty's strength to
block the door and prevent her from barging in on Mr
Heath's prostate examination. Clem opened the door, en-
raged.

'What the hell's going on?' he demanded.

'I need to see you, Clem. Now,' Charlotte begged loudly,
but in a far more endearing tone.

Clem, realising he was obviously not going to be able to
calm Charlotte down without attending to her, looked over
at Olivia. For an instant she felt a blush rise as she remembered the last time their eyes had met. 'Would you mind
checking Mr Heath's blood pressure? If that's all right tell
him I'll ring him at home this afternoon. Give him my
apologies.' Clem's voice was totally calm, as if this type
of intrusion happened every day. He also looked disgustingly healthy, which ruled out the pizza being off.

Olivia nodded, suddenly irritated by this silly woman,
who assumed she was so much more important than everybody else was. Clem turned to the drama queen.

'Charlotte, go and wait in my study. I'll be there in just
a moment.' Charlotte, pacified now she had got her way,
strutted off. 'Betty, would you hold my calls, unless, of
course, they're urgent?'

'But what'll I tell the patients that are waiting?' she
asked. For the first time Clem sounded irritated. Charlotte
must have got to him after all.

'Tell them something came up. It's not as if they don't

know. After all, Charlotte's outburst was hardly discreet. Tell them what you like.' And he marched off.

'Perhaps they were made for each other after all,' Betty muttered furiously.

Olivia tried to appease Mr Heath as she checked his blood pressure.

''Struth, I wanted to ask Clem for a script for me heart pills.'

'I'll have him write it up and I'll drop it in to the chemist for you this afternoon. He really is sorry. Something came up and he had to rush off.'

'I may be old, Sister, but I ain't deaf. That blooming sheila Charlotte calls and he runs. I dunno, she doesn't care tuppence for anyone except herself. What he's doing messin' with her I'll never know. Kathy must be turning in her grave, knowing that madam finally got her claws in him.' He waved a gnarled, arthritic finger at her. 'Nothing good will ever come of it, I tell you. She should stay put in Sydney, the city suits her.'

Olivia smiled noncommittally and helped the old man down off the examination couch. Privately she agreed with every word. Charlotte. She was like an unopened red bill, stuffed hastily into your handbag. Something, no matter how hard you tried, you never really forgot, but at least until you saw it you didn't have to deal with it. Well, the time had surely come. The music had to be faced, but not here, not at work. The next opportunity she got she would confront Clem, ask him outright just what was going on between him and Charlotte. The truth must surely be better than this uncertainty.

Finally Charlotte appeared, tearful but a lot calmer. Oliva tried to hover, to hear any snippet of their conversation, but a patient arrived, waving a pathology slip under her nose, and as there was no one else waiting for her, she really had no choice but to get on with it. Clem walked Charlotte to her car, hardly part of the service.

Olivia tried to concentrate as she took Mrs Peacock's blood. Thankfully she had good veins and the needle went in without difficulty.

'Well, that was nice and quick. It makes a change to be seen straight away. Thanks for that.' She rolled down her sleeve. 'Are you all right, Sister? You look a bit peaky.'

'I'm just a bit under the weather, nothing to worry about.' Olivia gave her a smile. 'Those results should be back early next week. If there are any problems, Clem or I will call you.'

'No worries. Thanks, Sister. And you take care of yourself.'

Walking over to the window where the sharps bin was kept, Olivia carefully emptied the kidney dish into the receptacle. Cursing herself for not being able to resist, she stood on tiptoe and peeped out of the window into the car park. And instantly wished she hadn't, for she was just in time to see Clem gently embrace Charlotte. She was leaning against him, nodding. Olivia felt as if she had been stabbed. She watched as he opened the car door and Charlotte climbed into her sporty soft top—red, of course. She was predictable. Olivia just ducked in time as Charlotte sped off and Clem turned and walked back to the surgery. She certainly didn't want Clem to catch her spying on him.

'What on earth was I thinking, getting involved with another man, let alone another doctor?' she muttered.

Clem walked into the treatment room. He had no reason to be there unless he wanted to see her. He looked tired but smiled when he spoke.

'I'm really behind now. How are you this morning?' Gently he put his hand up to her cheek, but she pulled it down and turned away, unable to take this display of affection. There were questions to be answered first. 'Mr

Heath needs a script for digoxin. I said I'd drop it into the chemist for him this afternoon,' Olivia said tonelessly.

'Thanks for that. I'd better write it up now or I'll forget, and I've already messed him about enough this morning.' He looked at her quizzically and suddenly his voice was serious. 'Livvy, are you feeling all right? You look ever so pale.'

I feel pale, she wanted to scream. I don't know if it's my stomach aching or my heart and head for being so stupid. Instead, she replied in the same toneless voice, 'I'm fine, just a bit tired. How's Elsie Parker?'

'Still battling on. She's amazing really. I've increased her morphine and changed her anti-emetic, which hopefully will make her more comfortable. I'll go and check on her this afternoon.'

Betty appeared at the door. 'The natives are getting restless.'

'I'm coming now.'

Betty bustled away.

'Livvy?'

'What?' she snapped. Clem just stood there. She didn't look at him, she couldn't bring herself to. Whatever he had been about to say, he obviously thought better of it.

'Never mind, it will keep till after surgery. I've left my prescription pad in the study. Would you mind bringing it in to me? I'll carry on with the patients.'

'Certainly.'

It was a beautiful study. Heavy wooden shelves lined the walls, every inch crammed with books, ranging from medical encyclopaedias and journals to various classics and the latest blockbusters. His huge, untidy desk sent Ruby into hysterics, but Clem knew where everything was and could place his hand on what he needed in an instant. Olivia, however, was not privy to his chaos. She rummaged through the various files and pieces of paper, eventually finding the prescription pad.

Picking it up, her heart skipped a beat, for lying there under it was a pregnancy test card. The blotting paper still paling showed it was a fresh test. What's more, it was positive! Her hands shot up to her mouth, stifling the scream that welled inside as the test card clattered to the floor.

How could he? How could he have done this to her? How could he have let her into his bed, into his life? It all made ghastly sense now—that was what this morning had been about. As friendly as Clem might be to his patients, that had been no doctor's congratulatory hug she had witnessed them sharing, and Charlotte's behaviour certainly wasn't one of a normal patient. Had she needed any more proof, Betty bustled in, bearing the final nail in the coffin.

'There you are. He's screaming for his pad. As if we don't have enough to deal with, he's now decided to head off to Sydney tomorrow morning, so I'll be on the phone all day, cancelling his weekend house calls. I hope he's back by Monday or we'll be stuck with old Dr Humphreys for surgery. It's bad enough when he's on call. Don't go getting sick this weekend—he'll kill us all, he's that old.'

Listening to Betty's ranting, Olivia swallowed the bile that rose in her throat. 'Why's Clem going to Sydney?' she asked, trying desperately to keep her voice even.

'And youse are supposed to have the brains. That's where madam lives, remember? I hope he's not going to propose. I mean it, I'll give him one week's notice.'

Numb now, she made her way back through the patient area. Clem's office door was open, and without bothering to knock she walked straight in and gave him the pad without a word.

'Thanks,' he muttered. Looking up, he saw her face and quickly came around the desk. 'Sit down. You really are pale.'

'I said I'm fine,' she snapped, near to tears and determined not to let him see.

'You don't look it.'

'Well, I am. How's Charlotte?' He was smooth—not
even a flicker of guilt marred his concerned expression.

'Much calmer. She's off to Sydney, thank goodness. I'm
just about sick of her dramas.' He sat down on the desk
and gently picked up one of her slim hands. Olivia sat there
frozen, her lips white, anger welling up inside her, only to
be drowned by a huge wave of sadness for what might have
been.

'Livvy, we really need to talk.'

'So you keep telling me, but we never seem to get there.'
She damn well wasn't going to make this easy for him.

'I know. Look, I haven't been completely up front with
you. I wanted to be sure about something before I bothered
you with it, but things have suddenly started to happen—
shall we say, a rather unexpected turn of events?'

Olivia's jaw dropped. Was that how he saw Charlotte's
pregnancy? Some minor inconvenience to an otherwise
normal day? But Clem continued talking, seemingly oblivious to her reaction. I have to go to Sydney tomorrow
morning, but I really need to speak to you before I leave.'

'You've got patients waiting,' she pointed out.

'I know. What about tonight? I'll take you out for dinner.
We can talk. I won't get sidetracked, I really need you to
say yes.'

He was almost begging her. It was Jeremy all over. What
did he think he could possibly say to her? That he wanted
them both? Or that the baby was a mistake? Hadn't he
listened to a word she'd said about Jeremy? Did he really
think she'd be so stupid all over again?

'What about Charlotte?' There, she'd said it. She held
her breath, scrutinising his face for a reaction.

'What about her? I told you, she's gone, she won't disturb us.'

Suddenly she couldn't bear the sound of his voice. It was so kind, so convincing. Maybe she should go out with him, hear what he had to say. Aware she was weakening, Olivia stood up sharply. What did this man do to her? She needed to get out, to think things through. She was scared, so scared that she'd lose her head and accept his story, only to be tortured all over again. 'Actually, you were right. I don't feel well. I think I'm going to have to go home to bed.'

'What's wrong?'

'I've probably just been overdoing things. Look, I'll take a raincheck on dinner and grab an early night.'

'Let me have a look at you.'

He looked so worried, as if he really cared. Surely there must be some explanation. Maybe he and Charlotte had had a one-night stand for old time's sake. Maybe… No, she reminded herself firmly, don't make excuses.

'No.' She almost shouted at him. 'I just need a rest. If you'll excuse me.' And not even bothering to say goodbye, she rushed out of the surgery, only stopping to grab her bag.

When she got home Ruby was there, busily sweeping the floorboards and desperate for news on the baby.

'You're early. Come on, I'll put the kettle on and we'll have a nice cuppa. Youse can tell me all about the baby. The way Betty's carrying on, it sounds like she delivered it. She didn't, did she?'

Olivia shook her head. Normally she loved Ruby and didn't mind whiling away the hours with her, but right now she really needed to be alone.

'Ruby, I don't feel too good. I'm just going to go and lie on the settee. Do you mind finishing up?'

Ruby fussed over her, laying her down and fetching a

pillow, but Olivia could tell she was hurt by her dismissal. 'Come over tomorrow morning,' Olivia suggested. 'I'll fill you in then. I really am tired.'

Appeased, Ruby tucked a rug around her. 'I knew it was too soon for youse to be back at work. You rest there, pet, and I'll get out of your hair. Can I get you a drink?'

'No, but thanks.'

Ruby hesitated. She really didn't want to leave. She'd never seen Olivia looking so awful, except those first couple of days after she'd gone missing.

'Is there anything I can do?'

'You could light a fire. I'm frozen.'

'But it's thirty degrees outside,' Ruby exclaimed, then, seeing Olivia shivering on the couch, she did as she'd been asked. Expertly arranging the wood, she lit a match and fanned the tiny flame till the fire burned merrily. 'Shall I fetch Clem? You look worse than you did fifteen minutes ago.'

'Ruby, please, don't.'

Ruby looked unsure, but Olivia insisted.

'I mean it. He knows I'm sick. That's why I came home early. I just need to rest. Promise me you won't go dragging him over.'

'Well, if you're sure…' She hovered for a moment then reluctantly packed up her things. 'Call if you need me.' She departed.

Olivia lay there for how long she wasn't quite sure, but gradually the room grew darker. Only the light from the ebbing fire filled the room, casting long shadows. Gazing into the glowing embers, she searched for answers.

How could she have let it happen? The last thing she had been looking for had been another relationship. Hadn't she only come to Kirrijong to straighten her head and stop her making a foolish mistake? Now Jeremy felt more like a distant memory than the man for whom she had wept

such bitter tears. Instead she had gone and fallen completely in love with Clem.

'I love him,' she whispered to the dying flames. And
somehow acknowledging the truth out loud made her feel
calmer. Perhaps in a couple of months she'd be over Clem,
too, but Olivia knew better. This was the thunderbolt, the
once in a lifetime the world spoke about. He had made love
to her, tapped wells of passions never explored. Opened the
gateway to a nirvana she hadn't realised existed.

Yet how could she love him when she obviously didn't
know him? The man she loved would never have been
kissing her, making love to her, if he had Charlotte, however unwelcome, waiting in the wings. The Clem she knew
would never have asked her out to dinner tonight if he'd
just found out he was to become a father, even if it was,
as she guiltily hoped, a mistake borne out of a brief fling.
The Clem she loved would face the music and to heck with
the consequences. He certainly wouldn't have let Charlotte
speed off alone to Sydney.

Olivia's mind whirred. She simply didn't understand.
Perhaps she had totally misjudged him and fallen in love
with a fantasy figure; maybe it was a classic case of a
patient falling for her doctor, or even just a rebound, to get
her over Jeremy. If that was the case it had worked, but
somehow it had backfired, for the cure was more agonising
than the original disease. None of these excuses gave her
any comfort yet the cold, hard truth was worse. She loved
him, full stop, end of sentence. No ifs or buts, just a whole
load of questions.

Yet did it really matter how she or even Charlotte for
that matter felt? Whatever mess he had got himself into,
Olivia was sure it was a reaction to his grief. Clem wasn't
free to love either of them. His heart belonged to Kathy.
How could she, with all her hang-ups and insecurities, even
begin to compare with a woman who had been so perfect,

trusting and gentle, the antithesis of herself? The only thing Kathy had done wrong had been to die and leave him, and it wasn't as if the poor woman had had a choice about that. Clem had his beloved memories. The ultimate other woman. How do you compete with a ghost?

The dull pain in her stomach spasmed suddenly, making her catch her breath. Olivia lay there in agony for a moment until gradually it eased. She was frozen to the core—perhaps a warm bath would help, she decided.

Watching the bath fill, she leant over to get the bubble bath but the pain in her shoulder intensified. The same nauseous feeling of the morning engulfed her. A spasm in her stomach hit her again, so violent it forced her to her knees, doubling her up on the bathroom floor. Something was wrong, terribly wrong.

Olivia tried to stand but her legs were trembling convulsively. She let out a whimper of pain and terror as she collapsed to the floor. 'Oh, God, help me, please.' She couldn't move, but just lay there, listening to the sound of running water, watching helplessly as the water lapped slowly over the edge of the bath. She had to get help. Had to get to the phone.

Slowly, so slowly, inch by inch, she dragged herself along the floor. The pain was so overwhelming, her muscles so fatigued, she was tempted just to lie there and rest a while, to let the bliss of oblivion descend on her, but an inner instinct, coupled with her training, told her she had to get to the phone. Had to let someone know of her plight. If she gave in, stopped now, then that would be it. The phone cord was just within her grasp and with a final, superhuman effort she stretched her fingers and pulled at the wire, bringing the phone crashing to the floor beside her.

The numbers were swimming before her eyes. Concentrating, trying desperately to focus, she somehow dialled Clem's number, praying she wouldn't get the answering machine or his voice mail.

'Clem speaking.' His voice sounded so calm, so normal. It was hard to believe he was unaware of the agony that was going on at the other end of the line. She tried to call his name but the words wouldn't come, just a tiny gasp. 'This is Clem. Is anybody there?'

She heard the urgency in his voice. Anyone else would have hung up, assuming a wrong number or a hoax call, but as a doctor this terrifying scenario had happened before.

'Clem,' she managed to croak, then inwardly cursed herself. If she had only one word left in her, why waste it telling him his name? But the heavens were listening and thankfully he recognised her voice.

'Livvy, Livvy, is that you?'

The fact he recognised her voice and the knowledge that help was on the way gave her some strength. 'Help me. Please,' she gasped.

'I'm on my way. Just stay there and don't move.'

She couldn't reply. The phone fell out of her limp hand and she lay there motionless on the floor, her breathing rapid and shallow, her skin deathly pale.

Clem frantically grabbed his medical bag and sprinted the short distance to the house, hammering loudly on the door, berating himself for not bringing the spare keys. Racing around to the side of the house, he saw Olivia through the bedroom window. Lying there so pale and still, he thought she must be dead.

In one movement he kicked out the window and opened the latch, desperate to reach her. Beside her in an instant, he saw she was still breathing. The relief was so intense he closed his eyes for a second and struggled to stay calm, then his sheer professionalism took over.

Her pulse was rapid and thready, she was so pale she

was practically exsanguinated. She was obviously, to his trained eye, bleeding out from somewhere.

He rang Betty, misdialling twice.

'G'day. Betty—'

'It's Clem, I'm at Livvy's,' he barked. 'She's critical. 'Organise an ambulance. Tell them we're going to need an airlift as well and that I'll ring with the details as soon as I can. Get Dougie and Ruby to come over now and tell them to bring the emergency blood from the fridge. Betty, hurry or we'll lose her.' He hung up, not waiting for a response, knowing Betty would come good when it mattered.

His training and experience were so ingrained that he treated Olivia methodically, managing to insert a drip into her hopelessly collapsed veins and squeeze lifesaving plasma substitute into her.

Dougie and Ruby arrived, horrified by what they saw. Clem was leaning over Olivia's inert body, oblivious of the pool of water they were both in from the overflowing bath. Dougie ran and turned off the taps as Ruby rushed over with the blood.

'Tell me what to do.'

'Squeeze this drip through. I'll get another IV line started and get the blood into her. Don't move her—she may have fallen. I don't think so but I'll put on a cervical collar to stabilise her neck just in case.'

Betty, with wisdom and insight that defied her scatty nature, arrived then, dragging the portable oxygen cylinder. She was purple from the exertion.

Clem looked at her gratefully. 'Good work Betty.' He slipped a green oxygen mask over Olivia's face, and for a fleeting second her eyes flickered.

Frantically Clem grabbed her hand. 'Livvy, Livvy, it's all going to be fine. We're getting you to hospital now.' In desperation he turned to Ruby. 'Did you see her eyes move? Do you think she can hear?'

And in that second Ruby knew. This wasn't a doctor speaking, this was a frantic man. His face held the same intense pain she had seen two years before. How clearly she remembered the week before Kathy had died, when she had taken her final turn for the worse. Betty had come running then, too, with the oxygen.

She knew then that Clem loved Olivia. They all did. In the months she had been there they had all grown to love and care for this tall, awkward, icy woman who could be so uptight and distant one minute and as vulnerable as a child the next. To see her lying there now, so fragile and helpless... Oh, poor, poor Clem. It must be like waking from a nightmare, only to be plunged straight back into the same hell all over again. He couldn't lose Livvy, too. God couldn't be that cruel.

They all battled with their emotions as they watched her limp body. Dougie coughing noisily to cover up his tears, leaving when the road ambulance arrived to help Bruce prepare a landing pad and light the flares. Ruby stood, trying to stay calm, with her hand on Clem's shoulder as he knelt over Olivia, oblivious of the ambulance officers working around him.

Betty had no such reserve and sobbed openly. 'What happened, Clem? What happened?'

He shook his head slowly. 'I'm pretty sure she's got a ruptured spleen.' His voice was quiet, flat.

'But how?' Betty's hysteria magnified Clem's frozen calm. 'Did she fall?'

'I don't think so. Glandular fever can cause an enlarged spleen. Very rarely it ruptures. I think that's what has happened to Livvy.'

'She will make it, though, won't she? I mean there's things they can do for that?'

Clem shrugged, utterly defeated. 'She needs more blood. She needs surgery, preferably half an hour ago. We've done all we can. It's out of our hands now.'

It took just over an hour for the helicopter to arrive from the base hospital, but it seemed like an eternity. They nearly lost Olivia twice, but just as it all looked hopeless the whirring of the chopper blades seemed to inject some hope into them all. Even Olivia stirred slightly and opened her eyes. She tried to focus on Clem's face, and for all his intuition he mistook the love that somehow shone in her dull, sunken eyes as gratitude for finding her again.

'You're going to be fine. The helicopter's here now.'

She tried to shake her head. That wasn't what she wanted to hear. She wanted him to tell her he loved her, to tell him she loved him, even if it was all too late. She tried to speak, but her mouth wouldn't obey her and only a small gasp came out.

'Hush, Livvy, don't try to talk now. We're all here. Everything will be all right. You have to trust me.'

And despite all the questions left unanswered, all the uncertainty, she did, no matter what.

His beautiful strong face was the last thing she saw as once again oblivion descended.

CHAPTER TEN

THANKFULLY Olivia knew nothing of the helicopter ride to Sydney. In a no-win situation they bypassed the nearer base hospital, after being informed the theatres were in use and the intensive care unit was full. They all knew that if Olivia was to stand any chance of survival she would need the best intensive care available. Bag after bag of blood was squeezed into her *en route,* as Clem knelt on the floor holding her lifeless hands, terrified that if he let go then so might she.

As the city lights neared and the crew expertly prepared her for a speedy exit from the helicopter, he had no choice but to let go. Helpless, he watched as the doors opened and she was rushed away. He wanted to run after her, to shout to them to do their best, that they couldn't lose her, she was far too precious. But his voice was lost in the whirring chopper blades, and all he could do was make his way to the theatre waiting room. He had told them all he could about her condition, all they needed to know.

The fact he loved her didn't matter to them. Everybody was someone's child or parent, lover or friend. All life was valuable, and they would give Olivia their best shot, in the same way he did each day, the same way Olivia did.

While he was sitting in the lonely waiting room, drinking endless cups of revolting machine coffee, a receptionist came in and asked for details. Gently she tried to get information out of him, but all Clem could manage was Olivia's name and current address. He didn't even know her date of birth. He loved this woman with every inch of his being and yet he couldn't even answer the most simple of questions about her.

'I'm sorry,' the receptionist answered, confused when he stalled on her date of birth. I thought you were the next of kin.'

'I'm her doctor.'

'I see,' she answered, still none the wiser. Doctors didn't normally pace the floors and cry openly over their patients, not to the receptionist anyway. 'Is there any way you'd be able get the information?'

He gave her Betty's number—she could pull out Livvy's résumé, 'I want to be informed the minute she gets out of Theatre,' he said, trying to regain his composure.

'Of course, Doctor.' The receptionist turned to walk out.

'She isn't just a patient to me, you know,' Clem called to her departing back, though why he had to justify himself to her he wasn't sure. 'I love her.'

The receptionist turned. She was used to grief. 'So I gathered. I hope things go well.' She smiled sympathetically. 'She's got the best surgical team on tonight. If it was my loved one that was sick, they're whom I'd want to be operating. Well, from what I hear anyway.' She blushed, suddenly remembering she was talking to a doctor.

'Thank you,' Clem said simply, glad that even though it had been to a relative stranger, he had at least acknowledged his love for Olivia.

The wait was interminable. Never had he felt so helpless. He knew, and yet couldn't bear to think of, the battle that would be going on in the sterile theatre. The wheels of bureaucracy would have swung into motion and by now Jeremy would have been contacted.

Jeremy. He had never met him, only spoken to him on the telephone, and yet he hated him with a passion. Hated him for causing Livvy so much pain. The bastard hadn't even had the decency to marry her yet he was listed on her résumé as the emergency contact. He was probably on his way now. Clem just hoped he had stopped to inform her parents in England.

His heart went out to them and the terrible events that would unfold when they picked up the phone and heard the devastating news. Would they all come? Was he going to meet the people who had made up Livvy's world before she'd come to Kirrijong? Beautiful, complicated Livvy.

Sitting in the bland waiting room, the television playing an old black and white film, he stared blankly at the screen. The film ended and a newsbreak followed. How could it not be the headlines? Why were they talking about some attempted bank robbery when his beloved Livvy was fighting just to stay alive?

Standing as he saw someone dressed in theatre blues approach, Clem tried to interpret the grim, weary face before she spoke, desperate for a clue.

'Dr Clemson.' She held out her hand and Clem shook it. 'I'm May Fordyce, the consultant surgeon on tonight. I operated on your patient.' The formalities over, Clem knew the news was coming and for a second he didn't want to hear it, terrified in case Livvy hadn't made it.

'She's more than a patient.' It was only fair to warn her. He didn't want the details to be too graphic.

Miss Fordyce nodded briefly. 'Your initial diagnosis was correct. She had indeed ruptured her spleen.'

'Is she…?'

'No,' she replied, but there was no jubilation in her voice. 'She made it through Theatre, but really I'm amazed she did. She's lost a lot of blood and she's had a massive transfusion. We're worried about disseminated intravascular coagulation.'

She waited for a response, for some recognition to flicker in Clem's eyes. Then she realised she wasn't speaking to another doctor but a scared and desperate fellow human being, and gently spelt the grim news out.

'You and the air ambulance team did a marvellous job of resuscitating her with fluids. When she arrived in Theatre we performed an urgent splenectomy. She made it through but she's critical. She's extremely weak and the volume of the blood transfusion is causing a lot of concern. We're having a lot of problems with her blood coagulation and we're trying to prevent her from going into renal failure. The next forty-eight hours will be crucial.'

A hundred questions flashed into Clem's mind, but for now the answers were immaterial. The need to see her, to touch her, surpassed everything. 'Can I see her?'

'They're just settling her into Intensive Care. I'll let them know you're waiting.'

For ten minutes he was allowed to see her. Just ten precious minutes. Gently he held her hand and told her all the things he had meant to say but somehow had never quite managed. Ten precious minutes where he told her just how much he cared and how happy she had made him, maybe without even realising it, and that he was sorry, so sorry that he couldn't have done more. Could she hear? There was no way of knowing but he knew that he had to say it now, for it might be his only chance.

Lovingly he arranged her long red curls. Walking over to the sink, he moistened a hand towel and wiped away a streak of blood that had splashed her cheek. 'You'd have me for breakfast if I left it,' he whispered gently into her ear.

'We need to do some obs.' The sister hovered by the bed. 'And she needs to rest.'

'I won't get in the way, I'll just sit here, if you don't mind.'

The Sister hesitated, not sure of this situation. Was he her doctor, friend or lover? Whatever he was, he seemed nice, and she felt it only fair to warn him. 'Her fiancé has flown in from Melbourne, he just arrived. Miss Fordyce is talking to him now. I expect he may want to sit with her.'

'Her ex-fiancé,' Clem stated bluntly but it was no use. In just one short sentence he had been relegated. For a moment Clem had the craziest notion to pick Olivia up and just run. He didn't want to leave, didn't want Jeremy or anyone else invading, but he didn't have any say here. And the hardest part to take was that he wasn't sure whether Livvy would have wanted him to.

Olivia was the talk of the intensive care staffroom. Two doctors in love with the same woman. One blond, with film-star good looks and a slick charm, who flirted with the staff and praised them for their efforts. The other dark and ruggedly handsome, but moody and picky, questioning every test result, checking the obs charts. Both as different as chalk and cheese, each with a bristling loathing of the other.

Over the weekend Olivia mercifully gradually stabilised and, defying all odds, by Monday was ready to be moved to a small side ward on the high-dependency unit, an array of wires and monitors still adorning her, each relaying its vital messages to the nurses' station. It was here that she started to drift back to the world. Her eyes heavy, she opened them slowly, flinching at the late afternoon sun that flooded the bed. Her throat felt dry and sore, as if it had been roughly sandpapered, her arm, strapped to the intra-venous giving set, heavy and unfamiliar.

She felt a hand on her head and a familiar voice welcoming her back to the world.

'Darling, it's all right. You're coming to. Take it easy. You're in hospital but I'm here now and everything's going to be all right.'

'Be careful what you wish for—it might come true.' It seemed that Clem's prediction had finally come to fruition, for there, coming into focus, his blond hair white in the fluorescent light's glare, his face smiling down at her, was Jeremy. Battling with nausea and pain, she tried to make some sense, to orientate herself, the numerous drips and machines all so familiar yet so alien now they were attached to her own body.

'Jeremy?' she croaked.

'Yes, it's me. I'm here now and I'm never going to let you go again.'

'What happened?' she asked feebly.

'Your spleen ruptured. It would have been enlarged from the glandular fever. It's very rare but it happened. I just feel so guilty.'

He had a lot to feel guilty about. Olivia could recall that much.

'I should have come and got you sooner, never left you in the middle of nowhere with an out-of-date bush quack. I'm sorry, darling.'

Olivia didn't respond. Instead, she lay there, trying to piece it all together. With the benefit of hindsight, everything made sense now. That niggling pain in her shoulder, the dizzy spells. Her medical mind realised they had been signs she had been bleeding internally. The abdominal pain, which she had just assumed to be food poisoning, had, in fact, been her dangerously enlarged spleen leaking slowly, with the potential to rupture at any time. But with hindsight it was easy to diagnose. It had been no one's fault. She could hardly point the finger at Clem when she had point-blank refused to let him examine her, and she had avoided a proper examination with Dr Humphreys. Anyway, surely no one would have envisaged what was, after all, an extremely rare complication of a common viral disease.

So now here she lay, with Jeremy playing the part of the concerned fiancé to perfection, saying all the things that a few months ago she would have longed to hear. It was almost farcical. A more dramatic reunion she couldn't have dreamed of. Totally inappropriately, and to Jeremy's absolute horror, Olivia started to laugh. He jumped back as if he'd been shot.

'She's confused. It must be all the pethidine you've loaded her up with,' he barked at the entering nurse, the Mister Nice Guy routine quickly starting to evaporate.

Olivia drifted in and out of consciousness. Once when she opened her eyes she saw Clem gazing down at her. He looked exhausted. The tiny lines around his eyes seemed deeper and they shone with tears. She wanted so badly to talk to tell him how she felt, but she had just had a shot of painkiller and its effects were starting to take hold, the words coming out muddled and confused.

'Shh. Not now,' was all he said, and gently placed a finger to her lips. 'You rest.'

When she awoke she was sure she must have dreamed the encounter, for there beside her was Jeremy. 'Hello darling. You've been out for hours.'

'What time is it?'

'Nearly seven. I was just waiting for you to wake up. I'm going to head off to the hotel and get some dinner. It's been a long day.' So he was complaining now. It wasn't as if she had asked him to come. 'But I've got some good news. I spoke with your surgeon and she's going to arrange your transfer to Melbourne in a couple of days. Get you back on home ground and amongst familiar faces. That's just what you need.'

'And you wouldn't have to take any time off work,' she added sarcastically.

'Olivia, don't let's fight. I thought that was all behind us now.' He kissed her haphazardly on the cheek. 'I'll let the sister know you're awake—they want to change your dressing. I'd just be in the way. Goodnight, darling. I'll be here first thing.'

Olivia nodded feebly. She had to tell him he was wasting his time, but right now she couldn't deal with a scene. It could wait till tomorrow morning.

Expertly, Sister Jay changed her dressing. She was middle-aged and incredibly efficient, with a brisk, rather old-school bedside manner. Olivia lay there, staring at the ceiling, thinking of what she would say to Jeremy, as the sister completed her task and deftly tidied up the bedclothes. After checking Olivia's pulse, she gently patted her hand and for a moment her face softened.

'You're looking a lot better. You were pretty crook there for a while, gave us all a fright.' Bustling out with the trolley, she returned a moment later. 'Are you up to a visitor?'

Olivia nodded. What did Jeremy want now? But standing in the doorway was Clem. He looked as tired and as awful as she felt.

'You look like it should be you in a hospital bed.' She smiled.

'They've put me up in the doctors' quarters. It's not bad, but I'd forgotten just how noisy they could be. There was a wild party on Saturday night—it went on till four a.m.'

'Did you go?'

He knew she was teasing but he played along. 'Just for a couple of hours, but the girls were awful and the beer was warm.' He came and sat gently on the bed, careful not to make any sudden movement that might cause her pain. Tentatively he took her hand and it felt so natural she left it there. 'I've actually spent the last few days and nights loitering around the corridor, waiting for Jeremy to leave. I'm surprised I haven't been arrested. I needed to see you were all right for myself. I came in once but you were out of it.'

So he had been here after all. It hadn't been a dream.

'I know what time it is, roughly to the nearest hour, but what day is it?'

Clem smiled at her question. 'It's Tuesday.'

'And you're still here. Why?' Suddenly she remembered that Charlotte was in Sydney. Of all the stupid things to ask. He had been coming here anyway.

'That's what I wanted to talk to you about.'

It was all too much—she simply wasn't up to hearing it. 'Not now, please.' Pulling her hand away, she turned her head towards the window and stared at the bland beige curtains.

'You're tired, of course. You need your rest. Can I come and see you again?'

What was the point? But somehow she needed to hear some answers, no matter how much it hurt. She had to find out all the details, but not tonight. 'Jeremy's coming in the morning,' she said.

'I see,' Clem answered, and she could hear the defeat in his voice.

'But he won't be staying long,' she added. 'Perhaps around lunchtime?'

Clem nodded. 'I'd like that.' Gently he stroked her cheek, but she couldn't take it, too scared she might crumble. Instead, she turned her face back to the curtains.

'I really thought I was going to lose you,' he murmured.

For a second she wavered, desperate to feel his arms around her, but common sense won.

'Thank you for saving me,' she said tonelessly, and then felt awful, for despite everything else this man had saved her life. She turned and looked at him. 'Thank you,' she said with more conviction.

Clem gave her a quizzical look. 'I'll let you rest. Till tomorrow, then.'

Olivia awoke next morning to the sound of the breakfast trolley. The 'Hourly sips' sign above her bed had been replaced by 'Free fluids'. Never had a weak cup of insipid hospital tea tasted so good. Gradually the tubes and drips had been taken down and all that was left to show of her near brush with death was one small drain, a dressing on her stomach and one peripheral intravenous line.

Being a nurse had some advantages. She was now officially well enough to be moved down into the shared ward away from the nurses' station, but while the ward was relatively quiet they left her in the side room. Replacing the cup in the saucer, she contemplated whether to ask for a second, but knew she shouldn't push it. Strange how the simplest things gave the most pleasure. The orderly came and pulled back the curtains.

'You've got the best view in the hospital here.' A huge gum nut tree filled almost the entire window. 'Enjoy it. When you get moved it's the furnace to look at.'

With mounting trepidation she dreaded Jeremy's arrival. She didn't have to wait long.

'Morning, darling, you look better.' Jeremy waltzed in, looking as immaculate as ever. 'I might even talk to Miss Fordyce and see if they can transfer you today. It's not as if they're doing much for you now and, anyway, I'll be in the ambulance with you. I am a consultant surgeon after all.'

Olivia listened, silently fuming. Jeremy just assumed he could pick up and carry on exactly where he had left off. Didn't she have any say in this?

'Actually, I won't be going back to Melbourne.' The words tumbled out and Olivia held her breath.

'Why?' he answered, nonplussed. 'Were you ill in the night? Is there something they haven't told me?'

'No, Jeremy. It's something you didn't ask me.'

He stared at her, completely confused.

'You just assume that I've forgiven you. You just assume

that I'm coming home with you. Well, I'm sorry, it's not that straightforward.'

He was over to the bed in a flash. 'We've been over that. It's all over with Lydia. You know how sorry I am.'

She almost felt sorry for him. He was so spoilt, so used to unquestioning adoration that it hadn't seriously entered his head that she might not come back to him.

'It's not about whether it's over with Lydia or not. It's the fact it happened in the first place. Jeremy, I'm sorry, I just can't forgive and forget—it's over.'

Jeremy shook his head. 'No, Olivia. Don't do this.'

A student nurse appeared and started to take her blood pressure. Intimidated to be in the room with such a senior nurse and doctor, she kept blowing the cuff up too tight.

'For heaven's sake don't they teach you anything in nursing school?' Jeremy snapped.

'She's doing fine.' Olivia smiled reassuringly.

Once they were alone again, he begged her to reconsider. 'Please, Olivia, I've changed, I promise. Once we're married you'll see—'

'No! *You* did this to us, Jeremy. I would have always been faithful, I would have supported you in anything, but I can't get over your affair. It's just too big. It's over, Jeremy.' She saw the tears well in his eyes and she knew he was devastated.

'You might change your mind,' he begged.

'I won't,' she replied firmly.

Jeremy shook his head. 'There's someone else. That Jake Clemson. I knew it. What's been going on?'

'This has nothing to do with him,' Olivia answered sincerely, because it didn't.

'I don't believe you,' Jeremy stated bluntly. 'Are you two having an affair?'

'No,' she answered truthfully, though such was her honesty that she told him the painful truth. 'But we did sleep together, once. It meant far more to me than it did to him—he's involved with someone else. And, anyway, this has nothing to do with Clem. It's about us.'

'Oh, I'd say he had a fair bit to do with it,' he retorted angrily, then the rage in him seemed to die as he begged her to reconsider. 'Please, Olivia,' he implored, but his pleas fell on deaf ears. It was simply too late.

Even her name sounded strange now. He was the only person who had called her 'Olivia' in ages. Even 'Livvy' was underlined on all her medical notes, a legacy of her admission when Clem had attempted to give her details. The Olivia Jeremy had known didn't exist any more. In her place was a stronger person, who would fight for her ideals.

'I'm sorry, Jeremy.' And something about the certainty in her voice made him finally realise she meant it. For a second the anger re-emerged and flashed over his face, but it soon subsided into a look of total defeat.

'I'm sorry, too, Olivia. Sorry for everything.' He stood there for a moment, taking in the enormity of the situation. Finally realising what he had lost. 'Do you want me to go?'

She nodded, biting her lip to stop the tears.

'Can I ring in a couple of days? See how you're getting on?'

Again she nodded and managed a faint smile. 'That would be nice.' She meant it. Hopefully they could go about this in a civilised way, remain friends even.

He left then, and Olivia turned her face and wept into the pillow, knowing how awful he felt, knowing that despite Jeremy's actions he had loved her, but just not enough.

Wiping away the tears, she let out a gasp. The old gum was full of bright reds and greens. A flock of rosellas was feasting on the tree. For a second she was transported back to Kirrijong, sitting by the tiny stream, pondering her future. So what now? Where did she go from here? She couldn't go back to Kirrijong. It would be torture, seeing Clem every day, knowing he was with Charlotte. Watching her blossom, ripe with pregnancy, heavy with Clem's child.

For a second she considered going back to Melbourne, but only for a second. Her time there was finished. It would take a stronger person than her to return there and work alongside her ex-fiancé. She could even return to England. Now that the panic was over her parents had rung, saying they would wait a couple of weeks till they flew out. Although longing to see them, she was actually grateful for the reprieve. She wasn't exactly bursting with places they could stay!

The uncertainty of her future was a problem that for now could wait. First she had to get this morning over with. Saying goodbye to Jeremy had been hard, but she had already expended most of her grief about their break-up. But saying goodbye to Clem, that was another matter altogether.

Sister Jay appeared in the doorway, carrying a familiar stainless-steel kidney dish.

'Time for your pethidine injection, and when that's taken effect I was wondering if you'd mind if Hannah, the student, gave you your blanket bath. She needs to be assessed, but she goes to pieces if anyone watches her. I thought she might feel less threatened if I left her to it, and perhaps you could let me know how she does?'

Olivia agreed, though she doubted whether the poor girl would be any less intimidated after Jeremy's outburst.

'That's fine, but I don't want the injection, thanks.'

Sister Jay checked Olivia's prescription chart.

'Are you sure? It's been a while since your last one and you're still written up for regular analgesia. The physiotherapist is coming later to sit you out of bed, which is going to hurt. Don't try to be brave. You've been through a lot.'

But Olivia was adamant. 'Really, I'd rather not.'

Sister Jay shrugged and left.

Her stomach hurt, it hurt like hell, but the pain was nothing compared to seeing Clem for what was to be the last time. She wanted a clear head for that. Wanted to be sure she understood everything he said. It was also imperative to her that she memorised his face. If she was going to live the rest of her life on dreams, she at least wanted them to be accurate.

Hannah clattered in, blushing furiously as she pushed a huge trolley laden with jugs and various pieces of linen and toiletries.

'I've come to give you a wash,' she ventured nervously.

Olivia's heart went out to the young woman. Nurses hated looking after other nurses at the best of times, and poor Hannah had drawn the short straw. Wincing with pain, Olivia leant over and opened the bedside drawer. Nothing, not even a comb.

Hannah set to work and Olivia lay there, pretending not to notice the tepid water splashing her face and trickling into her ears. Lying on her side as Hannah gingerly washed her back, she eyed the goodies on the trolley. Fern-scented talcum powder, pink carbolic soap—hardly the stuff to bring Clem to his knees. Not, she reminded herself firmly, that that was on the agenda.

'Just stay there. I forgot to get the lanolin cream for your pressure areas.' Hannah hastily covered her with a towel.

'Just a moment,' Olivia called. 'Hannah, I know it's awful for you, having to bathe me, and you're doing marvellously,' she added as the young girl's eyes widened, anticipating criticism. 'But what I really need, more than anything else, is to feel human again. Is there anything in the store cupboard that doesn't reek of disinfectant? And is there any chance of borrowing someone's mirror? I know I look a sight and obviously I didn't bring anything with me.'

Hannah started to smile. 'Are you expecting a visitor?' she asked perceptively.

It was Olivia's turn to blush. 'Well, sort of.'

'Then we'd better get you sorted. I shan't be long.'

Hannah returned moments later with her own make-up bag. 'When Sister Jay asks, I gave you the best blanket bath ever.'

'Absolutely. The best,' Olivia agreed as she rummaged through the bag. They even shared the same taste in perfume.

Hannah combed the knots out of her hair, while Olivia shakily managed a touch of mascara on her lashes and a dash of blusher. She knew she must still look awful but it was a huge improvement. Hannah had found what was probably the only hospital gown that actually had all the ties and didn't constantly fall off your shoulders. A quick spray of perfume and she felt close to human again.

'Thank you so much.'

'No worries.' Hannah smiled, confident now the barriers had been broken down. 'I'll just do your obs and then I'll leave you.'

For all her inexperience Hannah wasn't stupid. As she took Olivia's pulse, Clem arrived. Feeling her patient's heart rate suddenly accelerate, she knew it had nothing to with the operation. She quickly wrote down the obs and with an almost imperceptible wink she left them alone, gently closing the door behind her.

'How on earth do you manage it?' Clem laughed. 'You've been to hell and back and you still manage to come out looking gorgeous.'

'Hardly gorgeous,' Olivia replied lightly, 'but I certainly do feel much better today.'

'I've just been talking to some fans of yours.'

'Who?'

'Lorna and Pete. Our namesake is on the next floor.'

'Our namesake?'

'Baby Oliver Jake. He's doing very well.' Olivia leant back on the pillow.

'Oliver Jake,' she repeated. 'They didn't have to do that. He's doing well, you say?'

'Exceptionally. It's still very early days and there's a long way to go, of course, but all the signs look good. They want to pop down and visit you, but I said to give it a couple of days.'

Olivia nodded. Finally some good news.

'That would be nice. I expect I shan't be inundated with visitors. When are you going back?'

He sat down on the bed, achingly close. She so badly wanted to reach out and touch him, but kept her hands firmly beside her.

'That depends. I've managed to arrange a locum.'

'Dr Humphreys? Are you sure that's such a good idea?'

Clem shook his head.

'No, I've actually hired someone who's seriously considering the job of running the hospital. It's worked out well. It gives him a chance to see whether it's what he wants to do, and if it is, he can have his say in the final touches to the hospital.' He looked closely at her, watching her reaction as realisation struck.

'But I thought you'd be running it,' she said slowly, utterly confused.

'I know you did. That's what I've been trying to talk to you about.'

Her mind raced.

'I was actually coming to Sydney at the weekend to have dinner with an old friend and colleague, Craig Pryde—though I wasn't expecting to travel by helicopter,' he added.

Olivia stared dumbly at him.

'You know how I missed paeds?' he said gently.

Speechless, she nodded.

'Well, I've known Craig for many years. He's a paediatric consultant here at this hospital. He's going to be retiring next year, and his senior registrar just resigned unexpectedly. He's asked me to consider the position. When Craig retires I'd probably be offered the consultant's position. It's a great opportunity.'

Agonisingly slowly, realisation dawned. His future was moving on and she hadn't even been in the picture. Of course he would come here. Charlotte would never stay permanently in Kirrijong.

Olivia's pledge to concentrate and remember every word quickly went out of the window. Fighting just to hold back the tears as Clem went into detail, she was unable to take in the rest of what he was saying.

'So what do you think?' Clem concluded.

Olivia swallowed hard and forced her eyes to meet his, determined to retain at least a shred of dignity. 'It's a bit of a shock, I admit, but if you're sure it's what you want then go for it.'

She tried to sound pleased for him, to inject some enthusiasm, but it was asking too much. Maybe she should have had the pethidine after all.

'But this isn't just about me. I need to know how you feel.'

'Why?' she asked simply. Her feelings didn't come into it. Shouldn't he be having this conversation with Charlotte?

'Livvy, haven't you heard a word I've been saying?'

Olivia shook her head dumbly.

'I wanted to discuss it with you but it all happened so quickly and we never did seem to get around to having that talk. Then you were taken so ill. I've been trying to ask you to come with me. I know you've got Jeremy to consider and I didn't want to interfere, but I can't sit on the fence any longer. I know we haven't had much time together but surely you feel it, too?' His words tumbled out and for once he wasn't the strong, confident Clem she knew.

It was Olivia who spoke calmly. 'Jeremy and I are finished. We have been for ages. It just took a while for him to get used to the idea,' she said.

Hope flickered in his eyes then faded as he saw the look of confusion on her face. 'This surely can't be that much of a shock. You must know some of how I feel? I've been trying to tell you for long enough.'

'I know about Charlotte. The baby, I mean.' She held her breath.

'How?' he asked, bewildered.

'I found the pregnancy test card.'

'But that's got nothing to do with us.'

Olivia put her hands up to her ears, trying to block out the sound of his voice. She couldn't bear it. Couldn't bear to hear the excuses and lies. 'Oh, I'd say it had rather a lot to do with us, or maybe I'm just being old-fashioned. But I still think a baby needs a father. I thought we'd at least agree on that.' She stared defiantly at him, waiting for the excuses, the pathetic attempt at an explanation. She was stunned to see his look of incredulous shock change to one of anger—not the usual flashes of temper she had grown used to but a black rage that descended on his tired face. And what was even more disturbing was that she saw the disappointment in his eyes.

'You think it's my baby?' His lips were white, set in a thin line. 'How could you think that of me?' he rasped. 'How could you, Livvy? Is that the kind of guy you take me for?'

This wasn't a reaction she had anticipated. Agonisingly, realisation dawned. She had made the biggest mistake of her life.

'What else was I to think?' she answered defensively.

'Obviously you didn't think. You just assumed. Hell, I know you've been hurt, but how dare you tar me with the same brush as Jeremy?'

'I didn't want to,' she pleaded, 'but it seemed so obvious. Ruby said—'

'I don't care what Ruby said,' he replied sharply, trying desperately not to shout. 'I told you never to listen to her. Why didn't you ask me?'

'I did. I asked if there'd ever been anyone since Kathy.'

He looked at her perplexed. 'Go on.'

'And you said, "What do you think?"' she responded lamely, knowing how inadequate her excuse sounded.

'So it was easier to assume that I was sleeping around. "What do you think?" "What do you think?" His voice was rising now. 'My heavens, couldn't you see what I was trying to tell you? Since Kathy died I haven't been able to focus, let alone look at another woman—until you, that is. That night when I came to your door drunk I was terrified. Terrified because I knew I'd fallen in love and you seemed so wrapped up in Jeremy. Terrified because I finally knew it was time to move on.'

'But you used to go out with Charlotte. Surely you can see why I thought—'

'Oh, please.' He stopped her flood of excuses. 'One town dance fifteen years ago does not constitute a relationship, unless, of course, you're listening to gossip,' he said nastily. Then, seeing her start to cry, he let up.

'Charlotte's baby has nothing to do with me,' he finally explained, 'save the fact it will be my niece or nephew. She's got herself mixed up with Joshua, my brother, and I've been acting as an unwilling go-between. She's here in Sydney now, hoping he'll relent and marry her. The poor kid, it will probably turn out an absolute horror with those two spoilt brats as parents.'

What could she say? To have been so terribly wrong.

'Sorry' just didn't seem enough. All this time he had been trying to tell her he loved her while she had been thinking the worst.

'So you never slept with Charlotte?' She hesitated, taking in the enormity of what Clem was telling her. 'I was the first since Kathy.' Their one magical night together was suddenly magnified. She felt privileged and also painfully guilty, for Clem had been right—they *had* rushed things. She should have known that it had been his first time since Kathy. She should have been aware that, despite the joy and tenderness they had shared when they'd made love, there would have also been some pain and recrimination for Clem. No wonder he had seemed detached after they'd made love. No wonder he had needed to talk. It was something she should have known.

Seeing Olivia lying there utterly desolated, Clem felt his anger evaporate. This was hurting her as much as him, and the last thing he wanted was to cause her more pain.

'Yes, Livvy, you were the first since Kathy, and I hope the last. I can never go through this again. I've loved you from the moment I met you. I wasn't looking—in fact, I nearly ran a mile—but I couldn't escape it. It's just taken a while for me to get used to the idea. I was so sure I was going to spend the rest of my life alone, and then you came along. For the first time in ages there was a reason to get up in the morning, a face I wanted to see, and someone's opinion I wanted to hear. And it terrified me.'

Olivia lay there, slowly taking in what he was telling her.

'I know it's asking a lot for you to move your life here so I can chase a dream job. And before you even think it, it's not a "consultant's wife" I'm after. It's you, Livvy, and it always will be. I know you're going to need some time to think about it but, please, hear me out first. I can be so bloody-minded sometimes and I know I can be unreasonable, but I truly love you. I'd never hurt you.' He ran a shaking hand through his hair.

She felt like the judge and jury listening to the closing argument.

'I want to marry you, take care of you and show you that love can be good. But, Livvy, if you can't trust me, if you're unable to believe in all we could be together, we should forget it now. I can't live under the shadow of doubt—it's not fair on either of us.'

And for once there weren't any questions that needed answers. Everything Olivia needed to know was there in his eyes.

She took a tentative step off the cliff edge she had been balancing on for so long. Away from the uncertainty of the past and into the future.

'I don't need time to think about it.'

The jury was back; the verdict was in.

He stood there quite still, and she saw the apprehension in his eyes disappear as she held out her hands to him. In a second she was in his arms where she belonged, where she felt safe and loved. Whatever the future held, it would be with Clem beside her to share in the good times and catch her when she fell.

His strong arms pulled her into his ever-loving embrace and his mouth, tentatively at first, met hers, and then he kissed her with such a depth and passion she thought he might never stop. Delighting in each other's touch, neither heard as Sister Jay entered. She coughed loudly and Clem reluctantly let Olivia go.

'I didn't realise you still had visitors,' she said in a pro-prietorial voice. 'Miss Morrell should really be resting.'

Clem stood up like a scolded schoolboy.

'I've just had a call from Admin,' Sister Jay continued. 'It would seem there's some mix-up with your paperwork.

With your next of kin being in England, whom should we put as your emergency contact?'

Olivia caught the glimpse of mischief in the elderly woman's eyes and turned her face to Clem as he sat back on the bed beside her.

'That would be me, Sister,' he said, taking Olivia's hands. 'Dr Jake Clemson, Ms Morrell's fiancé, assuming, of course, that she'll have me.'

Olivia, suddenly oblivious of their audience, answered him with a kiss.

Leaving them to it, Sister Jay gently closed the door and, sitting at her desk, started to fill in the form.

'Well?' said Hannah impatiently to her senior.

With a smile Sister Jay put down her pen. 'I think we can take it as a yes.'

with whoever next of kin being in England, where should we put as your emergency contact?'

Olivia caught the glimpse of interest in the older woman's eyes and guessed her face no doubt as he face had been the last to fade.

'Fine, would be the 'Sister,' he said, using Olivia's name. 'In Jake Chessell's? W- Moore's name, meaning of course, that she'd have me.'

Olivia pushed, thoughts of Jake stopping, aware of him with her patient.

Leaving them to it, Sister Lovegood closed the door and paused at the desk, paused to fill in the form.

'WHY,' said Hannah incongruity to her senior.

With a smile sister Joy put down her pen. 'I think we can talk now over.'

OUTBACK FIRE

by

Margaret Way

Margaret Way takes great pleasure in her work and works hard at her pleasure. She enjoys tearing off to the beach with her family at weekends, loves haunting galleries and auctions and is completely given over to French champagne 'for every possible joyous occasion'. She was born and educated in the river city of Brisbane, Australia, and now lives within sight and sound of beautiful Moreton Bay.

Don't miss Margaret Way's brand new novels
THE CATTLEMAN (part of TO MUM, WITH
LOVE available in March)
& THE CATTLE BARON'S BRIDE
on sale in May 2006, from Tender Romance™!

PROLOGUE

THEY rode out at dawn. Their mission was specific. To hunt down "Psycho" the wild bull camel that was harassing the herd and attacking anybody unfortunate enough to come on it unawares. The situation had become so dangerous it was now necessary to kill the beast. Only a few days before one of the stockmen mustering clean skins on the desert fringe had encountered the raging animal and paid the price. Psycho had attacked without provocation kicking the stockman in the chest. The consequences had been serious. The man had to be airlifted to hospital and was still in a critical condition. He would have been dead only for the arrival of three of his mates who had startled the ferocious beast into slewing off.

When the rogue came on season, for it was the male camel instead of the female that came on heat, Psycho would pose even more of a threat. He had a fearful reputation for attacking other male camels with passionate fury, his strength and wildness driving them away to leave him with a harem usually twenty or more females he jealously guarded and impregnated.

Of recent times Psycho had taken to making open-mouthed dives at the tribal people who crisscrossed the station on walkabout. McFarlane had been informed of the attacks. His people were frightened and wanted protection.

Camels weren't indigenous to Australia. They and their Afghan handlers had been imported into the country in the early days of settlement to transport goods all over the dry trackless regions of the Outback; camels were ideal beasts

of burden in just such conditions. Their wild descendants,
some quarter of a million and they lived several decades,
were a dreadful menace. They roamed the desert from one
end to the other doing considerable damage to the fragile
environment. McFarlane tolerated them. By now they were
part of the Outback and there was a certain romance to the
sight of them silhouetted on top of a sand dune at sunset.
Unfortunately the time had come for Psycho to be destroyed before he turned killer.

Six of them made up the party that morning. McFarlane,
his overseer, Chas Branagan, Garry Dingo, the station's
finest tracker, two of his best stockmen and the boy, Luke.
Fourteen years old but already judged by the others to be
a man. The boy stood six feet, a superb athlete, with an
excellent head on his shoulders. He was a fine shot, a talent
he had been born with, as well as having extraordinary
endurance for his age. In fact he was well on his way to
becoming a consummate bushman like his father, Chas.
He had the same remarkable sight, hearing and sense of
smell. Skills that would be needed on the hunt.

McFarlane realised he had become very fond of the boy.
Indeed he was coming to look on him as the son he might
have had. The tragedy was his wife; the one woman he
had ever truly loved had died in childbirth leaving him
with the precious legacy of a daughter. His beautiful
Storm. While her mother slipped prematurely out of life,
Storm had come into the world at the height of one of the
fiercest tempests that had ever passed over his land.

Tragedy and triumph. Sometimes the two went hand in
hand. Like Storm and high drama. Storm had never been
an easy child. Tempestuous and outspoken she spent her
young life rebelling against his dictates when he had only
put them in place to protect her. Freedom was what she
wanted. Total freedom. The right to roam the station at

will. "Like Luke does." That was the catch cry "Like Luke does."

There were always outbursts against Luke. Big flare-ups of jealousy and resentment.

"You treat him like a son! He's *not* your son. He's *not* my brother."

How many times had he heard that? Storm fought his affection for Luke every step of the way. She overplayed her little princess and the pauper act most times the two of them were together. Luke being Luke, was gentle and tolerant with her, unfazed by her histrionics.

As for Storm, the light of his life, didn't she know her father adored her? When Storm was sweet, she was very, very sweet, irresistible like her mother. If she'd had her way she'd have joined them this morning. Imagine! A girl barely twelve, even if she could ride all day. Storm couldn't accept the confines of her femininity. She lived in a man's world and she wasn't about to come to terms with it. His difficult little Storm. How could it be otherwise? This was a child reared without a mother's gentling touch.

They skirted around the lignum that rose up like jungle walls, the party dividing up as they rode into the desert, ringed by heat waves that danced in the blinding glare. No tracks so far but then they had to contend with the rising wind that wiped them out almost as soon as they were made. Such a place of desolation this no man's land! The great flights of budgerigar that flashed green and gold overhead and the marauding hawks were almost the only living things. The grazing cattle had stripped the perennial cover from the slopes here and the blood-red sand moved at will.

Sand and spinifex.

This year of drought, even the spinifex wasn't so dense. Other years it covered the sand like a bright golden carpet.

After two hours or more of fruitless search the party broke up, frustrated but not willing to give up. Psycho should have been spottable but he wasn't. Wild animals had a way of disappearing into the landscape. Chas and two of the stockmen took off for the low eroded foothills, shimmering in the quicksilver light of the mirage. McFarlane, Luke and Matt, the other stockman, worked the undulating dunes, so red they were alight. It was getting hotter and hotter, the sun scorching out of a cloudless blue sky. So hot in fact McFarlane knew he was losing concentration. Not yet fifty he had lived a hard, dangerous life, and it was taking its toll. Broken ribs, a bad leg injury years back in Vietnam that still gave him a lot of pain especially if he was too long in the saddle. A tired man became careless. Matt had dropped back, skirting the mounds of dried up springs. He rode ahead with Luke a few feet from his shoulder.

Everything was silence. Infinity. The blood-red dunes ran on forever in great parallel waves; the tall seed stems of the spinifex called up glittering aboriginal spears. Nothing to signal the presence of the camel as it watched them, its shaggy, dull ginger coat an excellent camouflage. It stood within its crude shelter of desert acacias, its dark crested humped outline hidden by the thick gnarled trunks and weight of branches. McFarlane saw the wild camel as his quarry. Psycho in a particularly vicious mood saw McFarlane as his.

With extraordinary cunning the rogue camel waited for the optimum moment to break cover. It gathered itself for the charge then galloped directly at McFarlane with terrifying speed, its hump grown massive over the years, swaying, drumming through its nostrils its blind rage at the threat to its territory. In the crystal clear air of the desert the sound was deafening, travelling far. McFarlane slumped half sideways in the saddle trying to ease the pain in his leg, felt the hairs at the back of his neck stand up. For an instant he was deadly afraid then he wheeled his horse sharply but that stout hearted animal quailed in the face of the camel's blazing charge. It reared then thundered to the ground throwing the unsettled McFarlane out of the saddle and onto the sun-baked earth.

The boy, Luke, looked on in horror, a cry caught in his throat. For a split second he was frozen, then all thoughts of his own safety left him. He was ice cool, bracing himself for what lay ahead. This wasn't anything he couldn't handle. Every lost second almost certainly meant tragedy. There was only time for one shot. It had to be perfect. Clean. Humane. Conclusive.

Eye to the sight, finger on the trigger Luke waited…waited…his handsome young face strong and resolute. He was already beginning to squeeze the trigger. The camel was slobbering hugely, saturated in foaming fury. Its rank smell pervaded the air.

The shot cracked away echoing across the desert and bouncing off the boulders strewn about like giants' marbles. The camel died in mid-flight. It crashed to the ground, thrashed for an aftermoment then rolled motionless to one side, its body making a deep impression in the sand.

Urgently Luke dismounted and rushed to McFarlane's prone figure. Perfectly in control one minute, he was now uncertain. Anxiously he went down on one knee, eyes checking. ''Mr. McFarlane?'' he cried hoarsely. Every last man, woman and child on the vast station depended on this man. To many of them he was their guardian.

McFarlane lay for a moment, racked in pain and panting, thick dark hair and deeply tanned skin clogged with red dust, his grey akubra lying a foot away. Eventually, with air in his lungs, he managed a quiet ''I'm fine, boy. Fine. No need to worry. That was a close one.''

Luke nodded, shoving his hat to the back of his dark auburn head. ''Any closer and you'd have been trampled.'' Now the danger was over, his voice broke with emotion.

''No way! Not with you around. You're a man and I'm proud of you.''

McFarlane heaved himself into a sitting position, wincing as he reached for his wide-brimmed hat. He settled it on his head, then allowed the boy to help him up. A fine boy. Brave and loyal. ''I guess you could say you saved my life,'' McFarlane pronounced, his deep voice showing an answering emotion. He rested one large, strong hand on the boy's shoulder. ''You stood your ground in the face of fear. I promise you I won't forget it.''

The colour flushed into the boy's dark cheeks. He murmured something inaudible. Nevertheless it was one of those moments in life that are never forgotten.

CHAPTER ONE

BY THE time they finished yarding the brumbies every crinkle, every crevice of his face was ingrained with red dust. After a day of intense heat and real feats of riding through the rough country Luke was desperate for a shower and a long cold beer. He was due up at the homestead this evening for dinner and a game of chess. The Major loved his chess. He loved the right company. They were both accomplished players and they had long enjoyed an easy companionable relationship.

Nowadays Athol McFarlane, for so long a lion of a man, was going downhill right in front of the younger man's eyes. It deeply pained him. After the deaths of his parents Athol was all he had. He owed everything to the Major. Everyone on the station called him that. A carryover from his early days as a much decorated army officer in Vietnam. It was a term of affection now. No one was sure who started it. It certainly hadn't been Athol McFarlane. Those were the days he didn't care to talk about. *Ever.* Still only in his early sixties the Major had ongoing problems with his leg, an injury he had sustained in the war. What exactly those problems were, Luke never could find out, and he sure as hell had tried, but the Major didn't like to talk about his state of health although it was obvious to everyone who cared about him that he was deteriorating. And Luke suspected in constant pain, though there was never a word of complaint. The only complaint that passed the Major's lips were: "When is Storm coming home?"

He knew the old man missed her terribly. He missed

11

her, too. Sometimes he thought like a hole in the head. Other times like a hole in the heart. He never could contend with his feelings about Storm. He only knew it didn't pay to delve too deeply. She was beautiful. He had a vision of her out riding, cloud of sable hair flying—she hated wearing a hat even in the intense heat—not that it had affected her flawless ivory complexion, green cat's eyes sparkling with life and health.

He knew she was clever. She designed and made exclusive jewellery that sold as far away as New York. Necklaces, pendants, bangles, rings. You name it. And the beautiful people flew from all over just to have a piece designed by Storm McFarlane. Not bad to have an enviable reputation at twenty-seven. No husband. Two fiancés that never managed to get her to the altar. High time she was married, the Major said. He wanted to set eyes on his grandchildren before he died. So far Storm hadn't obliged. What was she waiting for? Superman? Only a rare man could satisfy her, he thought with black humour. Storm always had been damned near impossible to please. Certainly he had never succeeded except for those odd times when they acknowledged a bond. More than a bond. God knows what it was.

When he reached the comfortable overseer's bungalow that had once housed his small happy family, Luke went straight to the bathroom, stripped off his dusty clothes and ran a warm shower. After such a day, it took a while to feel completely clean. He had to soap his hair as well to rid it of the dust, then he allowed the water to run cold, luxuriating in the blessed sensation of feeling cool. Here he was twenty-nine and one of the greatest things in life was a shower!

My God!

Not that he hadn't had his own little romantic flutters. A few months of thinking maybe this is it, then the initial burst of interest and excitement drained away like the water in a clay pan. A few of his ex-girlfriends still hung in there. That was the amazing thing. He hadn't really lost a one. Carla was the most persistent without a doubt. He really liked Carla. She was good company, good-looking and she was good in bed. What the hell was the matter with him? Like Storm it was high time he was married. Deep inside he mourned the loss of his family. He had to make a family for himself. With the right woman. But who? A woman like Storm, who never failed to move and outrage him was out of the question. Storm McFarlane was trouble with a capital *T*.

Luke towelled himself off and slicked back his hair. Now and again he caught glimpses of his father in his mirrored reflection—the high cheekbones, the set of the eyes and mouth. But his colouring was purely his mother's. Though the worst of the pain had banked down to liveable he missed his parents every day of his life. He remembered as though it were yesterday getting the message to go to the headmaster's office. He sensed it was something important but never in a million years did he expect to see the Major, handsome and dignified seated in the headmaster's study.

The Major had come personally to break the terrible news. His parents had been killed in a three-car collision driving back from Alice Springs. One of the cars driven by a tourist was found to have been travelling on the wrong side of the road. His parents had been in the wrong place at the wrong time. He was then fifteen years old and a boarder at one of the country's most prestigious private schools. His parents had been determined he would have a good education but they could never have afforded *that* particular school with its proud tradition, splendid amenities and brilliant alumni that read like a Who's Who. The

Major had seen to it. Wouldn't take no for an answer.
Wore Luke's dad down.

After the accident the Major had flown Luke and Storm
back to the station for the funeral. Storm had insisted she
be picked up from her boarding school so she could be
there. Although her hang-ups had always centred on Luke
she had been great friends with his mother and father. Particularly his mother who thought the world of "the little
princess."

As a mark of deep respect his parents had actually been
buried in the McFarlane family cemetery on Sanctuary
Hill, some five kilometres from the homestead. He remembered how Storm had stood white-faced beside him holding his hand. He remembered how she had given him real
comfort for once, hostilities set aside. He hadn't forgotten.
Although Storm had to return to school he had stayed up
at the Big House with the Major trying to master his terrible grief, but never coming to terms with it, then he, too,
had to return to boarding school. After that, university.

Luke had graduated from college with an OP1, the top
score, something else that had set Storm off. She had
scored an excellent OP3. After that, the Major insisted he,
along with Storm, go on to higher education which after
all he had wanted himself. Luke'd worked hard and made
the Major proud, picking up an honours degree in Eco-
nomics. He'd been free to choose his own life after that
but all he had ever wanted was to be a cattleman like his
dad. Running a huge operation was big business these
days, not just learning the game. Luke revelled in Outback
life. It was in his blood and he had never felt truly at home
in the city. He'd told the Major this in a long discussion.
It was then the Major had confounded him by offering him
his father's old job. Overseer of Winding River Station. A

top job with big responsibilities. The two outstations now came under his jurisdiction.

These days he was the Major's right hand man. Visitors to the station, those not in the know, often mistook him for McFarlane's son. His rise had been meteoric but no one in a tough competitive world had ever questioned his ability. To prove it the Major was leaving more and more to him to the point where he was virtually running the whole operation.

Dressed in a clean shirt and jeans he walked up to the Big House pausing outside to admire it. He always did. It was a magnificent old house completed in the late 1870s by Ian Essex McFarlane a wealthy pastoralist who had come from the colony of New South Wales to take up this vast holding in South West Queensland. The house had been planned on a grand scale, all the more extraordinary for its remote desert setting, two storeyed, built of warm golden sandstone with a slate roof, its deep verandahs supported by slender white pillars with unusual lotus capitals forming a striking colonnade, the upper verandahs encased in white wrought-iron lace with very attractive fretwork. Semicircular stone steps led to the deeply recessed front door and he took them two at a time, passing into the spacious entrance hall its parqueted floor strewn with oriental rugs. Noni Mercer, the housekeeper, came out to greet him, smiling up into his face. "Hi there, Luke. Hot old day!"

"You want to try running down brumbies," he answered, returning her smile. Noni was a thoroughly nice woman. He was fond of her and had good reason to be. In her late fifties, short and compact, with a great heart, she had a bubble of grey curls and contrasting snapping dark eyes. "I have to tell you, Noni, I'm ready for your cooking."

"Aren't you always!" Noni blushed with pleasure. She ran her eyes appreciatively over Luke's rangy figure. He stood straight and tall, superbly built, a few inches over six feet. She had watched him grow up. Watched him turn into this almost unbelievably handsome young man with hair like a dark flame and those miraculous blue eyes. His lovely little mother, Rose, God rest her soul, had had just that marvellous colouring.

Noni had a very soft spot for Luke Branagan who never once used his high standing with the Major for his own gain. Straight as a die was Luke. How he and Storm weren't the greatest friends Noni could never understand. She had an idea Luke secretly carried a torch for the tempestuous Storm, though he would never let on, even under torture. Sadly, in Noni's opinion, and she cared deeply for Storm, that young woman had her feet set on a different path. Yet when she saw them together? Noni heaved a soft sigh, which made Luke dip his handsome head to look into her eyes.

"What's up?"

For such a big strong, dynamic guy Luke was in touch with women's feelings. "Nothing, dear," Noni evaded, then felt compelled to burst out with what was on her mind. "When is Storm coming home?"

His handsome face tautened. "Hell, Noni, why ask me? I'm not one of Storm's favourite people. You know that."

"She's been running with that for a long time," Noni gruffly scoffed. "Personally I don't think it's true."

"Well she sure doesn't *love* me," Luke's vibrant voice deepened. "And she doesn't confide in me, either."

"More's the pity!" Noni regretted. "The Major hasn't been terribly well today, but he's so looking forward to seeing you. You're not far off the son he never had."

"Maybe that's the problem, Noni," Luke's expression turned a shade bleak. "Storm hates to see it that way."

Noni couldn't do other than nod her agreement. "I just wish she'd come home." She turned her head quickly as slow, heavy footsteps sounded along the upper gallery. "That will be the Major now," she said softly. "I know Storm has a busy life. She's so successful and that's wonderful. She always was a clever little thing. Remember how she used to collect all those little bits of opal and quartz around the station?"

Luke's handsome mouth compressed. "I distinctly remember finding a lot of it for her. She was in heaven when the Major used to organize those prospecting trips to the gemfields for us. I made quite a few finds myself but I always handed them over to Storm."

"You would," Noni said. For all her tantrums Luke had always been honey-sweet to that little girl. Sweet and calm and understanding. Maybe he should have told her off. He was well capable of telling off the toughest and the roughest.

"Agate, amethyst, carnelian, garnet, sapphire, topaz, beryl," Luke was saying, his brilliant blue eyes reflective. "That's what started her off on her career. The Major always encouraged her. Now she's getting to be a big name."

"It's marvellous," Noni a recipient of several beautiful little pieces, smiled. "Storm is delighted when people fall in love with her work."

"She's not happy with guys falling in love with her," Luke commented dryly. "Two fiancés to date. Neither could get her to the altar."

"You're not married, either," Noni pointed out slyly. "You're quite a pair!" Personally she thought each had ruined relationships for the other.

As they were speaking Athol McFarlane appeared at the top of the central staircase then came very slowly down towards them. He was leaning very heavily on his stick but Luke and Noni knew better than to go to his assistance. The Major scorned help. He was independent to a fault.

"Well, Luke," he boomed, and his gaunt face lit up. "Come tell me all about your day. Noni has been fussing for hours lining up all the things you like to eat."

"She spoils me," Luke grinned, knowing it was true.

"And you're worth every bit of it." The Major nodded his thatched grey head that once had had Storm's raven sheen. "You've been the greatest help to me these past years. Devotion and dedication. Not a lot of men are as capable of it as you, son. You keep bringing your dad to mind. A splendid man. Not that I had any illusions he wouldn't have wanted to strike out for himself one day. With *my* blessing, mind, but that was not to be." Athol McFarlane's expression grew grave and introspective. "Come along now into the study. You might have to fly over to Kingston at the end of the week. About time to pay them a surprise visit. Noni will let us know when dinner is ready."

"Will do, Major," Noni gave a comic little salute and made off for the kitchen, thanking God Luke was around to ease the Major's pain and loneliness.

Above the fireplace in the Major's book-and-trophy-lined study hung a painting of Storm. It had been commissioned on the eve of her twenty-first birthday. He found himself looking up at it with a brooding silence. No lavish ball gown for Storm. No deep *décolletage* that would have shown off her beautiful shoulders and breasts. But the painting, like Storm, compelled attention. She was wearing riding clothes, white silk shirt and close-fitting beige mole-skins, a fancy belt with a heavy silver-and-opal studded buckle she had designed herself around her narrow waist. Her long black hair was blowing free, her head slightly profiled, skin luminous, her almond-shaped eyes the same rich emerald-green as the bandanna that was knotted carelessly around her throat. One beautiful long-fingered hand was on her hip, and the other clasped a white akubra with a wide snakeskin band. How many times had he seen her stand like that? Maybe a thousand. As a background the artist had used the wonderful colourations of the desert; the cloudless cobalt-blue sky, the purple hills, the gleaming gold of the spinifex dotting the red ochre plains. The setting lent the painting a kind of monumentality. The young woman up there looked so vivid, so real he had the sense she could very easily step from the frame.

Into his arms?

And then?

He never saw it without getting an erotic charge. He was under no illusion Storm couldn't move him powerfully. Nothing easy or relaxed about it. Blinding pleasure and sometimes more than its fair share of sexual hostility.

The Major, observing Luke quietly but intently, took his usual seat waiting for the young man to join him. "Could I ask you something very personal, Luke," Athol McFarlane queried, meeting that direct sapphire gaze.

"Sure, Major, as long as you leave Storm out of it," Luke returned deadpan.

McFarlane laughed. "What impresses me most about you two is neither of you can find anyone else while the other's around."

Luke, taken by surprise, didn't answer immediately. "You're suggesting a love-hate?"

"More often than not it's Storm waging the war," McFarlane answered ruefully. "I would have thought she'd be long over it by now."

"She'll never be over it," Luke answered, a mite tightly.

"I can't accept that," the Major growled. "I want to see her, Luke." It came out far more plaintively than he ever intended.

Luke stared across the table, perturbed by the Major's tone. "What's up? What's the matter? I wish you'd confide in me."

"Nothing to confide," McFarlane lied. He wanted desperately to tell Luke he was dying but he couldn't. He wouldn't even tell Storm. "I'm just feeling tired and old and lonely except for you," he evaded. "You're my adopted son, Luke. You know that."

"If there was anything badly wrong you'd tell me?" There was a serious almost stern expression in Luke's face.

"Sure I would." McFarlane tried to lighten that gaze.

"Why don't I believe that? I'm here to help you, Major."

The Major responded by grasping Luke's forearm. "Don't you think I know that, son? But it's four months at least since Storm was here."

Four months, one week and three days. "She leads a full life," Luke pointed out. "Even I've picked up the magazines Noni leaves lying around the place. She's beautiful, gifted, she has a fine family name. It's only to be expected she'd get invited everywhere. And she has her work. Her commissions."

"She could do them here." The Major's heavy eyebrows drew together. "I've offered many times to convert a couple of rooms into a studio, workshop, whatever she wants. God knows there are enough rooms empty."

"Have you told her how you feel?" Luke asked.

McFarlane sighed. "Yes." It wasn't strictly true. He always played hardy when she rang.

"And she *still* won't come?" It was hard to keep the censure out of his voice. Storm had plenty of time for parties and all the social functions.

"Maybe I haven't asked the right way." McFarlane dropped his gaze evasively, sighing heavily.

"You must know it's on account of *me*."

"I don't accept that, Luke." McFarlane shook his head.

"I think you might *have* to, Major," Luke countered knowing the Major had been living with the fiction one day he and Storm would get together. God, could you believe it? "Storm has always seen me as the usurper," he added with quiet force, opening up his own wounds.

"Rubbish! That's irrational." The Major's protest was overloud.

"Aren't human beings irrational when their deepest emotions are involved?" Luke held the Major's gaze until he blinked.

"You're a man of integrity, Luke," McFarlane said. "Storm knows that in her deepest being."

Luke's expression became sombre as he studied the other man's gaunt face, thin body and arms. "Would you like me to go to Sydney and fetch her?"

McFarlane looked up quickly. "You're far too busy to do that," he protested but his face brightened and he squared his shoulders.

"Everything is in hand," Luke pointed out. "I've got Sandy well trained. He can stand in for me for a day of two. Of course if you want me to check out Kingston?" Luke referred to a Winding River's outstation.

"It can wait," McFarlane said without a second thought.

"Actually it *can*. I've got the situation sorted out. Webb was the troublemaker."

McFarlane scarcely heard, his voice picking up strength.

"When will you go?" Luke studied him. It sounded as if time was of the essence.

"When would you want me to go?" Luke watched him carefully, evaluating the change.

"What about Friday?"

The day after tomorrow. Luke's mind worked overtime. The Major hid his desperation well but Luke sensed, no *knew*, there was something terribly wrong. He wished he could talk to Tom Skinner, the Major's doctor. Get things straight, but the Major would never forgive him for going behind his back. He had tried to get something out of Tom, to little avail. Whatever the true state of McFarlane's health the file was confidential. But there was the evidence of his own eyes. The Major was a sick man. He knew it. Storm knew it. Where the hell was she? Surely her concern for her father would outweigh every other consideration? Her long-running cold war with him?

"So?" McFarlane asked as the young man opposite him fell silent.

"No problem!" Luke flashed his white smile. The smile everyone waited for. "I won't let Storm know I'm coming in case she jumps town, though I will check to see she's in residence."

"What about young Carla?" the Major suddenly side-tracked.

"You could give me a clue?" Luke drawled, not wanting to discuss Carla.

"Dammit, Luke, you know what I mean. You and Carla used to be close. Is it still on?"

Luke picked up a paperweight and palmed it. "On and off. Carla and I are friends." He set the crystal paper-weight down.

'You're a darn sight more to her than that, my boy," the Major scoffed. "I've got eyes. The girl is head over heels in love with you. Her dad would be thrilled to have you for a son-in-law. Like me he only has a daughter to inherit.''

Luke, a generation younger, was very much attuned to women's issues. ''Don't underestimate Carla,'' he said. ''She's got a good head on her shoulders. She knows the business as well as her dad. She could take over.''

The Major shrugged. ''It's too hard a life for a woman, Luke. You know that. It's tough, dangerous and you want a man as boss. Even Storm realises that. Accidents happen all the time around stations especially remote ones like ours. What woman is willing to put herself through that? I'm only trying to find out what the position is with you and Carla.''

''Why exactly?'' Luke asked, with a look of dry humour.

The Major blew up. ''Hell, son, you're as close-lipped as I am. I care about you, that's why. I like Carla, too. She's a smart girl and a looker but I think you can do better.''

''Such as Storm?'' Luke asked directly.

''Surely you can understand that,'' McFarlane asked. ''Your lives are entwined. No matter what, there's that bond. Nothing in this world would make me happier than to see you and Storm together.''

Luke gave a hollow laugh, his eyes drawn to Storm's portrait. ''It would take an eternity for Storm and I to patch up our differences,'' he said thinking Storm's childhood had been damaged by the desperate need to be the only one in her father's life. She should have had brothers and sisters. She should have had *anyone,* except him. In his own way, without warning, the Major had set them both up.

Now the Major was saying very seriously, ''I know

Storm has given you a rough time—and you've let her.
She's the only one who could get away with it, but she
knows your worth. She *knows,* Luke, even if it would kill
her to admit it.''

"My thoughts exactly," Luke quipped. "It's just a
dream of yours, Major. An impossible dream.''

"But you care about her?" McFarlane challenged.
"You can't look me in the eye and tell me you don't. I
know you too well.''

"Then you'd know I would never waste time wanting
a woman who didn't want me,'' Luke said emphatically.
What the hell else was he doing if not that?

"Just bring her home, Luke,'' McFarlane begged with
overwhelming intensity. "That's all I ask. If there's a God
in his heaven he'll make things come right.''

... ...

CHAPTER TWO

IT WAS getting on towards late afternoon before he touched
down at Sydney's light aircraft terminal taking a cab into
the city where he booked into a hotel. Storm herself had
rung her father only the night before, in the course of the
conversation letting it be known she wasn't going out of
town that weekend. She was to be chief bridesmaid to Sara
Lambert, a young woman the Major knew from her occasional visits to the station. Luke knew Sara, too. At one
stage she'd had quite a crush on him that mercifully
passed. So with any luck he would find Storm at home.
Or if she did happen to go out for the evening, which he
was sure she would, he would sit it out until she arrived
back. In a curious way he realised he was elated at the
thought of seeing her again. A good idea to check the hype
now. Storm could be in one of her moods. Moods or not
he was certain of one thing. This time she was coming
back with him before something bad happened.

When he arrived at her seriously up-market apartment
block he had no difficulty getting past security. The man
at the desk knew him after seeing him a few times in
company with Storm and the Major. In fact the man appeared to think he was Storm's brother.

"Go right up, Mr. McFarlane," he said breezily. "I saw
Miss McFarlane come in a couple of hours ago. Didn't see
her go out, though I've been away from the desk on and
off."

He waved his thanks and moved towards the lift amus-

25

ing himself by thinking Storm most probably would be overjoyed to see him.

As it turned out Storm wasn't in but a very smart-looking older woman dressed in a blue suit emerged from the adjoining apartment to tell him Storm had left for a party at the Drysdales.

"You know them?" She must have been bored because she looked as if she was ready for a chat.

"Heard of them certainly," he replied. Every year the Drysdales made The Rich List. "I'm here on an errand for Storm's father." He smiled.

"Then you'll be waiting a long time," the woman said almost flirtatiously. "Those parties go on all night. Then there's Sara Lambert's wedding tomorrow."

"Yes, I know Sara," he said, unaware he was frowning.

"Look here, why don't you simply turn up?" the woman said. "I'm sure the Drysdales won't mind. Not if you're a friend of Storm's. They adore her."

"Who doesn't?" he said with the faintest edge of irony.

"You know Storm obviously." The woman's bright eyes were agog.

"I grew up with her." He told her casually, then lest she got the wrong impression: "I'm the overseer on the McFarlane station, Winding River."

The woman stared at him as if transfixed. "Really? It must keep you very busy?"

"It does. I don't have a lot of time. I should fly back tomorrow. Sunday by the latest."

"So go along to the party," the woman suggested, sensing his urgency.

"What, in this?" He pulled at the sleeve of his leather bomber jacket.

"My dear, you look *marvellous,*" the woman breathed and gave him the address.

The Drysdale mansion was right on Sydney harbour, which was to say on one of the most beautiful sites in the world. The imposing Italianate-style house with matching landscape grounds was ablaze with lights. There again he had no difficulty in gaining entrance. Like a gift from heaven, Sara Lambert, Storm's friend, had been invited to the party. They caught sight of each other as they approached the massive wrought-iron gates, open but flanked either side by attendants to vet the guests.

No male was dressed casually as he was. They either wore dinner jackets or well-tailored suits. Sara didn't appear to take much note of that. She rushed to his side, grabbing hold of his arm.

"Why Luke!" she carolled. "How lovely to see you! It's been ages and ages."

"Sara." He bent to brush her flushed cheek. "Your big day tomorrow. I wish you every happiness."

She beamed up at him, a very attractive blonde with sky-blue eyes. "I'd have sent you an invitation only you might have put me off going through with it," she said roguishly. "Only fooling. I love my Michael."

"I'm sure you do."

"Storm didn't tell me you were coming tonight?" She took his arm affectionately, as though they were the greatest of friends.

"Actually, Sara, she doesn't know."

The blue eyes rounded. "You can't be serious?"

"I'm absolutely serious. I'm here on behalf of her father. Literally a flying visit. The Major's not well."

"Oh!" Sara kept moving toward the gates where an attendant smiled and nodded to her then let them through. Easy as that! "I'm so sorry. I do know the Major has ongoing problems with his leg. Storm keeps me informed. A lovely man, the Major."

"I think so."

"And he thinks the world of you," Sara told him warmly.

"Unlike Storm," he said in an easy, languid drawl that masked a lot of hurt.

Sara laughed. "Maybe she's in denial. You two go back a long way."

"That we do." He left it at that.

Moving in line, they were almost at the front door: Luke without an invitation, Sara waving to other couples who had not yet worked their way into the house.

"I really don't think I should go in, Sara," he said. "If you wouldn't mind telling Storm I'm here? I'd like to speak to her for a few moments, then I'll be off."

"Oh for God's sake, stay!" Sara turned up her face to him, tightening her hold on his arm. "You're going to have to tell me what's been happening in your life. How's your girlfriend, Carla?"

"She's fine. I won't go in, Sara," he said firmly. "Apart from the fact I wasn't invited, I don't look the part." Not that he cared but he was old-fashioned enough not to want to gate-crash.

For an instant there was the same old hero worship in Sara's tone. "You look terrific! Like an ad for Calvin Klein. Great jeans and a cool leather jacket go anywhere."

Despite his wishes they were somehow through the grand double doors urged on by the press of guests to the rear. The entrance hall to his eyes was overly resplendent, more like the foyer of some sumptuous European hotel. Huge, even allowing for the swirl of laughing, chattering guests, all beautifully dressed, the women flashing spectacular jewellery. He presumed the handsome middle-aged couple in the centre were the Drysdales; something Sara immediately confirmed.

He moved back, to one side, taking Sara with him. "If you could just find Storm. I'd appreciate it."

Sara all but ignored him. "Don't you want to meet Stephanie and Gill?" she asked.

"Oh God! I think I'm about to," he said, watching the hosts break away from their other guests and walk towards them, looking highly interested.

"Sara, darling!" Stephanie Drysdale cried.

Lots of Euro kisses.

"This is Luke," Sara offered brightly. "Luke Branagan. He's Athol McFarlane's right hand man. Storm's father."

"Of course!" The hosts, husband and wife started to beam. Handshakes all round.

"Forgive me for gate-crashing your party," Luke smiled, "if only momentarily. I'm in Sydney to see Storm. I have a message for her from her father. It won't take long but it's important. Hence the flying visit. I'm needed back on the station. The Major hasn't been well."

"Nothing serious I hope?" Stephanie Drysdale asked, waiting on the answer.

"His health is a matter of concern, Mrs. Drysdale," he said.

"Well we must get Storm for you." Stephanie Drysdale turned to her husband. "Gill, why don't you show Mr. Branagan into the study while I find Storm. You'll want to be private." She hesitated a moment. "Are you going on anywhere else this evening, Mr. Branagan?" she asked.

"Luke, please." He gave her a smile. "I might catch a movie while I'm in town."

"Goodness! In that case we'd love you to stay." She flashed a glance at her husband, who nodded his handsome head in agreement. Sara, too, smiled excitedly.

"I'm not exactly dressed for the occasion," he pointed out amusedly, glancing down at his jeans and high boots.

"Don't worry about that. You look fine." Actually Stephanie Drysdale was thinking she had never seen a man looking so utterly divine.

Gilbert Drysdale led him off to the study while his wife and Sara went in search of Storm. Guests were wandering around everywhere, champagne glasses in hand, laughing, talking, relaxed. They continued through one of the opulent reception rooms along a corridor until they came to the darkened study.

Drysdale switched on the lights, illuminating a very functional, very masculine room in complete contrast to the rest of the house. Gracious like his wife, Drysdale stayed on for a moment to ask more of Athol McFarlane's health then he excused himself saying he had better get back to his guests. Luke took an armchair, upholstered in a rich dark green leather, allowing his eyes to wander casually around the room, his mind preoccupied with this coming meeting. Four long months since he'd seen Storm. It felt like years. Sick of her, sick with her. Hell it was like a disease!

He heard the tap of her high heels along the corridor, an excitement in itself as he forcefully inhaled a lungful of breath. She was there! Sweeping into the room in a cloud of some beautiful elusive perfume that made him flare his nostrils, a subtle blend of gardenia, orange blossom, freesia? What would a man know? What would a mere male know about the miracle of Woman? She bedazzled him in her sexy little sequined top in lime-green with a long side split ruffled skirt that had to be chiffon over silk, the tiny green iridescent beads that were sewn all over it catching the light. Her thick raven tresses were dressed more elaborately than he had yet seen, the volume increased so it winged back from her forehead and cheeks and spilt over her bare shoulders. Knowing her so well, he could see she had gone pale, her green eyes glittering like the emeralds she wore in her ears.

So near, yet so far! She made his head reel and she was using up his life.

"Luke, what is it? What's the matter?" she asked urgently, closing the study door behind her and leaning back against it.

It was quite a pose, a sizzler, but he knew it was unconscious. "Hi there, Storm," he said, getting slowly to his feet. "I'm really happy to see you, too. No need to panic. Your father sent me."

She could hardly speak for her surprise. Luke, as handsome, as inflammable as ever. "About what? Has he taken ill?" Though her heart quickened with fright, it came out like a challenge.

"You mean you didn't know?" he clipped off, his mood darkening. "Your father has been ill for years."

She couldn't bear the censure in his beautiful blue eyes. "I only spoke to him last night. He was perfectly all right then."

He could feel the familiar tension invading his body. "Don't be absurd, Storm. His leg gives him hell as you know."

That had its effect, too. "What are you accusing me of, Luke?" she asked heatedly, wondering if their clashes were to be repeated forever.

"Well, now we're on the subject, I'm accusing you of neglect."

She flushed, the upsurge of colour increasing her beauty. "Don't you always pick the right words," she said bleakly. "I love my father. I ring him regularly."

"But you don't visit."

She shook back her long hair. The overhead light had burnished the ebony waves with purple. "I have a *career,*

Luke. Can't you understand? I have commissions I must complete. And I get them from people with the money to afford them. Like the people who are here tonight. I just can't rush off at a moment's notice.''

He looked at her unsmilingly. ''Well you're going to have to. Your father wants you home. I think you should come.''

She laughed. It was almost certainly not humorous. ''*You* think…*you* think. Oh, yes, you decide what's best.''

''Don't start,'' he begged. ''I've had just about enough. You know and I know that you stay away because of me.''

''How you kid yourself!'' The truth didn't lessen the pain.

''I don't. You can't put anything over me. I'm not your father to be wound around your little finger. Busy or not I want you to come back with me. You have the wedding tomorrow, but Sunday.''

She stared at him, absorbing the aura of power that surrounded him. ''You can't be serious?''

''I'm always serious with you. Your father wants you.''

Anxiety was like a knife against her heart but she knew her father. He thought bringing her home was his right. Twenty-seven and he still treated her like a child. ''It can't be that serious, Luke. He would have told me.''

''Are you sure of that?''

''So you're calling the shots now?'' She was as defensive as ever. There was so much bottled up inside her it might never get out.

''I always act in the interests of your father. It's over four months since you've seen him. I have to tell you he's gone downhill since then.''

''Oh God!'' She all but swayed into a chair, the slit in her long skirt revealing one long, slender leg. ''I ring him every week without fail. Why does he never *say* anything? Why is everything so secret?"

"You know your father," Luke sighed. "He plays it close to the chest. Besides the last thing he wants to do is cause you anxiety."

"And what about you?" There was the pain again. Not jealousy. Rejection. "You're always there aren't you? He has you to confide in."

"Well he doesn't," Luke responded curtly, all the feeling he had about her cruelly twisting. "I tried to speak to Tom Skinner but Tom clams up."

"Do you really think I haven't tried to speak to Tom myself?" Storm flung up her head. "Tom does what Dad tells him. Just like everyone else. Including *you*."

"And you of course are the rebel?" He let his blue eyes wander over her body, so beautiful and so insufferable. "I'm sorry if it interferes with your professional and social life but I feel you should come home if only for a few days."

"Is that an order?"

"It's a request. Don't close your heart, Storm."

"Then it's that bad?" Her almond eyes glittered with unshed tears.

"I wouldn't be here otherwise. We're never going to be friends, Storm, but I do care about your father," he said, fighting down the mad desire to crush her in his arms.

"And he *loves* you." She had been exposed to that early. "What is it about you men that you value your sons above your daughters?"

"I don't accept that," he said, thinking to have a little daughter like Storm would be utter joy.

"It's true in Dad's case. I spent years of my childhood wishing I were a boy. Wishing I were you." She shook her head. She had been wounded in so many ways perhaps no one would understand.

The pathos of that stung him. "I'm sorry, Storm. I never asked for any of it."

"Of course not." Her smile was bitter-sweet. "It was your destiny. What are you really after, Luke. We both know you're ambitious. Is it Winding River? I swear you'll never get it." Her feelings for him, so complex, manifested themselves in inflicting hurt.

His eyes flashed. "If anything happens to your father, Storm, I'm *out*. Nothing on God's earth would persuade me to work for you. And you couldn't run the station yourself. You've taken no interest in it for years."

"Who needed my interest?" she said, in reality a victim of her father's blind injustice. "Who needs me when they've got you?"

"God, Storm, I'm not a monster," he rasped. "I'm no substitute for you when it comes to your father. He *idolizes* you, but you've always been too hot-headed to accept that. So he's one of the old school who thinks women have to be protected and provided for; shielded from the harsh realities of life. I understand perfectly how important your career is to you. I applaud you. But your father has given you everything you've got including your apartment."

That he knew was a double blow. "You know that?" she asked.

"You just told me." He moved restlessly, rangy and powerful. "How could you have afforded it anyway? It's only these last few years you've been making real money. I expect that your father makes you a handsome allowance. That dress must have cost a fortune." It was exquisite revealing her beautiful shoulders and the swell of her breasts. "The sandals. The emeralds in your ears."

"My mother's emeralds, Luke," she pointed out dryly.

"Columbian. Real emeralds are very hard to come by. You don't know everything."

He drew a deep steadying breath. "Look, why don't we put our little range war aside. I didn't come here for *you* I came for your father. Because I care about him. Like you he's given me just about everything but I work very hard to repay him. In fact I break my back."

"It's just like I said, Luke," she continued with the right mix of irony and humour. "You're hero material. The son Dad always wanted."

"And therein lies a lifetime of grief."

"I don't think it would be excessive to say you stole my birthright."

"That cuts deep. You know I didn't steal anything," he retorted with some passion. "Chance affected our lives."

"It certainly put paid to any civilised relationship between us," she said, hiding her sick regrets. "I used to think when I was just a girl the two of you deliberately tried to exclude me."

As a man he could understand that. "Now you know better." His expression gentled.

"Maybe I can't see the light even yet." Abruptly her tone changed. "Did you fly Dad's Cessna?"

He responded curtly to the near taunt. "The quickest way to get here."

"When do you intend flying back?"

"As soon as you're packed."

She searched the eyes that blazed out of his tanned skin. "You truly think it's that urgent? Dad likes to keep hold of us both. He says he's proud of my success but he'd have been far happier if I'd stayed at home dancing attendance on him. No, don't shrug it off, Luke. *Listen.* 'You're an heiress. You don't have to work!' What he really meant was he wants me to be financially and emotionally dependant on him. I'm not such a fool I don't know my own father. He's an important man, much respected, everyone speaks of him with such admiration—the way he reared me single-handedly.

"I've had a lot of time to think about it. Dad is first and foremost the big man in a man's world. He's lived like that all his life. Athol McFarlane, the cattle baron. The Major. A man among men. He's always said he never married because of his grief. He could have had any woman he wanted. He didn't have to marry a one of them, and you know there were a few. Dad didn't really want to remarry. He might have been having second thoughts about a son but you came along. Ready-made. To make the grand plan complete, you lost your parents."

He thrust a hand through his hair, the light above him capturing its dark fire. "I don't appreciate your talking about my parents."

"Why not?" she flared. "You talk all the time about mine. Anyway I was close to them, Luke. Don't forget that. Your mother used to call me Princess even if it was a joke."

"It was no joke," he told her. "You gave her joy."

Storm's green eyes turned deeply reflective. "Some people might think my father was rather cruel. Maybe unknowingly, he's not the most sensitive of men, but he never for one minute sees a woman as an equal."

It was perfectly true. Women to the Major were ornaments to be worn on a man's arm. "That might be, Storm," he agreed, saddened all at once. "But in his own way he loves you dearly."

She pressed back in the armchair. "That love has been a bit destructive, wouldn't you say? I'm also thinking this could be just a stunt to get me home. Since he's been so inactive Dad sits around making plans. Much as I love him I know he manipulates us both.''

''Agreed. I'm no fool, either.'' The muscles along his chiselled jaw bunched. ''I can only give you my spin on this. Your father is genuinely ill. Noni agrees with me. God, Storm, I didn't fly all the way here for a psychological analysis, informed as it may be. You're bitter and you feel betrayed. Maybe your father *is* ruthless but in the most benign way.''

''As though there's any such thing.'' She half smiled, a poignant movement of her lovely full mouth.

He had to look away. ''If you love your father as much as you say, you'll come. No one is asking you to bury yourself in the wilds. A few days. Hell, can't you spare him that?'' An image of the Major's gaunt face filled his mind.

Storm winced at the implication she was pitiless. In truth she felt defeated. Defeated by her love for her father, defeated by the messed up feelings she had for Luke. It seemed to her she had fought the both of them for most of her life.

''All right, you both win.'' She rose in one graceful movement, holding his eyes. Eyes that had haunted her every move. ''It won't be easy but I'll be ready on Sunday. Does that suit?''

''That will be fine,'' he said. ''You won't regret it.'' He was struggling not to stare at her, but the compulsion to do so was too strong for him. Her green almond eyes were so brilliant they might have had tears in them. ''I should go,'' he said, keeping a safe distance from her with the pure force of his will.

''Actually Stephanie is determined you stay. You could be the toast of the evening if you wanted to.''

"Don't be so ridiculous," he answered shortly, hostility flickering back and forth between them.

"That's a good thing about you, Luke. You have no vanity."

"Go on, anything else?" She had begun to walk to the door, now he followed her up.

"Surely Carla tells you how wonderful you are?" She swept about unexpectedly the sarcastic comment dying on her lips when she found him so close. Their bodies were only inches apart. Taller than average, Storm always felt at such a disadvantage with Luke towering over her. The physical shock of those blue, blue, eyes. That rich red hair! My God! It was like a detonator going off. Her heart quickened and she felt this great surge of what could only be excitement. This was a *man*. She felt his sexuality in every cell of her body.

"I wonder what would happen if we were cast up together on a desert island?" He gave her a mere shadow of his illuminating smile. Yet it drugged her. "No Major. No Winding River?"

"No past," she added as her defence mechanism kicked in. "We can't escape it."

His expression that had created such an erotic disturbance in her changed. "I'll go." Their relationship had not developed as other relationships did. He would be a fool to think anything could change. "Would you thank Mrs. Drysdale for her kind invitation but explain now you're coming back with me I have more things to attend to."

Incredibly she felt keen disappointment. "Don't let me put you off. Sara may be getting married tomorrow but I think she's reliving the intoxication of her holidays on the station. And you didn't even kiss her. Or *did* you?"

He dipped his dark red head. "I have to say I don't remember. There are so many girls I've kissed."

"I know," she answered. "You're notorious for getting women to fall in love with you."

They were making their way down the corridor when a tall, well-built young man with floppy blond hair dressed in immaculate dinner clothes, trailing Sara in his wake, approached. "Storm darling! I'd been looking for you everywhere until Sara told me you were trapped in the study."

"I did *not!*" Sara didn't hesitate to say indignantly.

"Good grief isn't that Alex, the ex-fiancé?" Luke murmured, lowering his head to be close to Storm's ear. "Pain in the neck, as ever."

The ex-fiancé had recognised Luke, too. "Well for goodness' sake!" he cried, without enthusiasm, "if it isn't…" He pretended to think for a moment. "Luke?"

As though he didn't know. Storm had brought him to the station several times during their year-long engagement. Luke nodded amiably. "I've been called that all my life. How's it going, Alex?"

"Great! Just great." Alex and Sara drew closer. "I thought Sara might be pulling my leg when she said you were here."

"Surprise visit." Luke offered laconically.

"Oh, what for?" Alex zeroed right in, his expression challenging but a mite troubled.

"Family matters, Alex," Storm said in a cool voice. "It's not Luke's job to explain."

"No, no, of course not," Alex smiled at her backing off. "Nice to say hello to you, Luke. I expect you're off now, message delivered?"

"As a matter of fact he's staying!" Sara tripped over to Luke and clung to his arm. "Stephanie took quite a fancy to him. On sight."

"This guy is clever!" Alex feigned admiration, at the same time noticing Branagan looked extraordinarily good. "I have to say he does bring in a whiff of the great outdoors." He gave a condescending smile.

"Well now you know what a cattleman looks like." Sara smiled brightly. "Pretty terrific, I'd say. Everyone seems impressed. Except, maybe you, Alex," she added, taking a shot at him.

"Not at all. You misunderstand me," Alex dropped his languid tone, moving toward Storm and taking her hand. "Storm, dearest, can't I carry you off? Everyone's missing you."

"Oh, I don't think so," she gave a little laugh, gently withdrawing her hand. "I must see Luke to the door. We have a few things to finalise."

"You're not going surely?" Sara looked up at Luke's handsome profile, her sweet expression registering acute disappointment.

"You heard the lady," Luke mocked, glancing towards Storm. "I'm being shown the door."

"Of course you aren't." Storm shook her head.

"No, actually, Sara, I do have things to attend to, but it's been great seeing you." Luke bent to kiss her cheek. "Every good wish for tomorrow. You're going to make a beautiful bride."

"Yes, I am!" Sara beamed. "Why don't you come along? You're here not a thousand miles away. We can always fit in one more friend of the bride. It would be lovely wouldn't it, Storm?" She glanced at her friend. "You should see the dresses. They're gorgeous. Storm, as my dearest girlfriend is chief bridesmaid. She's wearing a beautiful gold matt satin and guipure lace gown. She'll look out of this world."

Luke nodded. "She's got a talent for doing that. Don't

worry. I'll see it in the papers and magazines. It doesn't take all that long for them to reach us. Thank you for the thought, Sara, but I must decline. There are errands to run for the Major.'' True enough but the thought of seeing Storm in her bridesmaid's finery was more than he could bear.

"How *is* the Major?'' Alex asked belatedly. This when he'd been shown lavish hospitality on his visits.

"Not as well as we want,'' Luke said, then sketched an attractive little salute, more to Sara than Alex. "I'll say good night. Enjoy yourselves.''

"Hurry back, Storm,'' Alex pleaded.

"Bye, bye, Luke,'' Sara called as he moved away with Storm at his shoulder.

"You'll make my excuses to Mr. and Mrs. Drysdale, won't you?'' Luke double-checked as they arrived at the front door. Guests crossing from one splendid reception room to the other glanced at them with bright curiosity but Storm didn't appear to notice.

She indicated they step outside, the night breeze lifting her hair and wafting her perfume to him, an alluring intoxicant. "Of course,'' she promised, then as an afterthought. "How are you getting back into town?''

"I thought you'd never ask,'' he mocked, gazing back at her while he moved down a step. "Same way I got here. By cab. I've got my mobile or I might just keep walking. It's a beautiful night and it's not that far.''

"Too far for most people,'' she smiled, thinking how they both had been raised. Alex fit as he was, would never have considered it. "What time Sunday?''

He shrugged his wide shoulders that tapered to a narrow waist, expelling sex appeal in every pore. "I'd like to make it early but I doubt if you'll be ready for an early-morning start. Not after the wedding.''

She responded from long habit as if she'd been challenged. "You think I'm going to get drunk?"

"No more than usual, but I think you'll be tired. It's a late-afternoon wedding. The reception will go on for hours. Is the ex invited?"

"What do you think?" Paradoxically she wanted to reach out and touch him. The night around them was playing tricks.

"It sounds as though it might be on again." He launched into an excellent imitation of Alex's well-bred languid tones. "Storm, darling! I've been looking for you everywhere."

"You always did have a gift for mimicry. Remember when you—" She broke off. "It isn't on again with Alex. Not that it's any of your business."

"No more than your inquiry about Carla," he returned directly. "We have to stop off briefly at Mingari by the way. I have some freight to unload."

"Sure it's not just an excuse to see Carla?" She shot him a glance; the greenest flame. "How is she anyway?"

"You'll be able to see for yourself," he returned mildly. "She always asks after you."

She smiled without humour. "Do you know I think that has something to do with you? So what time in the morning?" She didn't look at him but stared over his head at the starlit night.

He took the rest of the steps with two easy strides, looking back at her, her lovely figure silhouetted against the light from the great chandelier in the entrance hall. Such a complicated existence he led. This was one woman denied him. "I'll be outside your apartment block at eight o'clock and that's a concession," he said more crisply than he intended.

"You really believe I still can't get up at dawn?"

"A rhetorical question, Miss McFarlane." He bowed. "Let me say instead I believe you can do anything you set your mind to. Not that it always works. To put it bluntly you've made as many mistakes as I have. Good night. Enjoy the big day tomorrow."

"I will." She remained still where she was watching him stride down the drive. Where Luke was concerned she was very, very vulnerable. It was something she had known all her life.

CHAPTER THREE

SHE was ready waiting for him at the front of her apartment building when he arrived in a hired car he must have organised the day before.

"All set?" He was out of the car moving towards her, perpetually virile, vivid, dynamic. She had to concede a glamorous figure with that superb lean body that made the most casual clothes look great.

"Two pieces of luggage," she said, colourful enough herself in a violet silk shirt tucked into skinny black trousers, high black boots, an Armani leather jacket draped around her shoulders. It was late winter in Sydney but it would be a lot hotter where she was going; except at night when the desert gave up its heat and the temperatures dropped dramatically.

Both looked and sounded brisk. A feat for Storm because she had quite a headache from the wedding. It had gone off so wonderfully well it had turned into a bit of a circus towards the end. She told Luke this in answer to his questions while he loaded her expensive luggage into the boot, then she slipped into the front passenger seat, trying to disengage herself from all physical sensation. Luke's aura was so powerful it scarcely let her breathe. In fact she reasoned she had spent most of her life fighting to get out of the shadow of the two most influential men in her life. Her father and Luke. God knows what she thought she had been doing getting herself engaged; first to Patrick, some ten years older and a very successful lawyer, then to Alex, more her own age who worked for his father in a leading stock broking firm. Alex couldn't fight out from under his father's shadow, either. She didn't think he ever would, but she was doing all right. Her name was a current buzzword since she was a finalist in the De Beers Diamonds International Award. It had been won by a fellow Australian—a brilliant young man with his amazing diamond mask. Not bad for more than 25000 entrants worldwide. Her father had told her he was thrilled for her when she rang to tell him the exciting news. Her piece, an elaborate creation for the hair, when elaborate jewellery was the fashion, her father, strangely enough had never asked to see it. She had heard much later that Luke had told her father it was an "incredible honour and he would have loved to travel to see the piece." He never had. A pity!

"What in the world's wrong with you?" Luke asked eventually as they approached the freeway. It was fairly early on Sunday morning and things were blissfully quiet. No crowds, no traffic jams to contend with.

"Lost in my thoughts." She glanced at him for a fraction of a second, not wanting him to intrude too much on them.

"You're not interested in conversation?"

"I thought you had me under heavy fire, Luke."

"Not at all." He shook his head. "I just want you to see your father face-to-face. I want you to give me the benefit of your opinion. I also want you to give him the comfort only *you* can bring."

"You should have been a politician," she said dryly.

"I've never wanted to be anything else but a cattleman like my dad. One of these days when I'm no longer needed on Winding River I'm going to start my own operation."

"Are you really?" she asked somewhat cynically when she knew perfectly well Luke was indispensable on

Winding River. Highly intelligent, well educated, Luke at twenty-nine was no pale substitute for her father. He was an extremely astute businessman, which he had to be these days in a fiercely competitive market. As well he was a consummate cattleman, and a born communicator. Luke was Luke. Dammit, Luke was unique.

"It's my dream to run my own show." Luke was almost talking to himself. "The Major and I see practically eye-to-eye on most issues, but occasionally I would have preferred to back my own judgement."

"Good grief, a criticism of Dad." She gave a little laugh, flinging her glossy hair over her shoulder.

"Think about it, Storm," he urged. "Don't I always say what I think, but you have to remember the Major has been too good to me to ever forget it."

Couldn't Luke *see* her father, in lavishing so much attention on him, had taken it from her? Storm sighed and gazed down at her ringless hands. She could have Alex's ring back anytime she wanted. "The thing is, Luke, Dad knew what he was doing. You always had that marvellous potential. That quality that sets men apart. You don't think Dad missed it. He always had you lined up for a top job. He thinks ahead. He has to after all, but he manipulates people. He manipulates lives. I'm not trying to make him out any sort of a monster or exorcise my own personal devils but I wouldn't need to be a genius to work Dad out."

He frowned as though the Major could do no wrong. "Since you're being so candid, could I say sometimes you sound like you hate your own father?"

"You're out of your brain," she said wearily, her equilibrium destroyed. Wasn't that the reason she stayed away?

"Am I?" Luke asked ironically. "There's a whole lot of angst there."

"I have to agree with you," she said sweetly. "Put it down to the way I was raised." Storm put her head back against the headrest and closed her eyes. She was a woman of intuition after all. She knew in her bones, even if Luke, blinded by devotion to her father, didn't, the Major was planning something that would involve them both. Whatever it was they would be expected to obey.

After hours in the air they finally landed on Mingari Station's airstrip, Luke making a perfect touch down despite the strong cross-winds. He was as good a pilot as he was everything else, she thought, yielding to admiration. Magnetic to women. All of her women friends had noted his brief appearance at the Drysdale party, professing their amazement some lucky woman hadn't snaffled him up. A lot had tried, she'd replied. Storm had her pilot's licence, too, but she hadn't been keeping up with her weekend flying times as much as she should have been. She's been too darn busy. The Mingari hangar was coming up.

My country! She thought as she gazed out the window. This infinite red land shimmering beneath the blazing blue vault of the sky. The liberating feel of it! The scent of the bush, the sunlit trees, the sight of horses and stockmen, working dogs, great herds of cattle. This was where her heart was and she had been driven away. It was like a great weight on her heart the way her father had cut her out of what she always thought of as her heritage. He had excluded her from all station business. He'd never discussed with her anything pertaining to the McFarlane operations, which were big. Women weren't supposed to bother their pretty little heads with such things. A woman's job was to look after her man. Have the babies. Run the homesteads. There a woman could reign supreme. She could be as active as she liked in women's affairs, but she shouldn't aspire to learning the business.

For years she had tried, bewildered by her father's attitude in this day and age. She had a good brain—she had to accept there were a few limitations attached to her sex— but letting her into the charmed circle, the men's club, would have made life tolerable. Why were heirs much more valued than heiresses? she agonized. She couldn't understand it. For years it had made her singularly unhappy. Sometimes when she faced the naked truth she saw clearly that Luke had always treated her as an equal. Maybe even put her up on pedestal. Instead of being a comfort, it had made her resent him. Other feelings she had for him were so subterranean she had even managed to keep them from herself.

Carla, who had never been under such restraints, was waiting for them near the hangar, waving, smiling, almost dancing up and down in her excitement. No sign of her father, Phillip Prentice, a close friend of the Major's. Carla, unlike Storm, was very much a part of the Prentice organization although Carla had two older brothers who worked with their father to run the huge station. Mingari was Winding River's nearest neighbour on the northwest border. This was the Channel Country, fabled area of the giant cattle kingdoms irrigated by the countless maze of waterways that ran into the Diamantina, Georgina, the Barcoo and Cooper's Creek. Rivers that flowed towards the greatest salt lake in the world, Lake Eyre, Mowana Mowana to the aboriginals. Mowana Mowana rarely filled, perhaps a few times in a century. But when it did! The sight was even more miraculous than the coming of the wildflowers after rains.

"Storm, how wonderful to see you!" Carla rushed forward to greet her, a tall athletic young woman with short dark curly hair, lovely golden-brown eyes, clear golden skin and a shapely figure. The whole thing added up to a very attractive package indeed. "You've got *thin!*"

"Do you think so?" Both of them kissed air. Storm knew from way back Carla had never been one of her fans. Of course it all had to do with Luke. How ironic! "I was a bridesmaid yesterday. I had to make sure I was able to fit into the dress." In fact she maintained her light weight and still managed to eat sensibly.

Luke, too, scored a kiss. This time not the air but right on his clean-cut mouth, Carla's lips parted and clinging. She found she couldn't look to see how Luke was reacting. In fact the sight for some inexplicable reason came like a tremendous shock. It served to remind her just how complicated her relationship with Luke was.

Carla drew back, her golden-brown eyes dancing. She linked her arm through Luke's. "Let's go back to the house and have lunch. I bet you're starving."

Storm answered quickly, too quickly. "That would be lovely, Carla, but Dad will be expecting us."

"He won't begrudge us *an hour,* surely?" Carla asked with high good humour not relinquishing her hold on Luke. "Besides Mum and I have everything prepared. Just cold meats and salad. Nothing fancy. Dad and the boys are coming in. They just love to see Luke. And they'll be thrilled to see you, too, Storm. Jason has never forgiven you for getting engaged to someone else."

As though she'd ever looked sideways at Jason Prentice.

"All right, Storm?" Luke's eyes held hers a moment, allowing her to make the decision.

She couldn't be anything else but gracious. "Fine, Carla, you've gone to so much trouble. It will be nice to see the family again, but I wouldn't like to delay too long.

I've been so busy lately my visits home have become precious.''

"Wonderful, then that's settled!" Carla turned a sparkling face to Luke's. "You've left me on my lonesome too long," she said decidedly provocatively. "Amy and Wes Richards are all set up to give a big party in a fortnight's time. Coming along?''

"Well I've been invited." Luke smiled. "I'll be trying to make it. It all depends what goes on back home.''

Home!

It was said so simply, Storm thought. Luke had staked his claim.

Mingari homestead, though it couldn't vie with the grandness of Winding River's homestead, nevertheless had its own charm. A large colonial-style building painted white with dark green shutters and a green corrugated iron roof, had been added to over the decades so that it rambled over a considerable area. Station horses grazed in a paddock nearby, and a kangaroo with a joey in its pouch hopped leisurely away into the lightly timbered grounds dotted with flowering bauhinias, as they swept up the drive.

Karen Prentice was waiting for them on the wide verandah, still so slim and attractive she looked more like Carla's sister than her mother. Both women had their sights firmly set on Luke. Carla in hopes of a husband. Karen doing her best to help her daughter. Neither of them was about to give up and it wasn't as though they hadn't been trying hard. Storm on the other hand was just a mite tricky; the Major's only daughter but not a great favourite. Storm had gained the impression for reasons of their own both women considered she offered some threat to their plans. At any rate courtesy prevailed, even if the smiles wore a bit thin.

Clive Prentice and his fine-looking sons, Jason and Daniel duly arrived and the greetings began all over again. The conversation sparkled with camaraderie, the men shaking hands; Luke came in for some back-slapping. Storm thereafter became the object of Jason's exclusive attentions, which she found idiotic. Eventually they went into lunch served on the very pleasant plant-filled rear patio. More lavish than Carla had suggested, there were platters of thickly sliced ham, turkey and cold roast beef accompanied by two superb salads, one Greek, one Thai, a creamy red and white cabbage coleslaw, the Prentice men particularly liked, with plenty of warm crusty loaves fresh from the oven flavoured with goat's cheese, potato and rosemary. White wine was offered; the men drank a couple of cold beers, no more. There was work to be done. Storm declined the wine, her head was aching enough.

"Why you've scarcely eaten a thing!" Carla waited her moment to call attention to Storm's half-eaten plate, as though it offered clear evidence of anorexia.

"What I had was delicious, thank you." Storm set down her knife and fork. "You must forgive me but I have a headache."

"I expect you got up incredibly early," Carla said, her attractive face a picture of sympathy.

"I can't remember a time when I didn't," Storm laughed. "The wedding I attended went on into the small hours. I stayed until after one. I had to. I was the chief bridesmaid."

"I bet you looked absolutely beautiful," Jason drooled, the expression on his face suggesting he was visualizing the scene.

"The bride looked better," Storm replied. Sara really had looked radiant.

Although it appeared very much like the family was

hoping they'd stay longer, it was Luke who came to Storm's rescue, gently refusing coffee. "Many thanks for your hospitality." He swept them all with his marvellous white smile. "That was a great pick-me-up but we mustn't keep the Major waiting any longer."

"I'll drive you back to the plane," Carla offered, springing up to hold his hand.

"By the way, Luke." Clive Prentice, a good-looking heavy-set man stood up. "I've been racking my brain to try and remember that Argentinean rancher's name. The guy the Major invited out about eighteen months ago. A great polo player."

"Otero," Luke replied. "Richard Otero. A really nice guy. What made you think of him?"

Storm didn't catch the answer. Karen Prentice returned from the house with a couple of painkillers and a glass of water. "Here, Storm, swallow these down," she urged. "You should have told me at the outset about your headache, my dear."

"It's not all that bad." Storm took the tablets gratefully. "Thank you, Karen."

Karen nodded, waiting while Storm swallowed the tablets. "Tell me, dear, how long are you staying this time?" she asked, just barely disguising the fact she hoped it wouldn't be more than a week.

"That depends on how Dad is. He keeps such a lot to himself but Luke thought I should come home."

Karen raised her nicely marked brows. "He flew all the way into Sydney for you?"

"Dad's plane, Karen. Dad wanted him to."

"Of course," Karen backed off. "We're all so proud of you. You always were such a gifted girl when Carla hated boarding school. I know the Major misses you dreadfully but I'm sure he realises you *must* live in Sydney for your work."

"Actually I could work anywhere," Storm said, prompted into a touch of perversity, "and sell through a gallery or certain jewellers. A lot of my work these days is commissions."

"You mean you might consider coming home for good?" Karen looked pained then mustered a smile.

"As I said, Karen, that all depends on Dad," Storm reminded her gently.

Why did Carla and her mother have such trouble understanding she had no designs on Luke nor he on her? They were quite incompatible.

When they landed on Winding River she was surprised and touched to see quite a few of the station staff had turned out to greet her. Stockmen, some of whom she had known all of her life, the new jackeroos, station wives with little children, friends from the aboriginal community. Storm walked down the line shaking everyone's hand and bestowing a kiss on each and every child. One new baby had arrived in her absence but she was glad she had remembered to send a card and some useful things for the layette. It was such a delight buying for a baby that she had gone a touch overboard but the young mother, Kalle, now thanked her gratefully holding up her adorable child for Storm's sweet kiss. These were the moments Storm found so rewarding. The knowledge that people on the station really cared about her and loved to see her home. The thought exhilarated her and set her free of her slight depression. The headache had disappeared as well.

When she and Luke walked up onto the verandah of the homestead, Noni rushed out, her arms outstretched. "Hello, hello, hello, darling girl!"

"Noni!" She embraced the woman who had been her support during many a fractious time.

"Your dad is waiting for you in the conservatory," Noni said happily. "He's a bit emotional with all the excitement. Hi there, Luke." Noni beamed, looking past Storm to the striking young man lounging back against a pillar quietly watching. Elegant and full of energy. That was Luke. It was quite a combination.

"Hi, Noni." He returned the smile lazily. "We stopped off at Mingari—I had some freight to unload. Karen invited us to lunch."

"Nice of her and so difficult to get out of," Storm supplied. "I hope Dad wasn't getting impatient?"

"Just a bit!" Noni admitted, studying Storm with pleasure. Everything ran very smoothly as long as everything fitted into the Major's schedule. "So you won't want a cup of tea?"

"I never say no to a cup of tea, Noni," Storm laughed. "Still black with a slice of lemon."

"Well I must go." Luke uncrossed his arms, preparatory to moving off. "There's always something that needs attention." He stood on the top step.

Noni drew a hasty breath. "I think the Major is expecting you, too, Luke," she said, thinking the Major could have received Storm on her own. Just this once.

"Another time, Noni," Luke said with a faint note of wonderment. "I'm sure he'll want to see Storm on her own."

"Not true." Storm's green eyes swept him ironically. "Why should this visit be different to any others? You'd better come, Luke. We both toe the line."

"If that's what it is," he replied, his chiselled mouth tight. "Please tell the Major I need to catch up."

"Of course," Storm answered smoothly. It was wrong

of her but she couldn't stop. "When its all's said and done Dad is really at *your* mercy."

"Storm, love." Noni tried to intervene, taking a few small steps to come between them.

It lessened the tension a shade. "So long!" Luke's handsome features were taut as he walked off.

"That didn't help, love." Noni turned back at this beautiful, beautiful girl who often tore her heart out. "Luke is such a good man."

A bitter-sweet smile played around Storm's lovely mouth. "He's everything a man should be. Not sarcasm. *Really,*" she answered without a trace of humour. "Give me a minute to freshen up then I'll come down. How is Dad today?" She took Noni's arm as they walked into the entrance hall. "Luke told me you're both worried about him."

Noni sighed. "I'd say he's in constant pain now but he never talks about it, never complains. You're going to be the best medicine any doctor could order up."

Storm gave the housekeeper a little hug, a glint in her eye. "You flatter me, Noni," she said. "Dad had *two* children. Didn't you know that?"

Athol McFarlane stood up the minute his daughter entered the room. "Storm, darling," he said, his expression so charged with feeling it was fierce.

"Daddy!" Storm went to him, her green eyes filling with tears of sadness and guilt. Only four months yet her father seemed to have aged ten years. Not the work of time. The work of pain. The piercing grey eyes looked sunken and bruised, harsh lines were etched into his tanned skin, his once powerful frame gaunt and thin.

"It's so good to have you home." He hugged her as

though he never wanted to let her go. Something that opened Storm's heart until he said, "Where's Luke?"

Storm drew back, trying to recover her emotional balance. "He's gone back to work. He's concerned about losing time. He likes to keep on top of things."

"I wanted him to be here." McFarlane frowned, obviously put out.

"Aren't I enough, Dad?" she asked quietly, smiling a little.

"Storm!" It was a cry from the heart even as he refused to see he had created a wall between them. "You're more than enough, but I thought Luke should join us. Sit down, darling. Tell me what you've been doing?" He winced as he resumed his seat in a high-backed leather armchair with a rest for his feet.

"Perhaps you'd better tell me what you've been doing first?" Storm drew her chair closer to him. "You don't look well, Dad." A serious understatement but knowing her father she couldn't overstate it. "What does the doctor have to say?"

Her father didn't rise to that. "The same old thing. I'm wearing out. The leg gives me gip from time to time."

"Perhaps I should speak to Tom myself?" She didn't say she already had. Several times. "Would you mind?"

Her father's mouth compressed. "It's the worst possible thing you could do. I'll keep you informed."

"But you wanted me home, Dad," Storm persisted gently. "That must mean something?"

His dark bushy eyebrows drew together. "I don't think it's so unusual for a man to want to see his only daughter surely?"

"Only *child*."

He didn't attempt to study her meaning. "I've told you many times, Storm, I'd build you a studio. Outfit it with everything you want. Convert rooms in the house if you like. I don't expect you to stay with me all the time. You could fly off any time you liked for a week or so. Take a break. See your friends. Have a good time. I need you here, Storm. It's as simple as that."

There was a tremor in his stern voice now that further upset her. "Something is wrong, Dad. Why won't you confide in me?"

"Would it make any difference if I did?" he asked abruptly, brushing at his nose as if at an irritant.

"It would make a big difference," Storm said, succeeding in preventing her own voice turning cold. "I love you, Dad."

"You say it as though I doubted it," McFarlane calmed down, folding his large hands in front of him, his expression turning pensive. "But if you love me, Storm, you wouldn't go away."

Slowly she shook her dark head. "Don't do this, Dad," she begged quietly. "I have a career. I'm a success. I have a life."

"Your life is here!" Suddenly anger flared.

"I don't see it that way, Dad." Storm had never been one to be intimidated. She wasn't now but she was shaken by her father's appearance. "Please don't let's argue. I've only just arrived home."

But his anger hadn't completely vanished. "How long do you propose to stay?"

"As long as I can."

Her father moved restlessly, his shoulders slumped. "Where did you say Luke was?"

The headache that had disappeared began to throb. "What has Luke got to do with this, Dad?" Her voice gentled in entreaty. "I'm your own flesh and blood."

"Now that sounds familiar." McFarlane raised his head

to give her a half amused, half impatient look. "Dammit, girl, I've never understood why you're so jealous of Luke."

Storm rubbed her temples. "I have no defence, Dad. I just *am*."

"But that's just plain perverse," McFarlane burst out. "He's such a splendid young man," he continued, looking puzzled. "You two should have been the closest friends. I've seen the young men you've invited here over the years. The fiancés. God they couldn't hold a candle to Luke," he said with open contempt.

She tried not to bridle. It was pointless anyway. "But then I was in love with them, Dad. Or I thought I was."

His answer was a wry snort. "I can't tell you how relieved I was when you finally came to your senses. It's time you got married, Storm. But to the *right* man."

"Who is?" Her gaze was direct and challenging. No wonder people whispered, she thought. No wonder Carla looked at her with suspicion.

McFarlane brushed a hand across his thick thatch of hair, a temporising gesture. "A man you can give your whole heart to," he offered. "A man you can respect and admire. A strong man, Storm," he added with humour. "One who can keep you in line."

"You think women need keeping in line?" She gave him a little, crooked smile.

"By and large they do. Especially you. You've always fought the least suggestion of authority."

She felt a twinge of guilt. "So I did. But I'm not here to fight you, Dad. I'm here to offer comfort." She leaned forward and took her father's hand. "It's like I said. I love you."

"I love you, too, darling." He stopped abruptly. There were tears in his eyes.

Tears from her father! It shocked Storm so much she jumped up and hugged him, letting her cheek rest against the top of his head. "Dad, Dad," she crooned.

Her father patted her hand, his voice soft and unless she was paranoid, a shade triumphant. "Make sure Luke knows to come up to dinner," he said. "It will be wonderful, the three of us together."

Falls the shadow.

There was sadness in her eyes but Storm made a supreme effort to answer cheerfully. "Sure, Dad. I'd like to go for a ride this afternoon. I'll tell him then."

Noni arrived with the tea, freshly baked cookies and some little almond tarts, well pleased when Storm and the Major asked her to sit down and join them.

The atmosphere immediately lightened. Noni had that enviable effect on people, Storm thought. She sat back, beginning to entertain them both with an account of the wedding; her most recent showing; her sales to a couple of very-much-in-the-news society women, plus a wealth of light, amusing gossip. She wished it were always so simple to make her father laugh.

Late afternoon while her father was taking a nap: "Just like a child!" he said. "I actually need it." Storm took out one of her favourite horses, Rising Star, an ex-racehorse whose delight in galloping Storm found exhilarating. A good gallop would clear the cobwebs. She loved horses. Loved riding. She'd felt confident and comfortable on a horse's back. She had done ever since she could remember.

There were photographs of her up in the saddle at age three, hard hat on her head, little striped polo shirt, jodhpurs, shiny boots on her feet. Photographs of her on horseback at all ages. An impressive one of her at the Royal

National Show performing an advanced dressage movement. For a while there dressage had been her passion, until her passion for jewellery making had taken over. Rising Star was a wonderfully supple and responsive ride. Once on the open plain she gave the bright chestnut with the white star on his forehead her full rein.

There was magic in galloping. It was far, far better than driving a powerful Ferrari. One of her male friends had let her take his around a track at high speed. It was exhilarating, but give her a fast horse every time.

A half hour into her ride, when the sunset was turning the deep blue sky into a glory of pink, crimson, and gold with bands of indigo and orange on the horizon, she sighted Luke. He was on horseback, coming from the direction of one of the holding camps. The way he rode filled her with excitement. He was a wonderful horseman. For long moments she was defenceless against the stirring sight of him galloping towards her. Why was she so much in need of her father's love and attention that she took it out on Luke? Maybe if her mother had lived? God how she wished she had. It wasn't all that easy being a child, a young woman, in a man's world.

Luke reined in, his eyes a blazing blue against the golden bronze of his skin. His dark red hair contrasted brightly against the pearl-grey of his akubra. Never a sign of a freckle. Not one.

"Enjoying yourself?" he asked, allowing his eyes to move over her, glossy mane wind-tossed, those beautiful cat's eyes clear and sparkling.

"Yes," she answered shortly when she felt quite emotional.

"How did it go with your father?" he coaxed.

"Well. He asked where *you* were."

Luke made no immediate comment on that. "Let's ride

into the shade. You really should be wearing a hat for protection.'' He glanced at her as she came alongside him. As usual she'd let her hat slide down her back.

"How come you don't get freckles?'' she asked.

He grinned. ''You've wanted to know that ever since I can remember. The answer is the same as ever. I don't know. I'm not ginger like poor old Sandy, you know.'' He named a station hand whose freckles were so close together they resembled a mottled tan.

"Dark auburn,'' Storm said, a soft note entering her voice. Luke's mother had had the same beautiful colouring. Any kind of light fired that hair.

''Did you tell him where I went?'' Luke asked, as they rode down on a narrow, curving billabong. The pink and cream water-lilies floating on it were wondrously beautiful and fragile. Like creations in porcelain. Or enamel, Storm thought, her creativity stirring.

"I simply said you went back to work,'' she offered after they'd both dismounted. ''He wants you to come up to the house for dinner.''

Luke stared at her for a minute, then turned away. ''No.''

"Ouch!'' She glanced at his unsmiling profile. ''Would you like to tell him that yourself?'' She gave him a slight, dangerously provocative smile.

"All right I will.'' He bent to pick up a few pebbles. He had to keep his hands off her. He sent them skimming across the water one after the other. ''It's your first night home after all.''

"Let's start again,'' she said wryly. After all this had gone on for years. ''I'm afraid nothing is complete without you.'' There was no anger in her voice…just a resigned acceptance.

Luke straightened, staring out sightlessly over the dark

emerald lagoon. "It has far less to do with me than a symptom of your father's driving need of a son."

"Do you know I agree with you," she said. "Why didn't he remarry?"

A pause then, "You wouldn't have liked that, Storm."

That unnerved her, threatening her tenuous poise. "Are you saying Dad sacrificed his own desires to appease me?"

"It's possible." He turned at last to look at her. "Having your father's sole attention has always meant a great deal to you."

"And that's not normal?" she asked defensively, staring into his eyes.

"Perfectly normal for a little girl as isolated as you were. Every little girl needs her mother."

She felt such a rush of emotion she turned away blindly. "You're absolutely right." A moment slipped by. "I've tried to get away from you, Luke," she admitted, low-voiced though it seared her.

"I know." His voice equally tense came from somewhere behind her. "I've had to pay a high price for your father's affection."

"How do you mean?" She spun on her heel only to discover him standing directly in front of her. His aura was so powerful, so *male,* she found it intimidating.

"You've figured it out by now," he clipped off. "I lost out on *you.* Your affection."

"Surely it wasn't important to you." Deliberately she moved back a few paces, putting distance between them.

"You charmed me in your cradle." He, on the other hand, stood perfectly still.

"I used to hero-worship you." She found herself saying haltingly as though in the grip of a truth serum.

"Then all at once things changed."

She took a deep shaky breath, trying to suppress the

sharp rising excitement that was cutting through her like a blade. "Dad has ruled our lives," she muttered. "He set us one against the other."

He shook his head. "If he did, he never meant to."

That spooked her. "Why do I ever expect any fairness from you?" she flared. "I can never open my heart to you, Luke. You're always on Dad's side."

"Wake up, will you?" he begged. "I'm here for you, Storm. You might consider it's possible, too, you're never on *my* side. Any chance we could start again?"

"No, I just can't. I really can't," Storm said in a passion. "Too many years have gone by."

"What are you frightened of, Storm?" he asked, fearing his own loss of control. Very quietly he moved towards her, like he sometimes did in her dreams. "Why are you so frightened of *me?*"

She was so alight she felt she would blow a fuse. "Such arrogance!" Her voice rang out caustically. "I'm not frightened of you at all."

"If you back any further you'll finish up in the water," he warned, holding out his hand.

She ignored it, a pulse away from lashing out at him.

"I think you are," he continued.

The air between them vibrated with a tension that had them both catching their breath.

"What do I have to do to prove it?" She stood there, hands on hips, head thrown back, eyes flashing green fire. An attitude of defiance he had witnessed countless times over.

"Why don't you let me show you?"

He started to walk towards her again, his brilliant eyes intent on her, while she tried to fight back excitement and panic.

"Don't you dare touch me, Luke," she warned.

He gave a challenging shake of his head. "I'm genuinely amazed I haven't tried it before. For years you were too young, but you're old enough now. Two fiancés no less."

"I couldn't even count your girlfriends!"

So great was her tumult she actually considered the ignominy of flight. But he was there, one hand taking a fistful of her hair, the other strong arm snaking around her waist pulling her so closely into him she felt the impact of body against body in every last cell.

Luke allowed her to grind against him in a futile struggle, her beautiful, high breasts crushed against his chest, her long-fingered hands flailing wildly. Her breath was coming unsteadily through her parted lips, sweet and clean against his skin.

He lost control.

He was alight with desire. It pounded in his temples and in his brain. The times she had cut him to the bone! The infinite number of times she had played princess of the manor! When his mouth came down over the luscious cushion of her lips, she gave a cry, muffled but keening like a bird's.

"Surely you've been kissed before?" He couldn't stop himself from offering a taunt. The wish to hurt her as she had hurt him was overriding any thought of tenderness. He was unaware his voice sounded drugged with long-denied desire.

Fire crackled, spat, burned through Storm's veins. She'd been kissed many, many times but no one had evoked such a passionate, primitive, reaction. She had imagined him kissing other women. Carla, the rest. In his arms she was forced to admit it, but the reality of having his beautiful clean-cut mouth over *hers* was too overwhelming to describe.

She wanted to lock her lips and her teeth. She wanted to deny him any pleasure he might take from her mouth and her body but the voluptuousness of her own emotions were simply too much for her. It was as if he had taken possession of her.

The very thing she feared.

"Luke, stop!" No order. A plea, knees trembling, her head falling forward against his chest, the wild urge to fight him spent.

"When I'm so enjoying myself?" His resonant voice was husky, mocking.

"What are you trying to prove?" Her skin was pale with the force of emotion, her eyes huge.

"Only the truth," he said quietly, observing her extreme agitation.

"Well the truth is I *hate* you." She responded passionately, on cue.

"Goes without saying! But what do you actually *mean*, given that you kissed me back?"

Storm couldn't bear to consider that. "I did not!"

"Did so. We can play these silly games. You know something?" He put his gleaming head to one side. "You're the greatest kisser I've ever met and Carla's not bad."

She saw red as she was meant to. Luke was an illness, a fever. There was no escape from him anywhere. She moved with feline speed and suppleness. She lifted her hand in an arc, then cracked it sharply against his lean cheek. Fall of flesh upon flesh.

A moment frozen in time.

God! In the heat she felt chilled. Overcome by shame. Humiliation. A kind of despair. She really needed help with no help to be had. Where was the enviable control, the poise that was so much a part of her? It deserted her utterly on her home ground. As her arm began to fall he pinned her wrist, not cruelly but leaving her in little doubt of his vastly superior strength. "A warning, Storm. Don't do that again. Not *ever.*" His eyes were blue stars.

"No I won't." Her tone was full of self-disgust. "It's too demeaning. And you won't kiss me either. Understood?"

He smiled a little at the "turn the tables" mechanism she so often deployed, holding her intently with his eyes. "Now that I can't promise. Not when I've just got a taste for it."

"Have your little joke," she turned on her heel.

"What makes you think it's a joke?" he called after her, watching her take the grassy slope like a gazelle.

"You won't like it if I tell Carla." At the top she turned to threaten him, her cheeks flushed.

For answer he sketched an elegant little bow. "My life is in your hands!"

It was said with the utmost mockery. A sobering prospect to know it was true.

CHAPTER FOUR

A WEEK slipped away, during which time Storm kept a close watch on her father. His general health picked up having her near. His eyes were brighter behind his glasses. He was always able to summon a smile. He talked endlessly of the old days; how he met and married her mother. How beautiful she was. How much he loved her. How his very existence was threatened when he lost her.

"But I had you, my darling. I had to pick up the reins."

Her father was so happy, so at peace, Storm found it almost impossible to broach the subject of her return to Sydney. Sooner or later she had to. It was necessary to keep her work before the public, especially now when she was riding high on her little moment of fame. But the ideas kept coming. Not just for the swank pieces that brought in the money and had the most staying power, but for good contemporary pieces within the reach of young, sophisticated jewellery lovers. Experimental pieces. She had brought a sketchbook with her—she was rarely without one—and it was almost filled. She'd also been asked to custom-design impressive pieces of jewellery for men. One of her customers was a top male executive who swore by the healing power of carnelian for his legendary quick temper. Others thought turquoise brought good luck. Every gem was credited with a special healing power.

She'd sketched out a few blueprints for bold signet rings either sculptured in solid sterling silver or eighteen carat gold handset with semiprecious stones; lapis lazuli, amber, jade, malachite, opal with its beautiful play of colours, jet, onyx, fire agates. Working with these gems and having easy access to them, Storm felt their power more than most. Diamonds, rubies, emeralds, sapphires and pearls remained the top five. So many legends were attached to them but Storm was just as fascinated by the many semi-precious stones that passed under her eyes. Stones that had been known and used since antiquity. A few years back she'd made a jade pendant on thin-corded leather for her father to wear around his neck. She'd used the most sought after jade, too. An intense apple-green. She'd gone to great lengths to secure it. Jade was said to have healing power over bone problems if it was worn. Her father had taken the pendant in his hand, admired the workmanship, and given it back.

"A man doesn't wear jewellery, sweetheart," he had said in a kindly but dismissive voice. "Besides I don't believe in all that healing stuff."

She still had the pendant at the bottom of her mother's jewel case which was now hers.

Luke became a fixture at the dinner table. Something that worked wonders for the Major's moods, if not Storm's. Luke had the most marvellous calming effect on him. That's what's wrong with me, Storm thought. I'm not calm, volatile mostly. Periods of calm. Always acutely aware of Luke, she had become preternaturally sensitive to his presence. But she had resolved to be good. Pleasing the Major was paramount to both of them. With an effort on both sides, they kept up a charade, a pretence at a new intimacy the Major didn't miss but apparently rejoiced in.

In the daytime Storm took her father for trips around the station so he could call in at the various camps and worksite to speak to his men. Often they enjoyed a mug of billy tea and sometimes a slice of freshly baked damper.

At other times Storm parked the Jeep on high ground so her father could look down on the mob spread out across the plains or a party of stockmen fording them across the shallows of the permanent stream that ran through the station. His favourite port of call was to watch Luke break in the best of the brumbies though "breaking" scarcely described Luke's method. Luke was one of the natural born "calmers."

He had an innate love and understanding of horses. No one on the station knew of one he couldn't ride when horses aren't inherently rideable. The horses Luke handled were broken in superbly. Horse breaking is a highly skilled task. It involves mouthing, riding and educating. Brumbies unlike the station bred horses weren't used to the sight of humans. Station horses were well handled from an early age consequently they were even-tempered and relatively controllable. Brumbies, were something else again. Often their bucking at the riding stage was positively ferocious.

Over the years many a stockman had sustained injuries trying to ride a wild horse; crushed ribs, broken collar-bones, broken limbs, broken facial bones. It was a fairly easy matter to get oneself killed, especially if a horse was cornered in a yard. That particular afternoon, the "mouthing" over Luke was riding a big bay standing some sixteen and a half hands with obvious thoroughbred blood. The bay most likely was the progeny of one of the station mares and a brumby stallion. Brumby stallions were notorious for their attempts to run off station mares to join the harem.

"I thought *I* was good in the old days," the Major grunted in admiration as they sat in the Jeep watching proceedings. "I never had Luke's skill nor patience. He's turned so many of these rogues into good working horses."

"That's the Luke we know and love!" Storm quipped, watching Luke speak quietly, soothingly to the wild horse urging the animal forward. Luke knew better than anyone how to get himself into the horse's comfort zone. Nervous, unpredictable horses were time bombs waiting to go off. Luke knew how to control his own emotions, something that communicated itself to the horse. There were no punishments in Luke's methods. A horse reacted according to its natural instincts he always said. If that presented a problem, then the problem had to be solved.

They sat for a good hour along with several stockmen and the two young station jackeroos perched up on the fence. The youngsters new to Luke's horsemanship were thrilled by the display, one of the jackeroos calling out to Luke for "a go." Luke took no notice whatsoever if indeed he heard the boy. His concentration on the job in hand was too intense. No one had ever seen Luke land on the sand, paralysed with pain.

"Stupid young devil!" the Major snorted with a hard edge of irritation. "Tell him to stop, Storm."

"Okay, Dad. Take it easy. One is foolhardy at that age," she said lightly opening the Jeep door. "I used to want to ride a buckjumper myself, remember?"

"Don't I ever!" the Major said with a faint tremor. "Tell that lad if he can't keep his silly mouth shut he can push off. Go find some work. They simply don't know what's involved here. There are plenty of professional breakers doing the rounds, but I haven't seen one to match Luke. He can control even the most dangerous horse and they're dangerous animals."

Storm walked over to the high railed fence and tapped the jackeroo lightly. "Listen, Simon, keep it down. Calling out to Luke could distract him. That horse could start acting up any time."

Simon flushed. "Sorry, Miss McFarlane." He glanced back nervously to where Athol McFarlane was seated in the Jeep. "It won't happen again. Promise."

"That's okay, Simon." She smiled at him. "We all have to learn."

Luke's session broke up ten minutes after and one of the part aboriginal stockmen took over, an excellent horseman and one of Luke's "pupils."

Luke came out of the yard and crossed to where they were. The Major still seated in the Jeep, Storm leaning back against the bonnet. Father and daughter watched him with varying emotions. McFarlane with pride, gratitude and deep affection, a fatherly love that had turned Storm's world inside out. Storm with the utmost caution overlaid with a kind of emotional tumult that was close to McFarlane's love.

Vibrations came off Luke even at a distance she thought. He had the perfect powerful physique, very lean but in no way thin. Countless images of him were tucked away in her mental file. She thought she'd had it firmly shut and under lock and key but one explosive kiss had torn open the lock. The file lay open although it still seemed important not to look.

"Hi!" Luke acknowledged Storm with the same controlled smile he'd been giving her all week. Even then it had the ability to dazzle her. He walked around to where the Major was seated on the passenger side, leaning in man-to-man.

"I think we've got ourselves a darn good horse, Major. He's a cut above the usual bunch. Thoroughbred blood."

"I'd say he was one of Nahra's." McFarlane of course had spotted it. He named a station mare that had escaped to the wild some years before.

"My guess as well." Luke nodded in agreement. "With

a badly trained horse it takes a good man to work it. Can't have the men flat out trying to handle the horses especially in difficult terrain. That way they won't be able to muster. The bay has potential. Now, what about a cuppa?" He leaned back over the bonnet to include Storm. "After that session I'm as dry as a bone."

"Good idea." McFarlane's gruff tones mingled pleasure with approval. "I've enjoyed this last week immensely. It's a wonder to have Storm home at last. She's been able to drive me all over. It's good to see the men."

"They're working well," Luke assured him. "It's been a pleasure for them to be able to speak to you, too, Major," he reported.

"What about if I have a go at that?" Storm suggested looking towards the sandy enclosure where the aboriginal stockman was working another brumby. It was a much smaller horse, a filly. The stockman was working from the ground, a technique Luke followed especially when handling a horse with behavioural problems. It was a whole lot safer than trying to work a horse when mounted. Ground control was achieved first before the move to the saddle. Storm whose horsemanship was not in question, found that she wanted to try it. Being home was so utterly different in every way from city life. She loved it. It was so varied and exciting, but she still resented being kept out of the picture.

As it happened it was difficult to say which one of the men said "No" first. Her father or Luke. Maybe it was simultaneous.

"I'm not going to get hurt," she assured them coolly. "If Wally can handle it, so can I."

"I'd rather you didn't, Storm," the Major said, his relaxed expression turning to a frown.

"Fifteen minutes. Luke can watch me. It's just a filly. I can handle it."

"I don't think we could handle seeing you get hurt." Luke spoke quietly for both of them, himself and the Major. "Hazards exist, Storm, you know that."

"You don't say those things to Wally," she retorted.

He considered briefly. "A fortnight ago Wally struck his head on a rail post when a horse bucked high. The filly looks quiet now but she could smash into the rails in an attempt to go through or over them if she takes it into her mind."

"I know," she said in a crisp voice. "I was born here, remember? But I'd like to learn the technique."

"Okay so I'll show you." Luke gazed at this dark-haired, green-eyed "princess."

"That's a promise?" She turned to face him directly.

He struck his heart. "Or hope to die. But we won't be working with brumbies. I can tell you that. You know enough about horses to know any horse can present a serious risk. Let alone a brumby outlaw. Now what about that tea? Take pity on me, Storm." He smiled at her.

It was one of those moments when she felt he reached out and actually touched her. Not just with those beautiful sapphire eyes but his hand. He might have been laying it on her naked breast so erotic was her reaction.

She drew a harsh, shallow breath turning away. "Oh, all right. As far as that goes it's thirsty work just watching you." And waiting...waiting...waiting...for you to kiss me again. Opening the file a little had also opened up a great fissure, a deep, untapped vein of desire that threatened to rock her to her foundations.

* * *

The days merged into one another with a continuum of peace. One afternoon Tom Skinner flew in with another physician, a specialist in his field, which was orthopaedics. The door was closed on Storm while both men conducted their examinations and conferred. Her father was an old hand at shutting her out when she was desperate to know the true state of his health. Afterwards, when the two doctors stayed on briefly for a reviving cup of tea, Storm tried her best to get some information. A difficult task when her father sat opposite her finally snapping out testily he was "just fine." Storm drove the doctors to the airstrip, and with her father safely up at the house tried again.

"He's *not* fine, Storm" was all Tom Skinner would say. "He's a very sick man. Life must be hard for him."

"He's dying isn't he." It was a bleak comment, not a question.

Tom stared ahead, as distressed in his way as she was. "Your father refuses to acknowledge such a thing. He's a man who confronts his pain."

"He won't let anyone else do it."

"I know."

"It's rather cruel, isn't it, Tom? While Dad plays the stoic he refuses to let me come close to him." Would she ever get over feeling emotionally excluded?

"It's his way, Storm." Tom Skinner had known Storm all her life and he shook his head regretfully. But Tom was a man under strict orders not to divulge the full extent of his patient's illness. It could be days, weeks, months. Given McFarlane's iron will, a year. "Don't think for one minute you're not giving your father the greatest comfort," Tom consoled her pain.

"He still treats me like a little girl, Tom. You know that. Sometimes I think I can't take it any more, but I can't leave."

"I don't think your father trusts anybody outside of…"

"Luke?" Storm broke in.

"Storm, Luke is as desperate to get through to your father as you are," Tom told her. "In many ways your father is a most difficult man." Obdurate as granite, Tom thought.

Two nights later the crisis came.

Storm woke out of a troubled sleep with a sudden and profound belief something was terribly wrong. She sat up in bed listening as though the house around her would deliver up the answer.

Dad.

Her whole psyche sensed him very near her, like a low beam of light. The sensation was so strong it had her weeping, tears streaming down her face.

Dad!

She flew out of bed, shouldered into her robe, taking the quickest route via the verandah to her father's suite of rooms.

The bedside light was still burning. He was propped up against his pillows. His reading glasses sat low on his nose. His eyes were shut, his mouth open, strong jaw a little slack. The book he'd been reading was still in his hand, pages open.

Sweet God!

Storm just had time to cross herself before she buckled at the knees, falling half-way across the floor. She felt so faint she let her head flop forwards until the dizziness passed. She knew without going a step further her father's mortal life was over. The sensation of his being in her room was his spirit passing.

Finally she rose and approached the bed finding a small measure of comfort in the fact her father's expression showed no signs of agony. He didn't even look tired and worn as he had at dinner. He looked as relaxed as when he was dozing in his favourite chair. He was one of the fortunate ones. He had died in his sleep.

There was no pulse. No breath to fog the little mirror she found tucked away in a chest of drawers.

Storm bent and kissed her father's craggy forehead, speaking aloud. "Go in peace, Daddy. I love you." Her tears fell on his cheek and very gently she brushed them off. Death was such a dreadful shock even when one was expecting it. Never properly understood. Insurmountable to accept.

For a time, she didn't know how long, she sat in a chair beside the bed, holding her father's hand. Her weeping had stopped, though she was trembling so violently, her whole body was vibrating.

Her mind's eye seized on an image.

Luke.

Luke would want to know. Luke could confirm her father's death. Strangely she didn't think of Noni. Not yet.

Storm let herself out of the front door into the darkness of the night. A cold wind was blowing in from the desert but she was oblivious to it. The sky was ablaze with a million stars. Another one up there tonight. Up there in the Milky Way, the home of departed heroes.

She wasn't wearing slippers but she felt nothing underfoot. She continued along the drive, through the gardens and out into the compound to the first of the staff bungalows, a glimmer of white. It was the biggest and the best. Home to the station's overseer. She passed a bank of honeysuckle on the way, its perfume so sweet and haunting it would always stay in her memory of that night. Resolutely she moved on, seeming to glide in her filmy nightclothes, long skirt stirring and floating on the night wind.

She moved up the few steps to the verandah. The bungalow was in darkness but she didn't hesitate. She knocked on the door.

"Luke. Luke." Her voice unknown to her, rose in a poignant wail. In the depths of her grief she only knew she wanted him.

Inside the bungalow Luke came out of an uneasy sleep.

Was he dreaming? He was certain he heard Storm's voice. Nothing unusual about that though. He dreamt about her frequently. With a groan he fell back against his pillow only to hear the voice come again. She was right outside his door. For an instant his whole body froze. Only one thing could bring Storm to his door.

Even as he thought it he was up, pulling on jeans. He didn't linger long enough to grab a shirt. She was standing outside the door, staring up at him, eyes unblinking even though he had switched on the porch light.

"It's Dad," she said, her voice so soft he had to bend his head.

"Oh, Storm." He reached for her and folded her into his arms. *"Storm."* His mouth found the top of her head. Kissed it. Drank in the fragrance of her hair.

"He could have told us he was dying," she murmured brokenheartedly.

He held her and rocked her saying her name gently time and again. "Don't talk about it now. It's all over." She seemed barely conscious her face and mouth were against his bare chest, but even in the deep distress of the moment his body reacted. "I'll come up to the house with you." With sheer force of will he pushed back all sense of desire.

"Would you?" She lay her palms flat against him, lifting her head to stare up into his face.

"I'm always here for you, Storm." He could have

added: I've always loved you. But even in grief he had his pride.

It was the start of over one hundred hours of purgatory for Storm through which she suffered deeply. Finally Athol McFarlane was laid to rest in the family cemetery on Sanctuary Hill. The funeral had been delayed for several days with her father—that lion of a man—laid out in a cold room, until mourners from all over the country were able to organise travel arrangements to the remote station; extended family, life-long friends, important people within the industry, pastoralists, politicians. They came by charter plane, private plane, a whole convoy of vehicles that made the long, hot trek overland. All of them determined to pay their respects to a fine man, to the McFarlane pioneering dynasty.

Luke had taken charge, making all the arrangements. Storm had let him, too grief stricken, too wretched, too disoriented to get herself together for the task. She had no one now. She had never known her mother. Her father was gone. Totally orphaned at twenty-seven.

Luke knew how she felt. He had lived half of his life that way.

Only on the day of the funeral did Storm regain control. Perfectly dressed in an outfit that had to be flown in as was his, a two-piece black suit, lustrous pearls at her throat and her ears, black pumps on her narrow feet, her long hair drawn back into a coiled pleat, a black hat with a down-turned brim on her head. Luke marvelled at the transition from brokenhearted child to woman in control. Only once at the graveside did she buckle but he had his arm beneath hers to support her. Somehow they got through, though Luke could feel the agony in her.

Up at the house, though he stayed near her, she seemed

in perfect control of her emotions, but her beautiful skin that had taken on a golden glow after her weeks in the sun had a tell-tale pallor. Mourners approached her to offer their sympathy and she spoke to each one in turn, her face sad but never betraying the full extent of her anguish. That was for later. Noni and her helpers circulated, offering platters of finger food and sandwiches. Tea and coffee was served, as well as cold drinks and spirits for the men. The men expected it as her father would have expected it at a friend's wake. No matter what, people had to be fed. Most of them had come a long way.

Carla Prentice, who with her parents had attended the funeral as a matter of course, waited her moment to get Luke alone, the depth of her jealousy startling herself. For at least an hour he had hovered around Storm like a body-guard, his attitude clearly protective. As if Storm needed any protection. Carla seethed as she stared across the packed room to where Storm was standing talking to the Davisons, a wealthy pastoral family. Storm had taken off that very becoming hat—too becoming for a funeral Carla thought—the severity of her tightly pulled back hairdo un-expectedly flattering. It showed off the perfection of her profile and the long swan neck. A very cool one was Storm, Carla thought, her throat tightening, eyes flinty. What made her think she was so superior? Why did people approach her the way they did? Anyone would think she was royalty.

Karen Prentice joined her daughter for a moment, her voice flat with warning. "Take that scowl off your face, Carla. It's most inappropriate."

Carla brushed her curly hair from her forehead. "I'd no idea I was scowling," Carla retorted, a light flush staining her cheeks.

Her mother's voice was low and toneless. "My dear, you're looking at Storm as though you hate her."

Was she? Carla felt instant shame. "Sorry, Mum."

Her mother took her hand. "Don't think I don't know how you feel. Luke is overdoing it following Storm around. But then she has no-one really."

"She has plenty of friends," Carla pointed out, her voice strained. She was unable to take her eyes off Storm and Luke. Luke was talking to Senator Austin but he was only a few feet away from Storm. Even in the heat when most of the other men had removed their jackets, Luke still wore a beautifully tailored black suit, his black tie sombre against the snowy-white of his shirt. Carla didn't see him formally dressed that often, now she gazed at him with such longing it seemed too much to bear. How handsome he was.

She could hear the sound of his voice, dark with a little edge to it, so attractive her mother always said it was just plain seductive. It had certainly seduced her. No other woman had snatched him from her grasp and a lot had tried. When Luke had appeared interested she had taken a few necessary steps. Lied if she had to. Carla felt a wave of self-disgust sweep over her. She had never imagined she could act the way she had. Falling in love with Luke had made her a little crazy. Even Storm had the notion they were friends when Storm was the enemy, beyond competition. When Storm was around everything changed.

A woman close to Carla was weeping quietly, comforted by a friend. Carla felt like weeping, too. Not for Athol McFarlane. For herself.

Senator Austin moved off leaving Luke momentarily on his own. Carla came out of her spell to rush to his side, clutching his arm.

"Impossible to believe the Major has gone." Now she allowed a few tears to come into her eyes.

"Yes." Luke sighed deeply, looking over to Storm's slender black-clad figure. "There's a lot of grief facing Storm. I know how I feel. Bereft. The Major was kindness itself to me."

Carla nodded. "I know he was, Luke, but you were worth your weight in gold to him. These last few years you're the one who's been running Winding River. My big thought is how is the Major going to express his gratitude?"

"Meaning what?" Luke's voice was a little hard.

"Come on." Carla hugged him gently. "Don't get me wrong, Luke. I only mean the Major is sure to mention you in his will. For that matter what is going to happen here on the station? Storm has her own life in Sydney. She's anything but a countrywoman now. I expect when she's feeling better she'll return there."

"We haven't discussed anything, Carla. It's been such a shock even though we all knew the Major was ill. But Storm is her father's daughter. She'll make the right decision."

"She'd be mad to let you go," Carla said wholeheartedly, forced to face the danger.

"I may well be looking for something else myself," Luke surprised her by saying wryly.

"Really?" Carla's gold-brown eyes opened wide. Hope stretched before her. "You could just about walk into any job you liked. We all know you could handle the top job on any station no matter how big. And you're such a great businessman!" She sparkled up at him and pressed closer.

Luke made no response to that but said quietly, "I think Garth Fullerton wants to have a word with me. Would you excuse me, Carla."

"Of course" came the gentle reply. "I've been waiting to speak to Storm. My heart aches for her. Now might be the moment. That Isabelle person has been monopolizing her for ages."

"Storm, darling," Carla cooed, when she reached the other young woman's side. "Why don't you come and sit down. You've been standing such a long time. Could I get you something? A cold drink?"

"Ye-es, please, Carla, if you would." Storm was grateful for Carla's intervention. Isabelle Parish was a very nice woman, but she did tend to go on.

Carla, loathe to give up her place, put up a hand to signal one of the house girls who arrived with a tray of cold drinks. "Orange all right, Storm?" she asked.

"Mineral water if there's any." Storm sank into a chair, wondering if she could last much longer.

Carla put a glass into Storm's hand.

"Thank you, Carla."

"You're so pale." Carla was torn between genuine sympathy and self-interest. "Is there anything I can do for you? You're so brave. Everyone admires you."

"What else *can* I be, Carla?" Storm asked, the usual colour missing from her voice. "Dad would expect me to conduct myself well. Even at his funeral."

No tears, thought Carla judgementally dismissing the depth of Storm's feeling. In reality Storm was in shock, numb with disbelief.

"There must be hundreds here," Carla said, almost brightly, looking around.

"So many good people." Storm was struggling to hold onto her exemplary control.

"Luke has been a great support to you," Carla pointed out, a little awed by Storm's beauty and dignified manner.

"Yes, he has," Storm acknowledged. "I don't think I

could have endured it without him. He's shielded me from so much.''

Carla was tempted to say: *Far too much.* ''I can understand you're very glad he's here. In a sense you'll be lost when he moves on.''

''What?'' Abruptly Storm came out of her grief-induced haze. ''What did you say?''

Carla could see quite clearly she was disturbed. ''I'm sorry…I haven't upset you, have I?'' she begged. ''I thought Luke would have told you he has plans to move on.''

Storm felt the ground had moved beneath her feet. ''We haven't spoken about anything, Carla,'' she said, her throat gone dry. ''Has Luke spoken to you?''

Carla hesitated, a pitying look in her eyes. ''Luke and I discuss most things, Storm,'' she confided gently. ''You must know we've grown very close?''

Storm nodded. ''Of course.'' Luke had known Carla for years.

''It would be impossible to hold onto Luke anyway,'' Carla continued kindly. ''I know he considered he was under a tremendous obligation to the Major—the Major being so good to him—but now the Major's gone.''

''You sound as though that makes you happy?'' Storm looked up from the contemplation of her empty glass. Even through the pall of grief and depression she could sense Carla's inner coldness and dislike.

''I'm happy when Luke's happy,'' Carla said, reaching over to pat Storm's hand somewhat patronisingly. ''We can be serious now about our future.''

''What stopped you being serious before?'' Lacking in energy though she was, Storm faced Carla, at the same time removing her hand.

Carla appeared not to notice. She glanced over to where

Luke was standing in sombre conversation with other cat-
tlemen. "Luke has had such close ties to your family,
Storm." Her voice held faint disapproval. "I mean it's
really extraordinary the way your lives have become entwined. You could almost be brother and sister."

Storm felt a little of her unnatural control slip from her.
She stared back. "What nonsense, Carla." She shook her
head. "Luke has never been a brother figure to me. I'm
sure he'd tell you I've never been any little sister to him,
either."

"Maybe not." Carla seemed to blanch at the expression
in Storm's green eyes. Suddenly she regretted what she
had started. "But you are bonded in a way. I'm only saying with the Major gone Luke is free to lead his own life."

"He's always been free, Carla," she said.

With a huge effort Storm rose steadily to her feet.

By late afternoon everyone had left. Private planes, charter
planes, helicopters including a large Sikorsky helicopter
belonging to a multimillionaire grazier, charter buses,
4WD's. Storm had retired to her room but found she
couldn't lose herself in sleep. It would be hard enough
when night finally fell and she had to get through those
long, melancholy hours. Tom Skinner had left her with a
sedative. If the worst came to the worst she would take
that. For now she changed into her riding clothes and went
down to the stables where one of the boys, seeing her
coming, saddled up Rising Star.

She wanted to gallop to the ends of the earth. And beyond. Frightened of the searing grief that was in her;
frightened by what Carla had told her. So Luke wanted
out? Whatever happened between them, she'd always believed he would stay.

Why? She needed to face the fact she had been an arrogant, complacent fool. When had she ever shown her appreciation for all Luke's hard work, his many skills, not the least of them that visionary business brain, his loyalty and devotion to her father? Why had she ignored him when he said he would never work for her? She had grown used to Luke as a fixture in her life. As if Luke for all their differences would always be there.

What have I done?

On this day of days she had never wanted to hear she could lose Luke. Luke was too important. Not only to Winding River but to her.

She turned towards the endless mulga plains, then gave the mare her head, urging her on as though the two of them were hell-bent on winning an important race. They took an old broken fence, relic of a holding yard, she, perfectly still and balanced, as Rising Star soared over it athletically, comfortably clearing the top rung. The next one they came on, the mare, responding to Storm's reckless mood, took it at too much of a rush. Power and speed took them over but it had been a near thing. Storm chastened, eased up, her heart thudding.

Her father had gone from her life. In one fatal stroke she was on her own. Now Carla was telling her she and Luke had plans. It didn't seem possible Luke could make that kind of commitment to Carla then kiss her as he had done. Maybe it had been anger, accumulated years of resentments, but there had been passion there. On both sides, the depth of which had shocked her. She'd been perfectly well aware Carla had been pursuing Luke for years. Carla was a stayer, one hundred per cent committed to a particular course of action. Luke was a catch in any woman's language even without a family dynasty and everything that went with it. Power, influence, money. Carla's father was a very wealthy man. Rich girls could marry poor guys

if the guy had much to offer. Like Luke. Luke would fit
very nicely into the Prentice operation. It was big enough
to accommodate two sons and a dynamic son-in-law.

It couldn't be true! She couldn't make sense of it. She
had seen Luke and Carla together, sensed they had once
been lovers, but it was an attraction that had gradually
died. On Luke's part, she'd thought. She kept remembering
people did marry for money. It happened all the time.
Many a wedding she had attended weren't exactly love
matches. They were well-considered social and business
contracts. And they seemed to work when romantic love
as a sole basis for marriage was often not enough. Carla,
though she appeared so open and direct, was a woman of
wiles. A calculating woman. Luke had talked about starting up his own operation. Banks weren't lending as they
used to. He would need a lot of money behind him. Or a
rich father-in-law?

That wasn't Luke. She had come to see Luke in all his
facets. Except one. As a lover. Storm sighed deeply. It
seemed she had spent her life in self-deception....

She was overlong getting back to the homestead, not
caring she had strayed into the hill country. If dark fell
and she had to spend the night in the wild she would have
a few dingos for company. She was dimly aware of riding
into the lit stables, one of the boys helping her dismount,
taking the reins from her, all the time speaking soothingly
as if to an invalid. She couldn't describe how she felt.
Numb wasn't an appropriate word. There was too much
pain there, just barely papered over.

Half-way up to the house Luke, walking very purposefully, met up with her.

"Thank God you're home." His voice was worried.
"I've had a couple of men out looking for you for the last

half hour. Where were you? Not in the usual places, that's for sure."

"I don't honestly know. I was straying."

"Straying is dangerous. Don't ever go off without telling us where you're heading."

She could feel herself tensing. "Ah then, but I'm the boss remember?" It was the worst tack to take but she was dreadfully off balance.

"I don't care who you are," Luke said, locking her with his gaze. "You can't leave worried people behind you."

"I'm sorry, Luke. I appreciate your concern." The answer was truthful, edged with just a little touch of jarring irony. It was too well ingrained.

"So you're coming back to the house?" he asked.

"Nowhere else to go."

"You've barely eaten for days," he pointed out, the note of concern still in his voice. "You'll have to try something."

"I suppose." For an instant she felt like throwing herself into his arms. She was so weary. "It just doesn't seem to want to go down my neck."

They had reached the front steps, Storm starting up them slowly, Luke standing perfectly still on the drive looking up at her. "Aren't you coming in?" She couldn't bear to be without him.

He didn't miss the inflection of dismay. "If you want me to." His voice was a little rough.

"I don't want to be on my own tonight," Storm said and she didn't care how it sounded.

CHAPTER FIVE

THEY ate in the kitchen. Noni, fighting her own deep distress, had been sent off with her friend, Ellen, to take a break from so much trauma. Always a tower of strength, Noni had appeared close to breakdown, too vulnerable to insist on staying which she considered her duty. It was Luke who convinced her he would be there to support Storm.

After her ride, Storm took a long shower letting volumes of precious water pour down on her head in an effort to rid herself of the anguish that threatened to break cover. Thank God Luke had come for her when he had. She would never have forgiven herself had her father died without her.

''Dad!'' Her voice was thick with emotion. She simply couldn't absorb it.

Afterwards she sat quietly at the table watching Luke going about the business of making them something to eat. What am I she thought? A child? But she'd come to a crossroad. She was aware as well she had always been subject to intense emotions. Luke hadn't even asked her what she wanted to eat, realising she didn't much care. He moved with such supple grace. A man totally at ease with his own body. At ease with himself.

After a while she got to her feet to find plates and cutlery. Luke had already thrown a clean white cloth over the Victorian pine table with its four Windsor chairs. Now she replaced the large fruit filled silver bowl centre table, breaking off a couple of grapes and placing them absent-

mindedly into her mouth. The kitchen had a lot of atmosphere, comfortable and friendly in contrast to the formal
rooms of the house, which were overly grand, enriched by
splendours her forebears had acquired at some stage. Occasionally she'd had notions of redecorating, weeding out
certain objects and pieces of furniture but her father had
been adamant the house had to stay as it was.

"Now it's all mine," she murmured aloud. No joy in
it. A statement of fact.

"The big thing is what you're going to *do* with it?"
Luke asked quietly, adding dressing to the salad and tossing it until the various greens were lightly coated.

"God knows! It can't go out of the family."

"Unthinkable!" he said. "Isn't Bloomfield coming back
tomorrow?" He referred to the family solicitor, senior
partner in the firm of Bloomfield, Bloomfield and Merrick.

Storm nodded. "I asked him to stay over but he said he
had things to discuss with Scott Cunningham. Mr. Cunningham is a client as well. Anyway I'm in no frame of
mind to hear Dad's will. Are you?" She shot him a glance
that burnt out of her pale face.

"Just take it quietly, Storm," he advised, pouring lightly
beaten seasoned eggs into a hot pan that was foaming with
a little butter and oil. She could smell the fresh scent of
the parsley and snipped chives he had stirred into the mixture.

"You're certain to be mentioned," she said in a matter-
of-fact voice.

"Does that bother you?" He glanced over his shoulder.

"Of course it doesn't. You deserve far more than a mention for everything you've done. Dad wasn't the easiest of
men but you always knew how to keep the harmony."

"It wasn't difficult." With the omelette coming together

Luke sprinkled the surface with grated parmesan. "This looks good. I expect you to eat it."

"You're quite a dab hand at making omelettes." She watched him fold it with the ease of an expert turning it out onto a warmed plate and sprinkling the top with a little more parmesan.

"It's the ultimate fast food. It's nothing to work a four-teen-hour day. I needed to master something simple and quick."

Storm sat down again, contemplating the pattern in the damask tablecloth. "Perhaps that says a lot about you, Luke. You master anything you turn your hand to."

They ate in near silence. Luke poured some wine. "What are we celebrating?" Storm asked, her eyes seeking his. Part of her was deeply disturbed, the other part surprised at how good the omelette was; how fresh the chilled wine tasted on her tongue.

He studied her a long while. She was wearing not a skerrick of make-up, eyebrows, eyelashes like black velvet, skin flawless, her mouth a natural tea-rose. But her eyes were dark with intensity. "You need to unwind a little, Storm. A glass or two of wine will help relax you."

"I have to make sure it does." She sipped a little more, staring across the table at him, this unique man who was woven into the very fabric of her life. "I want you to know how much I appreciate all you've done for me these past days," she said a little raggedly. "I thought I could run my own life but losing Dad has been like a great earthquake." Her hand tightened on her glass, until the knuckles showed white.

"I understand," he said quietly. He felt pretty much the same way.

Another silence, stamped with tension.

"And when did you propose to tell me about your

plans?'' she fired at him much later, her voice so brittle it cracked a little.

''What plans?'' he countered, disturbed by the tremor in her hands.

Storm hesitated a moment, appalled by the thought she might cry. ''I may have this wrong but I gathered from Carla you only stayed on for Dad. Without him you'd planned to move on.''

Something near anger burned in him, showed itself in his electric glance. ''When did you learn this?''

She rubbed her eyes a little desperately. ''This afternoon.''

''You mean Carla broached the subject today of all days?''

''I don't think she could resist it. Is it true?''

He reached across the table and grabbed her trembling hand, his fingers very tanned against her ivory skin.

''Why would I discuss my plans with Carla before talking to you?''

''You tell me?'' God how her heart hurt!

''I'll tell you it sounds darned odd. Can you *ever* believe in me?'' His voice was taut.

''I'm sorry. Are you saying Carla is making it all up?''

''I guess I am. Carla isn't above pulling a few tricks. I could cite a case,'' he began, but switched off. ''What was your conversation about?''

''Lord, Luke.'' She nearly laughed. ''About you. Carla says among other things you and she have made a commitment to each other.''

''Have we really?'' he said, almost amusedly, the overhead light ringing his dark red head with fire. ''I think Carla finds the odd lie downright useful.''

''You haven't?'' She looked at him questioningly, relief welling inside her.

It showed. "You make it sound like it's very important to you." He gave just a glimpse of his beautiful, illuminating smile.

"It *is*." Her voice carried sincerity. "I know I've said a lot of things in the past—I was wrong—but I couldn't do without you. I couldn't run Winding River, let alone the whole operation. Dad made a point of keeping me sidelined. I had to turn my attentions, my energies elsewhere."

"And in doing so discovered your own talent," he replied, hoping he meant a hell of a lot more to her than a highly valued employee. "You're a creative person, Storm. Designing and making beautiful jewellery must give you a sense of accomplishment?"

She nodded. "It does, but now I'm left with one of the biggest cattle operations in the country and I know next to nothing about it."

"You can learn."

She held up a hand. "*Can* I?"

"You're a highly intelligent woman. The big question *is* do you *want* to run a string of cattle stations?"

At the thought fatigue washed over her, she swallowed, feeling the great weight of her new responsibilities. "I'd like to know as much as I possibly can. Besides who could I trust to run it outside you?"

"Actually you could find someone," he answered more crisply than he intended, the urge to take her in his arms so powerful he nearly buckled under it.

"I don't want to."

What was he? Overseer, business manager? Nothing *more?* "I don't know that it suits me to walk a couple of steps behind you, Storm." He saw very clearly how that might be.

She raised her beautiful shadowed eyes with the first sign of anger. "You mean you won't work for a *woman?*"

"I mean I won't work for *you*," he answered without a pause. "You know too well how to make it tough for me. We've had a very stormy relationship. Just like your name."

"I was jealous of you, Luke. You can't possibly know how it was." She sat back in her chair, pushing her freshly washed hair over her shoulders. "I could hear myself shouting but it was like a voice in the desert. Dad had such power over me and he used it. To my shame I have to admit I was terribly jealous. But you wouldn't turn your back on me now? You wouldn't leave me when I desperately need you?"

He stared into her black-fringed emerald eyes. "When my life to date has been Winding River? I'll stay on until I can find someone to take my place. I'm not irreplaceable, Storm."

She gave a little wry smile. "Dad seemed to think so and he would know. I'm not about to crawl even for you. I don't want to insult you, either, but I have no idea what Dad was paying you."

"Storm, darling, a lot," he drawled, tossing off his wine.

"Knowing Dad you must have earned it," she retorted, her heart jumping at the endearment even if it was sardonic. "I'll pay more." What was she doing talking about *money?* The mistress in the Big House! Without Luke she'd be lost in more ways than she could yet imagine or fully understand.

"Don't let's talk about this tonight," he said.

"Why not?" She met the molten blueness of his eyes. "It diverts my mind when I'm full of grief and panic. Were you *ever* in love with Carla?" She had struggled not to ask that, but lost the battle.

"That's my business," he pointed out calmly, the light falling on his clean, chiselled facial bones.

But once started, she found it difficult to stop. "I thought it was all over. She says it's not."

"I thought your involvement with Alex was over?" he countered, preserving his cool front in an excess of strong emotion.

"It is but that doesn't mean we're not still friends."

"The same goes for Carla and me." He shrugged.

Restlessly she pushed her plate away, her heart labouring. "You'd better tell *her* that. She's madly in love with you, Luke."

He heard the combined note of worry and jealousy with a rush of pure joy. "You know I think you're probably right but I made no promises to Carla."

"You *were* lovers?" She put it to him too fervidly, betraying the extent of her own involvement.

"And you and Alex and the guy before him weren't?" he asked dryly. "Don't let's get into an argument."

She bit her lip, then shook her head. "Not me. I'm going to be good from now on."

He reached over, caught her hand and lightly shook it. "Well then, you can try. We can't go on as we did before. You know that, don't you?" His voice was deep, quiet and steady. It carried great conviction.

Some of the great pain eased within her but she didn't answer. Storm hadn't yet learned to reveal her secret heart.

The wine made her drowsy; gave her a few hours heavy sleep. She awoke in the early hours, thinking she heard footsteps; her father's heavy, uneven tread along the corridor before he retired for bed. She sat up quickly, for one long, dislocated moment thinking the last terrible week hadn't really happened. It had all been a nightmare. If she got up now, opened her door and called to him, "Everything all right, Dad?'' he would answer, ''I'm fine, darling. Go back to bed.''

Except he would never speak to her again.

Storm found the bedside light switch, her breath ragged over the trip-hammering of her heart.

''Dear God!'' she said aloud. It was neither a prayer nor an outpouring of despair. Perhaps a bit of both. The digital clock read 1:40 a.m. With trembling fingers she pushed back the top sheet and the light coverlet walking through to the ensuite and turning on the light. She was bone-white, her eyes bruised and shadowed. She turned on the cold water, splashed her face several times, patted it dry, drank a long glass of water, then began to retrace her steps. Chanting carried on the wind. She listened with a kind of wonder. The aboriginal people who moved freely across the station had organised their own wake. Athol McFarlane had always treated them so well and respected their culture.

It was a beautiful moonlight night but Storm was almost blind to it. She padded out onto the verandah listening to the mournful singing from the camps. It had stopped at some point but started up again. Death, the final crisis of the life cycle, was always associated with ritual, she thought. For the white man and the aboriginal. In the Dreamtime death wasn't always inevitable, but someone in the beginning had taken the fatal step that set the precedent; like the story of Adam and Eve. Like her own people death, too, despite belief in an afterlife, was an extremely upsetting affair for the aboriginals. Athol McFarlane's death had affected every last man, woman and child on the station and the news had been communicated far in the desert tribes. The mourning ritual had gone on for many hours of the burial day, but after the wailing a great stillness would fall over the bush. The chants weren't only to accompany her father to the spirit world and see him safely settled, they were meant to give comfort to her. In a way they did but the mournful singing marked by clap sticks and sand drums added to her acute emotional distress. She found her heart breaking and breaking all over again. Grief would stay a long time in her veins.

Desperation carried her down the verandah to the large guest room where Luke was sleeping. There had been no talk of his returning to the bungalow. Storm hadn't wanted to be alone; Luke was very upset himself, so it had been agreed without words that he would stay in the house.

She cared nothing for her flimsy attire, too distracted by her need for comfort. The only person in the world she could look to for comfort now was Luke. Luke had known her all her life. Her father had loved him like a son. Probably in ways she as a female could never have attained. At any rate, more than her. But Luke at this moment was her only salvation. He, too, had been dealt a terrible blow by her long-adored father's death. So at the end a very complex but unbreakable bond held them fast.

Luke woke out of a fitful sleep to see her framed in the doorway.

For an instant he was blinded as if by an apparition. The radiant moonlight streamed through her long gauzy gown, delineating the lovely curves of her body, edging them in silver. Her wonderful glossy raven's wing mane tumbled over her shoulders dishevelled by sleep. She was the absolute essence of woman, the beauty, the mystery, the boundless allure.

While he watched spellbound she called pleadingly. ''Are you awake, Luke?''

He felt like saying he was immediately awake every time she came into his orbit.

"Storm, what's wrong?" He got up very fast, the moon illuminating his lean, hard body, naked except for a pair of navy boxer shorts.

"I know it's crazy, but I'm a little scared. I thought I heard Dad's footsteps coming down the hall."

He didn't blame her. It was a very strange night and the chanting at the camp was so melancholy it could push anyone over the edge. "Your father would never hurt you," he said gently. "It's your overwrought mind playing tricks."

"Oh, Luke," she said. "I can't believe he's dead."

"Do you want to go downstairs?" he asked, his blood running hot just looking at her.

"I want to stay here. Can I? I won't bother you in any way."

Her voice was as sweet as a little girl's. My God, could she really believe that? But helpless tears glittered in her beautiful eyes.

"Sure." He spoke with a kind of asexual comforting tone. "You take the bed. I'll take the armchair over there. You'll probably need your own pillows. I'll go back and get them." He went to move out onto the verandah but she plunged almost desperately past him into the room.

"I want you to put your arms around me. It's wonderful sometimes to have a man by your side."

He could have groaned aloud but he didn't. "Hey, Storm, this is going far beyond our usual exchanges. I can handle them."

"I've been awful to you all my life but I'm going to make it up to you. Carla even said she thought of us as almost brother and sister."

"Yeah?" he rasped. "Carla was simply trying to fool herself and she's no fool."

"All right, I know it's never been like *that* but you're

the only one I've got. I'm only going to lie down." She turned towards the bed and slipped beneath the thin cover. "Look at it, it's big. There's plenty of room. I'll be myself again tomorrow. Promise."

To take advantage of her would be the ultimate betrayal. He knew he could *never* do it. To his utter horror he agreed. "Okay. You're going to have to go off to sleep now because I have to make my usual pre-dawn start. No matter how terrible this week has been the work never stops."

"You've made it endurable," she whispered, as he moved onto the bed, lying down and tucking his arm beneath his head, his heart knocking so loudly against his chest surely she must hear it, but she turned her body towards him, a sorrowing child again, not a woman aware of her own extraordinary power. She lay barely covered by the thin sheet. He made extra sure he lay on top of it, though if it were an iron barrier, his body temperature would have melted it.

"Good night, Luke," she said softly, lifting her head slightly and kissing his cheek. "You couldn't be cruel to me if you tried."

She wasn't faking anything as another woman might have done. Not Storm though she was very seriously in need of him. His silence, however, contained grief, wonderment and the fiercest inflammable frustration that kept him very still, every muscle rigid with tension. He was a man like any other man. Not a superman. Didn't she know anything might set him off? A slender arm flung across his chest in sleep? Her satiny face burrowing into his neck? The scent of her assailed his nostrils, full of so much allure, so much sexual intoxication, he made a near infinitesimal movement of withdrawal.

She stirred. "Oh, Luke, don't pull away," she begged,

her heavy eyelashes already falling. Pull away? When he wanted to bind her so tightly she would never get away!

It took her two minutes to fall into a light sleep, her body relaxed, as though she knew even in her subconscious being with him kept her safe.

He loved her of course. He loved her fire. Her quick temper. He loved her in all her dimensions; the sweetness, the zest for life, her artistry. He loved her capacity for deep feeling. Her love of the land. He even loved the flashes of lightning that went off when they were on the verge of a huge argument. It was impossible to capture her yet here she was in his bed, sleeping on his shoulder, his arm going a little numb from supporting her head. It could fall off for love of her, he thought. Damn you, Storm!

Ten minutes later he dared to look down at her sleeping face. She was fast asleep now, lashes still. The room was almost stage lit bathed in moonlight. The deep V of her lace trimmed nightgown revealed the exquisite shape of her breasts. By this time he was feeling a little wild and he was a man who had long since learned tight self-control.

Time to move to the chair. But she seemed to feel his intentions even in her sleep. She flung out one arm just as he feared, turning her body further to be nearer his.

God, you've got to help me through this, Luke prayed. I'm a decent man. But I'm a man in love.

So appealed to, God heard. Eventually Luke slept.

Storm opened her eyes with a start, wondering briefly, wildly, where she was. The air hung with a pre-dawn silence that would soon be dispersed by the songs of a trillion birds. A soft, misty light was entering the bedroom, pearling down on her and a man's long muscled back, the skin polished bronze, velvet in texture. He was turned so

far away from her he was on the very edge of the bed.
The head on the snowy pillow glowed like a dark flame.

Luke.

He looked utterly beautiful. A marvellous man. She'd
been afraid of him for most of her life, so powerful were
her feelings of coming second best. The mystery was how
she had retained so much confidence in her personal worth.
She and Luke hadn't got on at all. She knew now it was
because she'd always been in jealous competition for her
father's attention. It was her father's doing; though he had
been genuinely unaware he was causing such damage. The
result was she had elected to take it out on Luke. Himself
a victim of tragic circumstances.

Desire such as she had never known spiralled in her.
Up…up…making her feel light-headed. She wanted to
stroke him, so badly she couldn't control it. Her fingers
reached out, feathering along his skin. It seemed like some
kind of miracle—he was here with her until she recalled
she had begged him to stay in case her grief and sense of
dislocation carried her away.

"Luke…"

She held her breath, her fingers deepening the pressure,
so she was caressing his warm flesh.

He came awake at once, slicking his hair back with his
hand. He turned towards her, with such a rush of joy it lit
him up like a torch. Such naked longing was in her beautiful green eyes he didn't hesitate. He pulled her down to
him with strong, powerful arms, pressing her to him.
Blinding desire drove out any other consideration but having her. God hadn't he imagined it? Too frequently. *This*
was unstoppable.

"Luke—"

Just saying his name was a release. Her voice broke, but
he muffled her murmurs with his mouth, kissing her so

deeply and in such a fashion, she gasped once forbidden little endearments into his mouth, her fingernails digging into the bare skin of his back.

Inhibition vanished like puffs of sand on the desert wind. "I want you desperately," he muttered, his voice half smothered by her cushioned lips. "Lord, don't you know that?"

She tried to draw back a little, overwhelmed by the magic, her cheeks flushed with body heat. She stared into his taut face, her eyes enormous, dark green. "Make love to me, Luke," she whispered. "I can't fight you any more." The haunting was over.

If only that were true! He wished it with all his heart, but doubt pursued him. He had lived through long years of rejection by this beautiful creature.

But she kissed him. A kiss that transcended his fears. The initiative entirely hers, the kiss lingered on with such bewitching seductiveness he felt the blood beat hot and heavy in his veins and pool in his loins. He would never forget the touch of her lips, the irresistible softness, the satiny texture. His hands moved compulsively in a great, primitive yearning to know her body, finding first the pearly mounds of her breasts, feeling the wild beating of her heart beneath his palm. Her nipples were tightly crushed berries, the electric tingling his fingers induced in her, transmitting itself to him.

To be with her was ecstasy. He felt as though he was drowning in a tumult of sensation. That in itself was a frightening thing. For him to give so much power to this woman. It was an enormous risk yet he was so violently aroused, in such a frenzy of intoxication; he was unable to resist the magnitude of the temptation. There was no past. Perhaps no future. He only knew there was the here and now.

She was reciprocating, her slender limbs spread and writhing in a high state of excitement as he went about exploring her body passionately, deliberately, intimately. She was perfect. Everything he had ever dreamed about. He would always have her…if only in his dreams.

Excitement mounted to a kind of rage. Delirium. He could hold back no longer, the hard trembling starting up in his arms. But he had brought her to the very peak of rapture so she was guiding him irresistibly into her body, her movements swelling, her rhythm matching his. He was taking her away; far into that enchanted world inhabited only by lovers.

The rising sun brightened the sky. Rosy light stole across the bed, bathing the beautiful, naked bodies curved and fused as one.

CHAPTER SIX

WONDERMENT shielded her from the worst of her grieving. The residual mists of magic clung to her through the morning and helped her rejoice in the celebration of *life*. After the dawn's transforming experience she had fallen asleep, awakening long after Luke had left. She hadn't had a chance to speak to him about how she wanted him to be in attendance at Robert Bloomfield's visit. However, it had been agreed over supper the night before he would greet the solicitor at the airstrip and drive him up to the house. Senior partner in the family firm of Bloomfield, Bloomfield and Merrick, Robert had been her father's solicitor ever since she could remember. He would arrive in time for lunch. After that they would retire to her father's study where Robert would read the will. Storm wanted Luke to be with her. Luke was sure to be a beneficiary. He had a right to be there and she would probably have some expert advice.

Storm felt certain of the will's contents. Bequests to charities, extended family members, goddaughter, two godsons, lifelong employees, that sort of thing. Certainly Noni would receive something. Noni had been a wonderful support. But the bulk of her father's estate, which had to be considerable—though she had no real knowledge of his affairs—would go to her as his only child. She had no great interest in becoming a very rich woman probably because she had been an heiress all her life. Privilege was part of her background, not that she didn't thank God every day for it. She would continue the practice of family philanthropy. Get involved.

She went about the business of preparing lunch, dreaming a little, feeling guilty as though she had had no right to dream with her father so newly dead but the height of intimacy she and Luke had attained had given her strength. She set the table, three places, in the formal dining room, overlooking the rear garden with its groves of native trees, dense plantings of agapanthus and silver and grey foliaged plants all of which withstood the rigours of the Dry. A small pond fed by an underground spring was full of perfect water-lilies the colour of the sunrise. Tiny black native bees hung like clouds above the huge blooms drunk on the nectar. She could smell the heady perfume as it floated through the open windows.

The station was synonymous with water-lilies. They floated every billabong, every lagoon, their beautiful showy heads standing high above the water, the blue, the violet, the purple, the exquisite fragrant pinks and the hardy white with their deep golden centres. She stood for a moment staring out, a little awed by the depth of her feelings, wanting to protect them. They were so very new, so tender, like a newborn babe. Feelings only Luke had been able to call up so effortlessly.

Their lovemaking had been breathtaking, full of intense excitement, surprises and blood rushing need. Her shattering climax had been totally unfeigned. He had played her body like the most sensitive instrument in a master's hands.

She had never known anything remotely like it and she was a woman who had imagined herself in love at least twice. It occurred to her how contemptuous, however benignly, her father had been of all her male friends, especially the men she had allowed herself to become engaged to. She thanked God now she hadn't done them much harm. Paul had another love interest, a fellow woman barrister who would suit him far better than she ever would; Alex was hanging in there, thinking persistence would win the fair maiden but she realised now she had fallen in love with Alex for the most superficial reasons. He was good-looking, good company, intelligent, ambitious, but she knew he hadn't even begun to tap into her body's needs, let alone touch her soul.

Time now she stopped betraying herself. Time she stopped the self-deception. Her accumulated resentments, her flawed perceptions had all but robbed her of Luke. Her father in championing him, showing his deep regard and admiration had perversely turned her in many a wrong direction. Time all that was stopped.

But what of Luke? Even at the height of passion, when not only their bodies but their souls were naked, neither had uttered one word of love. Surely her endearments had been so frantic as to be incoherent? Luke had told her he wanted her. She had revealed in every possible way she wanted him. Needed him desperately.

Surely that was love?

The word whispered aloud, quivered like a butterfly on the delicate petal of a flower. All this she found soul-shaking. Her feelings were so profound they scared her. Love was the most precious commodity in the world. The most talked about. The most desired. Once given it put great and dangerous power into the hands of the beloved.

The beloved! There was no terror in whispering it to herself. Luke, the beloved. Her love for him had taken root long, long ago but it had never been allowed to bloom. The high fence for her now was finding the courage to allow it full growth, full expression. Did one learn that overnight or were all the defences she had built up too strong to be knocked over at will?

One thing was certain. Luke being the man he was would not brook any continuation of her former touch-me-not behaviour. How ridiculous she seemed to herself now. The haughty little girl, the even haughtier adolescent, the cool cutting woman.

Shame on you, Storm.

The grandfather clock in the hallway chimed noon. It brought her out of her reverie. Robert Bloomfield was due to fly in within the next half hour. Everything was in readiness. Nothing elaborate. That was inappropriate. Tarragon chicken salad with a handful of shelled walnuts thrown in. She'd made it and refrigerated it a couple of hours before. No Noni to bake fresh rolls. There weren't any left in the freezer, either, so she had to make up a batch of little dampers sprinkled with poppy seeds. Noni had taught her a few things. The little dampers were delicious with or without butter. Even if Luke, unprepared, couldn't stay for lunch she hoped he could be on hand for the reading of the will.

She was waiting on the verandah when they arrived, a cool vision in white linen with one of her own beautiful silver belts with turquoise and agate beads roped around her small waist.

Robert Bloomfield, a substantial, clever-looking man with a shock of prematurely white hair and contrasting very dark eyes, mounted the short flight of steps to greet her. "Storm, my dear! How are you?" It wasn't simply social lubrication. The answer really mattered to him. He had known Storm all her life. Long sympathised with her vulnerable position as a lone little motherless girl in what was essentially a tough man's world. His dear friend,

Athol, had always sought to protect her but he treated her like a fragile exotic flower instead of a desert rose. Storm in reality was as hardy as they come. As she would have to be once she learned the contents of her father's will. If she so chose it was contestable, he would be willing to represent her.

Storm was raising her cheek for his kiss. "A little better today, thank you, Robert. I hope the trips back and forth haven't been too tiring for you?"

"Not at all, my dear." He turned his distinguished head to include Luke, whom he liked and admired enormously. But still…?

"I didn't want Luke going to the bother of having to bring me up to the house. I know how pressured he is even at a time like this." Station work as he well knew never stopped. Dawn to dusk sometimes into the night. Seven days a week.

Luke gave him his white shining smile. "No problem." But he shifted his gaze to Storm, his feelings so intense they blazed out of his eyes. Hours later and he still felt as though he were intoxicated. Their fusion was still imprinted on his body. The magic so potent he thought it would never fade. "I'll be off now. You're okay."

Storm didn't care acute disappointment sounded in her voice. "Couldn't you stay to lunch, Luke? I'd so like you to."

"I'll second that," Robert Bloomfield spoke up, approval on his face. "I'm sure there's much to discuss."

"That would be great but I don't think I can spare the time," Luke apologised. "The rains have started up North. Flooding already. The floodwaters will eventually feed into our river system. For that matter we could have flooding here."

"So it's all hands on deck for the bit muster." Robert

Bloomfield nodded, understanding the situation perfectly. "Perhaps later on in the afternoon, Luke?"

Luke tipped his wide-brimmed akubra. "I'll try to make it up to the house before you fly back, Robert."

"But aren't you coming to hear Dad's will?" Storm found Luke's eyes almost pleadingly. "I'm sure you'll be mentioned."

"Maybe." He shrugged. Hell he deserved something but not if there was going to be any fallout. "It all has to do with you, Storm. I'm not family."

"And you're not just a valued overseer either. Please, Luke, I need you."

It was the first validation of caring Robert Bloomfield had ever heard from Storm and it set him back. As long as he could remember Storm and Luke had shared a very prickly relationship. Of course it was all Athol's fault. The man should have remarried. He'd told him so. Had sons. In McFarlane's world sons were viewed as the big assets. Daughters were the decoration. Bloomfield was aware he had taken sides long ago. His sympathies to this day were with Storm. Consequently he waited on Luke's answer with some trepidation.

Luke put a considering hand to his jaw, obviously trying to work out how he could find the time. "Can you give me a good hour?" he asked. "Maybe an hour and a half."

"Surely," Robert Bloomfield agreed, when truly, he didn't think it was a good idea at all.

They ate a companionable lunch, afterwards walking around the home grounds. They were absolutely extraordinary to Bloomfield's eyes, especially in relation to the vast wilderness beyond. Yet the landscape designer called in at the turn-of-the-century had had the great foresight—in a time when gardeners persisted in trying to plant delicate exotics—to design a magnificent native garden that conveyed a great sense of place. Over the years more in Athol's mother's time—Lady McFarlane had been a passionate gardener—the vision had expanded. He remembered as a young man marvelling at the regiment of gardeners who laboured along with the remarkable Mistress of Winding River to create ponds from subterranean streams planting the water grasses and the magnificent water-lilies that in all parts of Queensland grew like weeds except these weeds took the breath away with their beauty.

There were no sweeping lawns and garden beds of bright beautiful flowers such as his own garden in Brisbane. The homestead's extensive grounds kept to the natural contours and extraordinary flora of the desert environment, with a few introduced exotics that could withstand the conditions. Yet the flowers here seemed to smell more sweetly than anywhere else, he thought, inhaling their fragrance which carried for miles. The native boronia! Glorious! It had to have something to do with the dryness and heat releasing all the aromas.

It was a very pleasant interlude tinged with the to be expected sadness. It wasn't long after they found their way back into the house that Luke arrived. He must have decided to take a quick shower and change his clothes because he was dressed in a plain navy T-shirt with a white logo across the front, light blue jeans, his dark, fiery head damp from the shower. He was a very striking-looking young man, Bloomfield thought, looking across Athol McFarlane's huge partner's desk at him. Those handsome chiselled features, the stunning colouring. But over and above that he was a man of the future. He had the brains, the toughness, the natural authority that was God-given, to run the huge McFarlane operation.

Only one thing. He wasn't McFarlane's son. McFarlane's natural heir. Storm was. Bloomfield didn't think Storm was about to celebrate the news he now commenced to read out.

It was just as she expected, sitting side by side with Luke in leather armchairs. Bequests to various members of the McFarlane extended family; a large very valuable painting of an evening landscape by a famous early colonial artist was to go to one of Athol McFarlane's long-time mistresses. Forever kept in the background, out of respect to the memory of his wife, she was now handsomely rewarded. A range of charities were also to benefit handsomely; a collection of rare first edition books were to go to Robert Bloomfield himself, a sterling silver tea and coffee service dating from the latter part of the eighteenth century to his wife, Gillian, who had been bridesmaid at Athol McFarlane's ill-fated wedding.

Then came the crux....

Storm listened with a sense of total disbelief, so shocked she looked outwardly calm. How her father loved playing games! How transparent his motives! All her life she'd been led to believe she would inherit Winding River along with its two outstations now Robert was telling them in a completely dispassionate voice she and Luke had been accorded an equal share.

"I don't believe this!" she interrupted after a while, shaking back her heavy hair. "Didn't Dad know what this means?"

The temperature in the room had shot up for all the ceiling fans.

"I'm afraid he did, Storm," Bloomfield looked over the top of his glasses as they slipped down his nose. "Luke is to be granted what is termed a life estate. This means..."

"I know what it means," Storm said with a return to her old fire. "It means that Luke has half share in the station for his lifetime."

"After which it passes to you should you outlive him, to your issue or appointed heir," Bloomfield concluded, himself shocked by his friend's actions.

"Good God!" Luke sighed so deeply it seemed to consume his splendid, lean body. "Whatever made him do it?"

Storm swung her head, her eyes startling green. "Surely that's obvious? He had no faith in me. Any male at all would be an improvement on a woman. *You* were a natural godsend."

"Don't blame me, Storm," said Luke, picking up a glass of water and drinking from it.

"I'm *not* blaming you," she cried, recognising she was. "This is a dilemma, Luke. What are we supposed to do? Share the homestead, share the profits?"

Bloomfield coughed, lowering his eyes to the printed page. "Actually, Storm, as Luke is expected and indeed *has* to continue working the operation *he* gets the profits."

It was too much for Storm. She jumped up, her cheeks firing with colour. "What! I can't possibly accept this. God, Dad must have hated me."

Luke fixed his eyes on her. "Sit down, Storm," he said, making Storm and the solicitor witness to his tough side. "This bequest is for the sole benefit of the station. But you don't have to accept it. If you feel an overwhelming urge to contest the will, go for it."

Storm felt she was in grave danger of bursting into hysterics. "God in Heaven!" she said, but managed to sit down quietly and cover her face. "People are going to start to wonder if you aren't in fact Dad's natural son."

There was a brief silence while Luke's brilliant gaze whipped over her. "I'll forget you ever said that," he said in a deadly quiet voice.

"I'm sorry," Storm apologised. She had shocked herself. "But could you blame anyone for talking? Can you blame me for wondering what the hell is going on?"

Bloomfield looked across at her beautiful, passionate face. "I do think it was too bad of your father not to explain all this to you young people. I know it has come as a great shock but you see what he was getting at...Luke summed it up. You couldn't at this stage run Winding River yourself, Storm. You'd have to get in a full-time manager and a darn good one at that."

"I could fix that." Luke was sitting straight now.

Bloomfield shook his head. "For someone else to come in was the very last thing Athol wanted. He wanted *you*, Luke."

"My God didn't he!" Storm's little laugh broke. "He couldn't have made it any plainer." Inside she felt as if she was being pulled in all directions.

"Luke has carried the whole operation splendidly, Storm," Bloomfield pointed out. "You must give him that."

"Of course I'll give him that." Storm clenched her hands. "Luke is extremely capable like his father was before him. Dad relied on Luke even more heavily. I know what Luke can do, but God!—" She broke off, devastated.

As was Luke who felt quite stunned. "This looks like heading towards another nightmare," he said. "What happens, Robert, if I renounce this bequest?"

"Your share passes to Storm, of course," Bloomfield informed him, suddenly seeing what a bad move that might be. Especially for the station.

"Then Storm can have it," Luke said, rising to his feet. "And while she's about it she can find another overseer. I can give her a couple of names."

Storm swallowed hard, trying to get herself together. "What's wrong with you?" she demanded, thinking she was losing her right arm. "Why are you on your high horse? Did you expect me not to be shocked? You're shocked yourself. Or *are* you?" The minute the words were out of her mouth she bitterly regretted them; a legacy of all those years.

Luke ignored her. "I'd offer to drive you back to the airstrip, Robert, but I'm sure Storm can attend to that. If you'd excuse me I was paid up until the end of the month so I'll get on with my job."

"Don't you want to hear the end of it," Storm cried to his back.

"No, thank you very much." Luke swung around to answer quietly. But there was no way his inner anger could be missed. It burnt out of his eyes and showed itself in the pallor beneath his golden-bronze tan.

There was total silence in the study after Luke had left. Bloomfield holding his heavy head in his hands, Storm fighting a tidal wave of tears.

"He has his pride, my dear," Bloomfield finally pointed out quietly. "That was an unfortunate remark you made in relation to prior knowledge. You know what a secretive man your father was. If he hadn't lost your mother I'm sure he would have been quite different. In fact he was as a young man. But losing your mother changed him enormously. It wasn't inborn. I do know he adored you.

"Perhaps not in the way you wanted but according to his own lights. Women have such a wonderful refining influence on a man. I bless the day I met my Gillian. I can't imagine what my life would have been without her. Your mother would have given your father a well-integrated, happy life as she would have given you. With the best will in the world your father didn't know how to go about it."

Storm looked at him with great sadness. "That's not the

case, Robert, if you look at his relationship with Luke. Even before Luke lost his parents Dad thought the world of him.''

Bloomfield nodded his head. ''Well, Storm, it must be said, Luke's that kind of a young man. Let none of us forget he did save your father's life. It greatly reinforced the attachment.''

''Of course but it wasn't enjoyable for me. I wanted to be brave and strong like Luke. Not Dad's pretty little girl. Luke and I are so terribly enmeshed. I know it was dreadful of me to say people would wonder if he weren't in fact Dad's son, but Lord, Robert, you know as well as anyone Dad idolized him.''

''And you bitterly resent that?'' Bloomfield asked quietly, thinking it might have broken someone else.

''I did,'' Storm said, ''but I thought I had confronted it, Robert. None of this is Luke's fault. But I'm too far gone casting him as the scapegoat.''

''Except he's scarcely that,'' Bloomfield reminded her. ''If you allow me to finish reading the will, Storm, you'll find that your father left you a very rich young woman indeed. You don't need the income from the cattle operation, I assure you.''

Storm considered that carefully. ''The money is not the point, Robert. It's the whole principle of the thing. Even from the grave Dad set Luke above me.''

Bloomfield looked understanding but pained. ''I wish you wouldn't see it like that, even though I do understand. I can't find a nice word for this, but I'm afraid you have to consider your father was a master manipulator.'' He spoke very seriously but Storm gave a poignant smile.

''I know that. Luke and I have even talked about it. Dad manipulated us both. He's still at it.''

''The perfect solution would be for the two of you to

marry," Bloomfield suggested, emboldened by what he had seen on his arrival.

"Oh, Robert!" Storm started up, staring at her own portrait. What a haughty piece she looked. A real firebrand. Was she really like that? "Luke and I have never had any romantic involvement."

"Are you sure of that?" Bloomfield asked gently. "Gillian and I always thought you set one another off. I don't think, my dear, you've ever given Luke half a chance."

Storm turned. "Luke isn't a half a chance person. It's all or nothing with him. I don't deny I've fought him for most of my life. Fought off his enormous hold."

"So you are attracted to him?" Bloomfield watched her carefully.

Her expression gave her away. "The very minute I start to get things into perspective something like this happens. I never in my wildest dreams thought Dad would *handcuff* us together. I loathe it."

"I'm absolutely certain, although he never said so, your father intended the two of you to marry," Bloomfield offered.

"That would solve everything, wouldn't it?" Storm replied with false blitheness. "Especially in regard to Winding River. Luke could run it. I could produce the next heir. After all that's a woman's job, isn't it? Having the babies, raising the kids. I had a career. Not that Dad ever saw it as one."

It was sadly true. "Surely you can continue your career, Storm," Bloomfield said. "You're brilliant and very widely sought after. Gillian loves the beautiful necklace and earrings you created for our twenty-fifth wedding anniversary. I love to see her in it. Surely you can work from anywhere even if you have to make business trips from time to time?''

''What are you suggesting, Robert? Luke and I should bury our differences and get married.'' The very thought took her breath away.

''Whom you marry is your business entirely, Storm,'' Bloomfield pointed out. ''I wish you all the happiness in the world. You have had every material want but I do realise in many ways you were emotionally deprived. Luke, too, for that matter. He lost his parents at a very vulnerable age.''

Storm dipped her head. ''And he never acted up. Not like me. Luke took it on the chin. Whatever he thinks of me, Robert, whatever the bond, Luke isn't a man I can twist around my little finger.''

''Not like the last guy, eh?'' Bloomfield gave her an owlish smile. ''What was his name?''

''Alex. He's still around. He won't know about Dad. He's in Hong Kong on a business trip.''

''But that's all over, the relationship?'' Bloomfield asked, looking at her a little sharply.

Storm shrugged. ''It wasn't really ever on. I've never found the man to satisfy me.'' Outside Luke, she thought. Luke had brought love-making to a fine art.

''I take it Luke's romance with the Prentice girl didn't amount to anything?'' Bloomfield continued very smoothly.

''Not for her want of trying. She's madly in love with him.''

''So would I be if I were a young woman.'' Bloomfield gave a little bark of laughter, then swiftly sobered. ''What are you going to do about Luke, my dear,'' he asked quietly. ''You realise you could contest your father's will. My firm will stand by you.''

"You believe I have a right to?" Storm asked in a tight voice.

"Most people would." He shrugged. "Athol could have left Luke a sizeable sum of money. Enough to kick-start a small operation. Luke has all the skills to build on that. He's a young man with a big future."

"And besides he has half of Winding River. Off the record, Robert, I don't want you to speak as a lawyer, but as a family friend, what do *you* think I should do?"

Bloomfield considered very carefully. "This is one you have to solve yourself, my dear," he said finally. "I'll back you whatever you do, but this cuts too close to your heart. I suspect to Luke's as well. You *are* the main beneficiary of your father's will. There's plenty more left of it to read. You and Luke share Winding River at least in Luke's lifetime. After that, as I said, it reverts to you or your heirs. Luke cannot take up a position anywhere else— I'm darn sure Clive Prentice would love to have him sign on at Mingari—but under the terms of your father's will he has to stay here and run the whole operation. For that he takes the income, which I suppose is fair enough. Being a top cattleman is hard, dangerous work and one has to have a natural rapport and authority with the men. So far as residing together in the homestead, that's something I can't possibly decide. God knows it's big enough to house a small army but there are the proprieties of course."

Storm was vibrating with nerves. "I've offended him deeply," she said. "It's one of my hang-ups."

"I'm afraid, my dear, you have. But knowing you I expect you can smooth things over. Angry or not I know Luke cares a great deal about you. I watched the two of you at the funeral. It seemed to me you share a very strong bond, whether you want it or not. Now sit down, again, Storm, so I can get on with reading the rest of the will. At the end you'll find yourself a lot better off than even you expected. In fact you'll be one of the richest young women in the country.''

So why didn't it cheer her up? Storm slipped quietly back into her chair.

When Robert left she would have to find Luke. Not to kiss and make up. Her father had just made him her honorary brother.

The mauve dusk came and went. Night set in. Luke didn't come up to the house. Not that she had been expecting him to. He was probably as shell-shocked as she was, but her feeling for him erased everything else. In the starry darkness the desert air was cool and crisp. It enveloped her. Lights were on at the bungalow and she mounted the steps marvelling how swiftly events had overtaken her. Her father's death; the funeral; her night with Luke; the power and passion of their union when they had both forgotten their place in the scheme of things.

Now this. The will. Just as their relationship flared into sexual radiance everything could crumble. Maybe there was even something inevitable about it. Like a doomed affair. She anticipated Luke would be uncharacteristically cold but when he opened the door to her knock so casual was his expression she might have been one of the station hands. ''May I come in?''

''If you wish.'' He was the picture of calm but he was angry. She knew it. It was all in his eyes. And she knew those eyes.

''Have we really come to this, Luke?'' She looked around the living room, which was comfortably, even cosily furnished, spotlessly clean and tidy, but smaller than her own bedroom at the house.

"I haven't got the answer to that question, Storm," he queried. "Are you going to sit down?"

"Thank you." She moved to a club chair. "I didn't handle the will reading very well."

"Truth to tell neither did I." He glanced towards her. She was looking all of a sudden very fragile in that masculine chair. "Have you had anything to eat?"

"I had some lunch."

"I was making coffee. Do you want some?"

"Yes, thank you."

"So what have you come to tell me?" he asked a little later, placing their coffee on the table between them along with a ham sandwich. "Go on, eat it," he prompted.

She felt too sad and weary. "Why did Dad *do* this, Luke? Help me understand."

"Why?" His cleanly defined mouth tightened. "No matter what you think not to enrage you. Your father lived his life as the man in control. Scott Fitzgerald once said that the rich are different, and it's not just that they have more money. Your father had the power to control lives. Whatever he wanted had to happen. You must know he had plans to marry us off."

"No, I didn't," she answered at once. "All I know is every single male friend I brought here he compared unfavourably with you. Surely he didn't think that was the right way to go about it?"

He frowned slightly. "Eat your sandwich."

She shook her head but picked it up and bit into it, surprised to find she was hungry.

Luke let her finish it before pushing her cup of coffee nearer her. "Like another?"

"You're definitely, but definitely a carer. That was good but I'd rather talk right now. Dad seems to have made you my honorary big brother."

Luke responded instantly losing his cool. "The hell he did! The things you say, Storm. You're really something."

"Must be one of the reasons you love me." She smiled at him, very wryly, trying to lighten the mood.

"Why would I love a terrible woman like you?" he said in the same wry tone.

She stared at him with intensity. "God knows!" She held her head. "Maybe I'm disturbed. Maybe we can't live without one another. Situations like this must exist."

"It's the strangest case I've ever struck," he returned dryly. "The person who made things so easy and so difficult for us was your father. He should have had a son of his own."

"I'd still have been shunted into a back seat," Storm said, knowing it to be true.

"But you wouldn't have resented *me* at all. I wouldn't have been part of the equation."

She shrugged. "Anyway, it's all hypothetical. I knew Dad would reward you for your hard work and dedication...I expected that."

"But you never expected he'd do something so intolerable. You do find it intolerable, don't you?"

Storm drew a jagged breath, unable to deny it. Even from the grave her father was affirming Luke's value as equal to hers. "Can't you understand it's been a blow?"

"Of course I understand." The words burst forth. "I've been understanding all the injuries to you for most of my life. We've been presented with a dilemma, which I understand can only be resolved if we marry. Simple, if we were so madly in love with each other no problems existed. But marriage is a pretty big hurdle."

"You wouldn't *marry* me?" she asked, acknowledging a perverse sense of outrage.

It brought an ironic smile to his mouth. "The only way

I'd want you to come to me is of your own free will. But the handicaps are very much in place. The Major has put me in a bad position. You might consider that.''

''In what way are you in a bad position?'' she retaliated, thinking they would be forever locked in conflict. ''Overnight you have half of Winding River.''

There was an endless, endless pause filled with a ringing tension.

''I thought I made my feelings pretty clear,'' Luke said, blue eyes electric. ''You can stick Winding River, ma'am. Get your boyfriend Alex to run it. Contest the will if you like. Argue undue influence I coerced your father into leaving me half the station. He was in very poor health. A dying man very largely dependent on me, not only to run the whole operation but for company. You sure as hell kept *your* distance.''

It was a struggle not to hit him, but she didn't make that mistake. She stood up, anger and anguish all over her face. ''I was wondering when you were going to say that. I've been dreading it actually.''

''Why not?'' his voice was hard with mockery. ''You go ahead and blame me for everything no matter what. The sad fact of the matter is you can *never* trust me. You'll always be harking back to days that would have to be left behind. That's where this feeling of *powerlessness* you have began.''

That did it. ''So what are you suggesting, peace at any price? What am I supposed to say, Luke, good on you. You *deserve* half my inheritance. Bighearted Storm. I think it's lovely Dad thought so much of you.''

''Hey,'' he said. ''I told you. I don't want it.''

''Then you're a fool.'' She tried to pull herself together, her anger shaming her by tipping over into desire. ''Only

it's not so straightforward, is it? You're not a fool. Far
from it. You know I wouldn't contest the will.''

Suddenly Luke could take no more. ''I think if you
don't want to risk getting manhandled, you should get out
of here.''

She wasn't even the heiress now. ''You don't scare me,
Luke. I happen to know you. You're nothing if not the
perfect white knight. Whatever I think of this arrangement,
it was Dad's decision to split the station between us. He
knew I couldn't work Winding River without you.''

''Try to concentrate when I speak to you,'' Luke said,
sounding very tough. ''That isn't a consideration. I told
you I could find you someone very capable to take over.
Two names come to mind. I'll give you both.''

''You won't stay?''

''Obviously this needs spelling out in big letters. N-O.''

The hardening of his mood, the things he was saying,
somehow frightened her. But she wasn't about to show it.
''You've been paid up until the end of the month. You
said so yourself.''

''Okay but I won't wait a minute longer.'' He clipped
off the words.

''You'll refuse Dad's request?'' She was thoroughly unnerved.

''Maybe you should just *go,* Storm.''

''All right.'' She had her pride. She walked to the door,
her eyes huge and brilliant in her pale face. ''Dad felt you
were crucial to our continuing success. I can't deny I'm
finding this hard, but I think so, too. We both need longer,
Luke, to think about all this.'' Deliberately she met his
condemning eyes.

As if she were tormenting him he thought. She looked
quite heartbreakingly beautiful. So much a part of him.
Even at this worst of times he wanted her desperately but

he would fight that to the death. One thing he'd learned: Storm had an infinite capacity to hurt him. "Good night, Storm," he said resolutely. "It's been one hell of a day."

"Tell me about it." She made a little sound like a sob. "What happened to us last night, do you know?"

He stared at her from his superior height. "You're all grown up, Storm. I guess it was sex."

She took a ragged breath. "Is *that* what it was?"

"*You* need to answer that. I couldn't."

"It wasn't just sex for me," she confessed, very softly as though she was speaking to herself. "It was *incredible*. Like something I've never known."

It would be madness to weaken. "Well I guess now it's all over," he managed to say coolly. "Sad for me. Sad for you. But that's the way it is."

Blindly she turned away. "I think I'll go back to Sydney in a day or two."

He nodded, cut to the heart. "Well that's what you were going to do anyway, wasn't it?"

She was quiet for a moment. "I feel dreadful," she said firmly. "I can't believe what's going on."

"It's absolutely clear to me. The thought of sharing Winding River with me has upset you dreadfully. As if you weren't upset enough already. I'd have been a lot happier if your father had left me his damned stamp collection."

She was too disturbed to smile. "He *did*. If you'd waited you'd have found out. There are other things as well. Personal things," she said despairingly. "You didn't even ask…"

"How very rude of me." He simply couldn't bear to look at her and not take her in his arms. "I'll walk you up to the house," he said briskly. "Are you going to be all right on your own?" Even now it worried him.

"What in a house where Dad's haunting every corner?" She shivered in the crisp night air.

"You always did have too much imagination."

"Unfortunately, yes." She breathed out audibly in mute appeal.

"I think we can work something out," he found himself saying. "You sleep in the bungalow. I'll go up to the house."

She raised her dark head. "I don't know." But she did know. She wanted to. Even if Luke wasn't there.

"So that's settled." He read her eyes. "You can collect a few things at the house then we'll come back here. I'll leave from the house in the morning, otherwise I would have to wake you." He had a sudden vision of her asleep beside him that very morning, brushing it down, but not the monstrous deep ache inside him.

"Thank you, Luke," she said quietly, like a sweet little girl. "It's such a very, very *big* house and it's so filled with *him.*"

At this point of time it was true. "What it needs," he said tautly, "is children. Lots of them."

"Oh, Luke." There was a little tremor in her voice. "I was thinking four." Sudden tears appeared.

That was his undoing. He gave way to the awful, tearing desire that was rising in him. He pulled her into his arms, so hard, he was certain it hurt her but he didn't care. He wasn't going to be overshadowed by that other dominant male figure in her life. Her father. He wasn't going to let anyone else have her.

Storm, too, felt the waves growing, curling over into great tunnels that were taking her under. She clung to him, frantic for more, only he released her abruptly, keeping hold of her shoulders.

"Whatever man you choose to father your children," he said, his voice harsh with emotion, "you're going to lead him one helluva merry dance."

CHAPTER SEVEN

THE bungalow had good karma. The instant her head hit the pillow, Storm fell into a deep dreamless sleep. Not even the birds woke her; her nervous exhaustion was so complete. She'd slept in Luke's boyhood bedroom that had charm and peace about it. She remembered the display cabinet in the corner. His mother had bought it to install in his room. It was filled with sporting trophies he had won at school and university. Luke had been, still was, a superb athlete. He excelled at polo but as her father's health failed he'd found less and less time to play it.

Three guitars hung on the wall.

She took one down and began to tune it, staring out the open window at the cascade of white bougainvillea like a bride's veil. She and Luke had once fancied themselves as musicians. They had entertained themselves, her father and friends who came to visit the station, with country and western songs, which always went over well. It had amused them a lot. They weren't half bad in those far-off days. Their voices had blended well. Still in her nightgown Storm sat down on the bed again and began to strum an old Irving Berlin song about loving somebody always…always….

Of a sudden she stopped playing, unbidden tears gathering in her eyes as she acknowledged Luke had *always* been there through the best and the worst of it. There was more joy, more pain, more anger, more *passion* in being with Luke than anyone else in the world. Just as there had *always* been the struggle to accept him. She'd been engulfed by her feelings; she was nothing beside Luke. In her city persona, she had become a confident, successful woman—much admired. On her home ground she was still the immature teenager whose great underlying wish to be number one with her father was never fulfilled. Not then, not now, not ever but she remembered Robert's words— her father had loved her in his fashion. When was she going to accept the circumstances of her life? When was she going to rise above the past? She had her own identity. She was a woman and revelled in it. She might have wanted to be a boy when she was a child, a tall, strong, clever boy who could easily compete with Luke for her father's attention. Now it seemed pathetic and well…sad. She was totally happy and secure in being a woman. In fact she was quite unable to contemplate her old primitive wish to be a boy. It seemed so ridiculous now.

Sometime she had to start a new life. A life free of her father, adored though he had been. Surely it was time? Her heart might still ache at the wounds of the past but she would have to let them heal. Her father obviously hadn't even considered her feelings in leaving half the station to Luke. Maybe he had even thought she was willing to share. After all he had left her a very rich woman. But in giving them each an equal share there was so much potential for conflict. They would have to marry to make it work.

She mulled the situation over long enough to agree with Luke's taking the profits. He would, after all, be in charge of the whole operation. He would do the work though she was darn sure she was never going to be sidelined again. She wasn't a fool, a butterfly by nature. She ran a business. A good business that was expanding. She'd had clients fly in from Hong Kong, Thailand, California, all over to have her design something special for them. All the things she should have been taught about Winding River's operations she was going to learn. Not that she'd encounter the same problem with Luke. She didn't doubt for a moment Luke would show her everything she needed to know. Luke was a man of today as opposed to her father who had always maintained she didn't really need to know anything about "business" and became quite rattled if she persisted. Even rattled with Luke who could do no wrong. Luke had often tried to include her in discussions but both of them saw clearly it had irritated Athol McFarlane too much.

Men were men and women were women and never the twain should meet. Except in bed. Athol McFarlane's thoughts on having a woman, even a daughter, as a business partner.

So she was going to drive Luke away? Knowing Luke it could happen very fast. What if he turned his attention to another woman? What if he married her? Would the new woman then become part-mistress of Winding River? She, herself, would be expected to make her residence in Sydney, visiting very infrequently. Luke had his share for life. The income for life. After that, if she survived him—somehow she couldn't bear to dwell on that—his share would revert to her. So in the end Winding River would come to her children.

Rather than start up a headache, Storm took a quick shower, dressed in the clothes she had brought from the house, a yellow T-shirt, above the knee cargo shorts, white socks and sturdy boots. She knew the aerial muster was going on today. Luke would be flying the helicopter. She'd find a good vantage point in the hill country and oversee the muster. She always found it thrilling. Afterwards she could do a bit of prospecting, picking up her stones. She'd found many a piece of opal matrix in the ancient hills. She might be lucky again today. She shoved her yellow akubra on her head, drank a glass of milk from the refrigerator

and picked up a couple of shiny red apples. She'd be going
some distance so she'd take one of the Jeeps.

Sometimes the station used the big helicopter operation
run by Grant Cameron, other times Luke took up Winding
River's reliable Bell 47. Luke was a high-calibre pilot.
Heli-mustering in a tough industry was both cost effective
and a time saving alternative to stockmen in a big operation like theirs. A half hour out she spotted the red helicopter flying low over the scrub. It was flushing out hundreds of cattle and rounding them up. Stockmen on the
ground were working in conjunction with the helicopter,
on motorbikes and horseback. If this year the rains a thousand miles to the tropical north of the state continued, or
a cyclone swept in, this vast riverine desert would go un-
derwater. The plains were so flat the water could spread
for fifty miles. In this part of the world it was possible for
thousands of square miles to be irrigated by the northern
floodwaters without a drop of local rain. It could work for
her given Luke's commitment to Winding River; he
wouldn't leave now and put all his hard work in jeopardy.

A breathing space for them both?

Storm parked the Jeep at the rust-red base of the highest
hill, picking her way carefully up the rocks to the flat-
topped summit. A single ghost gum on top of it. She had
a great view. Cattle were thundering towards the holding
yards. Once Luke swooped so low her heart jumped into
her mouth. What he could do with the helicopter was fantastic. Her father used to make the joke that Luke could
lean out to open the gates of the holding yard without even
landing, but Luke never did anything too risky. Apart from
person safety, air regulations were too strict.

She watched for quite a while then when the helicopter
swung inland, maybe to land, she began to pick her way
downhill fossicking through the ancient stones. Little liz-

ards were darting thither and yon but she took care not to touch them. The geckos if touched were so vulnerable their tails dropped off. A group of wild donkeys came to see what she was doing on their territory, but she shooed them off, hoping she wouldn't meet up with a feral camel. It was a station rule to refrain from shooting feral camels if possible but some of them were incredibly dangerous on their best days.

These hills and flat-topped mesas, so harsh and arid for most of the time, she'd seen them covered in the most beautiful delicate blooms after rain; wild hibiscus, morning glories, cleomes, lilac lamb's tails smothering the rough stones, the undulating waves of the green pussy tails massed to the far horizon. She was moving very carefully, for the hillside was covered in loose shale, when she spotted something glittering down below her, flashes of blue and green raised up along the serrated back of a chunk of rock. Opal?

She moved faster downhill, planting her feet firmly, treating the hill with respect, but to her horror her foot became snagged in the tangled old root of a spindly bush. She went hurtling like a train, trying desperately to retain her balance, her efforts undermined by the loose shale.

"Oh God!" she cried out, a sound that carried surprisingly far in the still desert air. She was sick with the fear of falling, smashing her face, her limbs into those rocks. It was a miracle she was staying on her feet. An instant after the thought she totally lost balance, ricked an ankle badly, before sliding helplessly down the slope....

She came to almost immediately she thought. Maybe a half a minute when she lost consciousness. She'd hit the back of her head on a half-submerged rock that had stopped her descent. She had blood on her hands. She'd thrown them out to protect her face. There was a powerful dull ache in her head. Storm could feel the lump without reaching back to touch it. But worse, far worse, she had sprained her ankle or... It was throbbing badly, swelling within her boot. Hell! She'd have to get herself out of this. The extraordinary part was for all the tumble her hat was still shoved down over her eyes. It might even have deadened the crack to her skull. Gingerly she went to sit up but as she did so her gaze fell on a snake in a defensive fanged position not four feet from her. A taipan, the largest and most feared venomous snake in the country, thus the world. Rich brown on top she could see its yellow and orange under spots. Its head was raised above its coiled body easily ten feet in length. It wasn't the first time she had encountered a snake, desert death adders, taipans. One lived with them in the interior but even the worst of them weren't aggressive unless threatened. Somehow that didn't give her a lot of heart.

There was no way she could move fast, not with her ankle. The snake could strike lightning fast if she startled it. What to do? She dared not throw anything. Instead of darting away it could attack. Between the throbbing in her ankle, her head, plus the glittering heat she wasn't thinking too clearly. In fact she felt woozy. She could stay perfectly still and the snake might lose interest and slither away. She thought it looked less alert. The head had lowered fractionally. They had antivenom on the station. That's if anyone would get to her in time. Storm held herself rigid scarcely daring to breathe. Go away, snake. Go away and find yourself some other little reptile to eat.

It seemed like an eternity until the taipan slid off disappearing into the sparse vegetation the same colour as itself. Just as well it hadn't been a dingo attracted by her blood. Very determinedly Storm began to move. Her ak-

ubra was protecting her face but the sun was scorching her
arms and legs. If only she could discard that boot! Her
foot was swelling so much the boot could hardly contain
it.

Where was Luke? He had always found her as a child.
But then it had always been Luke who had gone looking.
She even remembered what he used to call her, little
champ! She'd like that. Little champ. One of the boys.
She'd have to be a champ now to get down the hill....

Luke!

He waved to the men as he took the chopper back up.
He'd spotted the Jeep from the air and realised it was
Storm. She'd always enjoyed watching the aerial muster,
but she'd chosen a damned hot spot to do it not that there
was a cool place away from the curving tranquil banks of
a billabong. The strangest thing was he thought he'd heard
her call his name.

Luke!

That was crazy, but he'd heard it. Now he had a strong
urge to find out if she was okay. Probably she was fossicking around looking for white and crystal quartz, the
sparkling stones polished by wind-blown sand until they
resembled glossy gemstones. The Jeep he'd sighted far off
was empty. He saw her at the same time. Her yellow hat
and her yellow T-shirt were a blaze of colour against the
rust-red rocks. He knew instantly there was something
wrong. She appeared to be inching herself down the incline
lying almost prone, but she raised her arm to wave to him.

Little champ!

Now why did he think of that? Their shared childhood
of course. What a rebel she'd been! Always defying her
father's overly strict edicts, always trailing after them like
a little scout. In retrospect the Major had treated her more

like a precious porcelain doll than a living child full of courage and high spirits. Maybe the fact the Major had lost his young wife so tragically explained his overzealous sense of protectiveness.

He put the chopper down at enough distance to prevent the whirling rotors from showering her in sand. His mind was racing, trying to fathom what had happened. He suspected she had lost her footing on the loose shale and taken a tumble. Obviously she had injured either her foot or her leg.

He took the slope with a mixture of speed and caution, reaching her in the shortest possible time. He dropped to his haunches staring down at her with a face taut with anxiety.

"Where does it hurt?" Even as he spoke his eyes were running over her. He saw the blood, he saw the grazes. Her face was unmarked but she held her head gingerly. So far as he could make out, the worst problem was her left ankle. He would have to cut off the boot to release her swollen foot.

"I hope—I think, it's sprained." She spoke calmly enough, but she couldn't stop herself from gasping in pain. "I hit my head, too. I'm sure there's a great lump. And a bloody great snake," she gritted, "a taipan, kept me company for God knows how long before it decided to take off."

He listened in horror, opening out the sharp blade of his pocket-knife. "I'll be as gentle as I can."

"You'd better be," she said, but smiled.

As it was, she fainted while he swore softly in distress. He removed the damaged boot very slowly. It was ruined. The foot was very swollen. He didn't know yet whether it was a bad sprain or she'd broken it. He prayed the former though bad sprains caused the more pain. Sometimes, too, a clean break was quicker to heal than torn ligaments. She was coming around, moaning a little. "It's all right, Storm." He bent to comfort her, stroking her cheek. "I'm here."

She murmured something, her face ashen. He looked back down the slope trying to gauge the best route to take. He settled on the way through the clumps of spinifex that dotted the cratered terrain. The spinifex would hold the soil and the stones there were larger, flatter, like pieces of sculpture. He would have to carry her so he could take no risks. He walked his proposed route first, pitching away the loose stones that mantled the ground, leaving his foot-prints as a track to follow.

"I'm sorry, Luke," she gasped as he lifted her into his arms. "I'm sorry...sorry..." Sorry for everything.

Storm spent two days in Base Hospital where Luke had made the decision to take her immediately after the acci-dent. Her ankle was X-rayed. It proved not to be broken but sprained. With her youth and excellent state of fitness, it was anticipated she would make a trouble-free early re-covery. The blow to her head was treated with caution. When she arrived at the hospital she was found to be con-cussed, so she was admitted for observation and her cuts and grazes cleaned up.

In the afternoon of the second day Luke came for her, landing the helicopter on the pad to the rear of the hospital. He found her inside the foyer waiting for him. They had her in a wheelchair and the sight smote him.

"Hi, how's it going?" He bent to kiss her pale cheek, his heart exposing him as a man deeply in love.

"Fine. I bet you're mad at me?" Tears of weakness shone in her beautiful green eyes.

"Can't you feel it?" He gave her his melting smile,

remembering the very many times she had said that to him in their lives. "In much pain?" He knew she wouldn't acknowledge it.

"I'm okay. One of the nurses lent me a dress. It's easy, button through."

"That was nice of her." The dress was loose like a child's smock, made of some light flowery material. She looked beautiful whatever she wore. "And the headaches?"

"They're all but gone, Doctor."

"Which reminds me I'd better have a word with him," Luke said, turning his head to look around.

"He left, Luke. He's gone with Sister Maree. There's been an accident on Mingari. One of the stockmen, I think."

"Too bad. Now let's get you out of here. I'll need a wards man to help me get you into the chopper but I shouldn't have any trouble getting you out."

Which was the case when they set down lightly as a bird on the homestead's huge circular drive.

"Just let yourself come down to me," he urged, holding up his arms.

She felt such pain in her ankle, she shut her eyes as he gathered her body to him, holding her closely, strongly, as if she were as insubstantial as a five-year-old.

Her silky black mane brushed his cheek. Magic. Crushing him beneath a weight of desire. "Put your arms around my neck," he advised, his voice so gentle and soothing she felt like a filly he was breaking in.

"What would I do without you," she exclaimed. It was meant as a truce, a peace offering but somehow, maybe because of the pain, it came out edgy.

"I'm sure you'll find out," he said, his sensitive antennae out.

Inside the house he set her down on a sofa in the drawing room. "Okay?" He had never seen her so pale.

She looked up at him, so vibrant with life. "Thank you, Luke. If you could get the crutches out of the chopper I should be able to manage on my own."

"Not today anyway. I've contacted Noni. Told her about your accident. She wants to come home."

"Oh, that's a shame! It means she won't be able to enjoy a longer stay with her friend."

"Don't worry about that," he said. "She *wants* to come, Storm. Besides you need someone. I'm sure you don't want me to help you dress and undress?" He had an irresistible vision of her slender naked body.

Her face lit up with a wry smile. "I know you'd do a good job. I've put everyone out haven't I? This is such a very busy time for you." She smoothed the full skirt of her borrowed dress then she lifted her eyes to him. "You *are* going to stay?"

His expression gave nothing away. "I won't leave you when you're like this, Storm. I won't leave until the big muster is over. I owe that to your father."

"Not to me?" She looked searchingly into his handsome, familiar face.

"I quit before I let you ask for my resignation." He said it like a joke but she knew it was no joke.

"I suppose I deserve that?"

"Maybe, but all this can wait, at least for the time being. The both of us have enough on our plate."

"I know," she sighed, "but we have to discuss it sometime."

"I think I'll wait until you've got some colour in your cheeks," he answered dryly, beginning to turn about. "I'll make some tea. You put your foot up." He found a cushion and placed it. "How long does the doctor think?"

"Two, three weeks." She winced a little as her foot came to rest, an involuntary movement of her facial muscles. "I'll see how I go."

"You'd be best advised to do as the doctor says," he warned, knowing Storm. "Ice packs, I suppose?"

"Yes. Don't worry about me, Luke," she said in a conciliatory voice. "This is nothing. Just a minor setback. When's Noni coming home?"

He paused at the door. "We can't expect her until the day after tomorrow. She'll come in with the freight plane." His eyes moved over her as she lay on the couch. "I'll stay here at the homestead tonight so you can sleep easy."

She wanted nothing more. Nothing more than he should touch her. Love her.

"The things you do for me," she said.

Luke didn't return to the house until well after seven. Hours lost were hours that had to be made up. He had showered and changed, the dark flame of his hair temporarily subdued by damp. He found her in the kitchen, crutches beneath her arms, going from the counter to the table.

"Here, let me do that." He crossed the large room in a couple of strides.

She surrendered without a fight. "I never knew how difficult it is to get around on crutches. I guess I'll learn."

Concern touched his eyes. "I told you I'd attend to all this, Storm. You know you should be off that foot as much as possible. Hopping around will only slow progress. I'm sorry, I'm so late. It was unavoidable."

"No apologies, Luke." She gave him a grateful look. "Thank you for taking the time."

"So what's on the menu?" He looked to see what she had managed so far.

"Salad as an entrée, salad for mains, salad for dessert,"

she joked. "That's as far as I got." She sank into a chair, letting Luke take the crutches from her, then she sat forward to rest her elbows on the table. She had covered it with a pale blue damask cloth that shone in the light. "There's a ham in the fridge, fillet steaks. I managed to thaw some smoked salmon. Take your pick."

"If it's okay with you I think I'll go for the steaks." He was hungry.

"Of course. A man needs filling. I'll stick to the salad and maybe a couple of slices of the salmon. I haven't been doing anything so I'm not terribly hungry. How's the muster progressing?"

"Right on schedule." He dipped into the refrigerator and withdrew a couple of steaks. "When you're properly on your feet again I'd like to show you how things are run. You're a good businesswoman, you'll take it all in your stride."

Storm was briefly quiet. "No Dad to contend with?"

"The Major was one of the old school. There are many, many things you need to know."

"And you're going to teach me?" She stared into his handsome face.

"I'm assuming you want to learn?"

"Of course I do." The black wings of her brows furrowed. "And what better teacher?"

He ignored that although it wasn't said provocatively. "Like a glass of wine?"

"Sure." A thirst rose in her throat. "You'll have to go down to the cellar. I wasn't up to those stairs."

"Mind a red?" He paused at the cellar door. "No time to chill a white."

"Red will be fine. A good Shiraz."

He was back within moments, going to a drawer for the corkscrew. It came to her that she loved watching him move about. He had such method about him, a clear, cool, logical mind. No unnecessary shuttling. Economy of movement. It made her smile.

Over the meal he began to talk to her about the McFarlane operation, which was far more involved than she had imagined. She, in turn, spoke about her father's extensive portfolio, which she had inherited, not terribly surprised when it appeared he already knew pretty much the extent of it. Not that he claimed prior knowledge but it was evident to her her father had taken Luke into his confidence. In fact Luke raised suggestions, showing his own knowledge of the share market and how to play it. He even suggested a different broker, citing a name. "They're more on the ball than the crowd your father had been dealing with for years. You need new blood."

The conversation continued at an engrossed pace even after they moved to more comfortable chairs in the sun-room. Both were in accord, Luke seemed relaxed. What better time to approach the dilemma that lay between them and try to resolve it, Storm thought, deliberately introducing the subject. "You said once you wanted to start your own operation."

A small shrug though his body tensed. "Even your father knew that, Storm. I owed him so much. He gave me a home, a first-class education, even the damned clothes I stood up in until I could finally earn. But I made no secret of the fact I always wanted to be my own man."

"Dad would have admired that."

"It was scarcely why I did it."

"I know. I don't want to force you to reject your share of Winding River, Luke. It was Dad's wish that you have it. I promise you I won't go against his wishes. I have no thought in my mind of contesting the will."

"Why not?" He gazed at her with his intensely blue

eyes. "You'd probably win. Bring in the big guns. The thing is, Storm, it's too massive a bequest. Not easy to accept. Not easy for you."

She took a breath. "Dad wouldn't have been around if you hadn't saved his life?"

"Maybe that was exaggerated." He brushed the idea off.

"I don't think so. Dad himself said he thought he was done for. I won't fight your share, Luke. As far as I'm concerned you're entitled to the profits as well. You'd be working the whole operation."

A range of warring emotions crossed his face. "You know what your father had in mind?"

She nodded her dark head. "Pretty feudal wasn't he? He was practically *giving* me away."

Luke's shapely mouth set. "He thought it would work. An arranged marriage no less."

"Just like the good old days," she crowed. "So what would have happened had I married Alex or someone like him and you married Carla or her successor? Didn't he think it through?"

Luke answered, almost angrily. "Obviously not. You knew your father, Storm. What he wanted *had* to be. Of course as a business arrangement it would have worked fine."

She considered that, unnerved. "You mean you'd accept your inheritance if I consented to marry you?"

He studied her with his blue level gaze. Somehow she had changed out of the borrowed dress. She was wearing a little violet singlet top that showed off the beautiful neat shape of her breasts, with a sarong splashed with fuchsia and violet flowers, wrapped around her slender hips. It was as if he'd always known these hungers for her, yet answered crisply. "I don't mean that at all. When I get married, Storm, it'll be because I can't live without that one woman in my life, and she can't live without *me*."

At the look in his eyes her cheeks flamed and she dropped her gaze. "Are you telling me you haven't met her?" She cursed herself for being such an emotional coward.

"Oh I've met her all right," he clipped off, "but she's all locked away behind emotional barriers."

"Not of her own making...you know they weren't *all* self-inflicted..."

"Maybe not," he sighed, "but she's the only person in the world who can knock them down."

He carried her up to her room. They could have taken the lift that had been installed a few years back when the Major was having difficulty with the grand staircase, but there was too much pleasure in having her in his arms, no matter the inevitable torment.

"So what are you going to sleep in?" he asked after he set her down on the huge, canopied bed. Such a beautiful bedroom she had, fit for a princess.

"This will do." She glanced down at herself, not wanting to go to the least bit of bother. The briefs she was wearing matched the singlet. The sarong was simple to untie. "I'll splash my face and clean my teeth."

"I'll go get your crutches," he said. "Turn off the lights."

She didn't even wait, hopping the short distance into the *en suite,* grabbing onto the porcelain basin for support, her left leg bent up at the knee. By the time he returned she was hopping back to the bed.

"God there's no stopping you, is there?" he said, torn between amusement and dismay.

"I managed okay. The trick is to not put your injured foot to the ground."

"You will try to remember what I told you about making good progress?"

"Yes, brother, dear."

"Cut it out."

She felt a jolt. "I'm sorry."

"You're a cruel little cat," he said quietly.

"But I meant it sincerely. I am sorry. You know as well as I do my tongue always runs away with me."

"You don't have to let it. Are you sure there's nothing else I can get you? You might need painkillers during the night?"

"Then I'll call out to you," she said sweetly, putting her hands behind her head and making a plait.

"You'd better not," he warned.

"Why, what might happen?" she asked softly, her green eyes glowing.

His answer was curt. "What's going to happen if I don't get out of this room."

"So I'm sexually satisfactory at least." Something was pushing her into being provocative. Blind *need?*

"Good night, Storm," he said without a smile, turning on his heel.

"Good night, Luke. Aren't you going to kiss me before you go?"

"You're a mystery to me, Storm. That much I know."

"A woman should always be a mystery to her man," she came back at him.

"You're taking it for granted, aren't you, I'm *your* property?"

"Why not?" she said discordantly. "I'm yours. If you wanted to you could carry me off."

"As what, first prize?"

She threw herself backwards across the bed, her eyes filling with tears at the faint lash in his voice. "Don't go, Luke."

He groaned in frustration, struggling under the weight of pride and his pent-up desires, knowing himself trapped.

"Don't go," she whispered, turning her raven head that had already escaped its thick plait. Its silken coils swirled all over the pale gold brocade of the quilt. "Share my bed with me. Share Winding River." She extended one slender arm. "The way things are, there's no escape."

He agreed. How could he not? But the years of duelling had to cease. He wanted liberation. For himself. More importantly for her. Looking at her lying across the bed like that, his strong desires broke their leash. Impetuously he crossed to her bed, positioning himself directly behind her head, then he dropped to his knees, cupping the lovely alluring oval of her face between his hands. Storm, his heart's desire. "Witch!" he murmured, kissing her glowing eyes shut.

"All witches have green eyes." She flung back her arms, digging her fingers into the fiery thickness of his hair. "Kiss me until you can kiss me no more."

For the briefest moment he considered drawing away, a gesture meant to torment her as she had tormented him for years, but her pulsing mouth was just beneath his. "Have you thought I could hurt you," he muttered, "knock your ankle?" It was a genuine concern.

"I don't care." She looked into his marvellous face, the risk of some pain to her ankle counterbalanced by the anticipation of the priceless pleasure only he could give her. "I can't promise I won't scream." She gave him a slow, tantalising smile.

"Then I'll have to be very, very gentle."

In one exquisitely controlled movement he rolled the

violet singlet off her, slipping it over her head. "You're so beautiful!" Her skin gave off such a lustre in the light. Like ivory satin. "*So* beautiful," he repeated, laying his head between her breasts, inhaling the seductive scents of her woman's body. "I can hear your heart pumping," he murmured, revelling in her heart-breaking, open-mouthed sighs of rapture.

"It beats for you," she whispered, never once looking away from his eyes. So then, very slowly, Luke moved onto the bed beside her, careful where he was placing his long, lean body, feeling the huge bed take his weight. Such intimacy he had only dreamed of! He pressed his mouth to the blue pulse that beat so wildly, betrayingly in her throat.

CHAPTER EIGHT

LUKE had just finished talking to the station's resident saddler when he spotted the light aircraft coming in from the north east. A few minutes more and he could confirm his educated guess: a single engine Piper. It could only be one person. Carla. Her father had bought it for her a few years back. No toy, but the vehicle best suited their unique way of life. He knew what Carla wanted. She wanted to check out what was happening on Winding River. It was no secret Noni had taken leave. That left him and Storm alone. In that extraordinary way women have, Carla had long divined his heart despite all the dramas and clashes between him and Storm. Carla had seen straight into the secret places, though he had never discussed Storm with her at any time, nor had he ever risen to the barbed remarks Carla had thrown his way.

He had stopped his relationship with Carla almost at the time Storm had broken off her engagement to Alex. Carla had taken it better than he hoped, making him promise they would always remain friends. He thought that was so. Carla always appeared to have accepted the shift in the relationship. It struck him unpleasantly from time to time that Carla had instigated a few breaks of her own with a couple of his former girlfriends. Carla had always been ready to sew disinformation, even downright lies, always denying them convincingly when questioned. Scheming he had come to see was at the centre of Carla's being. Outside of that when she got what she wanted, she was good company. But his feelings for her had never amounted to being in love even if their relationship had transcended the merely sexual.

Now he saw he had trouble. Carla was another one who believed she could never lose.

He arrived at the airstrip moments before she set down, waiting for her to complete her after checks.

"Luke, how's it going?" She rushed to him, her attractive face lit up in a bright smile, that in no way reflected her central tensions. "I heard on the grape vine about Storm's accident. With Noni being away I thought I'd do the neighbourly thing and volunteer my services. It can't be easy for her until her ankle heals."

What was he supposed to do? Give her coffee and send her on her way. Storm wouldn't be agreeable he knew. The two were not close.

"That's kind of you, Carla," he said, unwilling to hurt her by refusing her quick kiss. "I suppose you got your information from the hospital?"

"As a matter of fact, yes. One of our stockmen broke a few ribs and his collarbone. A bullock pinned him between a gate and the fence."

"He's okay?"

"He'll live," she said cheerily. "How is it up at the house? Pretty dismal I should think. Storm adored her father."

"Yes, she did," he answered quietly.

"Not that she was the best daughter in the world to him." Carla gave him a quick you'd-have-to-agree-with-me glance.

Instead he retorted. "What's that supposed to mean?"

She reached up to pat his shoulder. "Now, now, don't get hot under the collar about your pal, Storm. Honestly, the way you two grew up! It was damned near incestuous." She gave a little laugh.

"It was damned near nothing of the kind," Luke responded in a voice that should have warned Carla off. "I hope you don't go around repeating that sort of thing?" He could well believe that she might.

"Sweetie." Carla was all innocence. "A lot of people think so. The Major treated you like his son and heir."

His strong jaw tightened. "The Major has gone now, Carla. I'd appreciate it if you don't stir things up and put our friendship at risk."

Her brown eyes, her best feature, shone with ready tears. "As if I'd ever do that." She began to walk towards the Jeep, speaking over her shoulder. "I expect the will has been read?"

"You surely don't think I'm about to discuss it with you, Carla?"

She scanned his taut, handsome face. "Knowing you, no. I'm sorry about what I said before," she apologised. "I know what Storm means to you. But even you can't deny she didn't visit her father as often as she could have."

"She rang him regularly," Luke said abruptly, looming over her. "She has a career, you know."

"Ah yes, the brilliant jewellery designer!" Carla exclaimed. "I expect if she hadn't sprained her ankle she'd be back in Sydney now?"

Luke recognised this couldn't go on. "Carla, what did you really come for," he asked quietly. "I'm not going to have you upsetting Storm. I somehow feel that's your aim."

A red flush whipped upwards from her throat. "What a terrible thing to say! Is that what you think of me, Luke?"

He looked over her head. "I can't help remembering some of the mischief you've made."

She struggled to deny it then realised it was impossible. "You know what they say? All's fair in love and war."

"That's all over, Carla." He regarded her with a mixture of sympathy and wariness. "I never led you to believe I was after a commitment."

"Of course you didn't." She tossed her head. "You laid it straight on the line. We were two adults in need of comfort. Speaking of comfort, Storm must be one of the richest women in the country?"

He tried to keep his cool but she was making him angry. "That's her business, Carla. She'll be very rich certainly."

"I just hope the Major left a sizeable legacy to you?" she asked him with considerable directness.

"Why do you say that?" he parried not about to take her into his confidence.

"Because he knew your worth," Carla almost jeered. "We all know Storm will head back to Sydney. Probably she'll sell up. She can't run the operation."

"You obviously don't know Storm," he said crisply. "She'll never sell Winding River. The McFarlanes pioneered this part of the world."

"So? Not all the old families are still around. It makes sense for her to sell it. I know Dad would jump at the chance to acquire it. The banks are lending again. If we sell off a few interests... This is one of the best operations in the country. In these last few years that's largely been due to you. We could make plans, Luke. You and I."

So she had never chosen to believe their relationship was over. "Carla, the last thing I want to do is hurt you," he said, his face set, "but there's no *we*. Stop knocking your head against a brick wall."

She looked up at him and put a finger to his lips. "Shh! It may appear like that to you, but to my way of thinking you're the one who's doing the head knocking. You just won't accept you'll never get Storm. She's way too big a prize. Even for you."

After last night that thought didn't strike him. "Carla, this conversation is getting downright depressing. Feeling like you do I think it's best if you fly off home. Our relationship failed, accept it once and for all. If we're going to pay attention to the grape vine, I've heard you and Les Marshall are pretty close."

She stiffened as though she'd be thrown off balance. "Les is just a playmate. Nothing serious. A woman likes to feel wanted."

"Men do, too," he said. "Listen, I can offer you a coffee."

She smiled. "That's nice of you, Luke, but I really did come to see Storm. You're making me out a bitch with an unpleasant taste for making trouble, but my motivation couldn't be purer. I want to be of help. I know Storm isn't a friendly person but Mum was on my back to come over. We really feel for Storm. Everyone does. Why can't you give me a bit of credit?"

"Maybe because I've learned my lesson," he said suavely.

She stood looking into his eyes. "For a sweet man you have a cruel streak. At least take me up to the house to say hello. I can see what Storm thinks. If she doesn't need a woman's help I swear I'm prepared to fly back home."

"Is that a promise?" he asked in a very wry tone.

"Trust me, Luke," she exclaimed, thinking if he did, he'd be dead wrong.

Storm heard Carla's voice before she saw her. She'd been sitting quietly in the sunroom, perfecting some of her blueprints for a new collection of jewellery when the sound of Carla's bright confident voice broke into her concentration.

Oh Lord, she thought, mourning the temporary loss of privacy. She and Carla had never been close. In fact they had seen little of each other over the years for all the two stations Winding River and Mingari bordered. They had gone to different boarding schools. Carla had not gone on to University preferring to come back to the Outback. Storm had forged a career in Sydney.

Then there was *Luke*. A state of affairs that now had a tremendous bearing on their never too friendly relationship.

A minute later and Carla all but bounded into the room, as eager and attractive as usual, dressed in a pink shirt and matching jeans that set off her tan. Luke was a few steps behind her, looking not altogether happy.

Briefly their eyes met.

"Storm!" Carla gave a little sympathetic cry and rushed forward to drop a peck on Storm's cheek. "Poor old you! We had news of your accident. Mum and I decided that the nice, neighbourly thing to do was for me to come over. You must be finding it difficult hopping about on crutches?" Her eyes went to the crutches Storm had placed beside her.

Storm felt quite unable to be ungracious. "That was kind of you, Carla. You flew yourself over?"

Carla nodded, looking towards Luke and smiling as though the three of them were the greatest of friends. "I came prepared to stay a few days. That's if you want me." There was a little catch in her voice as though being wanted was important to her.

It threw Storm slightly, making her revise her recent impressions of Carla. Still, she didn't want Carla's company. She had Luke. But how to convey that without hurt? "That'd be nice, Carla," she said injecting as much warmth as she could, "but Noni is coming home tomorrow."

A light flush swept Carla's face. "That's great! Good news. I knew she'd want to be with you. Until tomorrow then," she suggested, her gaze going back and forth, a little anxious. "Until Noni arrives. Mum and I felt sure you'd want another woman on hand."

Storm's mind filled with wry humour at that. "That was kind of you both to think of me, Carla, but I've been managing okay."

Carla's voice became more persuasive yet. "It's important you don't try to do too much, too early," she warned. "I know you'll be wanting to get back to Sydney as soon as you can. I see you're doing some sketches." Her inquisitive eyes flew to the table.

Storm nodded and gently closed the sketchpad. "A new collection. It's not really the time to be doing it but I made a commitment. I sell some of my jewellery through an art dealer who arranged a showing of my work with that of a simpatico artist. The combination worked well in the past."

"You're so clever," said Carla in an admiring undertone. "Please don't think I'm here to get in your way. I only want to be on hand should you need help."

Storm wondered how she could possibly get out of this short of rudeness. She didn't want that. "I do have Luke," she pointed out gently, allowing her gaze to settle on Luke's tall, rangy figure.

"Not *all* the time!" Carla protested, just barely keeping her feelings of outrage to herself, "besides we're all into the big muster, aren't we, Luke?" She looked to him for back-up.

"We're going well," Luke remarked so briefly, Carla pulled a face.

"Oh dear, it almost sounds like you don't want me to stay?" Her face fell visibly, the expression in her golden-brown eyes full of hurt.

Storm lacked the toughness to tell Carla to go, "Oh please, Carla," she said, "stay overnight by all means. It's a long way home."

Carla made a lightning recovery, turning to Luke with now dancing eyes. "I brought just one overnight bag with me. It's in the Jeep. I'll go with you and get it. Mum and I would hate to think we left Storm alone with her swollen ankle. Let alone her grief. Never underestimate the importance of friendship I say."

Despite her professed wish to be "on hand" for Storm, Carla spent several hours of the afternoon going in search of Luke before finally catching up with him at Cash's Crossing. This was a drafting camp near the river where branding, earmarking and other operations were being carried out. Calves and mothers in particular were always treated as gently as possible. Not only were the most humane methods in operation, gentle handling was a big asset to beef production for docility of temperament in cattle was an important factor in increased beef production. On no account was rough handling of the stock on Winding River permitted under punishment of "the sack."

Carla returned to the homestead towards sunset full of everything she had seen around the station; loudly applauding Luke for the many improvements he had made; how wonderfully *quiet* was the big muster.

"Dad always says the boss of any outfit has to have great people sense as well as great cattle sense. Luke is marvellously skilled at both. I know I shouldn't be asking this, Storm…"

So *don't,* Storm pleaded inwardly knowing if a question had to be so prefaced it was better left unasked.

"...but Luke tells me the Major's will has been read," Carla continued, eyeing Storm off. Storm felt a stab like betrayal then she reminded herself of Carla's devious nature. She kept silent, so Carla rushed on.

"Of course it was just in passing," Carla explained, "he didn't go out of his way to tell me or anything. Feeling about Luke as I do." She gave Storm a bright-eyed glance. "I just wondered if the Major had left him anything. I expect he did. The Major was such a wonderfully generous man. Luke is a living testament to that."

Count ten. Why ten? She asked herself. She really needed half an hour. "Surely if you discussed my father's will, you and Luke being so close, he would have told you?" Storm asked very coolly.

It didn't put Carla off, she shrugged. "You know Luke. He's a bit like the Major the way he keeps things to himself."

Storm considered. "My father did remember, Luke, Carla." Her tone she kept even. "I'd rather not discuss it however."

Carla's eyes lit with little golden flames. "Substantial, I would say, from the expression on your face. I know he'll get around to telling me. It's no secret Luke wants his own cattle run. He's a man who likes doing things his way."

It really was time to shift, if she could. Storm eyed her crutches. "I'm absolutely certain Luke and Dad saw eye-to-eye," she said.

"In most things I guess, but Luke did have concerns..." Again Carla left it up in the air; to be guessed at. "That's the difference between us, Storm," she pointed out kindly. "You never bothered your head about the McFarlane operation. I quite understand that. Your interests are artistic. In my own case, I wanted to know exactly how Mingari works. Dad sometimes says I know more about it than the boys.''

Storm didn't doubt it. The Prentice boys weren't overly bright. ''I'm sure you'll be a great asset to your husband,'' Storm said. ''Whether he's a cattleman or not. Just for the record, Carla, I always wanted to know about the station but Dad thought women and cattle operations didn't mix. I guess in many ways, however, as much I loved him, he was the ultimate chauvinist.''

Carla gave her a shocked look, then a faint smile. ''What a thing to say about your father.''

''Dad wouldn't have minded.'' Storm shrugged. ''He was the first to recognise that quality in himself only he thought it was greatly to be desired.''

''You *do* have a sharp tongue.'' Carla's tone was censorious.

''I like to tell the truth, yes.'' Storm moved restlessly, causing Carla to jump up.

''Now what are we going to have for dinner tonight?'' she asked in very bright tones. ''I'm not quite as good as Noni but pretty close. Mum always saw to it I knew my way around a kitchen. We never had a live-in housekeeper and cook like you.'' She gave Storm a look that set Storm's teeth together.

''Noni's *family,* Carla, not just an employee. Many's the time I've cried on Noni's shoulder.''

''You have?'' Carla looked amazed. ''I can't imagine you crying, Storm. You always seem so self-contained. We were all amazed how composed you were at the funeral. I found it so hard…now I thought we might ask Luke up for dinner? Does that suit you?''

Storm had the sense of brushing up against a steamroller. "Carla, I couldn't have stopped you asking if I tried."

Carla hadn't been exaggerating when she said she was a good cook. In fact she had pulled out all the stops over dinner, turning it into a gala occasion when it was only a handful of days since she had attended Athol McFarlane's funeral and found it very hard. Surely not the most sensitive woman in the world, Storm thought, and this is not to impress me. She was impressed all the same.

"Where did you find all this?" she had to ask, unaware there was so much produce at hand.

"You'd be amazed at what you have in the cold room." Carla looked smug. "Noni has stocked up on just about everything you can think of. The little pasta entrée was very easy. I'll be happy to give you the recipe. I know Luke loves pasta. The aged beef was to hand. All I've added is a grilled vegetable salad with anchovy butter."

"I wish I were more hungry to do it justice," Storm said without malice. "I'm not the country's most brilliant cook."

Carla's reply was instantaneous. "I'd be glad to give you a few lessons. You don't have to ask Luke if he's hungry!" she added, looking at Luke's near empty plate with satisfaction. She touched him affectionately on the hand. "There's lots more."

"All in good time, Carla," Luke said smoothly.

"You're going to love dessert."

"There's more?" Storm concentrated hard on not groaning.

"I have to remind you, Storm, the way to a man's heart is through his stomach."

"Maybe that's just an old wives' tale," Storm said.

"My dear Storm, but it *is*. Mum says it's absolutely critical a woman knows how to cook."

"It would seem so. This *is* turning into a banquet."

Carla started to laugh. "Come on, this is a nice meal. Remember the reason I'm here. I want to look after you." She turned her head to Luke. "I think you're going to love my peppered pineapple with vanilla coconut ice cream. It might sound funny but it's delicious."

"Carla," said Luke, "your mother must be very proud of you."

Afterwards they had coffee out on the verandah, the black velvet sky incandescent with stars. The evening had gradually merged into Carla's telling one preposterous story after another, but Storm had to admit quite a few of them were funny. Carla liked to act out the various parts, changing her voice frequently to suit the character. She was an excellent mimic, leading Storm to remark she would have made a good actress.

Carla looked at Storm quickly to see if she was joking, which she wasn't. "For God's sake, Storm," she burst out, "the very last thing I'd want is to strut my stuff on a stage."

Luke lifted his head a fraction from the back of the chair to say, "You don't have to relinquish the idea, Carla. All the world's a stage according to our friend, Shakespeare."

"But darling." Carla touched him lightly on the arm. She was always touching him: his shoulder, his hand, his arm, his cheek. "There's nothing more I want than to be a good station wife."

"And mother of a brood, I hope?" Storm broke in. "Being the only one isn't a great blessing."

"Well, you would know," Carla laughed. In reality she was quite miffed at Storm's exotic appearance. It just had to be for dramatic effect to put her in the shade. From somewhere Storm had got hold of an Indian sari, glowing emerald in colour, printed with gold medallions with a wide gold border. She had draped it around herself in a surprisingly expert fashion, Carla thought. I mean how many times had Storm worn a sari? Yet tonight she looked like a young maharanee or something with that mane of raven hair and those cat's eyes that echoed the colour of the sari. It was all so threatening Carla thought. No one should be that beautiful. The sooner Storm was back where she belonged the better!

Storm, not entirely unaware of the trend of Carla's thought, leant back in her peacock chair, her injured foot resting on a cushioned footstool. For a while now she had been pretending to listen to Carla while taking the opportunity to study Luke's striking face as familiar as her own, yet she never tired of looking at it. He had such a beautiful mouth. A sensual mouth. It had left its imprint on her. It had left its imprint on Carla. Small wonder Carla still wanted him. Certainly that was why Carla was here. Not to be on hand for her. To be near Luke. To impress on him she was the kind of wife he needed. Luke's breaking off the relationship with Carla had only strengthened Carla's resolve. Love affairs were sad, Storm thought. Someone had to lose. And so she felt pity for Carla who despite her determined camaraderie had no love in her heart for Storm. In fact she was coming close to hating her.

By ten o'clock Storm was tiring of what struck her as an incongruous *mñage à trois*. As the evening wore on Carla adopted an increasingly proprietorial attitude towards Luke, her manner intent on conveying to Storm their brief affair was far from finished. Luke countered with a few sardonic remarks that should have urged her to change tack, but Carla chose to ignore them.

"What about a walk?" she suggested, as though the evening's entertainment wasn't over. She looked towards Luke, pressing his arm. "We won't leave Storm long. Just a quick stroll."

"Don't feel bad about it," Storm said, when Carla was looking anything but glum. "I feel a little tired anyway. I'll say good-night. Many thanks for cooking dinner, Carla. It was excellent."

"Why you hardly touched a bite!" Carla exclaimed. "I'll help you upstairs. We can take the lift. What a help to have it in the house like this."

Luke side-stepped Carla's suggestion. "It's okay. I'll carry her." He stood up, as superbly fit as a man could be. "Straight up the staircase, along the hall. I don't like to see you struggling with those crutches."

"Hey, I thought I was getting good."

"She *is* good," Carla maintained stoutly, in no mood to see Storm in Luke's arms.

"Not good enough for me." Luke shifted his chair out of the way, then moved over to the peacock chair where Storm reclined. "Ready?"

"My hero!" Storm sighed lightly.

Carla didn't like that. She didn't like it at all. Worse, she found she couldn't bear to see Luke cradling Storm in his arms. Something about the attitude of their bodies deeply disturbed her. They looked so comfortable together. No, comfortable wasn't the word, though Storm's body accommodated itself easily to Luke's. They looked like…primitive emotions surfaced…they looked like *lovers*. There wasn't the tiniest doubt in her mind. Oh God, Carla thought. They've slept together. Their body language said it all.

"I'll tend to the dishes," Carla called, watching Luke carry Storm up the grand central staircase. Why didn't he drop her, Carla thought, instead of doing a Rhett Butler. Before she could stop herself she made a bee-line to the rear staircase, which gave onto the upper gallery. From there she swept out onto the verandah inching down to Storm's bedroom, as though there might be an orgy in progress. She was taking a risk, she knew. Luke might walk out onto the verandah, but she thought not. The French doors and the wooden shutters were fastened back. And there was cover. Golden canes in big glazed pots were set at intervals all along the verandah, their billowing fronds providing shelter.

For years, and no exaggeration, she had done everything in her power to make Luke Branagan notice her. Finally she had succeeded though her strategies, frenetic as they were, hadn't been good enough to hold him. She had always known about the strong bond between Luke and Storm but that had been kept in balance by endless conflicts. Now this! How and when had it happened? When had the gulf been bridged?

By the Major's will? Luke had been named as a major beneficiary. That was a little difficult to swallow. Storm would be mad and she didn't seem mad at all. Determined to know, no matter the cost, Carla stole along to the bedroom, positioning herself stealthily beside one of the golden canes that flanged the bedroom door. Jealousy was slicing through her with the sharpness of a blade. She felt a twisted sense of betrayal. Didn't Storm McFarlane have enough without taking Luke? She was a witch. There were a few still around. One of those dark-haired, green-eyed women that cast spells. Storm didn't want Luke. They'd been combatants for years. She just wanted to show her power. She could hear them talking inside the bedroom, their voices low.

"I think Carla knows," Storm was saying, sounding like she was dismayed.

"Knows?" That was Luke. "You mean about us? It wouldn't surprise me. Carla's very sharp. I suppose it's all spelled out the way I look at you."

Carla heard the sigh. I don't want your pity, Storm McFarlane, she thought. I want you to disappear to Sydney and never come back.

Then Luke spoke and Carla sobered enough to listen. "I'm afraid you're right," he said. "But Carla has to face facts. Noni will be here tomorrow. Carla will be free to go home."

So he can't wait to get rid of me, Carla seethed. Off with the old and on with the new.

"I think Carla thinks her dislike of me is going unnoticed," Storm said in her cut-glass voice.

"Well it's not going unnoticed by *me*." Luke's attractive tones slightly hardened. "There are two sides to Carla," he added thoughtfully. "She could make a good enemy."

Too right I can! Carla thought, her passion for Luke dissolving into a fuming rage.

"Then be careful when you go for a walk with her." Storm gave a little laugh.

Carla thought Luke would answer, but there was silence. A silence that stretched unbearably. Overwhelmed with jealousy Carla peered around the shutters only to see Luke bending over Storm, seated on the bed. They were kissing.

And such kissing! Carla felt the hot blood rush to her cheeks. He had never kissed her like that. Those were light-hearted pecks compared to what she was seeing now. This was a grand passion. She wasn't such a fool she couldn't interpret that. Why was she worrying about being seen? If she beat a drum they wouldn't even hear her.

Carla turned on her heel and fled the way she had come. Still full of vain hopes. Still full of plans...

Noni arrived home midmorning, surprised to find Carla had come to visit, but encouraged by the pleasantness of Carla's manner, her competence and her regard for Storm's well-being. Carla seemed so genuinely friendly, Noni, who had never really taken to her before now, revised her opinion.

It was Carla who thoughtfully made morning tea and served it in the sunroom. Afterwards, she excused herself so Storm and Noni could have a private talk. There were many things Storm wouldn't say to her, Carla had decided, but she would confide in Noni, loyal family friend and retainer. When that happened Carla proposed to be somewhere within earshot. She felt not the slightest shame at the thought of eavesdropping. Sometimes it was the only way one could flush out confidential information.

In the end it took an interminable half an hour for Storm to bring up the subject of her father's will, a half hour during which Carla was supposed to be packing her overnight bag and putting the guest bedroom to rights. Carla, however, had taken up a position on a lower step of the rear staircase, cramming her ears to hear what was being said in the sunroom.

There was the whole tiresome episode of Storm's accident. Who hadn't been confronted by a snake? Carla thought and almost groaned. General talk about people Carla didn't even know, then just when Carla was about to give up and go upstairs Storm began to tell Noni the terms of her father's will.

Bingo! Carla kissed her fingers.

Starting with the bequest to Noni herself. Far too generous for a servant, Carla thought, barely controlling a sniff.

Then the bombshell! The unexpectedness of which had Carla on her feet, tiptoeing closer to the door. Luke had inherited a half share of Winding River. Something called life estate. Not only that, before Carla could even catch her breath, the news he would take the profits providing he continued to work the whole operation. It came like a blow that almost knocked Carla out. In one stroke, Athol McFarlane had made Luke a rich man, a real player. Whatever else she had imagined, a splendid lump sum, she had never for one moment anticipated Luke would be given equal share with the Major's only daughter. Her immediate thought was, it was unfair. So the Major had doted on Luke almost like a son? Luke wasn't his blood.

There was absolutely no way Noni expected it, either.

"But darling girl how extraordinary!" she cried. "It seems a great deal for *affection,* though I know no one has worked harder than Luke. He certainly deserved recognition, but this, it quite takes my breath away."

My sentiments exactly, thought Carla, continuing her detective work.

"Dad had plans, Noni," Storm explained. "I think his dearest wish was to see Luke and I married."

Tears of outrage came to Carla's eyes.

"Luke would keep the station going. I would provide the heirs."

Silence again. Carla pictured them side by side. "But how do you feel about this, dearest girl?" Noni still sounded like a woman in shock. "How does Luke? I know it would have come as a great surprise to him."

Surprise. *Indeed!* Carla fumed.

"It did. To us both," Storm said. "I'm afraid I reacted so badly, Luke threatened to leave. He said he wanted no part of any legacy. He wouldn't work for me—'' Storm broke off, thinking she heard a small sound. ''Was that something?''

Carla waited for no more. As if she had taken wings she swooped up the stairs making for the guest room. She accomplished it with such quietness and such speed by the time Noni came to the door of the sunroom to investigate, the rear hall and the surrounding area, were quite empty.

''Nothing, darling,'' Noni said reassuringly. ''Nothing at all.''

It seemed graceless in the extreme to send Carla off without lunch so after unpacking her things and settling in, Noni returned to her domain, pleased to find it spotless, to organize lunch. Her mind was still trying to cope with Storm's news; the fact Luke had inherited half share in Winding River had put her own sizeable legacy on the backburner. Luke was a truly exceptional young man. She really cared about him. It was Noni's own view that he would make a fine husband for her beloved Storm. The more she thought about it, marrying would seem to solve the problem. At the same time it could have thrown them into a new dilemma. What a master manipulator the Major had been, God rest his soul. Noni went out to her vegetable garden to find the making for a salad.

Meanwhile on the front verandah Storm and Carla made casual conversation, Storm trying her hardest to be friendly for all she found it a little heavy going. Carla, waited her moment. Then let the chips fall where they may! Finally it came. Storm passed some remark about Luke's having to visit the outstations, giving Carla the opportunity to insert gently, sounding troubled, ''It must have come as an awful shock Luke inheriting half of Winding River?'' She looked at Storm, her eyes full of sympathy. "I know in your place I would be devastated."

Storm could hear Carla's words, but they seemed to be coming from a long way off. In fact it was difficult to describe the full impact Carla's words had on her. Anger uppermost. A horrendous pain like a stab to the heart. "Wherever did you get that information from, Carla?" She stared at her, not believing it could have come from Luke. Not Luke! Not now she had delivered herself up to him.

"Why, Luke, of course," Carla confessed, sounding a little frightened. "He told me when we went for a walk last night. Please don't tell him I told you," she begged. "He'd be very angry with me. It was supposed to be a secret to share."

Was it possible she was telling the truth? Storm thought grimly. A lie could easily be found out. "What else did he tell you?" Storm asked.

"Oh, Storm, I'm sorry." Carla put her hand to her burning face. "I should never have said anything but I thought we were friends. It was the last thing I expected to hear. Luke told me it was only for his lifetime. He did explain that. That helped a bit. The station will revert to you. As it *should*."

"And Luke told you all this last night?" Storm asked, aware her tones were very blunt.

Carla hung her head. "I can see I've made you very angry. But, Storm, my sympathies are with *you*. Why if Dad did that to me…" She gestured helplessly.

Her whole heart wanted to believe in Luke but this smacked of the truth. Where else would Carla have got it from?

"Regardless of whether Luke is angry with you or not, Carla, I intend to speak to him about this."

"And ruin my chances with him?" Carla's eyes filled with tears. "Storm you can't be so cruel. I love Luke."

"Then I'm very sorry for you, Carla. He doesn't love you."

There was a look of total denial in Carla's eyes. "Maybe not now but he *will* in time. There's no life for him with you, Storm. For any number of reasons. You're always looking down your nose at him. He *hates* that. He hates the way you've always played the lovely lady of the manor."

"Did he tell you that?" Storm's voice suggested she was highly sceptical.

"Storm, surely you know Luke and I have spent a lot of time together. You were off in Sydney most of the time. You got yourself engaged twice. Luke had to have someone to confide in. Is it so hard to believe he'd confide in me?"

That seemed to echo endlessly in Storm's head. "I suppose not," she said eventually. "And how would the fact Luke has inherited half share in Winding River affect you? I've told you, you've lost any hold over Luke."

"That's not what I sense when I'm alone with him. He trusts me unlike you. Anyway, surely he can sell out to you?" Carla's trim body was taut with excitement.

"Did he say that?" Storm's brain was spinning.

"Luke is a man who considers his options," Carla said, respectfully. "I know his first thought was simply to go. He's a proud man. But I suppose you convinced him not to leave you in the lurch. I wouldn't want that either. You'll go back to your career, Storm. We all know that. You get your face in all the glossy magazines. All the time. I know you're not a social butterfly, or anything like that, but you *are* social. It occurs to me you could even sell to Luke?"

She'd come this far she might as well go on. "How would Luke come by the money?" Storm asked.

Carla's triumphant expression shaped itself into careful consideration as though this were a question intended to be taken very seriously. "There are ways, Storm," she said at last. "Luke has friends. Dad thinks the world of him. So do the boys."

"And they're prepared to demonstrate that devotion?" Storm asked with barely concealed sarcasm. "When you go home, Carla, with your news, which I haven't the slightest doubt will travel far and wide, you can tell your family I'll never sell Winding River. This is part of *my* heritage. My children will inherit it."

Carla's mouth turned down. "That's a long way off, Storm," she pointed out. "Lots could happen between now and then. Luke may be agonizing over the right thing to do now, but in the end, I believe he'll take up his inheritance. One thing I do know—" she leaned forward, staring directly into Storm's eyes "—whatever power you have over him and I grant you you're beautiful, you'll never turn him into your lackey. He'd rather..."

"Get it all out, Carla," Storm urged, thinking this confrontation was the last thing she needed. "There's something else?"

Some alarm bell went off. "Forgive me," Carla suddenly muttered. "My feelings are running away with me."

"I'd go along with that," Storm answered wryly. "You're a guest in this house, Carla." An uninvited one. She didn't have the heart to mention it.

Carla paled a little. "I'm sorry if you think I've behaved badly, Storm. I have no wish to hurt you. Believe me, I'm your friend."

Storm turned her dark head slowly. "I have a big problem with that."

"All right you're not one of my favourites." Unexpectedly Carla laughed. "You have everything. Money, looks, a career. What I'm really trying to say is lay off Luke."

For an instant Storm felt like crying for them all. Instead she looked out over the drive with its magnificent central fountain. She could hear Noni's footsteps in the hallway coming closer. She was immensely grateful. "Carla," she said quietly, not responding to the other woman's challenge, "I cannot fail to tell you, you've got problems. There's *nothing* between you and Luke except maybe the embers of a friendship. I'm sure under the circumstances you won't want to stay for lunch."

Carla looked back over her shoulder. She too was aware Noni was almost upon them. Noni, the devoted family "friend." "Listen to the lady!" Carla said with a bitter laugh. "I only came to see Luke anyway."

Storm looked up at Carla as she stood swaying like a boxer on her feet. "You surely didn't think I thought otherwise?"

CHAPTER NINE

ONE of the ground staff drove Carla to the airstrip. Storm didn't wave her off. She felt close to collapse. To lose her father, then to have to stabilize her emotions after hearing his will; to consummate her subterranean passion for Luke, to be disabled with her injured ankle. Now Carla with her revelations. It was too much to handle. Surely if Carla were sane she wouldn't continue with her obsessive quest for Luke? Was it possible he continued to encourage her? More likely Carla was a little mad? Not that it wasn't possible to lead a normal life and still obsess about relationships. She wouldn't have believed Carla at all except there was no way Carla could have known. Only three people, four counting Robert, knew the contents of her father's will. Robert, even if he had been in the house, was the soul of discretion. His very livelihood depended upon it. She had only just told Noni. Noni for any number of reasons she ruled out. That left Luke himself.

He and Carla had gone for a walk last night. It was a known fact, at one stage Luke and Carla had been more than friends. Carla when she had no obvious cause of making mischief was good-looking, vivacious, a born country woman with all the necessary skills, and she could be entertaining. Was it possible Luke needed to talk about his life-changing bequest with someone else? Someone he trusted? Luke had to know Carla cared about him deeply. Carla was on *his* side.

Noni coming back into the sunroom where Storm was

supposedly resting with her foot up, saw the play of emotions move across Storm's face.

"What an odd girl!" she exclaimed, sinking into an armchair opposite Storm. "One minute she's staying for lunch the next she's off." Noni had been trained to ask questions but she waited.

Storm couldn't help the deep sigh that ran through her, leaving her drained. "You didn't happen to mention anything about Dad's will to her?"

There was a brief awful silence.

"I'm amazed you ask me, Storm," Noni's sweet features registered deep hurt causing Storm's eyes to fill with quick tears.

"Oh, forgive me, Noni. I don't know why I asked. It was a stupid question."

"Except you're not stupid, my girl," Noni pointed out bracingly. "Something was behind it?"

Betrayed? "Carla appears to know just about everything in connection with Luke's inheritance. How Dad left him a half share. How it was a bequest for life. How afterwards it would revert to me or my heirs. Only three of us knew, Noni."

Noni pressed a hand to her head. "You can't possibly think Luke told her?"

There was a bleak expression in Storm's eyes. "They went for a walk last night. I know Luke was shocked by the sheer size of Dad's bequest. Luke can't say everything to me. Maybe he needed to confide in a friend."

But Noni had a talent for sounding out emotions. "Dearest girl, he's *not* in love with Carla. I can tell you that."

"He must have thought he was in love with her at one time?" Storm stared back a little helplessly, looking more vulnerable than Noni had yet seen her. In fact she looked fragile.

"Just as you thought you were in love with Alex and that other fellow," Noni countered reasonably.

"Then how *did* she know, Noni? I don't think I could bear it if I thought Luke had taken her into his confidence. She mentioned something else that was telling about Luke. She said he would never be my lackey."

"He never said that," Noni answered promptly, with scorn.

"Maybe not those words. But he did tell me he wouldn't work for me. That was before the will was read."

Noni was tempted to say what she thought and gave into the temptation. "You're in love with him aren't you?" she said gently.

"*In* love with him?" Storm was almost in tears. "Noni, I love him. I've always loved him. But unthinking, unknowingly, Dad pushed us apart. His latest attempt to bring us together hasn't had much success, either."

Noni knew all the facts; recalled them. "I've watched you two for many long years," she said. "I looked on helplessly while your father, with the best of intentions, did a lot of harm. You *must* accept, Storm, your father loved Luke. Luke was just the sort of boy, the young man your father would have wanted for a son. It affected you badly, but in your father's eyes his love for Luke had nothing to do with his love for you. You were his beautiful, gifted daughter. But in his eyes no woman could be strong enough, exceptional enough to run a cattle empire. The Major wasn't about to throw a lifetime's work away. Or the McFarlane heritage."

"So he devised a scheme whereby Luke and I would marry, little caring if there was fallout?" Storm said, her eyes sad.

"It's up to you, Storm," Noni said, her voice firm but comforting. "Your life has been complicated for so long.

It's time to free yourself of the bonds. Talk to Luke. I'm sure he'll come up with a perfectly reasonable explanation.''

The muster was ahead of schedule which gave Luke a lot of satisfaction. Most of the herd was now within a day's journey of water. He'd been up very early that morning to greet four of the stockmen coming in from the skeleton camp where they had spent the night. They were strung out perhaps a half mile apart, stock-whips cracking, driving the bellowing beasts in the desired direction towards water. Very soon he'd know where all his cows and calves were. It was time to delegate a few of his jobs so he could visit the outstations. He had intended doing that, but the Major's death had changed everyone's plans.

As always no matter what he was doing his mind drifted back to Storm. He had taken such delight, such exhilaration in the beauty and passion of their coming together. It had overwhelmed him so much so he had difficulty dealing with this business of his half share. Storm, initially shocked and angry and he didn't blame her, now seemed to have accepted the situation far better than he could. It was a great honour, but he had difficulty coming to terms with the magnitude of it. The magnitude of winning Storm, like plucking a star from the sky. With a half share in Winding River, running it as he wanted, he had the world at his feet. They needed to take in another station. Central Queensland for preference, not big in Winding River's terms, but providing lush green feed for at least six months or so of the year. He had just such a station in mind. The bulk of the cattle would be straight Brahmin. Storm had a good mind.

When things settled, perhaps after he had a chance to visit the outstations, he would discuss it with her. He just hoped she hadn't been too irritated by Carla's comments and performance last night. Carla's wish to hold onto him seemed almost neurotic. God knows what Carla would think when she got around to hearing the Major had left him a half share in Winding River. She would hear it if he took up his bequest. She would hear it and half the world if either Storm fought the will or he forfeited the bequest. He had come to see Carla had a strange pattern of behaviour. She had gone to considerable lengths last night to make it appear to Storm their short affair was far from over. At the same time she was seeing Les Marshall. Sex was very important to Carla. Les would be sure to oblige.

He returned to the bungalow at dusk, found a little note from Storm asking him to come up to the house for dinner. Noni must have delivered it, he thought, pleased in one way Noni was home, but mindful in another Storm now had a chaperone. No glorious night in Storm's bed. He was still light-headed at the thought of it. He couldn't possibly let her get away. He loved her. Extravagantly. She knew that of course. He had always loved her.

He knew the minute he saw her something was wrong. He had been an excellent student of her every expression, every mood, though she covered up well. Noni ate with them, the meal hour quiet but companionable. Afterwards Noni withdrew to the kitchen, refusing his offer to carry in the dishes.

"I'll pile them all on the trolley, dear." Noni smiled. "You two enjoy the cool of the verandah. I'll bring coffee out shortly."

She allowed herself to be carried, looking absolutely beautiful in a light dress that was the colour of lilacs he supposed. Or maybe jacaranda. Her face was so close to his he wanted to kiss her, his eyes travelling to her mouth as lustrous as a rose. The scent of her intoxicated him. She smelt so delicious, cool even when the temperature soared.

The moon was out with a glittering trail of stars, so close to hand one only had to reach out.

"You've been very quiet," he remarked, after he settled her comfortably in her favourite peacock chair.

"I'm finding it a bit wearing not being able to get about," Storm explained, inside shaking with nerves.

"The swelling is subsiding." He glanced approvingly at her ankle.

"At best I might be right in about another ten days."

Behind Luke's handsome head was the dazzling sky and the moon. She fixed her eyes on it. If only issues didn't constantly present themselves.

"So what's wrong?" he asked when she finally looked back at him. "I suppose it has something to do with Carla?"

"Why would you say that?" She levered herself up a bit, straightening her shoulders.

"Carla suffers from delusions," he drawled. "That was only an act last night. There's nothing between Carla and me. You of all people should know that." How could she not?

She picked up a cushion and held it to her like a child. "Except you do talk to her?"

"About what?" Luke's strong features tensed. Hadn't it always been like this? Why did he allow himself to hope things would be different?

"Oh, Luke!" Storm expelled a long sigh, her beautiful hands working a little. "I know there's a perfectly good explanation?"

"I repeat, about what?" A thousand confrontations crammed his mind.

She looked at his taut face, such an aching in her. "All

right, Carla said you told her in confidence about Dad's will. How you inherited a half share. How it was termed a life estate. How—"

"And you believed her?" He cut her off abruptly.

"Only because there was no other way she could have known." Storm's eyes pleaded with him.

"I bet you told Noni," he said.

"Yes, I did. I love Noni. She loves me. She's been with me since I was a child. I trust her."

"But you don't trust *me*. You'll sleep with me. You lose yourself in my arms. I can arouse you again and again, but it's only sex—a great charge of emotion. Maybe it even makes you feel wicked."

"Luke!" She was shocked to the depths of her soul.

"Who the hell am I anyway?" he demanded. "Just the kid your father took on. The kid left without a father and mother. Hell, you've hated me all your life."

An answering anger flashed through her. "Hate you...hate you..." How she longed to spring up. "I *love* you. I've been ill thinking about all this."

"You love me do you?" He moved towards her like a panther, pinning her face in his hand. "Let's hear your little cry of pleasure." He bent his head and took her mouth, in his fevered state letting his hand shape her breast, feeling the instant swell of the nipple. He kissed her long and hard, as if they were about to be estranged and he wanted her to remember.

"Luke," she whispered. "Please stop." She had to, *had* to beg his forgiveness.

Immediately he stepped back, full of self-loathing. "I don't know how it is or why it is I let you do these things to me. But it's all over, Storm. I won't be your scapegoat for the rest of my life."

Pressing her hands down on the sides of her chair, Storm

managed to stand up, in her agitation putting her injured foot to the floor.

"Aaaah!" She couldn't control the whimper of pain.

He couldn't *not* help her. Even now. He went to her, took her weight, pressing her back into her chair.

"Tomorrow I'm going to visit the outstations," he said in a perfectly hard voice. "I'll be gone probably a week maybe a little more. I'll let you know. I don't know why I'm bothering to tell you this, but I told Carla nothing at all. It would be impossible feeling the way I do... did...about you. But I'm not swallowing your distrust any more. I don't know how Carla came by her information, but I think you might consider Carla is not above snooping."

"That's it!" Storm's knees were trembling. She suddenly remembered the little sound she had heard when she and Noni were talking in the sunroom. "That's it! She overheard me talking to Noni. Oh God, Luke, you must let me apologise."

"Don't bother!" His voice rasped, his eyes like blue fire. "I thought I loved you, Storm. I thought I loved everything about you even your astonishing aberrations. I wanted everything from you. I wanted it all. I wanted to marry you. I wanted you to have our children. I was fool enough to think we could start again with Winding River to be held in trust for the heir who was strong enough to hold it together. But it's over. You've given me too much pain."

Sick with emotion, Storm held out her hands to him. "Don't do this to me now, Luke. You've always been able to forgive me no matter what I've done."

"Not any more." He looked around him blindly, hardly seeing anything for his upset. "I've known no other home but here on Winding River. It's time now to move on."

* * *

It was the longest ten days Storm had ever known. She filled in her time as best she could, working on her collection—the ideas weren't coming—replying to Sara who had sent her a long, loving letter from Rome, where the news of Athol McFarlane's death had reached her; replying to innumerable sympathy cards; replying to Alex who had been told of her father's death on his return from Hong Kong. Alex wanted to come and visit her.

"I'll throw up my job if I have to," he told her. "I just want to be by your side."

She thanked him for his genuine expressions of sympathy and his many kindnesses to her, but told him at this sad time she needed to be on her own.

The only tiny ray of sunshine was the fact she was able to put her foot to the ground. Could in fact walk on it. She had mended well. She confided in Noni how Luke had reacted—in any case Noni had guessed something had gone terribly wrong—so both women were feeling powerfully disturbed. Luke had become the linchpin in their existence. Recognising he could go out of their lives left them with feelings of acute depression.

Storm agonized over how she could put things right. Possible courses of action seemed to occupy her mind every single hour of the day and into the night. She simply couldn't envision a life without Luke. Her entire happiness hinged on his being there. She was part of him and he was part of her. Now their alienation made her feel terribly isolated. How very easy it was, she now discovered, to realise the worth of a loved one when the loved one decided to go his own way. It probably wasn't even unusual in relationships but it always came as a great shock. Why hadn't she heeded the warnings? It seemed her time of grace had finally run out.

Luke had left word when he arrived on Duranji,

Outstation One, and when he left. There was a great sense of relief that the days were passing and soon he would be coming home.

Home.

It struck Storm cruelly it was just as Luke had said. He had always *lived* on Winding River but it had never been his home. It was up to her to change that. Her task was to get them started on a new life. That's if he would ever forgive her. Knowing Luke she had to consider seriously that once he had made a decision he would stick to it. Winding River had been a battlefield far too long. Outstation Two, Mungin, was more remote, two hundred miles to the northwest. Luke arrived at the designated time, took off at a designated time. His inspections were complete. He would arrive on Winding River around 3:00 p.m. that Friday afternoon. Over an hour and a half later, Bill Davidson, the head stockman came up to the homestead a worried man. Luke's flight was overdue, when Luke was a man who stuck to his schedule. Bill had already contacted Mungin only to be told everything had been fine when Luke left. If he had kept to his flight plan he should have landed on Winding River.

"The weather was brilliantly fine when he left," Bill was saying. "Scorchingly hot!" No electrical storms in the area predicted. "Of course he could have put down for some reason or other," Bill continued, looking anxiously at Storm for some kind of agreement. Storm, however, felt such a clutch of fear it was like her heart had seized up. Bill continued to ramble on, as though talking was a relief, his forehead furrowed with all sorts of anxieties. Storm vaguely heard him say something about the automatic distress signal. It hadn't been picked up. Both knew, none better, how many lives had been lost in light aircraft crashes throughout the Outback.

The sunset was glorious, turning the riverine desert to a land of molten gold. But for once Storm didn't feel her heart lift at the spectacle. The imperial sun sank behind the great pyramids of fiery red sand dunes. The brief lilac dusk set in with thousands of birds flying into the billabongs in multi-coloured clouds. Somehow Storm had come to grips with her tearing panic. Air Services Australia Search and Rescue was informed, Storm giving all necessary information, her voice falsely calm. Controlling the tone and speed of her delivery helped her keep sane. No radio contact had been made by Luke. Neither could he be reached by radio. No distress signal had been picked up. Search and Rescue had the flight path, which would make the task of finding Luke, and his aircraft less difficult but these occasions were always time for worry. Full-scale operations would begin at first light.

It was going to be a long, long night for everyone on Winding River. There had been plenty of drama over the years. They all had their memories of the Major. But Luke was *young*. Someone special. Nothing could happen to Luke. Station people relied very heavily on each other for support and comfort. Storm turned to Noni at this anxious time. Both of them far too uneasy to think they could find a few hours oblivion in sleep, but both women tried very hard to keep their emotions under control. There was always the possibility of total electrical failure. Luke would have to make a forced landing. He would have to find a clear space to use as a runway. There was a whole inland out there. Mulga country. Spinifex country. Desert. There wasn't much leeway for making a mistake. The only comfort was, Luke was an experienced pilot.

He loved flying with a passion. It was an immense exhilaration. The twin engines roaring into life, soaring into the blue. He loved the colour blue. He supposed everyone had a colour they loved best. Blue was the sky. Blue was peace and freedom. The vast ancient land drifted by beneath him scorched a fiery red by a million suns. It was a wonderful feeling to know he was part of it, this great sunbaked land with its ancient plateaus and its isolated mesas. He rejoiced in the connection. Beneath him lay the desert; the Dead Heart credited with many deaths. Explorers, pioneers, pastoralists, later day tourists who for reasons he could never understand didn't heed the warnings. Some came from a world where there was abundant water everywhere. Down there water was the difference between life and fearsome death.

Up here in the cobalt-blue sky his mind always seemed clearer. Perhaps it was because he was totally alone with his thoughts and the simple exultation of flight. As always during these past, heat filled, hectic days he had been wrestling with what he was going to do with his future. The disabling truth was he could not contemplate a future without Storm in it. No escape for him, he thought wryly. His love for Storm was a raging fever that might never be cured.

The Cessna had been cruising as smoothly as a Rolls-Royce so it came as a tremendous jolt to see his entire instrument panel shut down. Total electrical failure. That meant he had lost all communication. Battery? Choke in the fuel pipe? His mind hit on two likely possibilities. Things happened despite regular maintenance. The twin engines were still humming efficiently but he had no other option than to make a forced landing. And as quickly as possible. He dropped altitude descending to a height where he could search for a reasonably safe landing strip. In this area larger than the United Kingdom there were no highways to hand. No dirt roads. No grassy paddocks. No nice, helpful people. Plenty of mulga country. Spinifex country. Blood-red sand. A land majestic but frightening in its ruggedness. He was well off course before he spotted a wide sandy flat that was dotted with golden spinifex in seed. That would have to be it. He turned downwind in preparation for the landing.

A few hairy moments coming in to land, the spears of the spinifex scratching the undercarriage, the gnarled and twisted trunk of a mulga almost clipping a wing. A desert oak loomed up and for a few heart-stopping moments when his whole life seemed to rush by, he wondered if the Cessna would stop in time.

It did and he swore aloud in his relief.

Once on the ground he looked around him with an awe he had never lost. The immensity, the great silence, the unmistakeable brooding challenge thrilled him, fired his imagination.

I am the desert. I am the Dreaming Place. I will still be here when man is no more.

The landscape was so highly coloured it almost hurt his eyes. Ancient pottery baked hard. He had the shivery feeling he might easily have been the first white man to ever have looked upon it. This was forbidding country for anyone who didn't know it intimately. The sun at its peak generated temperatures of more than forty-three degrees. Ally that to the excessively dry atmosphere, and a man could dehydrate within forty-eight hours, leaving a mummified corpse. He always carried water without fail. He was a skilled bushman. He had lived in this environment all his life. He had learned well at the feet of the tribal elders. He knew where to dig for water. He knew what plants to eat. He *could* survive but he was pitted against the cruellest environment in the world. The desert.

Surrounded by so much primordial splendour he felt no

fear. He wasn't going to perish. Maybe it would take time but Air Rescue would find him. Besides he had to live to tell that woman, that Storm McFarlane, he was going to marry her. There wasn't anything she was going to be able to do about it, either. He knew her mind better than she did.

He turned to make his inspection of the Cessna, discovering like he thought the problem was battery melt down. In the near distance he could see a family of dingoes on the prowl, ears pricked, at the alert. Further off a couple of camels were running wild and his mind harked back to the day he had saved the Major's life. Even now he could feel the Major's strong hand on his shoulder, hear the deep rumble of his voice:

You stood your ground in the face of fear. I promise you I won't forget it.

He had saved the Major's life. Now it had come to him his destiny was to give his daughter the best possible life. To love her and involve her in all his plans. She had such energy in life. So had he. They needed to combine it for the future. For their children. For Winding River. By now she would have learned the news. He hadn't turned up on the station. Communication lines had been broken. He knew in his heart she would be desolate if anything happened to him. If nothing else, they had to get their love out into the open. Once settled they could work together to find answers.

So heartened, with the vision of Storm very clear in his mind, Luke went about the job of preparing to spend the night in a desert where the great heat of the day would drop to a comparative freezing.

It had been a terrible night for both of them. By mid-morning they still had not received word, though they all

clung to hope. A full-scale search was in operation. The
downed aircraft would be spotted. Luke would be safe and
well.

Thirty hours. Thirty minutes. Forty seconds. Storm
thought. All that morning in torment. It was like living
with a knife in her breast. To have parted in such anger!
It was more than she could bear. Why had they spent so
much time in arguing? More to the point why had she?
All their lives it was Luke who had shown the understanding, the tolerance. She, especially vulnerable as a girl child
then a young woman, had railed against Luke's position
in her father's life. For this maybe her father was to blame
but she was old enough now to get her futile hang-ups
under control. She would do anything, be anything, give
all her money away, to have Luke safely back in her arms.

Driven by emotion the anguish that would never empty
out until Luke was safely home, Storm gathered branches
of white bauhinias in flower from the home grounds;
sheaves of the sun-loving zinnias and masses of greenery
taking the Jeep to Sanctuary Hill. Of course the flowers
couldn't possibly survive, not in the heat, but her grief
directed her to strip the orchid trees and pile up the gorgeous open-faced zinnias that flowered profusely even in
the dry.

Once at the cemetery, Storm lay her floral offerings first
on her parents' graves. They lay side by side. She moved
a distance away, past her ancestors' graves with their mon-
umental headstones to where Luke's parents had been laid
to rest. Again side by side as husband and wife should be.
The white bauhinia branches she lay on the graves of the
women, the mothers. The multicoloured zinnias she strew
over the graves of her father and Luke's. How the lives of
the two families had been intermingled. How could she
possibly let Luke leave when his parents were here on

Sanctuary Hill? It was unthinkable. All her life she had been afraid to trust. But it wasn't too late. Dear God, don't let it be too late. Storm bent her head and prayed with the greatest intensity she had known in her life. Prayed that Luke would be found safe and uninjured. She prayed all the old hurts would go away. The love she had for Luke couldn't disappear into a void. She prayed for her family. She prayed for Luke's family. Unwilling to leave this strangely peaceful spot, she was forced to seek shelter beneath the magnificent desert oak that grew near the entrance. Sanctuary Hill was surrounded on all sides by a tall wrought-iron fence with double wrought-iron gates hung from stone pillars to lock it in.

Another scorching day and Luke was out there in the desert. Even with the shelter of the wing the heat would be intense. She knew he would be carrying that precious commodity water. None of them travelled any distance into the desert country without it. Worn-out by her sleepless night and the crushing weight of anxiety Storm allowed her lids to fall...

A voice somewhere spoke her name. She was dreaming. It was Luke. The tears started up behind her shut eyelids. The bond between them was so strong he could reach her even in sleep.

The hand moved from her wrist to her face, stroking, caressing, the voice repeating her name.

"Storm...Storm!" So much love in it. Longing. Concern. Her splendid white knight.

"Darling, everything's all right. You can open your eyes. I'm here. I'm really here."

Maybe the dream was playing a cruel joke. He *wasn't* really there. But strong arms reached for her. Flesh and bone. She was drawn to her feet. Those same arms locked themselves around her like they would never, never, let her go. Not even in eternity.

She lifted her head and stared straight into Luke's blazing blue eyes. They were all the more jewel-like because his eyes, like hers, glittered with tears.

"Luke! Oh thank you, God!" She sagged against him overcome by relief and joy, unable to say any more because he lowered his head; kissed her with such a flame of passion it burned itself into her. "I couldn't go on without you," she told him emotionally when he allowed her breath. "I love you with all my heart."

"As I love you," he answered immediately, voice vibrant with emotion. "I could never go away and leave you. I could never die without telling you, you're all the magic, all the wonder in my life."

"Can you forgive me?" she beseeched him, touching his beloved face with a wondering hand.

He shook his gleaming dark red head. "There'll be no talk of forgiveness between us. The old days are past. What we're going to talk about endlessly is our future. You and me. I want you to marry me, Storm. I want it as soon as it's respectful to your father. I want you to be my wife, the mother of my children. I want us to be together in this life and the next. I want when the time comes, a long, long way off, we'll lie here side by side. Maybe our daughter will come to cover us with blossoms. White as a bridal veil. Marry me, Storm. I won't take no for an answer."

She hugged his lean body to her, her hands digging into his hard-muscled back. "I'll marry you. I promise. I wish it were tomorrow but I think it must be April. April is a lovely month. Would you like an April bride?" she asked radiantly.

He gathered her to him; held her right up to his heart. "April is perfect. Heaven. I can't wait to see you in your bridal finery walking towards me."

EPILOGUE

APRIL IN THE CHANNEL COUNTRY
THE MIRACLE OF THE WILD FLOWERS
THE BRANAGAN-McFARLANE WEDDING

The Branagan-McFarlane wedding celebrated on historic Winding River Station received wide coverage in the press. It was an open secret the stunningly handsome bridegroom, the late Major Athol McFarlane's protégé had received a half share in the famous station in recognition of his services to the family but that seemed neither here nor there when the bridegroom was to continue running the McFarlane operation as he had in the past. It was reported the happy couple was to make the station their home although the bride, an acclaimed jewellery designer would continue her career selling her beautiful pieces through favoured outlets.

Three hundred guests had been invited to the wedding. They came from all over the country and overseas. A famous women's magazine was allowed coverage on the understanding the substantial fee in the form of a cheque would be made out to the Sydney Children's Hospital, a charity dear to the bride's heart. Everyone who attended the wedding could speak of nothing else for months on end. The floodwaters the station had received during the Wet had receded leaving a wonderland of wildflowers on a gigantic scale. Flowers to the horizon! A total transformation of the desert landscape; millions and millions of everlastings holding up their pretty paper faces, white, yellow and pink, the fluffy flowered mulla-mulla, the crimson of the desert peas, the masses and masses of other wildflowers that traced their coloured embroidery across the vast land. It was a sight no guest, especially those who had never witnessed such a miracle, were likely to forget.

And the homestead! Glorious! The bride had refurbished it. What exquisite taste! The wedding ceremony was held in the old ballroom where everyone got quite teary at the obvious love that bathed the happy couple in radiance. The beauty of the bride was a great talking point. Her gown was *fabulous!* Strapless with a romantic billowing skirt of ivory delustred satin, the hem and some twelve inches of the grand traditional skirt, like some primitively inspired piece of jewellery, were encrusted with various coloured beads, brilliants and crystals, in an amazingly beautiful aboriginal motif.

The bride's lustrous mane of dark hair was drawn back from the face but allowed to cascade down her back. She wore the traditional long bridal veil simply caught so as not to detract from the quite wonderful piece of jewellery she wore around her throat. A combination of stones her adoring bridegroom had found for her since childhood, sapphires and opals, mixed up with precious and semiprecious jewels. It was extraordinary and it added the drama quite in keeping with the bride's vivid style of beauty. The bride had four attendants and two flower girls, twins. All of them looked lovely on the big day, the enchanting little girls modelling silk representations of the station's wildflowers, as diadems on their golden curls.

It was all so passionate, so rife with promise; the

guests were quite carried away by the emotion of it all. The bridegroom was described at every turn as "simply smashing." An understatement in the eyes of his deliriously happy bride.

As one important family dowager was later heard to remark as she watched Luke and Storm whirling through their wedding waltz. "Those two are soul mates! Just look at the expression of love on their faces. It's so transparent it gives me goose bumps. Mark my words— which everyone did—this is a marriage that will last!"

She said it again at the family christening some eighteen months later. Storm and Luke gave a big party to celebrate the birth of their first child, the most gorgeous, the most adorable little girl child. The child had her father's hair; perhaps a couple of shades more to rosy-red. At six weeks old she didn't have the expected navy eyes. Emily's eyes were a clear beautiful green. Could anything be more perfect?

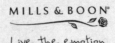

MILLS & BOON®

Live the emotion

0106/01b

Modern
romance™

FOR REVENGE...OR PLEASURE? by *Trish Morey*

Jade Ferraro is a cosmetic surgeon, and Loukas Demakis
is certain she's preying on the rich and famous of Beverly
Hills to attract celebrity clients. He has no qualms about
seducing top-secret information from Jade. He begins by
buying her dinner – and then he uncovers the truth...

THE GREEK'S BRIDAL BARGAIN by *Melanie Milburne*

She was a rich girl and he was the housekeeper's son
– and their innocent affair was destroyed. But now Kane
Kaproulias has Bryony Mercer in the palm of his hand...
Her family is penniless and the tables have turned. Kane
has waited a long time to have Bryony right where he
wants her – in his bed, as his wife!

HER TYCOON PROTECTOR by *Amanda Browning*

Shelby Greer is horrified when she learns a mysterious
man is threatening to harm her to get revenge on her
father. Her bodyguard is Gray Compton – sexy and
charming. Shelby wouldn't mind spending night and day
with him – if only he wasn't the man who once ruthlessly
spurned her advances...

BOUGHT BY A BILLIONAIRE by *Kay Thorpe*

Leonie rejected Vidal's proposal because of his arrogance,
his womanising – and his powerful sexuality, which left
her trembling. But now the Portuguese billionaire is back
in her life and he could make her his mistress. But Vidal
doesn't want a mistress. He wants marriage...

On sale 3rd February 2006

*Available at WHSmith, Tesco, ASDA, Borders, Eason,
Sainsbury's and most bookshops*

www.millsandboon.co.uk

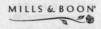

0106/02

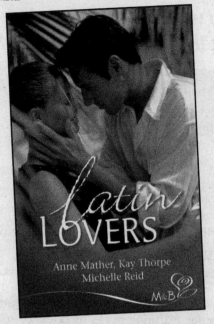

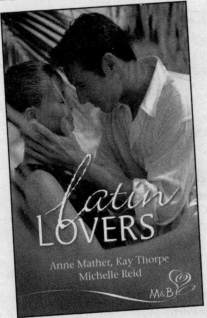